PENGUIN CANADA

COPPERMINE

KEITH ROSS LECKIE has worked in the film and television business as a dramatic scriptwriter for more than thirty years. His credits include multiple movies and miniseries, including *Everest!*, *Shattered City*, *Milgaard*, *The Arrow*, and *Lost in the Barrens*. He lives in Toronto with his wife and children. *Coppermine* is his second novel.

Visit his website at www.keithrossleckie.com.

KEITH ROSS LECKIE

COPPERMINE

PENGUIN
CANADA

PENGUIN CANADA

Published by the Penguin Group

Penguin Group (Canada), 90 Eglinton Avenue East, Suite 700, Toronto, Ontario, Canada M4P 2Y3
(a division of Pearson Canada Inc.)

Penguin Group (USA) Inc., 375 Hudson Street, New York, New York 10014, U.S.A.
Penguin Books Ltd, 80 Strand, London WC2R 0RL, England
Penguin Ireland, 25 St Stephen's Green, Dublin 2, Ireland (a division of Penguin Books Ltd)
Penguin Group (Australia), 250 Camberwell Road, Camberwell, Victoria 3124, Australia
(a division of Pearson Australia Group Pty Ltd)
Penguin Books India Pvt Ltd, 11 Community Centre, Panchsheel Park, New Delhi – 110 017, India
Penguin Group (NZ), 67 Apollo Drive, Rosedale, Auckland 0632, New Zealand
(a division of Pearson New Zealand Ltd)
Penguin Books (South Africa) (Pty) Ltd, 24 Sturdee Avenue, Rosebank,
Johannesburg 2196, South Africa

Penguin Books Ltd, Registered Offices: 80 Strand, London WC2R 0RL, England

First published in Viking Canada hardcover by Penguin Group (Canada),
a division of Pearson Canada Inc., 2010
Published in this edition, 2011

1 2 3 4 5 6 7 8 9 10 (WEB)

Author representation: Westwood Creative Artists
94 Harbord Street, Toronto, Ontario M5S 1G6

Manufactured in Canada.

LIBRARY AND ARCHIVES CANADA CATALOGUING IN PUBLICATION

Leckie, Keith Ross, 1952–
Coppermine / Keith Ross Leckie.

ISBN 978-0-14-317581-0

1. Murder—Coppermine River Valley (N.W.T. and Nunavut)—Fiction.
2. Inuit—Coppermine River Valley (N.W.T. and Nunavut)—Fiction. 3. Royal North West Mounted
Police (Canada)—Fiction. 4. Coppermine River Valley (N.W.T. and Nunavut)—Fiction. I. Title.

PS8573.E337C66 2011   C813'.54   C2011-905307-1

Visit the Penguin Group (Canada) website at **www.penguin.ca**

Special and corporate bulk purchase rates available; please see
www.penguin.ca/corporatesales or call 1-800-810-3104, ext. 2477 or 2474

TO MARY,
FOR HER LOVE AND SUPPORT,
AND FOR GIVING ME ALL MY BEST IDEAS.
THANK YOU, BABY.

To love another person is to see the face of God.
—VICTOR HUGO

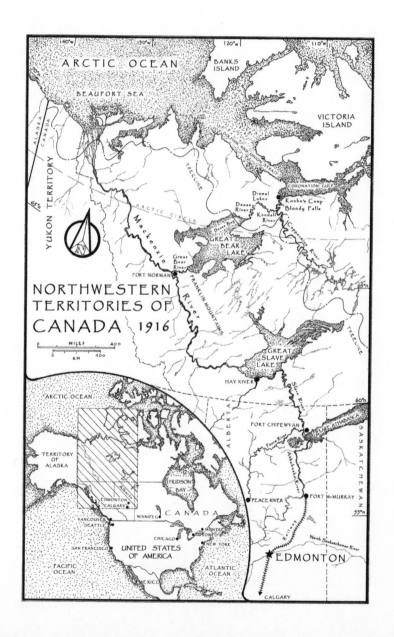

NORTHWESTERN TERRITORIES OF CANADA 1916

AUTHOR'S NOTE

This true story of the murder trial of Sinnisiak and Uluksuk came to me in 1992 as I was researching a screenplay for the CBC movie *Trial at Fortitude Bay* (a contemporary trial in the High Arctic). In the summer of 1917, the Coppermine story was the first jury-system trial of an Inuit in Canada and became a huge show trial, attended by journalists and students of law from all over North America. The press referred to it as "modern law meets Stone Age man."

The story fascinated me for eighteen years. I planned to write it as a novel, but I had created three produced miniseries for CBC, and they were looking for another. So, somewhat reluctantly, I signed on to script the Coppermine story. I researched it, travelled to the important sites, and fashioned it into the outline of a four-hour dramatic miniseries. Then a regime change occurred at the CBC, and Coppermine and most other projects portraying Canadian history and long form projects were scrapped.

As a long-form writer, I was out of work. That's when my wife suggested I go back to the original idea and take a year to write Coppermine as a novel. With my son and daughter in university and a mortgage to pay, it was a daunting prospect. I hadn't written a novel in twenty years. I had a good sense of story and dialogue, but was my prose up to scratch? Could I internalize emotion? As a writer in film and television for three decades, I write as if the viewer may change the channel at any point. Is this a good thing?

What you have in hand is the result. Its strength is in the narrative and the characters, all inspired by real events and people. *Coppermine* is one of those stories that I find just as compelling today as on the first day I discovered it.

I would like to warn historians and explorers that I have taken dramatic liberties. If you're looking for precise historic accuracy regarding this case, please refer to Gordon Moyles's *British Law and Arctic Men* or McKay Jenkins's *Bloody Falls of the Coppermine*. For instance, the rapids on the Coppermine River where Jack and Angituk dump their canoe in Part One are, in fact, a day's paddle above Bloody Falls, but for dramatic reasons, I represent them a distance below. John Hornby did not testify at the trial, though his statements were discussed. The impressive exploits of Royal North West Mounted Police Inspector Denny LaNauze and Corporal Valentine Bruce are distilled into one character—Jack Creed. The love story may or may not have taken place, but it was inspired by a real person. For these and other historical and geographic offences, all I can say is that I may tamper with facts for dramatic reasons, but I do my best to tell the truth. My job as a scriptwriter and now a novelist is to mythologize the true stories I love.

Let me paraphrase the words of Mr. Twain: Everything here is absolutely true, except what isn't, and it should have been.

Please enjoy.

PROLOGUE

JULY 6, 1913
FORT NORMAN
NORTHWEST TERRITORIES

The young priest stood on the rough planks of the Hudson's Bay Company dock at Fort Norman feeling the thousand-mile thrum of the Mackenzie River against the haphazard structure of spruce logs, nails, and ropes under his boots. He savoured the brilliant light of the short-lived Arctic summer sun on his face, anticipating the little steamboat that would bring to him his new companion. His melancholy eyes searched the southern horizon of that vast river through the wind-washed Arctic air, its clarity rendering every image with a dreamlike aspect that only became more intense the farther north one ventured.

Father Jean-Baptiste Rouvière had come to the sub-Arctic two years before, and his thin body and tentative movements were a testament to the burden of his work. He had this day made his way by canoe from his camp into Fort Norman well ahead of the loosely scheduled arrival of the riverboat. He sat down now on a warm spot of exposed granite shield and took out the new journal he had ordered from the Hudson's Bay store. He had been keeping some notes over the last year, though he had been forced to use them for kindling when the desperate pain in his frozen fingers trumped the importance of record keeping. Now, however, he was determined to write the whole of his experiences—past, present, and future—in this sturdy little book. And he had also vowed to himself always to carry dry kindling in his pocket in order that this record would remain safe.

He looked out again at the seabirds that hovered over the wide river hundreds of miles from any sea. Ravens croaked and muttered in the spruce trees above him. Settling himself on the warm rock and with one eye on the river, he began to write:

> It is with humility I begin this journal of my work as your brother in the Lord and in the name of Christ and His mother the Immaculate Mary. I have been deeply blessed by my special mission here in the North. I was chosen by Bishop Breynat himself. Please forgive me my moment of pride in this. The Bishop told me there were stories of an isolated tribe of Eskimos up on the Coronation Gulf—the Copper people—who had never seen a white man, who worked with stone tools and never knew the rest of the world existed. A culture frozen in time. There were rumours they were violent savages, witches and cannibals, but to the Bishop they were the children of God yet to be claimed.
>
> "Go to them. Bring them to the light," he told me. I was to travel even as far north as the Coronation Gulf of the Arctic Ocean, and find these last few primitives, these Eskimos, some of the most isolated and backward human beings in the world. A kingdom of ignorance. He told me to convert them to the one

true faith so that, as he put it, "we may send a few specimens to Paradise." And I tell you, I rejoiced in the assignment. A challenge and adventure in the Lord's name. Dare I say it? In the footsteps of Peter? And so I had gone, and gone willingly. *Ecce ego mitte me.* Here I am. Send me forth. I have been here for two years.

The winter was very hard in the little cabin on the Dease River. It was relentlessly, crushingly lonely. I had not anticipated how in the Arctic the regimes of light and time are so very different. I have lived through a nightless summer and a dayless winter. The guide I hired, Mr. John Hornby, a somewhat erratic young man, took me to a tiny, damp, poorly built cabin on the edge of the treeline where the winds seeped freely through the log chinkings, still three hundred miles from my goal: the mouth of the Coppermine River. Then, after we'd had only one single contact with the human creatures I sought, the Englishman left me to go trapping for the entire winter!

But there remained for me that first contact with the people, the brief, seductive taste of possibilities so soon after my arrival. In early October, before Hornby left me, we made a trek north from the Dismal Lakes almost as far as the southern reaches of the Coppermine River itself. I was delighted to find a small hunting band of the very Copper Eskimos I was after, and I rejoiced that the Bishop's mission might in fact be fulfilled. They were not the hostile savages I had been warned about, and once their curiosity overcame their initial fear of me, they became friendly companions and good hosts. Hornby and I camped together with them for a few precious days and they fed us, gave us furs, and attended when I tried to speak to them. Such lovely, good-hearted creatures!

But Hornby did not know their dialect. Their language was impossible to him, and though their eyes were politely interested as I showed them the Cross and the pictures of the Crucifixion, of Heaven and Hell, of angels and devils from my illustrated catechism, I knew they had no idea what I was talking about. And as I looked into those amiable, confused faces I felt I was in the presence of very ancient men. Stone Age men. From long before even the Christ. Willing, curious, hospitable, but very much from another, long-ago world. So much to say to them. So far to bring them.

And then one morning they vanished. They must have gone north again, for Hornby had said the Dismal Lakes were as far south as they ever roamed. And after this first contact, this brief liaison with those beings I so passionately hoped would become my flock, Hornby took me back to the cabin and I was left alone to face almost two months of the Arctic night locked inside the blue-black vault of the winter sky.

When there were still two hours of light in a day, a Métis trader came by the cabin and stayed with me for two nights before continuing south. I took great pleasure in speaking French with him, a rough man with rude jokes. I indulged myself to laugh at his stories. The trader in return allowed me to say Mass and give him Communion and even hear his three-year confession of life among the Cree, the sexual contents of which severely shocked me! And then he left me, carrying my long letter to the Bishop speaking of my very modest accomplishments—and making a special request. I was careful not to have it too forceful. I asked in my letter to be sent a companion. Someone skilled in languages.

I learned to chop firewood from the scraggly little spruce at the edge of the treeline. Hornby taught me how to fire the Winchester .44 calibre rifle with the heavy brass cartridges to hunt elk or caribou. But I had enough tinned food to survive. I celebrated blessed Christmas alone, saying the Mass and eating tinned corned beef and beans as a blizzard howled around me. Despite my repairs, it blew through the broken insulation of Hornby's sorry cabin. I prayed a great deal and wrote letters to my family and superiors, unsendable until the spring, and I memorized the Scriptures again, prayed more, and, as the blizzards swept in on me from the big lake to the south, held on. I had forgotten to wind my watch, and when I found it had stopped I did not know at what time to reset it. I didn't know what was day and what was night, when a day ended and the next began. The dark was endless. Time became meaningless. Was it an hour ago I last ate, or a day, or a week? No way to tell.

I had heard of it, been warned of it: the sickness that comes from weeks without sunlight in the wilderness. The Mackenzie delta Eskimos called it *perleromeq*, a psychosis whose symptoms are a feeling of deep sadness, of profound weariness, of utter defeat.

They told me it can render a man comatose or drive him to extreme violence or cause him to run naked out into a minus-forty-degree night to embrace the relief of death.

It was not until early January that I felt the chilling touch, the first weight of this deep depression brought on by relentless darkness. I began to imagine that Satan had taken up residence inside me. I refused a dialogue with him. I stopped praying and was sure my leather bible was hot to the touch. I felt the irony that I had come to bring the light of Christian knowledge to these people, the very light of Christ's spirit, and now I was denied virtual light, the sustenance of solar light, and my doubts were increasing every day that it would ever return. Sometime a little later—and I am ashamed now to mention the contemplation of a mortal sin, but I write it down so that it illustrates the depth of this depression—I fashioned an effective noose and chose the beam most likely to support my weight and not allow my toes to touch the frozen dirt floor.

Then quite suddenly one day a strange, thin, growing light pushed through a crack between the logs. What was this light? I opened the door against the drift of snow, squeezed out, and scrambled up the snowbank to stare into a glow coming from the gap made by the Dease River between the scrub trees. And then there it was: the sun. It stayed only a moment, peeking over the earth's horizon. It moved neither east nor west, but appeared for a few moments as I watched to simply roll over and disappear again, the glow remaining for almost half an hour. This was all

I needed. Hope. A promise. A covenant with God. I
was not forsaken in the darkness. Satan had departed
and I became almost myself again. It had been a little
longer than forty days and forty nights in the darkness
by my calculations. It had shaken me, what I saw as
a weakening of my faith, and I promised myself this
would never happen again.

As the days returned and the sun strengthened, so
did my resolve to continue the mission. I had been
excited by the meeting in the autumn with a few of
the people who would become my flock. Soon, as the
days lengthened, I would go north as far as I had to
and find the rest. I would establish a beachhead for
Christ, bring enlightenment to these good, ignorant
people. At the mouth of the Coppermine I would
create a little outpost of the Kingdom of God.

The letter came to me in early May by way of two
Royal North West Mounted Police officers checking
in on me. These good-natured men, who stayed three
nights, brought me playing cards (we played Wisk!),
a fine round of ripe Oka cheese from our brothers in
Quebec, tinned fruit, a bottle of Hudson's Bay rum,
and the tragic news of the sinking of the *Titanic* the year
before with great loss of life. But the best thing, the
most amazing thing they brought me—these pleasant
messengers of hope—was a letter from Bishop Breynat.
He was sending me a priest! Father Guillaume Le
Roux. Young and fit, a Breton gentleman, a student of
philosophy at Liège, two years of service in Rome, an
intellectual, and, most important, a linguist! I could
not have asked for anything more in a man to share
my mission. And my dreams.

FATHER ROUVIÈRE STOPPED there in his writing and looked up, his eyes squinting against the glare of the low sun on the surface of the Mackenzie. He sensed something coming. He stood up and took a few steps forward out onto the dock; his heart beat faster. The little steamboat had swung into view, carried sideways on the treacherous current, crabbing its way toward the makeshift landing. He waited for it there, his open, still-youthful face reflecting both his failures here on the edge of the world and the anticipation of his dreams fulfilled.

PART ONE

One

APRIL 12, 1916
CARIBOU MOUNTAINS
NORTHERN ALBERTA

All night, beneath an amazement of stars, Corporal Jack Creed of the Royal North West Mounted Police pushed a course due west through the knee-deep snow of the black spruce forest. The ponies with their grim burdens followed in an easy line. There was the sound of his breathing, the jingle of tack, and the muffled hooves but little else on this still night. Creed glanced back from time to time, making sure the bodies had not shifted. He hadn't had sufficient rope to secure them all properly and if one slipped off, the wolves that were following would be on it in a heartbeat.

The senior officer of the patrol, Inspector Armstrong, had been a tall man. The pony that carried his body was a small quarter horse. It was an unfortunate match. Slung across the pony's back, the Inspector's fingers brushed the snow. Creed should have trussed the arms up as he had with Cunningham and Reas, but the day was fading and by the time he had the others loaded and secured, the evening temperatures had plummeted despite the fact that it was nominally spring. The

Inspector was stiff and Creed couldn't bring himself to force the frozen flesh of the raised arms to the man's sides. He just bent him over the horse—his core not fully frozen—and roped him down. So now in death Inspector Armstrong reached out with bare, lifeless fingers, probing the passing texture of the deep, crystalline snow.

Jack Creed was confident inside his five-foot-nine-inch frame, a good balance between strength and speed that had benefited him on the playing fields of Upper Canada College in Toronto, where he excelled at football and cricket, captaining the first eleven. At UCC he knew he was above his station, but he didn't mind. His father, a cattle farmer outside Peterborough, after a few prosperous years had paid good money to send him to the college to rub shoulders with the Eatons, the Gooderhams, and the Masseys. He had enjoyed the friendship of his wealthy classmates but was not really of their world. Off the cricket pitch he read everything he could get his hands on, from Tolstoy to Twain, Conrad to Kipling. His father called him a dreamer, but Creed wondered how that could be a bad thing.

Creed had also been called handsome by various women, not infrequently, but this too meant little to him. His intelligent brown eyes saw the world around him with clarity, often a sense of irony, but never cynicism. He believed in humankind, despite the battering his faith in it had taken by what he had seen so far in his twenty-eight years of life. He looked to an improved future.

The aurora borealis crackled and whispered behind him on the trail. He tried to whistle the lights down closer. Sometimes it worked. They were keeping him company. Creed found corpses very poor company. He looked back again. All seemed secure. His eyes held on the slightest figure, slung across the pinto. Reas was just a boy, a farm kid from Weyburn, Saskatchewan, proud as hell of the uniform he wore—the broad-brimmed stetson on the saddle horn, military tunic under his fur coat, the woollen trousers with the yellow stripe. All of that would be sent back to his mother. It still deeply troubled Creed to see a boy cut down so suddenly, even after his months on the front in Belgium. He thought it'd be different here.

Like his older brother, Charles, before him, Creed had joined the Canadian Expeditionary Forces in 1915, against the strong wishes of their father. One son was enough. He needed him on the farm. He called him a fool. In retrospect his father had been right, but Creed had been determined to go and find Charlie.

Creed pulled his hand from his mitten and slid it inside his fur coat to rub at his shoulder, where an old wound was aching from the efforts of the day, or perhaps the ache had been triggered by the memories that had surfaced from the smell of gunpowder and blood. The third body, on the last horse, was his friend Cunningham, a good, seasoned officer. Begley had recognized this threat and shot Cunningham first. Creed would deeply miss Cunningham. They had shared a non-cynical nature. They could spend congenial days on the trail together and not say a word. On the trail there was really little need for talk, and when you did, it had to mean something.

THEIR SPRING PATROLS had been fairly routine. The officers separated to do solo rounds of two dozen hunters and trappers in the north section of the Caribou range. That had been the best time for Creed. It had been a hard winter, with little or no game. The Mounties brought extra flour and tinned meat and fruit to the desperate. It gave a lot of satisfaction to put sweet slices of peach in the tin cup of a starving man. The four officers had met up again south of Buffalo Lake for the final leg back down to their detachment at Hay River.

There was one last call: check on a couple of trappers named Ross and Begley at a remote cabin high in the Caribou near the source of the Buffalo River. No one had seen them all year. In the last of Ross's letters he had said that Begley had been acting odd, arguing, hoarding food, and stealing his things. And some who knew Begley said he could be unpredictable. The Ross family in Halifax was concerned and had asked the Mounties to look in on them during their patrol.

The Mounties came upon the small, well-built trappers' cabin mid-afternoon. An old fire was smoking a haunch of meat hanging on a neat tripod outside. The camp seemed well kept, with firewood stacked against the wall, a line of laundry drying.

Creed turned, his saddle creaking, to look out at the view of the mountains, young peaks extending to the west, plenty of snow still on their flanks and summits. He noticed Cunningham too was taking in the vista and nodded his approval. No question they had found a beautiful spot here, and Creed caught himself thinking how fine it would be to live in a place like this for a year or two. Do a little trapping, as he had done in Ontario as a boy. There'd be trout in the streams lower down. A few books and a deck of solitaire cards for wintering. Lonely. A long way from humanity, true. But Creed had had enough of humanity for a while.

"Dismount," Armstrong told them. They did so and approached as a foursome.

"Sir, why don't Reas and I just flank you a little over toward the trees?" Creed suggested.

"I don't want to spook 'em."

"Maybe just unholster our weapons then, sir?"

"This isn't a damn machine gun nest, Corporal. This is just a social call."

"Yes, sir."

Armstrong hailed the inhabitants of the cabin in a strong, congenial voice. "ROSS! WALTER ROSS? EUGENE BEGLEY!"

There was nothing for a minute, then distant ravens bickering aloft and a light wind in the trees. Finally the door unlatched and a big man came out to them wearing a long, heavy buffalo coat in the warm weather. He came several steps toward them. His small, pig eyes were a little wild, but they had all seen those bush eyes many times in the camps they visited. He would settle down with talk.

"Are you Begley?"

The big man nodded, his eyes still a bit startled. There was a wafting stench coming off him that made them all step back. Ross, they thought, must be the clean and tidy one.

Inspector Armstrong spoke to him calmly. "We're on spring patrol and thought we'd stop by. See if you're all right. If you need anything. Any messages or letters we can take back for you?"

"No." The word came out like a croak from a man who hadn't been speaking much recently.

"We're pleased to see you doing well." Armstrong gestured to the meat on the tripod. "This has been a bad game year."

Begley smiled and nodded, his wild eyes softening a little.

"How's Ross?"

"Good," he told them. "Off after partridge."

"You're both in good health, are you?"

"Never better."

"We'll wait around a bit. Say hello to Ross."

It was apparent Begley didn't like this idea. "Could be gone a couple days."

"Maybe we could have some tea," Armstrong suggested. "We brought tea, sugar, flour, and tinned peaches and apples."

Begley weighed this idea for a moment. "Sure. Come inside."

Begley turned and walked back toward the cabin. Reas carried the bag of supplies. Creed casually unclipped his holster cover and folded it over inside the belt.

"Hell of a nice place you've got here, Begley," Armstrong offered. "How was the trapping this winter?"

"Good. I'll show you my furs." Begley stood to one side of the door and gestured them all inside, smiling through his yellow teeth.

As he passed the smudge fire, young Reas stopped. The bag of supplies fell from his hands. He was looking at the fire. He took a step toward it, gasped, and fell to one knee, choking.

"What the hell, lad? You all right?" Armstrong asked him.

Reas was retching into the sandy soil of the path. Armstrong took a step away.

Creed bent down to Reas. "What is it, Jimmy?"

The boy recovered enough to speak one word. "Toes."

"What?"

The boy raised his hand and pointed at the haunch smoking over the fire and said, "It has toes."

Cunningham took a step closer to observe. "Jesus. He's right."

Begley raised and fired point-blank the double-barrelled shotgun he had taken from under his big coat. He hit Cunningham and then Armstrong, just as Creed was withdrawing his pistol. Begley swung the butt against Jack's head and he fell stunned to the ground.

When full consciousness returned, Jack sat up and found blood blinding one eye. Through his good one Jack looked over to see Begley pounding young Reas's head in the mud with the butt of the shotgun. The big man moved at an astounding speed. Jack located his old revolver beside him, but the cylinder had opened and slid off the spindle rod and the bullets lay in a semicircle in the snow. Jack, his head roaring like a forest fire, found the cylinder and slid it back on the rod. There was one bullet inside. He located three more in the snow with his bare hand and loaded them with the calm, focused care he always had when he knew a mistake or hesitation would mean his life.

Creed was overcome by a stench and turned to see Begley standing above him, the shotgun raised again over his head. Jack locked the cylinder plate, cocked the hammer, extended his hand, and fired the first round of the small calibre into Begley's chest between the open lapels of the buffalo coat. Begley hardly flinched. The butt of the big man's shotgun came down an inch from Creed's face, deflected by his arm, glancing off his shoulder. Begley raised the gun again. Creed fired twice into the exposed chest. Begley looked down at him, his pig eyes vacant, the gun still held above him. Creed fired his last shot up under Begley's chin and the big man dropped dead on top of him.

He crawled out from under Begley and applied snow to the goose egg on the side of his head and cheek to stop the bleeding. He was relieved his collar bone hadn't been broken by the butt of the shotgun, but it was badly bruised.

Creed dug a shallow grave beside the cabin and, using the pinto, dragged Begley to it. He dug another, smaller one beside it for Walter Ross, and Creed buried what was left of him. First off, there was the smoked haunch. The head and hands were on a shelf inside the fetid cabin; Begley must have been keeping them for company. And there were some clean bones Creed found in a pot behind the cabin. Creed arranged them all neatly, respectfully, in a rough semblance of their original divine organization. He placed three layers of flat rocks on the graves to stop the wolves and wolverines from digging them up.

One of the four ponies had taken some shot and was lame. He didn't want to leave her alive for the wolves or bears, so he gave her the last apple from the can he ate for dinner and then led her into the woods and shot her. He used Cunningham's large-calibre Colt to be sure the job was clean. She would distract the wolves from the graves.

Three ponies, three bodies. Creed didn't mind the long walk back to the fort at Hay River. It was very still. Not a breath rustled the frost-encrusted forest. Nothing between him and the cold and silence of outer space. His buffalo jacket, hat, and heavy mitts kept him warm. With the northern lights in front of him, the temperature staying even, and the hard snow crunching beneath his high brown boots, he indulged himself in the old feeling of euphoria that came from surviving an action when others have not. He was overcome with a sudden, reckless arrogance, even though it could just as easily have been Cunningham leading the horses. Or all their haunches could currently be smoking over Begley's fire.

Creed chuckled out loud at this grisly image and wished he could share it with the others. He could almost hear Cunningham's laughter. Of course, one day it would be his turn, but tonight he was very much alive, only hurting here and there. And he had a spiral of twisting green celestial flames for companionship in the black sky above him. He felt fine and strong. Today had been a good test for judgment and control. A song came to mind that had been popular in the trenches. He sang it under his breath.

> I'm always chasing rainbows,
> Watching clouds drifting by,
> My schemes are just like all my dreams,
> Ending in the sky ...

HAY RIVER WAS A RAMBLING, low-lying Royal North West Mounted Police detachment town on the south shore of Great

Slave Lake. Creed reported his grim news to the sergeant in charge. The community suffered a deep shock over the loss of a quarter of the detachment, including the commanding officer. Creed oversaw the local doctor's autopsies, a science he had given some study to, and then attended the burial of his three colleagues in the little RNWMP cemetery.

A breeze off the lake kept the blackflies at bay. Armstrong's pale, thin wife and wide-eyed daughter were at the funeral, and he spoke condolences to them and reassured them their father and husband had done his duty honourably and not suffered. He felt badly for them, alone in this rough land, and hoped they'd go back to her family in Minnesota. At the funeral a photographer tried to take Creed's picture and he turned angrily away from the camera. Creed hated photographs and shied away from attention.

A telegram came to the Hay River office ordering him to report back to his commanding officer in Edmonton. He had only been on loan at Hay River. He had his clothes washed, had a bath and shave, and put on his khaki field uniform in time to board the riverboat south to Fort McMurray, and from there, the train to Edmonton. Lulled by the gentle rocking through the hilly lake country and forests of scrub, white spruce, and aspen, he slept for a couple of hours, and then woke to the new topography of a few gatherings of poplar and white birch and the flattening prairie grasslands. He wrote a letter to Cunningham's wife in Toronto and one to Reas's mother in Weyburn to post in the city. Creed was good at these letters. He had written scores of them in France, always trying to put in a personal memory or two. As he finished the Reas letter he looked out ahead to see in the distance the multi-storey brick buildings of Edmonton, and as the train slowed for its approach into North Station he took a deep breath to calm himself and prepare for his re-entry into civilization.

EDMONTON HAD BOOM-TOWN enthusiasm. First it was the lucrative fur trade, then it was cattle transported east on the new railway. Then, during the gold rush of '97 and '98, it turned from a sleepy town to a city, a staging ground for the almost-impossible overland route to the goldfields of the Klondike. Edmonton hosted, provisioned, and fleeced those hardy souls, men and even a few women, who set off through forests and muskeg, across rivers and mountain ranges on vehicles as diverse as steam-driven tractors featuring enormous wheels and wind-driven wagons. They dragged flatboats hundreds of miles and pedalled bicycles until they sank to their hubs. Very few Klondikers who set off from Edmonton ever made it as far as the goldfields, and a swath of abandoned supplies and vehicles lay scattered for five hundred miles across the hostile topography that had defeated them. But the merchants of Edmonton counted their money and the city prospered.

Soon the promise of gold had waned, but the population in the east had grown and their demands with them. Now wheat was king and Edmonton grain farmers became rich. Then, with the war looming, her vast coal and oil deposits became her principal currency: a deep, rich seam was located directly under the main street of the town.

Wartime Edmonton had its share of boom-town cowboys, soldiers, roughnecks, and railway workers, but on the surface the city retained a certain Victorian dignity and order that her citizens energetically endorsed. It might be a western boom town, but it had class. The city had been well designed, laid out in a grid: streets going north and south, avenues going east and west, each given a number, with a few exceptions, such as the central Jasper Avenue. The city extended north and south of the broad, winding North Saskatchewan River in almost equal measure, with the downtown and government offices on the north side.

There were numerous churches of all Christian denominations. In the summertime, garden parties and strawberry socials were popular. There were riverboat rides out of town to picnic sites on the open prairie, bands accompanying with both classical and popular music. And on the short winter weekend days there were snow festivals with skating on the river, complete with Chinese lanterns and cauldrons of hot chocolate, often fortified from hip bottles and flasks in defiance of the prohibition.

It was apparent that Edmonton valued order and good government, and the citizens could be outspoken if the government didn't please them. There were labour strikes and public demonstrations against higher taxes. The good people of Edmonton were pleased with themselves and what they had accomplished. Deemed the capital of Alberta in 1906, the city had an image to maintain, unlike that crass cowtown to the south called Calgary.

The Edmonton RNWMP office and barracks had been completed only two years before. The patterned brick structure was nothing less than a castle, with battlements and towers, a fine stone entryway, and an extensive courtyard with lawns and gardens. A full moat was abandoned as impractical only in the later stages of construction. There was even a secret subterranean tunnel leading down into the river valley, presumably in case the inhabitants had to escape an attack by a marauding army from, say, Calgary. Or if the Cree and Blackfoot and Blood tribes, inspired by the ghost of Sitting Bull, put their differences aside to make an assault against the capital. This bold structure was built to provide tangible evidence to anyone inclined to oppose it of the strong and impassive presence of the law.

CREED IMMEDIATELY REPORTED to his commanding officer. Superintendent G.S. Worsley was tall and lean, with old-fashioned sideburn whiskers, a Church of England monarchist who believed his life's work was extending sound English principles into the Northwestern Territories of Canada. He tolerated Creed's Scots Presbyterian upbringing as a lesser evil. "At least you're not an Irishman or a papist, " he had told him. He was pleased to find a man who favoured extended, lonely patrols in the North. In this, Creed was a rare commodity. In turn Creed liked Worsley, despite his political views.

Creed entered the large, well-appointed office. On the wall were several English prints showing glorious battle scenes from the Crimean, Boer, and Napoleonic wars. Worsley was reading the report Creed had telegraphed from Hay River. Creed saluted him, standing at attention in front of the desk. Worsley called him to ease and expressed his sadness at the loss of his colleagues, the three good men from the Hay River detachment.

"How is the head injury?" The bruising from Begley's shotgun butt was still quite visible.

"Fine, sir. Looks worse than it is."

Worsley gestured with the pages in his hand. "Good report, Creed. On a sad, unfortunate episode. No way of predicting it."

"They were all good men."

"Yes. Well, congratulations on how well you handled it all under the circumstances."

"I appreciate that, sir." He waited a respectful moment. "Sir, Cowperthwaite mentioned to me there was another assignment. Someone lost beyond Fort Norman."

The Superintendent put down the Begley-Ross report and pushed it to one side, studying Creed. Though the man had been under his command for seven months, to Worsley he remained something of a mystery. He knew Creed had been a soldier early on in the war in Europe, and he noted how Creed's experience of the trenches lingered in his occasional long, haunted looks. Worsley had seen a nervousness in other veterans too, but in

Jack there was something else: a spiritual burden, a *gravitas*, a sadness. Worsley had not pursued it, of course; the man had a right to his privacy. And he had become one of Worsley's best men at a time when men were scarce.

"You just got back, man. And this could be a long one. I think you should take some time off after what you've been through. I'll send Svenson. He'll make a good job of it."

"What is the case, sir?"

"Don't worry about it, Creed. Really. Take a rest. Stay here in Edmonton and help me with enlistment. Manpower is the problem now, with the war sucking away every available man. And you have your ... friendship with the magistrate's niece. Take some time in town. You have a bright future here in Edmonton."

"Thank you, sir, but can you tell me about the mission?"

The Superintendent paused, showing minor irritation at Jack's stubbornness, and then began. "All right. This report comes from Ottawa. Two years ago two papist priests ... oblates ... Fathers Rouvière and Le Roux, went north to 'convert the heathen.' Rouvière had been up there for a couple of years, guided by a trapper named Hornby. Rouvière was joined by Father Le Roux at Fort Norman, early summer of 1913, where they provisioned."

Worsley turned and gestured to a map of western Canada on the wall behind him, his hand tracing a line of breathtaking distance north from Edmonton. "Then from Fort Norman by canoe up the Bear River and across the Great Bear Lake to the Dease system. They had a cabin some miles up the Dease as a base. That summer they travelled past the treeline and portaged over the watershed up through the Dismal Lakes. They were sending letters and reports back with traders every couple of months. Those letters stopped more than two years ago. Some Cree said they saw them well north of the treeline. They may even have got as far north as the Coppermine River, inside the

Arctic Circle. Then recently a Métis trader showed up at Fort Norman with some of their belongings—some clothing, a rosary, a prayer book. Everyone believes the worst. Father Rouvière's a good friend of Bishop Breynat, and Le Roux is a second cousin of the French ambassador in Ottawa, with a wealthy family in Paris. Anyway, our orders come from the Office of the Attorney General. They want all the resources of the police dispatched. Well, until I re-man Hay River, I don't have much in the way of resources. I think the damn priests are probably just lost somewhere, unable to get letters out and so on. Svenson's a good man for the job."

"I'd like to take it, sir."

"I think you should sleep on this, Corporal."

"What are the specific orders, sir?"

"You go north as far as you can, possibly to the Coppermine River, find the priests, and bring 'em out."

"What if they don't want to come out?"

"Persuade them. Get at least one of 'em back to Fort Norman, anyway, and telegraph their people and Ottawa will be happy. After that they can do whatever the hell they want."

"And if they're dead, sir?"

"Conduct the appropriate investigation. If foul play is suspected, make an appropriate arrest."

"Yes, sir. Does Cowperthwaite have all the area maps, post locations?"

"This is the Coppermine, Creed. It's never been charted. No police posts. No credible maps at all beyond the mouth of the Dease River or south of the Arctic Ocean coast, except a few sketches from Franklin."

"Franklin? *The* Franklin?"

"Yes. An earlier expedition. The trapper Hornby operates along the southern edge, but he doesn't go into the Coppermine.

Other than that, Franklin was the last white man we know of to get that far. Except maybe the priests."

Worsley was gesturing again to the map behind him, pointing to the Mackenzie River delta near the border with Alaska. "See, the Mackenzie delta here has whales ... and Hudson Bay has furs ..." He indicated the huge bite out of central Canada named after the captain whose mutinous crew put him and his young son out to sea in an open boat to perish. "But the Coppermine"—he pointed to the 100,000 square miles of empty, uncharted space between—"has nothing. It's a wasteland. Samuel Hearne spoke of copper deposits, but no one's had the courage to go and find out. Probably the most isolated place left in all the Americas."

Superintendent Worsley turned away from the map. "There is one other element to this you should be aware of. It was in the orders from Ottawa. As empty and isolated as it is up there, it's ours. Ottawa sees this as an opportunity to show the world a Canadian presence there, whether it's a rescue or a burial."

"Understood."

"You'll need to pick up a translator in Fort Norman, if you can find one."

"My Cree's good and I have some Inuktitut."

"Copper Eskimo's all different, they say."

"I prefer to travel alone."

"Take a translator, Creed. You don't have time for language lessons."

Creed hesitated, then nodded. "All right."

"You'll have to winter up there, of course, so take a year's worth of provisions. Cowperthwaite'll help you with all that. Any questions?"

Creed's heart beat a little faster. An honourable mission. Months of solitude.

"No, sir."

"You're sure, then?"

"I'll go."

"You don't want to talk to Miss Harvey first?"

"No, sir."

Worsley paused a moment to study him. "I'm sure you have your reasons, Creed, but you should think about spending more time in the city. With people. Maybe after this one."

"I'll think about it, sir."

IT WAS AFTER DINNER and several officers of "D" Company were smoking in the mess. Corporal Dewey, his boots up on a table, blew three perfect smoke rings from his cheap black panatela before posing the question.

"So, at what point do you decide to eat your partner?"

The contents of Creed's Ross-Begley report had been circulated.

"You have to be damned hungry," Svenson, a tall, muscular blond man with a stained moustache, concluded.

"Or damned irritated."

"Two winters in a one-room cabin could do it," a little Yorkshireman named Woodard speculated.

"My question is," Dewey continued, "was it the irritation or the hunger? When you can't stand him anymore, do you slit his throat and then say to yourself, 'My, what a tender little shank.' Or is it the other way around? And what the hell d'you eat first?"

Corporal Lyle Cowperthwaite spoke through the laughter and speculation. "This is all sick, and you're ruining my digestion. Begley was obviously an insane murderer." Cowperthwaite was slight, with jet-black hair framing a pleasant, cherubic face often given over to indignation.

"What if we were out on patrol and I died of starvation before you, Cowper?" Dewey inquired. "Would you die before eating me?"

"Yes!"

"You'd be a goddamned fool."

"Come on, Cowper. If the man died of natural causes—" Woodard prompted.

"Doesn't matter. Human flesh is sacred."

"So is human life. Isn't it?"

"This case isn't about survival. This is about the murders of four men. Almost five. Imagine what Creed's been through. Surprised he's still sane."

"Assuming he was."

"What's that supposed to mean?" Cowperthwaite glared at Dewey.

"Creed's a bit of an odd duck."

"He's just quiet, unlike some!"

"Do we know anything about him? Where he's from? What he did before the force?"

"He put in his war service, like Ralph and Frank here." Cowperthwaite gestured to a trooper with a glass eye and another with a wooden leg. "I heard he saw the worst of it."

"Was he wounded?"

"Don't know."

"Don't get me wrong, he seems a good fellow—"

"Jack Creed is one of the finest troopers—"

"Oh, shut up, Cowperthwaite. We all love Creed. We're just talking ..."

All fell silent as Creed entered the barracks and put down his knapsack.

Cowperthwaite stood up. "Hi, Jack."

"And here he is," Dewey said expansively.

There were reserved greetings all around, several condolences for the lost men, and acknowledgement of the tough patrol. Creed smiled thinly, a little awkward in their midst as he shook their hands, warmed by their respect. He ended with Cowperthwaite, who leaned in to ask quietly, as if in collaboration, "Did you take the new assignment?"

Creed looked at him. "Yes."

"Up to the Coppermine. Alone?" Dewey asked. They all knew.

"They're short of men at Hay River. I don't mind."

"My God, man, it's almost to the North Pole."

Sergeant Freeman looked up from his book through wire-rimmed glasses. "You'll be meeting Paleoeskimos." Freeman enjoyed a photographic memory. While most of the troopers owned a couple of books, Freeman's parents had sent him an entire *Encyclopaedia Britannica*, which he'd set about reading from page one, and he retained most of it.

"Oh, listen to who's got to the Ps."

"Paleoeskimos: probably the most primitive humans on earth. Quite distinct from our Indians, you know. Closest relatives: the Chukchi people of northern Asia and the Koryaks of Siberia. It's now universally accepted that they crossed the ice bridge from Siberia thousands of years ago." Freeman looked around at the faces, pleased with himself.

"Well, I think it's brilliant," Cowperthwaite continued. "Patrolling that far north. Rescuing people, bringing civilization to the remote corners of the country."

For a second Creed's face flashed impatience. "I don't want to bring civilization anywhere, Lyle. Just want to see that the priests are all right. There any hot water left?" Creed was in a hurry.

"We saved you some."

Creed was headed for the showers, checking his watch and taking it off.

"You know, Creed," Dewey said, examining his panatela, "you'll almost be up to where the Franklin expedition was lost."

Creed hesitated in the doorway. "I'll give your regards to his ghost."

"He's probably found the Passage by now," Svenson speculated.

"You know, they were eating each other at the end," Dewey said, looking to get a reaction out of Cowperthwaite.

"Oh, shut up, Dewey. It's never been proven. I can't believe Englishmen would eat one another."

"I don't know, but if that's the local cuisine, Creed, better pack a bottle of Worcestershire."

Creed smiled as they laughed. Dewey slowly, carefully, blew another ring. Creed could hear their talk in the mess as he turned on the shower and waited for it to warm up.

"Eating human flesh. It's unthinkable!"

"You know, Cowperthwaite, I've often thought, with some carrots and onions, you'd make a nice little stew."

The laughter rose again. Creed smiled, then he turned and stepped into the luxury of almost-instant hot water.

AS CREED LEFT THE BARRACKS and walked quickly down Jasper past Wellington Terrace and into the market district, he was shocked by the city noise and congestion. Horse-drawn wagons vied with muffler-less motor cars, honking trucks, and pedestrians. So many people, heading intently in all directions, like a disturbed school of trout. He made hesitant progress through them toward his rendezvous.

She was waiting at the corner of 103rd Street and smiled broadly when she saw him. Nicole Harvey was the most beautiful woman Creed had ever seen—curly golden-blond hair cropped in a modern style, a healthy blush to her flawless skin, inquiring hazel eyes, a perpetual smile on her full, responsive lips, and beneath the stylish cotton dress the generous curves of a woman. When she spoke, his words dried up. When she took his hand, his strength left him. When she laughed, his knees weakened. What Nicole Harvey saw in Creed, he had no idea. But here she was.

She had come west from Toronto to live with and care for her favourite uncle, Horace Harvey, a respected magistrate whose beloved wife had died of diphtheria two years before. Nicole loved and confidently embraced the West, though she maintained an eastern sophistication. After only a few weeks of seeing each other they had, surprisingly, made love, once, in the library when the magistrate and the servants were out and they had had more than one glass of sherry. They had been a little awkward in a pleasant way, but quite successful, and neither regretted it. Nicole had been excited and pleased by it all. A second opportunity had not arisen, and to invite her to a hotel room seemed sordid.

She hugged him and kissed him on the cheek, then saw the bruising on the side of his face. "Oh, darling, what did they do to you, poor thing? Does it hurt?"

"No."

He was relieved she did not ask for the details of the killings. It was another world and he was happy to be in the comfort of this one, with her, enjoying the waft of her perfume, the closeness of her body, the music of her voice, if only for a short while. As they walked west on the new cement sidewalks of Jasper Avenue, gazing in the shops, she held on to his arm and talked away about fashions, and news that Creed had missed: the discovery of a fresh oil field northwest of the city, the capture of the German-held town of St-Eloi by a Canadian regiment, discussions with the Americans about them joining the war, a woman who had killed her husband with an axe while he slept.

"But my question is," Nicole teased, "did she use the blunt end or the blade end? It didn't explain that in the papers. The blunt end is less messy."

"Guess it depends on how she felt about him."

She released her sparkling laugh that made men on the street turn and look. "You're funny, Jack."

They stopped for a moment while Nicole dug in her handbag for a silver cigarette case, and with a furtive glance up and down the street she put the Sweet Caporal between her lips. Her uncle Horace disapproved of women smoking, but he would still be in court. Creed vaguely disapproved himself, not because she was a woman but because the smell reminded him of the trenches. Everyone smoked in the trenches. The smell of tobacco and rum before an attack, the smell of tobacco and blood after. But here, as he lit it for her, he found he could not take his eyes off her full lips on the cigarette and the way they parted when she exhaled.

And yet he had chosen to leave her again and go north. Something powerful within him rallied to the offer of extended solitude. How could he explain it to her when he didn't understand it himself? He was determined to tell her now. He was going to leave her and the friendly exuberance of this young town again, and go off, much farther this time, into the barren lands for a year.

"I assume you're going to take me to the garden party on Saturday night? I have a new gold dress that will look smashing beside your blue serge."

"Garden party? Where is it?"

"At your barracks, you donkey. Don't they tell you anything? Mayor Henry and his wife will be there, and some of the cast from *Gloria's Romance*."

"Who's Gloria?"

"It's a play, Jack. At the Majesty. Billie Burke's in it. With a five-piece band. I went with Harold and Ruby last week. I'd go again if you want. I'll get tickets for Thursday night."

"I'd like to, Nicky, but I have something to tell you."

At his serious tone her lips reconfigured into the slightest of frowns.

"I'll be going away again for a while. Another assignment."

"Going where? You just got home."

"Two priests have got themselves lost up north."

"How long will you be gone?"

"Months. Maybe a year."

She stopped and turned to him in shock, throwing the cigarette into the street. "A year! That's not fair! You don't have to do that. They can't make you. Someone else can go. I'll have my uncle talk to Worsley. They can find someone else. It's ridiculous—"

"Nicole, the priests could be in trouble. I want to go."

The hazel eyes appraised him. The real pain suddenly reflected in them startled him. "You *want* to go? You *want* to leave me? I thought you loved me. I thought we were going to talk about ... a future together. "

"I would like that. I'd like that very much."

"Then why is it you want to go off and live like some nomadic hermit? Do you hate me so much?"

"Of course not. It's my job. It's what I have to do."

"I don't understand you, Jack."

"It's not you, Nicole. You're wonderful."

"Then what is it? Why do you want to leave a comfortable life with people who care about you and go off into the bush where you'll freeze to death or drown or get eaten by a bear?"

Her rising, angry voice projected well even in the din of the traffic and pedestrians slowed to look at them.

"I just need to be out there a little longer. I don't think it'll be forever. Maybe this will be the last time."

She was fighting back tears as she studied him. She knew he was a good man and she believed he was fond of her. She had let him make love to her once and had never regretted it. He was polite and congenial and would make such a good husband, but she sensed within him the presence of doors that were closed to her. Though he listened and said the right words, she sometimes sensed she never had his full attention.

"Please don't go."

Creed looked at her in silence.

"It would just help if I knew why you're doing this. Going back out there. What do you get out of it?"

Creed thought about this a moment and came as close to the truth as he ever had.

"Peace."

Nicole's lips trembled. "I have to go." She turned and walked away from him. Though he wanted to, he did not follow.

JACK TOOK NICOLE to the garden party at the barracks on Saturday, and she was right—her gold dress and his formal blue serge uniform complemented each other beautifully. She smiled proudly when guests found out he was to leave again.

"Oh, you know Jack, hightailing it for the bush every chance he gets. I try not to take it personally."

She is magnificent, Creed thought as he watched her put on a brave face despite the pain he caused her. *She's probably too good for me.*

He was scheduled to take the train north on Tuesday. She was civil with him as he prepared to depart, and even made jokes. They did not discuss the trip. On the evening before he left, there was a small gathering at her uncle's house and she toasted his journey and wished for his success and safety, and he marvelled again at her poise and selflessness.

She dutifully saw him off at the station the next morning, and for the first time since he had told her of the mission, there were tears. They embraced and kissed, but then she looked into his eyes.

"Jack, I love you. You're the only man I want. Please take good care, my darling. I don't want to lose you. You find those priests. You do what you have to do, and come back home to me."

"All right. Thank you for understanding, Nicky."

"Fine, then. Good luck."

She did not kiss him again. She stood for an awkward moment, then before the tears got worse, she turned and left him. For a moment he felt the hollowness of regret. He hated that he was such a disappointment to her. But there was nothing he could do. He turned and stepped onto the train.

CREED WAS THINKING about that moment now as he stood on the deck of the little steamer named, with a determined lack of imagination, the *Mackenzie River*, making its way north between the shifting sandbars and the deadheads of that noble waterway. She had said she loved him, at the station. He had said nothing in return of love. He had never been sure of what that was and whether he was capable of it. He hoped so. But did he love Nicole? This he didn't know.

Creed was in his field-uniform shirt sleeves, and in his hand was the journal of Samuel Hearne's travels in the Arctic, *A Journey to the Northern Ocean*. It was an early edition, a gift from Cowperthwaite. Hearne had been the first white man to see the Arctic Ocean, in 1771, and his personal impressions, told in a florid but accurate accounting, would be pleasant company on the voyage. He had that and *The Valley of the Moon* by Jack

London and Ford Maddox Ford's new novel, *The Good Soldier*. Lyle Cowperthwaite had also given him a dubious collection of Robert Service poems with a bookmark at "Clancy of the Mounted Police":

> In the little Crimson Manual it's written plain and
> clear
> That who would wear the scarlet coat shall say
> good-bye to fear
> Shall be a guardian of the right, a sleuth-hound
> of the trail
> In the little Crimson Manual there's no such word
> as "fail."

Creed had left the simple-minded book on the train.

He now felt the power of the huge river beneath the sturdy little boat and looked across its vast surface, which cut between the Franklin Mountains in the east and the Mackenzie range in the west, their snowy summits in stark contrast to the deep azure skies. He looked up to see an immense golden eagle riding the thermals high above the river, too high to spot prey, apparently just for pleasure. And Creed considered for a moment the bird's point of view. He imagined what he himself must look like, a tiny, warm creature carried on the wide water in a little vessel far below, hardly more than flotsam. He was heading into the great North again, moving even farther away from the clamorous din of humankind with its righteousness, arrogance, and death. And Creed realized suddenly why he loved the North so much. He could now answer the question she had asked of him. It was the freedom of insignificance within this enormous country that breathed life into his ailing spirit and lifted the weight from his heart.

Two

Fort Norman was an unplanned gathering of log buildings
and shacks at the confluence of the Mackenzie and Great Bear
rivers. The only sense of order came from three log buildings
of similar dimensions: the Hudson's Bay store, the Anglican
church, and the Royal North West Mounted Police detachment.
The detachment had the best location, on a high point of land
that overlooked both the Mackenzie and Great Bear rivers and
faced lofty Bear Rock on the far shore to the north, an orphan
of the Franklin Mountains. A quarter mile out of town, as if
in rejection of the vulgarities of the settlement, in the middle
of a treeless field, stood the Roman Catholic Mission of Saint
Theresa. Creed gazed at it all as the boat approached the landing.

All of the trees near town had been reduced to stumps, which
gave the settlement the barren, deforested look of a Belgian
battlefield. This impression unnerved Creed for a moment
as the steamer nudged up against the ramshackle dock, which
offered a weary groan. The crew secured her and threw down
a narrow gangplank. Though no rain had fallen for days, the
streets held a perpetual layer of sticky mud several inches deep.
Creed had the distinct impression that no female influence had
ever been brought to bear on the creation and maintenance of
Fort Norman.

Creed stepped off the gangplank onto the rough and shaky dock with his pack and duffle. The three-man crew unloaded crates of supplies to the Hudson's Bay agent while the captain barked orders, impatient to carry on downstream to the delta and the lucrative whaling stations on the Beaufort Sea.

Along the shore of the Great Bear River, a family of Cree— mother, father, older daughter, and two young boys—filleted pink salmon and hung them on a sturdy cedar rack to dry in the thin sun and wind, sharp knives flashing as they worked. Skinny dogs fought over the discarded offal in the shallow eddies. Both man and beast stopped to watch Creed, the lone passenger, disembark from the *Mackenzie River*. He raised a casual hand toward them and the family responded in slow motion, holding hands or knives slightly aloft. The dogs went back to fighting and Creed made his way up the mud road toward the detachment.

THE BURLY RNWMP SERGEANT, Eli Farrell, CO of the Fort Norman post, had never heard of Creed. Farrell had only recently been appointed and was clearly drowning in administrative paperwork.

"We're the last people they tell what's going on half the time," he said, pawing through the papers on his desk. "We're way down on men here. Everyone's taken off for Europe to fight the Hun. Lost two more good men last week. They get talking and dare each other, eh? But what can you do? Just the way it is."

Creed tried to remain patient. When Farrell finally did come up with the week-old telegraphed memo from Edmonton, he seemed to blame Creed personally for this interruption to his schedule.

"Didn't know you were coming so soon. It's going to take a little time to organize all this. With the war rationing, we don't have much in terms of provisions, and I don't know what kind of boat to put you in. Our canoes are all out or stripped down. I could get you Mason's riverboat, but you'd need a crew and I don't think they'd want to cross the big lake. We have a York boat one man could handle, if you like to row."

"I don't like to row. When will the canoes be back?"

"Hard to say. A couple days. A week."

"How about an interpreter? Copper dialect."

On this count too, Farrell was pessimistic. "Let me ask around."

"You realize time is an issue here, Sergeant. With any luck I hope to get up there, find the priests, and get out before deep winter."

"I'll tell you what. I haven't had my breakfast yet. Why don't we just step down to the mess for an eye-opener."

The mess was the biggest room in the detachment and featured a long rough-hewn bar with a large cracked mirror behind it. Creed met two congenial constables, Willis and Oberly, drinking coffee. Farrell, his hands trembling slightly, poured Hudson's Bay rum and tomato juice into a melonite tumbler.

"Would you care for one?" he asked Creed.

"No, but I'd have some of that coffee."

Oberly poured him coffee.

Farrell drank half his tumbler. "I swear it keeps me in the pink."

Creed did find it unusual for an RNWMP sergeant to be drinking on duty at midday, but he had become used to it, of course, in the trenches of Europe. Rum was often the only thing that kept body and soul together there. And so it worked with Farrell, for he was quickly transformed into a positive, decisive officer.

"We'll get you the provisions you need. Find a canoe. Have you on your way day after tomorrow. So, what can we tell you about the priests?"

"You remember them? Rouvière and Le Roux?"

"Of course. They came through here in '13. The one, Rouvière, had been in the area a couple years before that and travelled alone up to the treeline looking for Eskimos to convert. Nice fella. Little guy. Sense of humour. Liked to play cards, and he was good, too. He stayed the winter alone in one of Hornby's lousy old cabins up there. Hornby's something of a trapper, trader in the area. Bit crazy."

"Yes. I've heard of him."

"Willis and Oberly here went up to check on the priest that first spring."

Willis and Oberly had been listening and Oberly now spoke up. "That's right. We had some food and mail for him. He was pretty damn glad to see us."

Willis continued: "We tried to convince him to come back with us, but he wanted to stay and find those Eskimos. We were there a few days. Helped him chink up the cabin—it was in rough shape—and shot some game for him. He came down later that year, well after the big thaw, to meet the other one."

Oberly picked up the story: "Yeah, that's when the second priest joined him. Father Le Roux. A Frenchman, from France like. He was supposed to be good with languages, which would come in handy when they finally found some Eskimos to tell about Jesus."

"What do you remember about Le Roux?"

Oberly took a moment to gather his impressions. "Tall man. Big. Kept to himself. Kind of moody. But could just be his way."

"They provisioned here?"

"Yeah. Set off in an eighteen-foot canoe up the Bear. They didn't take a lot. Travelling pretty light if they figured on wintering up there. They planned to get back up to the cabin, then head north again toward the Coppermine to hunt for Eskimos. But that was the last we ever saw of them."

Creed turned back to Farrell. "So you would see regular letters from Rouvière?"

"Yes, he'd get out letters every couple of months by way of some half-breed trapper or trader in the area. We'd forward it on to Montreal or sometimes Winnipeg—Rouvière had a sister there. Then, a few months after Le Roux arrived, the letters stopped. I believe Oberly and Willis were on patrol in the area again and went to check in on them in November. They found the cabin deserted."

Oberly continued: "No one had been at the cabin in a while. The river was freezing up. We went north for a few days on foot as far as we could. There was no sign, no Eskimos. Then the big snow got heavy, food was low, days short. We headed back south again. Then last winter that breed came through here with a rosary and a prayer book with Le Roux's name on it and we got worried. Sent the report."

"How would I get in touch with Hornby?"

"That's a tough one. He can be a hard man to find. Could be on the Dease or up the Mackenzie or on over to the Bay. But if you're up there, he might find you," Willis told him.

"Have you gentlemen discussed what might have happened to the priests?"

The three officers looked at each other.

"I tell you what I think," Farrell said quietly. "Our Cree will tell you. Those Copper Eskimos are a vicious bunch. *Ejaka* the Cree call them: half man, half animal. Bad actors. Aren't many who've met them and lived to tell the tale. Sure as a pussy's a cat, they murdered those poor priests and stole their guns. If you think you can find out more, Godspeed, but that's awful big country up there."

"Well, I have my orders."

"Why don't you at least take Willis with you? Knows the

country up to the Dease. He has an amazing number of awful jokes."

"I'll be fine alone. No offence." Creed nodded to Willis, who was not offended. "But I will need an interpreter."

Farrell smiled at Creed's abrupt dismissal of his suggestion. He looked at Oberly and Willis for ideas. "Not much to choose from that speak Copper Eskimo. There's Isaac Klenenberg, but he'll be trading up the Mackenzie for another month. There's Old Charlie, I suppose, if he can still stand."

"That boy at the tannery, maybe. The breed," Willis suggested.

"That's true. He knows the Copper-speak pretty good, I hear."

THE TANNERY was off a small tributary of the Great Bear, and was owned by a half-Cree named George Fish. Three men, one white and two Indian, worked shirtless in the large open-doored shed over two big boiling pots, stirring the hides. There were two black horses in the corral. Beyond them, in the shadow of an enormous tamarack tree, a skinny figure sat intent on his work. Creed approached him. He wore an oversized checked flannel shirt and wool trousers with suspenders on a thin body. An old slouch fedora hat was on his head and his black hair hung down to his beardless chin, obscuring his face as he worked.

"Hello there. Are you Angituk McAndrew?" He pronounced it "On-gi-tuk" as he had been instructed.

The boy looked up at him for a moment, warily regarding the uniform. High cheekbones, slightly almond eyes, thin nose. Creed would guess about fourteen, maybe fifteen. Hard to tell. The boy nodded and continued with his work. His slender fingers were strong and quick with the knife as he sliced the hide off a muskrat. The back of his left hand had an unusual tattoo design of intermittent blue lines extending down the fingers.

"I need someone who speaks good Copper Eskimo. I'm going north, maybe as far as the Coppermine. Pays good. Dollar a day plus food included. You interested?"

The boy's voice hadn't completely broken yet. He spoke in a hoarse, adolescent whisper. "Maybe. How long?"

"Months. Could be a year. We have to find two priests."

The boy shifted his body slowly, turning toward him in his oversized clothes. "Priests?"

"Yeah. Seems they're lost up there."

The boy squinted at him in the sun, giving him the once-over, taking his own time to appraise Creed and decide. "Dollar and a half a day and I'll cook."

A dollar and a half a day was a lot.

"Can you hunt?"

The boy nodded.

"And you're sure you speak Coppertuk?"

"It's called Inuinnaqtun. My mother was Copper."

Creed held his eyes for a moment, noticing they were bright blue, before the boy looked down again to his work.

Kind of skinny and pretty young, Creed thought, *but he'll have to do. Not a lot of options.*

"Okay. Done." Creed extended his hand. The boy looked at it a moment, hesitated, and then they shook.

CREED REPORTED LAST to Father Ducot at the Catholic mission outside of town. The man was engaged in a lunch of Arctic hare and caribou tongues and asked Creed to join him. The priest was a little shocked to find the investigation consisted of only one man.

"We had some fatalities at Hay River and are low on officers. I'm doing the preliminary search for the Fathers."

Father Ducot gave him two photographs of Father Jean-

Baptiste Rouvière. One, taken after his ordination, showed a slight, clean-shaven, serious young man in a light cassock buttoned down the front, a crucifix placed jauntily in his sash, his eyes very distant as if in anticipation of future travels. The other showed him with a full beard and fur hat, a canvas coat over his heavy, skirted cassock, wearing snowshoes and standing outside his cabin beside a little man identified on the photo as Hornby. Father Ducot had no photograph of Le Roux.

"Father Jean-Baptiste is a very sweet man," the priest began, his accent soft. "I've been deeply missing his card games and his conversation. The winters here can be so oppressive. But he was absolutely determined to get up to the Coppermine and build his church. He promised the Bishop. He said to me, 'Souls are very dear and they must be gained one by one.'"

"His plan was to build a church?"

Father Ducot poured them another glass of claret. "Oh, yes. Ultimately."

"Where, exactly?"

"Somewhere on the Coppermine, or even as far as the Coronation Gulf at the river mouth, on the Arctic Ocean. So inconceivably remote ..." He paused for a moment as he contemplated this. "We were told that at certain times of the year some Eskimo people congregate there to hunt and fish. A big camp. And we had received information, you see ..." He paused again to wash down some tongue. "Information from a man named Bernard ... a boat captain in the Mackenzie delta. He had passed word that a missionary by the name of Fry had been commissioned by the Church of England ..." He almost spat out the words and took a second to recover. "... to prepare to mount an expedition toward the Coronation Gulf! A vexing rabble of Protestants, Freemasons, and materialists. Old-fashioned adherents of Darwinian theory who think they are the vanguard of progress!"

He had lowered his voice as if Church of England agents were lurking at the windows. "Father Jean-Baptiste was determined to get there first. I remember his words. He said he wanted to 'checkmate the zeal of the Protestant who comes to sow tares in our field.'" Father Ducot looked up from his dinner with sudden suspicion. "What are your affiliations, Corporal Creed?"

"I am unaffiliated, Father, believe me. I just want to see that your priests are safe."

Ducot accepted this.

Father Ducot allowed Creed to take with him the two photographs and a packet of letters that Rouvière had sent to him in the hope that they might provide clues to the missionaries' whereabouts.

FATHER DUCOT TOOK HIM behind the Catholic mission and pulled back a canvas tarp from a rack. Creed found himself standing before the perfect canoe. It had belonged to a prospector who was mauled by a bear and taken south for treatment, leaving it in the safekeeping of the priest. It was a sturdy little red sixteen-foot beauty built in Peterborough, Ontario, Creed's hometown. Creed had paddled these craft on Rice Lake and the Otonabee River from the first day he could pick up a paddle. There were claw marks along the gunnels and thwarts of this one, and some dark blood had pooled between the ribs. The encounter with the bear had occurred when the man was paddling in the shallows. The priest assured Creed the man had survived, but a recent letter had instructed him to sell the canoe; the prospector wasn't coming back. Ducot offered it to Creed for sixty dollars. Privately, Creed thought he should have given it to him for free. It was, after all, Ducot's fellow priests he was trying to find. But the price was firm and Creed paid it.

THE PETERBOROUGH PADDLED as prettily as it looked, cutting against the heavy river current of the Great Bear with tenacious efficiency as they left Fort Norman behind them. And the little craft comfortably carried their provisions: a wanigan box of tinned food, tea, salt, chocolate, lard, and tobacco to trade, as well as utensils and pans, two sealed bags of clothing, knapsacks with personal effects, a tent, sleeping bags, rifle and cartridges, axes and knives, a small oil stove, and a can of fuel.

The boy too seemed a reasonable choice so far. He didn't say much, but his paddle strength was well beyond what his thin frame promised. Creed's trust would be won slowly. Coming around the first slow bend, Creed put his back to the stroke, digging deep, twisting off with an efficient J. The boy felt the new power from the stern and matched it, and the canoe surged hard against the current. Creed loved canoeing. It was honest, repetitive work that got you somewhere, accomplished something, like piling sandbags or digging graves. You lost yourself in the motion and you could forget about the context.

That first day, the weather held clear and warm and they covered a respectable eleven or twelve miles against the current before making camp on a flat rock shelf that would hold the warmth of the sun long after dark.

"I'll put up the tent if you want to make dinner."

"What do you like?" the boy asked.

"Beans and the bully beef, I guess. Keep it simple."

The boy was studying the river. "I saw char. You want fish?"

"Sure."

A small coiled line with a silver spinner dangling from it appeared in the boy's hand, and Creed watched as he climbed nimbly over some broken boulders collapsed out into the river. He took a position facing the pool, behind the rocks in the lee of the current, where the fish would rest on their way upstream. He tossed the simple lure with a practised hand, letting out enough line for it to descend and hold in the current three inches above the bottom, where just enough light from the low sun would flash off the rotating spoon to seduce a fat char.

Creed turned and set to putting up the conical canvas tent. It was big and heavy, army issue, the same design they had had long ago in basic training and so familiar he could raise it in his sleep. These tents were useless in the trenches at the front, but this one would be practical here. Miraculously, all the pegs and poles were in the bag, though on the granite shelf he had to use rocks piled one on top of another to secure the floor and wall lines. He cut soft cedar boughs for inside.

Creed was opening the flaps to air it out when he heard the boy returning over the rocks. He had a nice four-pound char hanging limp on his line, more than enough for both of them.

"Nice work."

The boy nodded at the compliment but didn't smile. Within minutes he had a fire going, the fish gutted and slow-frying with a dollop of lard in the cast-iron pan. He mixed a little flour with river water, kneaded it into dough, wrapped it in a tight spiral around a moistened stick, and soon had it toasting away over the fire. Then he opened a can of green peas, and for dessert he gathered sweet blueberries and redcurrants from the resolute bushes in the crags nearby to complete the feast. Creed watched the whole process, quite impressed with the boy's resourcefulness. Considering the lack of choice, he had done well finding him. Only thing, he never smiled. Creed resolved to work on ways to get a smile out of him.

Over the next few days, the boy's cuisine did not falter. The fishing was productive and they were eating a lot of salmon and char, saving the tinned beef and beans for the future days of need. They spent their evenings and nights in the conical tent, which offered some relief from the mosquitoes, and Creed read his books. And though it often rained, the tent proved tight and dry. Each morning, as the boy made a breakfast of bacon, fried bannock bread, and coffee or tea, Creed would shave with water warmed by the little spruce fire and write a few lines in his journal. He had never travelled north of the treeline before, and as he warmed his hands at the fire Creed often wondered how they would handle much colder weather without fuel for warmth. He reminded himself that the priests had managed it. At least at first.

Father Rouvière's first letter to Ducot had been sent as he travelled for the first time up the Great Bear River. Creed's French was a little rusty, but it came back quickly and he was to find in the letters a sense of Rouvière's voice: earnest, sincere, humble, often expressing a youthful wonder. He found himself looking forward to meeting the man.

> What a river! The current is very strong and there are places where there is not enough water and the rocks threaten us. And sometimes the rapids go on for miles. Sometimes we have to climb out and push the boat to get forward at all!

Of the mission, Rouvière wrote to his friend:

> So far the good Lord has kept me well and I ask Him every day to preserve me to the end until I might fulfill this difficult mission which has been entrusted

to me, to introduce these people to the one true
Saviour. No one knows how many Copper there are
or what they are like and I'm sure there'll be some
tough nuts up there, but I trust they are too good-
hearted to put up much of a fight against grace. I rely
upon your prayers.

AS CREED AND THE BOY continued up the Great Bear, the sun
stayed warm on their shoulders and baked the earthen riverbanks, whose pungent aroma mixed with that of the pine and
willow trees into the wafting scent of fertility itself. They had
seen three moose, silky black otters diving in the shallows, and
many long-tail ducks and mergansers negotiating the quiet
eddies near shore.

On the fourth day, they met the Cree. Beyond a slow curve
in the river, and below a rocky peak on the north bank called
Mount Charles on Creed's rough sketch map, they came to a
set of deep rapids, the tunnels of black water arching their
backs over granite rocks like breaching whales. By his subtle
backward glance from the bow, Creed knew the boy wanted to
power through it. But the water was low, and Creed wanted to
be careful with the Peterborough. There was a portage path up
ahead and Creed's legs could use the break. He pulled them over
to the worn, muddy bank to face a two-hundred-yard carry.

With no need for discussion the boy hoisted the wooden
wanigan box with the band straining against his forehead and
slid a large canvas pack on top—eighty pounds of gear—and
was off, well ahead of Creed. Creed strapped the paddle blades
tight against the mid-thwart and, with a fifty-pound knapsack
on his back, hoisted the pretty red canoe up onto his shoulders,
his forearms resting, steadying, along the inside curve of the
gunnels, keeping the craft parallel to the ground.

The well-worn portage was not long, and he had tried to pack light for times like this. As he neared the end, where the water calmed again, he was startled by the unexpected sound of harsh voices. He tipped up the bow of the canoe to see.

They had surrounded Angituk—three rough-looking Cree. They wore a hodgepodge of fur and white men's clothing: canvas trousers, a waistcoat, a nautical cap, a soldier's jacket. Angituk had dropped the wanigan and was holding them at bay with his skinning knife and paddle. The men were hissing at him and murmuring threats and insults, but by the way Angituk held the knife they realized he could use it, and for all their bravado they remained cautious.

Creed rolled the canoe from his shoulders, dropping it on a bed of soft junipers, and called out in Oji-Cree. "Get away from the boy!"

They saw the yellow stripe on Creed's trousers and did as they were told, but they continued to glare at Angituk with contempt and suspicion and, Creed noted, even fear. The shortest man, in a bowler hat, sun goggles, and a wolverine vest, turned to Creed.

"Why is a white policeman travelling with a disgusting *Ayashkmew?*"

"Because it is my pleasure. Now go on your way."

"You are in danger. One night he will stick that knife in your back and eat you."

Angituk was embarrassed and would not meet Creed's eyes.

"That is no concern of yours."

The Cree in the bowler hat came close and spoke quietly to share a confidence with the white man. "Eskimos have magic. They are shape-shifters! They can become animals."

"Stop talking nonsense."

"Don't trust him."

"He is a good man."

"I tell you this for your own good."

Just then Creed noticed the heavy artifact hanging from the short man's neck. Creed took two steps toward him. As the man raised his hands in defence, Creed grabbed the crucifix and inspected it. It was an unusually large silver cross inlaid with mother-of-pearl. He turned it over to find the initials *J.B.R.*

"Where did you get this?"

The man looked worried. "I traded it from a Dene hunter up on Great Bear Lake a few weeks ago."

"What was his name?"

"I don't know."

"You don't know his name?"

"I don't know him. We were just passing."

Creed believed him. He bought the crucifix from him for two dollars and sent them on their way.

Before the Cree left with the bales of marten and mink furs they were taking south in their battered birchbark canoes, they looked warily at the boy, and the one in the bowler hat again warned Creed about him.

"Even a young one. They have magic. They can steal your soul. They can make you sick. You will die."

"You are like an old woman," Creed scoffed.

The short Cree's eyes flashed at this insult. He coughed up some phlegm and spat on the ground near the boy's feet. "Remember. You were warned."

They shouldered their canoes and their bales and were gone.

The boy looked up at Creed. "Thank you, Corporal. I'm sorry."

"Superstitious idiots."

They loaded the canoe and continued on their way without further discussion, but Creed found himself casually musing about the reaction of the Cree to the boy. Magic? He wondered what the signs would be.

That night at the campfire, Creed couldn't resist. "Is it true? Do you know magic?"

The boy thought about this for a while, the fire illuminating his features. "Our shamans know magic. The rest of us? We know about the spirits around us. That's all. We know how not to get into trouble."

"That's an important skill. Perhaps you can teach me," Creed suggested with a smile.

"I'll do my best," the boy replied, his face dead serious at the responsibility presented to him. Then he crawled into the tent to sleep.

THEY PADDLED UP the Great Bear for eleven days in all. The tall, thick pines surrounding Fort Norman gave way to a shorter variety as well as black spruce, whose numbers dwindled like the hairs on a balding head. They portaged five times and tracked that many times or more, walking in the ice-cold river, pushing or pulling the canoe over the rocky swifts and shallows the way Father Rouvière had done. Creed continued to read through the young priest's letters. One described his first encounter with the Eskimos. He and Hornby had made their way across the big lake and were at a camp up the Dease River, halfway to the Coppermine.

> Hornby was difficult this morning and went off hunting. I decided to take a walk in the opposite direction, northeast along the river. I'd walked half the day when I saw something at the top of a hill. I walked in that direction to see what it was and I saw several people in the cleft of the hill. Are they caribou? Are

they men? I can't tell at that distance. To make sure
I go toward the hill. There's no doubt about it: these
are Eskimos! Thanks, O mother Mary! The first step
of my mission fulfilled. Be pleased to bless this first
encounter! I was wearing my cassock and holding my
oblate cross. As soon as they saw me, they came toward
me, holding their arms to the sky and bowing deeply.
Immediately, I raised my arms aloft. The leader gently
took me by the arm and presented me to the others.
They called me by their word: *Kabloona*. They touched
me, shook my hands, touched the cross around my
neck. Immediately, I began to try to tell them by signs
that ... *celui qui est sur la croix* ... He who is on the Cross ... *s'y
est immolé pour nous* ... He was murdered for us! I gave out
medals, which I placed around their necks. All were
overcome with admiration. They brought me to their
camp to eat. I struggled to make them understand that
I had come for them. They are my new congregation,
and I will stay among them. O mother Mary, that with
your blessings we can convert them to the true faith.
The Eskimos are a really hospitable people. This first
impression was very favourable and I think if we can
meet them often it would be possible to do a lot of
good!

ONE AFTERNOON, only about a day's journey from the big lake
ahead, Creed and the boy arrived at a place where the riverbed
narrowed and the current gathered strength. Once again they
lowered themselves into the water up to their waists and tracked
the canoe, with Creed pulling on the bow painter and the boy
pushing from behind. They dug their boots into the gravel and
rocks of the riverbed and pushed, making slow progress against

the river, but Creed spoke with encouragement as much for himself as for his young companion.

"We're getting there. We're doing well. One foot in front of the other. We'll deserve that hot fire tonight, eh? Maybe we'll open that tinned ham. What do you think?"

Creed glanced back to see the boy nod in agreement.

"Yeah, the ham," Creed continued. "Warm it up in the tin. Maybe even peaches. Hell, we deserve it after this."

Glancing back, he saw the boy nod again, but he was tired and struggling. Creed's feet found their way between boulders on the bottom. The river was deep here, in some holes reaching to Creed's armpits. The boy was shorter. They could go in to shore, but the solid wall of low black spruce there would make for a hell of a portage. Creed studied the unaccommodating river ahead.

"Maybe we'll sleep in tomorrow. Just an hour or so. No one's going to complain ..."

Suddenly the canoe became much heavier and Creed turned to find the boy was gone. So complete was his disappearance that Creed scanned the empty shore for him. Straining at the painter to hold the canoe against the current, Creed stared at the river where the boy had been. Nothing. Then three fingers broke the surface. The boy was caught under the water.

Creed surged back to him and stared down at the boy, three feet below the surface, on his back, arms wheeling, one foot jammed and twisted between two boulders, his body held prone by the relentless current. Creed glanced downstream to where rocks would certainly take the canoe and all their supplies if he let go of it. He put the end of the painter between his teeth and submerged himself, embracing the boy and trying to drag him to the surface. The current was too strong. He worked his way toward the boy's boot, the pull of the canoe snapping his neck as he took its full weight with his teeth. The boot was jammed in pretty solid. With a lunge Creed went deeper, pulling the canoe back with him, and got his fingers under the sole. The boy's struggles were weakening. Creed yanked on the boot, the weight of the canoe now assisting his efforts. It didn't budge. The boy's arms moved in slow, helpless circles as the last of his strength ebbed. Creed renewed his grip on the boot and, this time with all his strength, pulled again. The air left in his lungs escaped in an underwater growl. The boot came free and he and the boy broke through the surface together, gasping in the air.

He helped the boy to some rocks in the shallows to rest. But for the bruised ankle, he was all right. Frightened and trembling, but all right.

"Thank you," he said, still breathing hard.

They camped that night on a gravel bar nearby. Creed gathered driftwood for a big fire to dry their clothes, and warmed the promised tin of ham. They opened the peaches for dessert. The boy was embarrassed by the whole episode, and Creed resisted his natural inclination to tease him.

They dried their clothes on a makeshift rack and stared into the fire. It occurred to Creed how little they had spoken to each other on this trip. It had been a relief at first, the boy's silence. It was as Creed wanted it. But after all these days, he realized he knew very little about him. And then, as if to deepen his curiosity, when Angituk was unpacking his dry bag, Creed noticed a thick leather-bound book that had half slid out onto the earth beside the fire. He was amazed to read the title: *Canterbury Tales.*

"Where the hell did you get this?"

"From Father Ducot."

"You stole it?"

"No," the boy said with sudden indignation. "He loaned it to me."

"Do you understand it at all?"

He caught the flash of anger in the fire-lit blue eyes and immediately regretted the question. The boy recited, like an accusation:

> And specially from every shires ende,
> Of Engelond to Canterbury they wende,
> The holy blisful martyr for to seek,
> That hem hath holpen whan that they were seke.

"Why would I not understand? It is a journey. Journeys are what I understand. Though Herman Melville is better at it than Chaucer. Twain is good too, but Conrad is the best of all."

The boy offered nothing further. Creed stared at him, astonished.

As the silence between them thickened, Creed realized he had lost the opportunity that night to pursue the questions in his mind about the boy.

THE NEXT AFTERNOON they approached the enormous inland freshwater ocean that was Great Bear Lake. Three hundred miles of water stretched out before them. A brisk northerly was whipping up three-foot breakers. Even so, it was nothing the canoe couldn't handle easily once they found deeper water beyond the breaking waves. The wind was dropping and clocking around slowly. It should be southeast by morning.

Creed and Angituk paddled in amiable silence, coming up to the mouth until they came in sight of a red beach. There, where the Great Bear River flowed out of Great Bear Lake, stood a large brown bear. For a moment Creed was sure he was seeing things. It stood in the shallow waters, nose elevated, taking in their wind-carried scent. It nodded to them several times. No stranger to bears, Creed was cautious, and he glanced down at the claw marks on the side of the canoe, determined not to share the fate of the previous owner. But as much as he paddled the craft out from the shallows, Angituk tried eagerly to take it in, closer to the creature with whom he was speaking softly in the Copper dialect.

"Close enough!" Creed finally told him tensely, but the boy was not listening, and as they drifted closer Creed felt an odd, dreamlike exhilaration.

The big bear—and it was larger than Creed had first realized—stuck his nose out toward the boy, his head bobbing at Angituk's words as if in agreement. They drifted within twenty-five feet and Creed saw that they were in very shallow water. The bear, if he followed an urge, could sprint to the canoe and be on them in three, maybe four seconds. Creed glanced at the old .38-55 lever-action rifle in front of him in its leather case. His hand went to it and the boy noticed the movement.

"Don't," he whispered in a tone that stopped Creed cold. His pistol was more accessible, but a pistol would never stop this brute, it would merely anger him. He forced himself to stay calm and simply observe the bear and the boy.

As he watched, he listened to the boy's youthful voice, an oriental murmur with a high, questioning lift on certain words and a rhythmic guttural consonant caught in the back of the throat, like a three-octave song. He was hearing the Copper language for the very first time. What had Freeman said at the barracks? A Siberian language. Even close to Chinese. And the beast actually seemed to answer in a series of grunts. It was to Creed as if the world held its breath. Then suddenly the bear turned west and lumbered slowly away, down the red beach toward a promising copse of black pine.

The boy watched the creature for a moment, then began to paddle again. Creed had the overwhelming desire to pose the ridiculous question, What did the bear say? He paused, and reformed the question in his mind.

"What did you say to the bear?"

"I told him who we are and where we're going. I should have explained—he is my *tornrack*. My spirit guide. In the North he is the white bear. Down here he is brown."

"What is a spirit guide?"

"When we are young, we look for a spirit helper in dreams. In my dreams it was always the bear. He helps me. He told us all is well, except a storm is coming tomorrow."

"That right?"

"That's what he said."

Skeptically, Creed looked at the scarlet horizon, which promised a fair day tomorrow. Not even a suggestion of cloud. He smiled at the thought of the bear predicting weather.

"I don't think so. Look at that sky."

The boy shrugged and began to paddle hard. Following his lead, Creed put his back into the paddling, powering over the breakers until they were fifty yards out from shore. They would head east up the south coast for an hour, give a little distance to the bruin and make camp on the beach. They'd need a good rest tonight, for tomorrow they would rig a small sail and set out, not knowing when they might touch land again.

Three

They headed out that morning on the vast, calm lake with a small canvas sail pushed by the gentle southeast wind Creed had predicted.

"You see? What do bears know?" he told the boy, who merely shrugged again.

Their destination was Dease Bay, directly northeast, on the far side of the lake. He was tempted to head straight across on this calm freshwater ocean, but the course would have taken them very far from land, almost out of sight. So he set a course to the east toward a large peninsula, keeping the shoreline well in view. They sailed with naive ease on the gentle swells all morning.

When the storm did hit a few hours later, it howled them along all afternoon, the contrary wind continuing its rotation clockwise from south, behind them, to southwest and finally west, off their port beam. With each shift Creed adjusted the sail to accommodate for the wind change. He had lashed keel boards that knifed down on either side, sixteen inches deeper than the keel, to guide a steady course, and he hiked out, leaning over the westward gunnels, showing the boy how to do it to keep the boat upright and the sail filled. They moved along quite nicely in the storm, with no advantage to be gained by paddling. The bow lifted or cut through the waves, and even the odd breaker so far offered little challenge to the sturdy craft. Now, with the wind from the west, Creed had to lean out over the gunnels more as a counterweight to the sail and the boy did the same. The rain came and went. They put on oilskin jackets. Mid-afternoon, the boy handed Creed fried char and biscuits and cold tea. Apprehensive at first, as the day wore on, the boy relaxed and his enjoyment grew steadily.

Through the day, Creed navigated by his compass. But now night was falling quickly. They could see only distant land off to their right. They had no choice but to sail on. Creed stared at the horizon backlit by the setting sun, the afterglow soon extinguished by the storm clouds looming ahead. The darkness swallowed them; the compass was useless without either a star to take a bearing from or light to read the instrument by. And with no horizon to orient themselves by, it was like sailing into a coal mine. The wind was back at her tricks. It came around again, finally northwest and freezing, building the oncoming waves to drive the little canoe too far east.

As they sailed blind, the northwest waves were the last natural guide to the northerly course they steered, but they had grown. The crashing roar of rogue waves broke in the darkness around them. For all her graceful lines, the Peterborough was a river craft with a low freeboard, and they were in the middle of an ocean. As they rode up each wave, Creed turned into it, praying it wouldn't break over the gunnels until they crested, then struggled to point the boat back on course, thirty degrees off the line of the swell. Each wave took a lot out of him and he did a survey of his stiff, frozen muscles wrestling with the paddle. For the first time he wondered if he had the stamina to ride out this storm all night. He wasn't sure.

The first wave that broke over the gunnels deposited a pailful of water. The added weight held the canoe down, and on the next wave the same thing happened again.

"Bail!" Creed called out to the boy. He heard him fumbling in the cooking wanigan and the bumping of a pot against the ribs of the canoe as he did as he was told.

They rode out two more big ones. In the blackness he could only judge the coming break by sound and rhythm. The wind whined in his ears like incoming German .77 rounds. Over the sound of the waves he heard thunder, and a second later the world was illuminated with a flash of vibrant, crackling white light. It revealed that the water in the canoe was deeper than he had thought, and the boy's blue eyes looked up at him in fear as he bailed for their lives. Then all was blackness again and they rode another big one, up and over, this time taking no water. But there was something else Creed thought he might have seen in the instant of total light, something breaking the distant horizon. Could have been dark clouds or his eyes playing tricks. He waited for the thunder, and when it came he watched where the horizon should be and sure enough, in the bright flash that followed, standing in black silhouette one hundred yards to the northwest, there it was.

"Land!"

The boy paused from his labours a moment to look. They stared into the darkness where the narrow slip of shoreline had now disappeared. Then came the biggest wave yet. Creed could not get the vessel turned in time. It hit them on the angle and there was nothing they could do. It swamped them, rolling them half over, the mast and sail in the water on the lee side and Creed and the boy with them. Creed jumped when he knew they were going over and he found himself under the canvas sail. The water was icy cold, and his heart pounded with shock as he fought his way to the surface only to be stopped by the spread of the canvas sail. He reached to his belt for his sheath knife but remembered it was in the pocket of his pack. He tried to swim to the edge but couldn't force back the boom, which the hull of the canoe held tight against her side in the relentless wind.

Another wave washed over them and the hull bounced hard off his head. The ice-cold water soaked his wool clothing under the oilskin, entered his boots, sapped his strength, and pulled him down. He tried to fight it, but he just needed a moment to rest. Despite the freezing embrace of the water it was good to be out of the wind. He'd just rest a moment in the darkness then find his way out from under the sail. He hoped the boy was all right. In a moment or two he'd try again.

He heard the rip of canvas as a knife flashed down close to his face. He felt a sudden tug on his collar. Then he was floating up through the tatters of the sail, into fresh air and the howling wind. He gasped the rich, cold air into his lungs. He opened his eyes. The clouds were thinning and a pale but constant suggestion of moonlight now illuminated the little Peterborough, awash but still stubbornly afloat. Creed turned to see the boy, the knife in his teeth glinting in the faint light, looking very worried.

Creed called to him. "I'm okay. We'll get rid of the sail and paddle her in."

The boy nodded.

Working together, they cut the stays of the makeshift mast and pulled it free of the supporting thwart. They retrieved and coiled most of the thick halyard, then let the mast, boom, and remnants of sail float free. They righted the canoe. The ties had held and all of their supplies, including their paddles, were still on board. Creed took his position on the windward side, Angituk on the lee, and they began kicking in the direction of the island. Not that the direction was clear—they were down in the water and could not see over the waves. The centre of the storm had passed them by, but once in a while a crack of lightning would offer more illumination and Creed would push himself up on the gunnels to gain height. The second time he saw them, much closer now, the tips of a few pine trees.

"There it is! To the left. Come on! Kick, damn it!"

They finally touched sandy bottom in a sheltered cove of a peninsula, a rocky oasis jutting well out into the lake. They dragged the Peterborough, heavy with water and supplies, half out of the water. They cut the lashings of the keel boards to release them and dragged the vessel higher to safety. They crawled up on the sand beach on their hands and knees in the lee of the wind, both gasping, shivering uncontrollably. The moon came out then, bright enough to cast clear shadows. When Creed's breath returned, he laughed and said out loud what he had said at several other moments in his life.

"Still here."

The boy looked at him as if he were crazy, but when Creed's honest laughter continued, the boy understood. He studied Creed again with amusement and then, as if bestowing a special prize, his teeth bright white in the moonlight, Angituk smiled.

"There you go," Creed told him triumphantly.

THEY SET UP THE TENT first to dry. There was lots of brushwood, and though it was wet, with patience Creed soon had a roaring fire on the beach. The sleeping bags and clothing had been in dry sacks that the water had not penetrated. They quickly changed out of their wet clothes, a distance apart in the darkness, their backs to each other as always, and soon they were before the fire eating hot pork and beans out of tins and staring into the flames, their exhaustion now beginning to take over.

"Our *isuma* is good, Corporal."

"What is *isuma*?"

Angituk considered his answer for a moment. "It is something everyone has, some much more than others. It is a mixture of wisdom and luck."

"It was mostly luck today. I'm sorry, I should have listened. Your bear was right about the storm."

"Yes, but they're not perfect."

Creed looked at him and laughed again. The weather bear is not perfect. Angituk smiled once more and Creed admired his flawless white teeth. Twice in one day, Creed mused. They stared at the fire in exhausted silence, their eyelids and the empty tins in their hands heavy and their bellies full.

"Angituk, I ... You saved my life out there."

The boy nodded slightly.

"Guess we should call it a night."

They lay in the tent back to back in their dry sleeping bags, Angituk on the edge of sleep, Creed writing in his journal a report on the events of the day, by the light of the small lantern. He finished his very short and objective description of the capsize and it struck him again what he owed the boy.

"Angituk? You awake?"

He heard a breath drawn and a mumble. "Hmmmmm?"

"Thank you again for today, Angituk. You're a good man."

Angituk answered in his sleepy, adolescent whisper, an inscrutable smile on his lips. "You're a good man too, Corporal."

A moment later, steady, shallow breathing filled the space between them.

Creed withdrew the crucifix from his jacket pocket and held it up to the soft light of the lantern. The mother-of-pearl inlay sparkled in his hand. A sudden pessimism came over him. Could the priests still be alive in this dangerous land? He tucked the crucifix away. Just before sleep claimed him, he remembered a section in a book by Vilhjalmur Stefansson, *My Life with the Eskimo*, published four years before, about the Eskimo belief that the world as we experience it is really a dream and dreams are the actual reality. He had sometimes had that feeling in Belgium. He must ask the boy about that belief.

Later that night he swam in the black sea with priests dressed in their full vestments. Le Roux chided him for stealing the crucifix and demanded it back. Rouvière took his hand to show him things and they swam forward in the darkness together. Creed awoke happy and more optimistic than ever before that the priests might still be alive.

THEY LEFT THE TIP of the eastern peninsula and for the next two and a half weeks they made their way across the Great Bear Lake, trying to stay within distant sight of shore. They spent two nights on the tip of another peninsula to the west, where it rained in curtains for thirty-six hours straight. They spent the time in the gloom of the tent while Creed wrote in his notebook and read Hearne's diary and most of Ford's novel about friendship and betrayal. The boy finished his Chaucer.

Creed noticed that each morning before they left land the boy would walk along the shore and carefully select a handful of coloured pebbles, sparkling quartz or pink granite, and put them in his pocket. After they had set out on the water, he would lay his paddle across the gunnels and carefully drop the pebbles one by one into the translucent depths.

"What are the pebbles for?"

"Gifts for the beings who live in the lake."

"What beings?"

"Lake spirits. They have to be treated with respect."

"What do they look like?"

"I don't know. They can take many forms down there. I don't

like to think about what they look like. Maybe they're invisible. Hope we don't see any."

"I hope they like your pebbles."

GOOD WEATHER HELD for them during the second week, and one morning they went ashore and cut another mast and boom, rigging a smaller canvas sail that worked for a few days until the wind shifted directly north again. By this time they could make out the thin black line on the horizon that was the north shore and they didn't mind the paddling. The north wind offered a challenge and they approached landfall well into the next dawn. The very basic maps Creed had been given at Fort Norman proved true, for they could see the mouth of the Dease River in front of them. It would take them farther north and west, to the cabin the priests called home.

As they approached the mouth of the river, Creed's eye caught something on the shore to the east, a structure of some kind that did not fit with the topography or flora. He guided their craft toward it, noting that he could see through the clear water to the stony bottom of the lake. The thing onshore that had drawn his attention was a large old York boat, wrecked on the shallow, rocky shore many years before. It was thirty feet long and made of thick planks, a huge open rowboat that would need a team of several strong men to row it, like a Viking long ship. The weathered mast was still in place, but the main propulsion would have come from the strength of men's backs. Could be the property of Hudson's Bay or private traders. Must have been blown up on the rocks by a southwest gale. Creed wondered what had become of the crew. As they drew closer, he could make out the battered nameplate, *The Jupiter*, and his first thought was how the hard men who had pushed this far north years before through this unforgiving land still kept a whimsical eye on the planets and stars. But then he recalled that Jupiter was the father of the god of war.

It was a relief to be paddling near shore again, with some shelter from the wind and rollers. Several hours beyond the mouth, now on the flat river, they were paddling past a high, rocky point and Creed had the feeling they were being watched.

"I feel it too," the boy told him, and together they scanned the high rocks, but they could see nothing.

To the north of Great Bear Lake, along the riverbanks, the black spruce and pine were noticeably shorter and more spare on the hills, and rather than solid forest, they grew in copses, gathering resourcefully in the sheltered valleys, behind windbreaks, leaving wide open spaces of rock and tundra. Creed and the boy were approaching the end of trees.

WITHIN AN HOUR of their being on the Dease River, the weather closed gloomily in and stayed with them for two days. Unlike those of the Great Bear River, the riverbanks here showed little sign of life. Even the fish made themselves scarce and not one responded to the boy's spinner.

On the second day they came around a bend in the Dease and entered a widening of the river that the rough map identified as Imaerink Lake—in Cree, "the place where people died." What had compelled Hornby to build his cabin on this cursed lake was beyond Creed. On the far side, at the eastern end, against the dark green of the stubby forest, stood the rectangle of a cabin. As they approached the shore, Creed's heart sank. The cabin was nothing but a burned-out ruin: the roof gone, rough doors and shutters broken open. In the sullen mists it had the morning-after look of a direct artillery hit. They landed the canoe in silence and Creed walked to the front door. The boy squatted on the shore beside the canoe, apparently wary of getting any closer to this place where spirits could remain. He began to sing a quiet song like a chant, a monotonous, meandering dirge in a minor key.

Creed approached the ruins. As he stepped across the threshold, a raven flew up through the open roof into the sky. Inside there were charred pieces of furniture and a scattering of notebooks, most of the pages ripped out to fuel fires on the dirt floor. There was a crude fireplace and hearth fashioned out of stones and clay. Broken dishes littered the floor. He picked up a handwritten page. In French, it recorded a meeting with trappers and Cree and some simple advice on finding the Eskimos. Creed poked around in the ashes with a stick for a while but found little more—a tattered magazine of French architecture featuring Notre-Dame, another of Vatican City, a few pages of a child's picture book of Bible stories, and a hymnal.

The boy's meandering song stopped suddenly and Creed was astonished to hear a clipped British voice call out, "I say, chaps! How goes it?"

Creed bolted out of the cabin to find a short white man in a tweed coat approaching. He had long, curly black hair, bright blue eyes, a full beard, and a face weathered well beyond his natural age, twenty-seven or twenty-eight. He had three tattered sweaters layered under his jacket, no hat, and his fingerless gloves held an ancient pair of binoculars. He carried a large-bore, long-barrelled rifle and his eyes were a bit wild. Creed approached the man slowly, cautiously.

"Good morning. I'm Corporal Creed of the Royal North West Mounted Police. This is Angituk." The gun swung vaguely toward Creed. The man had a smile on his face, but Creed appraised the unsettling eyes. "Just point that gun away, friend, if you'd be so kind."

"Oh, yes! Sorry. Of course." The man lifted the barrel, leaned the weapon against a rock, held out his hand to Creed, and almost shouted his name. "John Hornby! At your service, sir, yes, at your service indeed."

"Hornby! I was hoping to find you."

"As you have. How are things 'outside'? I don't get outside very often."

"Fine. Outside, things are fine."

Hornby shook his hand for a full fifteen seconds before Creed could take it back again.

"Oh, sorry."

Accompanying John Hornby was a small mixed-breed cur with large saddlebags across his back and a red paisley hand-kerchief around his neck.

"And this is Dawg."

"Hello, Dawg. What brings you up here, John?"

John's smile faded slightly as he pondered this question for a long moment. "My legs ... mostly. Had a canoe for a while when I was on the Snake."

"No, I mean what are you doing up here?"

John looked a little confused by the question. "I'm talking to you," he insisted.

"No, I mean, are you hunting or trapping or trading?"

John nodded and smiled pleasantly.

"Which?" Creed asked innocently.

"Oh, no, I'm not," Hornby told him solemnly. "We don't allow witches here. I mean, we don't burn them at the stake or anything, but you just can't do that sort of thing around here. We've warned the shamans."

Creed decided on a new tack. "Sorry about your cabin."

"Oh, yes. Miscreants. Wish I could find them and teach them a lesson."

"John, I understand you knew the two priests that rented this place from you? I'm looking for them."

"Yes! Rouvière! I brought him up here ... three winters ago. Lovely man!"

"I'd like to ask you some questions."

"Then we must have tea! Have you brought any tea? Been a dog's life since tea. No offence, Dawg."

WITH TEA IN HIS HAND, Hornby proved a surprisingly clear and concise narrator.

"When Father Rouvière first came here, the poor man hadn't spent a warm summer day in the Arctic, let alone an entire winter. He had few supplies, no cold-weather clothing or gear. He had a wool coat. Imagine. Wool. How long do you think a sheep would last up here in winter? One day at most. Father Rouvière had no hunting skills, had never even met an Eskimo, except for a few domesticated ones on the Mackenzie. He barely knew me. Imagine going up here with me? I even get scared thinking about it. But I got him set up in Norman. He loved to play Wisk and chess in the evenings."

Hornby went on to explain how Rouvière was at first almost beaten by the physical demands. "He was a skinny little guy. The wind'd cut right through 'im. Never thought he'd last, but he did. 'Perseverance triumphs,' as they say. Do they still say that?" Hornby stopped and looked pointedly at the silent Creed.

"Yes. Yes, I guess that's what they say."

"There was the one time we found some of the Huskies."

"Huskies?"

"Yeah. Eskimos. The Coppers. I call 'em Huskies. We were the other side of the Dismal Lakes, almost to the Coppermine when we found 'em. Father Rouvière looked like a kid on Christmas morning, he was so excited. They'd never seen a white man before. We might just as well have been men from Mars. You know, funny I should say that—because there's a strong argument it's true! There's a professor at Cambridge that's pretty much proven we're descended from Martians. I mean, ask yourself—would you rather come from Mars or monkeys?"

"The choice is clear."

"They landed long ago and left us here, don't you think?"

"Certainly it's possible. But what about the other priest, Father Le Roux?"

"Oh ... yeah." Hornby's expression darkened. "He showed up the next year."

"Tell me about him."

"First-class son of a bitch! A scold. Five minutes after I met him he was telling me I was living in mortal sin and had to get rid of Arimo. She's the Cree woman I live with in my other cabin on Dease Bay. Then he took some of my supplies and demanded I take them to the Coppermine. I told him to bugger off, and then I left."

"You left them?"

"Yes, I did. I felt badly for Rouvière—he was a sweet man— but I wasn't going to guide them if Le Roux was staying. Instead of going north, Dawg and I spent the season walking west to the Mackenzie River to see the land." Hornby suddenly fell silent.

"And did you ever see them again?"

"No. But I did see the Mackenzie River."

"But you believe the priests did go north after you left?"

"Yes. I heard they met a Huskie hunter who agreed to take 'em north."

"What do you think happened to them?"

"Oh, I think they're dead. Starved or froze or killed. Rouvière tried, but he wasn't so good on the land. I suppose the Huskies could be looking after them, but ... you see this cabin? I don't know if it were Dene or Cree or even a hunt party of Huskies came this far south and did it, but whoever, they wouldn't have torched it if the priests were still alive."

"Where would you look for them?"

"Up the Coppermine, of course. There's a gathering place for the Eskimos called Bloody Falls. Good fishing and hunting just ten miles from the Coronation Gulf. I'd head there."

"You've been there?"

"No."

"It's in Samuel Hearne's book. He witnessed the massacre of an entire Eskimo village there by the Chipewyans he was travelling with. So he named it Bloody Falls."

"I know. Samuel Hearne is why I'd never go there."

"What do you mean?"

"Some of the Huskies who escaped those killings saw Hearne standing with the Chipewyans and thought he was their leader. All the Huskies heard was that the massacre at Bloody Falls was led by a white man. That's why they hate us now. Long memories. One hundred and forty-five years. But that's why I've never gone into the Coppermine. Don't want to get my throat cut."

"Anything else you can tell me?"

"There's a well-known Huskie hunter up there I've heard of that usually camps near the mouth of the Coppermine. His name is Koeha. If anyone knows what happened to the priests, he will."

"We'll try to find him."

"And I've done my best to spread the word."

"What do you mean?"

"The 'understanding.' I told those Huskies on the Dismals the deal."

"What deal?"

"Well, the deal that if an Eskimo kills a white man, then a hundred white men will come and kill them all."

"I suppose a little terror goes a long way."

"I believe it might save a white man's life or two."

John Hornby excused himself then. He and Dawg were on their way to Hudson Bay. Again he shook their hands, thanked them for the tea, and wished them well.

"Now you be careful. There are some bad actors up there," Hornby cautioned.

"So I've heard. It's good to meet you. Appreciate the information."

Creed delighted Hornby with three bags of English Breakfast tea, which he put carefully in his knapsack.

"That's so wonderful, because you know English is exactly the language that Dawg and I speak when we're having our breakfast!"

"Right."

Dawg and the little man in the tweed coat went off through the stunted woods, due east, toward Hudson Bay.

CREED AND ANGITUK CAMPED for a night outside the gloomy burned-out cabin and Creed read more of the letters. Father Rouvière had spent several days in camp with the Eskimos after that first encounter.

> On the 17th of October my Eskimos left to go back north to the Coppermine for the winter. I had showed them the coloured pictures of Heaven and God and His angels, but I don't know how much they understood. I was able to note a few words, see a little into the language, but it was very little that I could gather this year. Eskimos have never farmed, so how do I teach the proverbs with no gardens, no

deserts, no vineyards or seeds, no sheep or shepherds, no bread, no trees for the Crucifixion, no notion of God? It is a labour so slow that I can scarcely see if I am getting ahead. But souls cost dear and they have to be gained one by one.

I tried to get some of them to stay with me for the winter. This way I could have learned their language fairly quickly, an indispensable step toward ministering among them, but they would not. Next year I must follow them north. Once I have established myself with the people, the chances of setting up a permanent mission base on the Arctic coast will be vastly easier. But so far away. It would be so lonely. If only I had a companion to keep me company and share this work.

In a later part of this letter to Father Ducot, Rouvière seemed for a moment to lose heart.

Would such a church on the Arctic Sea be successful? What do you think? Would such a base be a good idea or would it be useless? If they want me to abandon this mission and return to Fort Norman, I'd be happy to take up the community life again as soon as possible.

Did he believe this? Were his doubts this deep, or was he looking for reassurance and support from his Church? Creed wondered.

THEY PADDLED UP THE DEASE for three days. They picked blueberries on the banks and shot two wild geese for their dinner. They reached the pot-shaped lake that was the river's

source. There near their camp they found a place where a copse
of black spruce had stood and been cut down, but not with axes
or saws or any metal tools. The small trees had been bludgeoned
down, smashed and hammered with blunt blades.

"Copper Eskimo. Stone tools," Angituk explained.

Creed was struck by the brutality of the tree harvesting and
wondered at the fact that a people so primitive, without forged
metals, could still exist.

They were only a dozen miles beyond the priests' cabin when
Creed realized they had passed the treeline. There had still been
fingers of forest following the river into the barren lands, but
now the smooth rock rose up from the shore to touch deposits
of tundra between the granite undulations. The black spruce
were gone. The sporadic clumps of trees had been replaced
by dwarf willow bushes and grass and great stretches of open
tundra where all arboreal effort had ceased. The cold had won.

The second evening at their camp on the little lake, they found
a small herd of caribou and Creed shot a young female with the
.38-55. Before Angituk butchered it, he quickly made a small
incision to cut out a portion of organ meat, still warm, for them
to eat on the spot. Creed found it very good once he got past the
soft, bloody texture. A little salt helped. The boy tossed a portion
of the liver onto the ground. Creed asked him about this.

"An offering to the animal spirits who granted us this food."

The boy quartered the animal with his larger knife and they
found enough dried brush and twigs to slowly cook a haunch on
a stick. As barely cooked as it was, Creed had never tasted finer
meat. They took a package of it with them to sustain them for
the next two weeks, and the rest of the caribou Angituk cached
in a hole within the permafrost, with rocks on top to stop
animals getting to it. He piled more rocks overtop as a marker
for their return or for any other traveller in need.

When they could paddle no farther on the eastern edge of the lake, they climbed the ridge, carrying the Peterborough several miles over smooth rock. They had some difficulty finding the best way over the top of the watershed and had to retrace their path twice after coming to dead ends in valleys and creeks. They camped west of the high ground one night and the next morning made it to the top of the ridge, where they could see a thin promise of water in the distance. Several more hours of carrying the canoe beyond the high ground took them down to the beginning of the Dismal Lakes chain. According to the sketch map, they faced another portage beyond that to the Kendall River and finally reached the Coppermine.

The Dismal Lakes sat on a plateau surrounded by bare, rocky hills, some topped by year-round snow. The sharp, broken landscape was unmitigated by any foliage, and was mauled relentlessly by the wind and weather from the north. So dismal was the series of narrow lakes that the original explorers had spent no time in differentiating between the three or four of them, one flowing into the other. In the interest of precision, Creed thought, they could at least have written Dismal number one, Dismal number two, etc. Or perhaps Dismal, Miserable, Dreary, and Melancholy. The names suited the overcast landscape. But then, as if to demonstrate the contrary nature of the land, when the sun shone and a wind came up to blow the insects away, the little lakes revealed their pretty side, with golden light filtering through the grassy meadows that framed the shorelines.

One night during an endless sunset, Angituk snared a dovekie. He brought it over, still alive, so that Creed could appreciate the fine colouring of its wings and belly. It settled in the boy's hand, the legs held firmly between his fingers, and he stroked its back and murmured to it to remain calm. Gently he spread out a wing for Creed to see the distinctive patterns of black and white, and the little bird did not resist him.

"He's male. These markings attract the female from a great distance."

"Beautiful," Creed agreed, smiling.

Angituk stroked the creature a few more times. Then, as Creed watched, the boy suddenly pushed his thumb and forefinger through the skin, up under the protective breastbone, and deep into the chest cavity to find the tiny beating heart. He pinched it until Creed heard the pop. The bird was dead and still in a second. Angituk stroked it a little more and then went to prepare it for dinner. It would attract no more females in this life.

They were several days paddling on the Dismal Lakes before they found another portage, following the waters east until finally they carried again and wet their canoe in the waters of the Kendall River, which flowed swiftly toward the Coppermine between impressive canyon walls. The rapids on the Kendall became increasingly severe on the approach to the con-fluence, and they had to unload on a gravel beach and portage everything up over the shoulder of yet another high ridge. They stopped to rest on the way to the top.

On the portage trail, just below the crest of the ridge, stood a stone figure. Creed had seen pictures of these stone men. *Inukshuk*, Angituk called them. This one was as tall as Creed was. A topknot of long, mossy hair blew gently in the wind and gave the impression of life. The figure offered company and an important message: you are not alone in this land. Others have been here and will come again. One strange feature of this stone man was a small cylindrical stone that someone had embedded between the legs as an erect penis. Angituk found this a good joke, but seeing Creed's discomfort, he pulled it out and threw it away.

"There will be a cache between his feet. Have a look."

Creed lifted out several flat rocks to find what was there. He uncovered three delicate arrows wrapped in hide. Their shafts were made of willow twigs bound carefully by sinew, guided by feathers, and armed with small hand-pounded copper tips.

"These are beautiful. So delicate. Why are they here?"

"If you need them, you take them."

Creed unwrapped another item: two ermine-skin slippers with wooden amulets sewn into the toes. There were also six frozen char and caribou bones with meat. Creed put everything back. The boy watched him until he was done.

"Now, come and look at the land," Angituk ordered with a new authority that made Creed smile. He lifted the canoe again and followed him up to the crest of the ridge.

The height afforded a clear view, past the wild confluence of the Kendall, of the big river and the land known as the Coppermine. It was afternoon and the golden light gilded its vast features. They could see thirty miles of the broad river below them like a vein of earth, making its majestic way north in graceful turns through a barren, treeless landscape alive with endless tracts of wildflowers and carpets of thick, rich grasses. It flowed all the way to the Coronation Gulf of the Arctic Ocean. Angituk spied a herd of muskox along the river within rifle shot, the big glossy black creatures gambolling across the dark green hillside with surprising grace. The boy told him their name: "*Umingmak*: the bearded one."

The lead bull stared stonily at them from beneath his long horns, his guard hairs like a tattered cloak around his legs. Ravens and golden eagles circled in the skies. An Arctic fox looked up at them from the riverside, his nose searching in the tangled winds for a compelling scent. A plover scurried in front of Creed, trying to distract him from her nest close by with her fraudulent broken-wing display.

Creed noticed the boy's obvious pleasure. "What is it?" he asked him.

The boy was gazing out over the land. "*Aimavik*. Home."

"How long has it been since you were up here?"

"Seven summers." The boy turned to him then and looked into his eyes. "It's different up here. Do you feel the connection to the land under you?"

Angituk suddenly dropped to the ground and put his ear to the granite rock. "Try it!" Creed had never seen the boy so animated.

Creed went down on his knees, hesitated, then put his ear to the ground near Angituk.

The boy's eyes flashed. "Can you hear it? The Earth is asking, '*Il-viunna-hugi-vit?*'" He stretched out the phrase.

Creed listened. He was quite surprised to find there actually was something, a thrum or vibration.

"What does it mean?"

Angituk took care to make the translation accurate. "It means, 'Are you who you appear to be?'"

Creed looked at him, startled. "What do you mean by that?"

"It's not me. It's the Earth's question."

"The Earth should mind her own damn business."

"That's all right. The Earth is patient. She does not need an answer right away."

The boy smiled at him, stood up, easily lifted his heavy load, and descended toward the riverbank. Creed got to his feet. He turned and paused a moment to contemplate the view of the Coppermine flowing lazily to a sea beyond the horizon. He was impressed by this land, its essence of solitude, its indifference to civilization. He shouldered his knapsack, put the canoe once again on his sore shoulders, and headed down toward the compelling waters of the Coppermine River.

Four

They encountered the hunting camp just around the second embankment above the river. Nine Copper Eskimos, an extended family, were cooking dinner. They had three caribou-skin tents erected and were simmering a stew in a large soapstone pot over a fire of grass and twigs. They were startled enough when they saw Angituk, but when the *Kabloona* arrived they were terrified. The men grabbed their spears and bows to form a line of defence while the women and children gathered themselves behind and prepared to run away. Angituk called out to them in their language: "Don't go! We are Angituk and Creed. We are in a good mood. We have no weapons hidden. Who are you?"

The Eskimos calmed themselves a little at this and the women and children tentatively returned. Creed looked at them, noting their finely stitched clothing: caribou-hide coats with shoulders enlarged and pointed, a profile like a Japanese samurai's outfit he had seen in photographs, with shell and bead designs and amulets sewn into them. Their jackets were short, to the waist, with long tails hanging down at the back to sit on. There were fringes of various furs at the neck and cuffs, with a small pointed triangle of pelt on the bottom edge, below their stomachs. The clothing was fine-looking but far from pristine: food juices and fat drippings matted the thick hair. And as the people came closer, the bodily smells were almost overwhelming.

As Creed surveyed the small camp, he realized there were no forged metals to be found. No guns or metal tools. They used soapstone for their cooking vessels and whalebone for buttons and implements. There was a copper blade like a miniature scythe lying on a flat stone and a copper knife beside it, hammered out of the soft natural metal, but no forged metal of any kind. *These people are pre–Bronze Age,* Creed thought. *Two thousand years before Christ!*

Angituk was apparently enjoying himself, pleased to be among his people again and talking to them with enthusiasm. Though he knew no one in the group personally, he explained to Creed that two of the hunters had heard of his grandfather's people. He asked them questions and teased the children, quite at home. They were as curious about Angituk, the half-white man who could speak to them. They felt with their fingers his strange clothing and smelled him. He was like them but not really one of them.

The hunter-leader, with long hair to his shoulders and a wispy beard to match, solemnly approached Creed, staring up at him quizzically, more than a foot shorter. He offered his hand and they touched fingertips. The man felt Creed's skin and his brown hair. Others came forward, two men, an old woman, and a little child. They touched Creed's face and hands. They poked his body.

Angituk spoke with them and then explained, "I told them you come to visit and you mean no harm."

The old woman looked Creed in the eye. She had amulets and wooden ornaments in her long hair. Then suddenly her hand moved out and down and tightly cupped his testicles. Startled, Creed pulled away.

"What is she doing?" he gasped.

The old woman turned to the others and spoke triumphantly and the Eskimos all laughed. Angituk smiled and translated. "She says you are no demon. You are a man."

The leader looked plainly into Creed's eyes and asked a question. But before Angituk could translate, Creed had a question of his own.

"Can you ask him if he knows the hunter Koeha?"

Angituk hesitated. "He has invited us to eat with them."

"Okay, but what about—"

"They will like it if you eat with them and then they will tell you what they know."

A woman lifted a wooden board fashioned from driftwood off the soapstone bowl to show the caribou stew she and another woman were cooking for everyone. Creed peered into the dish of half-cooked muck—bone and fur and blood. "Jesus," he whispered as he looked into their eager faces.

"They'll feel good if you eat," Angituk reaffirmed.

Creed smiled at them and tried to sound convincing in response. "Yes. That would be nice."

"My people on the Coronation Gulf are much better cooks," Angituk told him. "But try it. It's not so bad."

He was given a heaping soapstone bowl of the slimy, repulsive mess and a clamshell spoon. Angituk was also given a bowl and he took two enthusiastic bites to encourage Creed to eat.

Creed looked down at the vile stew and, deciding not to taste it first, quickly swallowed two bites. He nodded and grunted with pleasure as he chewed the almost raw caribou meat and picked pieces of bone and hair from his teeth. The Eskimos nodded and smiled with approval, then they began to eat too, smacking their lips and moaning with satisfaction. Creed was relieved the pressure was off him and subtly put the bowl to one side. As they ate, they watched him out of the corner of their eyes with a natural curiosity. And Creed studied them. They had sewn pieces of animals into their clothing: talons and beaks of eagles, weasel skins, and the teeth and ears of wolves and foxes.

After offering tobacco, Creed asked through Angituk if they knew the hunter Koeha. The leader replied that he knew him well and that they'd seen him two weeks ago at his camp at the mouth of the Coppermine. Koeha was healthy and the fishing had been good. He would stay at that camp until the ocean was frozen in a few more weeks, and then they would go out and hunt seal on the ice. But the next question ended the congenial discussion.

"Tell them we are looking to find two white men—priests— who travelled this way three summers ago. Have they seen them?"

When Angituk translated this, using the words "white shamans" for "priests," every Eskimo stopped eating and looked fearfully at Creed. Some began to whimper.

"Ask them what they know."

Angituk spoke to the frightened people and they talked among themselves so he could not hear, all casting worried glances toward Creed.

Finally the leader put his bowl to one side and stood up. He gestured for Creed to follow him to the river.

"What does he want?"

"He wants us to go with him. He has something to show you."

Cautiously, Creed stood up and followed the leader. Angituk went with them some distance down the path toward the river and around an outcropping of rock to where they could look clearly north down the broad Coppermine, sparkling gold in the afternoon light. The leader pointed and said three days down the river was Bloody Falls. They should go there to look for what they wanted. The leader said some other things, speaking at length. Then suddenly he stopped talking and hurried back up to the camp.

"What was all that about?" Creed asked, studying the winding path of the river as it cut north through the series of ancient headlands as far as they could see.

"He said at Bloody Falls there is an old sled that we should see. He swears he knows nothing more. He and his people did not do anything wrong."

"What did he mean by that?"

"I don't know."

"Well, I have a few more questions for him."

Creed studied the river for another moment, then began to walk quickly back up the path. Angituk caught up to him, but when they came around the rock to the place where the Eskimos had been camped, they were gone. Only stone circles remained where the tents had been, the twig fire still smoking. They had packed everything and disappeared in a matter of minutes while Creed was speaking to the leader. Creed looked up to catch a glimpse of him on the ridge a hundred yards away, moving quickly south along the river.

"Hey ... HEY! What the hell?" Creed called out.

The leader looked back once and quickened his pace. Creed did not go after him. He turned to the boy.

"What else did he say?"

"He said they're sorry."

"What does that mean?"

"I don't know."

"Anything else?"

"Well ..."

"Yes?"

"He warned us that Bloody Falls is haunted by demons and bad spirits. So people don't go there anymore."

"Really? This sounds promising."

THEY DESCENDED the broad Coppermine in two days with minimal paddling. Steep sand bluffs lined the shore where the river had slowly, methodically carved its path over a hundred thousand years. The weather was fair and a multitude of birds entertained them. Creed's anticipation grew as they approached Bloody Falls. Here the investigation would begin in earnest.

Creed's good mood was in stark contrast to that of his companion. Never the voluminous raconteur, Angituk had now fallen into almost complete sullen silence, and it only gradually dawned on Creed that the boy was afraid. Despite his pleasure at returning to the land of his birth, the spectre of Bloody Falls loomed large for him. His association with the whites of Fort Norman had not shaken off his Native superstitions. The tale of "demons and bad spirits" had unnerved him, yet Creed was determined not to indulge the boy with any sympathy for his preoccupations. But neither would he tease him.

APPROACHING BLOODY FALLS from the south, Creed and Angituk avoided the quickening current on the east, which would suck them into the tumult. They landed at an eddy on the west side and pulled the little canoe up onto the gravelled shore. Taking only a small knapsack with his notebooks, Creed clambered up the shale to the top of the ridge to get a complete look at the place. At first Angituk stayed with the canoe, but as he watched Creed move quickly away, he stood and hurried after him.

In the midst of the flat, monotonous, barren lands, Bloody Falls was a dramatic feature. The expansive river passed through a narrow cut in the high, black-terraced granite ridge. Verdant carpets of grass covered the hillside across the river where muskox grazed. Two golden eagles flew in opposing circles off the clifftops. The oxygen-injected water was alive with char.

Bloody Falls was positioned at that rare latitude where both grizzly bear from the south and polar bear from the north came to fish and hunt and fight.

Creed and Angituk climbed up over the top of the ridge to where they could look down into the gorge a hundred feet below, the deep green water squeezed between two massive slabs of granite, the walls cut as clean as any quarry.

"You want to try running this?" Creed teased him over the intimidating roar.

The boy didn't reply as he looked down into the suicidal frenzy. He stayed close to Creed, looking around from time to time in worried expectation. His thin frame gave an involuntary shudder and he wrapped his arms around himself.

"What's wrong?" Creed asked him in a voice that sounded more irritated than he felt.

"Don't you feel them?"

"What?"

"The *inua*. Spirits of the dead."

"No."

At the bottom of the final set of rapids, the river spread out and flowed into a wide basin. Beyond that they could see it winding north through many headlands toward the ocean. To the right of them, across the river, was a rocky little plain, out of the wind, close by the best fishing spot at the bottom of the falls—a good place to camp.

"Look." Creed pointed, speaking above the muted roar of the falls. "That must be the Eskimo camp Hearne wrote about. Right there, on the other side. Where the Chipewyans attacked them."

Creed sat down and the boy sat beside him. Creed had read the passage in Hearne's book several times. July 17, 1771. A scout had found the Eskimo camp at the falls. The Indians Hearne was travelling with had put on war paint and sneaked up on the camp under cover of darkness. Hearne had gone with them but stood back from the actual attack. The Indians dragged men, women, and children, all of them naked, out of their tents and speared and knifed them to death. Hearne found the shrieks and groans of the dying "quite dreadful." He wrote of how one young girl had escaped the attack only to be speared to death at Hearne's feet. As Hearne pleaded for mercy for the girl, the two Chipewyans laughed and twisted the spears as she writhed on the ground between his legs.

Creed studied the flat, rocky plain across the river. He could almost hear the cries of the dying on the wind.

"Hearne was a son of a bitch," he found himself saying under his breath. He looked down at Angituk and noticed that the boy was shivering though the air was warm. "What is it?"

"My people."

"It was a long time ago."

"They're still here." His teeth were chattering.

Creed moved to him and rubbed his thin shoulders vigorously, then put his jacket over them. He was going to say something more but stopped himself. After a moment he stood up. "Let's go look for this sled."

Creed continued slowly along the high ridge on the west side of the falls. There was an ancient path worn smooth into the granite by a million feet over thousands of years—Eskimo, Cree, Dene, Chipewyan, but no more than a small handful of white men. There were some scrub trees and bushes growing here in the rocky clefts, watered by the mists that issued up from the rapids. It occurred to him that the path would be a difficult one for a heavy sled. There must be a lower path to circumvent the falls, and he was scanning the bushes down the slope when he heard feet running. The boy slowed suddenly as he neared, and walked up to him, trying to hide his anxiety at being apart from him in this place. He stopped a few feet away, put his hands casually in his pockets, nodded an acknowledgement, and gazed around with as much nonchalance as he could manage.

"I was thinking they wouldn't bring a sled up here on the ridge," Creed mused. "There must be a path farther down the—" He focused on something. "There it is."

Sure enough, down the slope on a level, grassy pasture sat a weathered qamutik. The priests' sled. Creed loped down the grade toward it. Angituk stood there conflicted, looked around, then slowly followed.

The weeds had grown up around the old sled. Scattered in the grass and bushes were the remnants of a canvas knapsack, blankets, a sweater, and trousers. Creed reached down through a thistle bush and brought up an old, weathered leather-bound notebook. On the second blank, gilt-edged page were the handwritten words: *Property of Father Jean-Baptiste Rouvière*.

On the other side of the qamutik, beneath the protection of two layers of flat rocks, he could make out the partial skeletal remains of a human body. He carefully removed all of the stones. What was left of the man lay face down, his bones and mummified skin and tissue held together by two tattered layers of long woollen underwear. The external clothing had been stripped off. Wolves and wolverines had dug under the rocks and torn at the extremities of the body, and were it not for the protective stones the body would have been scattered long ago. In several places gnawed bones were visible, and most of the left leg and arm were gone. Creed noted first what looked like a knife hole through the fabric just under the rib cage and a large black bloodstain around it. The skull had been traumatized at the back by some instrument creating a deep depression.

Kneeling beside the corpse, Creed noticed it was encircled by an oval of smaller stones. He tried to raise the skeletal body slightly to see the face. The body was lighter than he'd expected, dried out. The eye sockets were long empty, but the leathery skin and beard were mostly intact, stretched very tight over the skull, the teeth protruding. On the parchment skin that held the neck bones together below the chin, Creed noted a wide incision that would have pierced the jugular and opened the windpipe. On a tattered bit of what was left of the shirt was the embroidered name *Père Le Roux*.

Creed sensed Angituk behind him. "Looks like we've got a murder to investigate."

For the first time it occurred to Creed that another officer or two on this patrol might have been a good idea. He turned to look at Angituk, who was staring at the skeletal remains with equal measures of fear and fascination. The boy spoke in a whisper. "Spirits of the Dead are the most dangerous. They hate us for being alive."

Angituk began to back away slowly from the corpse. Creed felt a surge of anger and impatience. He stood and grabbed the boy roughly by the arm.

"I'll just bet they do. I think if I was stabbed and had my throat cut and my head bashed in, I'd be angry too! Look at him. Look at what your people did!"

He held the boy for a moment and forced him to look at the corpse. Then he let him go. The boy backed away a few steps, terrified, shaken, rubbing his arm where Creed had held him, unsure what to do. Creed took a deep breath and withdrew his notebook from the little knapsack. He started to sketch the murder site, drawing in the sled. He stopped before he'd gone far and turned again to the boy.

"All right. I want you to walk in circles around the sled,

increasing them by five feet each time you go around, and see what you find: personal possessions, books, clothing, or maybe the other priest. You understand?"

The boy looked miserable at the burden of this assignment, but he took a deep breath and did as he was told. He walked in ever-growing circles around the sled and the body, studying the ground through the high grass, hoping desperately to find nothing. Creed returned to his sketch, taking care with the position of the body and labelling the placement of other things he found: Rouvière's notebook, two spent rifle shells, a piece of blanket. He paced off distances. Angituk walked, murmuring an eerie little song, an *irinjelo*, a monotonous dirge in a minor key, a song meant only for dead ears.

"Spirits of the Dead," he sang to them. "Please don't bother me. I am no one really. I only wish you well. I am sorry you are dead, spirits ..."

With the little Kodak 3A autographic camera Creed had brought, he took systematic shots of the murder scene. The boy was expanding his circles as ordered, now thirty yards away. Creed felt a little badly for airing his temper at him.

Angituk continued in Inuinnaqtun: "Good Spirits of the Dead. I am not worthy of your interest. If you are interested in us, you should look at the white man, who is much more worthy of your attention. If you like, go and see about the white man. Deal with him, but please leave me alone. I am nothing."

"What are you singing about?"

"Nothing. I must make a noise with each breath so the spirits can't enter and strike me dumb."

"Oh, for Christ's sake," Creed mumbled, but unconsciously he too slowly began humming a note with each breath exhaled.

Creed sat down to make detailed notes in his book about the wounds he'd found on the priest. He was in the midst of describing the throat slash when the distant chanting stopped and the boy called out in a voice wavering with fear.

"Corporal!"

The boy stood frozen, sixty yards away, staring at something on the ground in front of him. Creed stood and walked quickly through the high grass, resisting the urge to ask questions. Judging by his expression the boy wanted to run, but he dutifully stayed beside his discovery. Creed came up to him and there, lying on its back, seen through the narrow gaps in two layers of flat stones that had been placed on top of him, was the weathered skeletal corpse of the second priest, Rouvière, in similar condition to the first. Creed removed all the stones as before. This one too had been partially eaten by animals, his right and most of his left leg gone and his left arm missing below the elbow.

Creed noted substantial trauma to the front of the skull. His outer clothing was gone and, like Le Roux's, his mummified body was held together by two layers of long woollen underwear. There was a large hole in his chest, an exit wound. Creed turned the body over, looking for the entry wound and the black bloom of dried blood. He found it high on the back, to the right of the spine.

Creed looked up at Angituk. "The bastards shot him in the back, probably running away." He felt another surge of anger. "What kind of a son of a bitch would shoot him in the back?" Angituk moved away from him. Creed took a deep breath to quell his emotions. "I'll need two or three days here. Set up the camp over there beside the sled."

The boy looked more fearful than ever. "Beside the sled? Not down by the river ...?"

"No. I want it right beside the crime site."

"But for water and fishing and ... escape ... we should be by the river. Not here."

"Just do what I told you."

The boy looked miserable.

WITH THE SUN LOW on the horizon, Angituk finished the last of the three *inukshuks*, four-foot rock statues on the perimeter of the camp, complete with moss headpieces for the wind to move and create the illusion of life that would ward off the bad spirits so prevalent in this place. He kept busy collecting sweet heather for the fire, snaring a beautiful ermine whose pelt was now stretched out and drying, and finding four plover eggs for the morning meal. He had set up the tent at the centre of the pasture and had a small twig fire going, over which was roasting the skinned carcass of a fat ground squirrel he had snared. He went back to feed the little fire with the dried bushes he'd collected and one good chunk of dry driftwood he'd found on the shore. He chopped it into small chunks with the Corporal's hatchet.

Angituk had enjoyed this trip to the Coppermine very much, more than he let on. But he wanted to move on from this evil place. The Corporal was a pleasant and generous employer and didn't waste words in the manner of other white people, as if somehow silence would bring them closer to death. So Angituk had worked hard for him, kept him fed and warm and safe. The squirrel was sizzling. They would eat it soon. There was time now to read a few pages of Kipling. As he opened the book, Angituk looked over to where Creed was working beside the second body, writing intently in his book. The boy studied him a moment.

CREED CONCLUDED the second autopsy to the best of his ability with the basic medical training he had. He was amazed that after more than three years anything of the corpses remained, but he reasoned that for eleven months of the year the bodies were frozen. The stones offered protection too. And in summer, fish and squirrels were in abundance in this location for all predators and for the lesser animals that cleaned up after them.

He worked through a theory for each murder based on the physical evidence and his experience. He believed Le Roux was killed first at the sled. The first wound was the knife to the torso, but he could still have fought back. The mortal wound was the knife cut to the throat, which would have killed him within a few seconds. The blow to the head was the finale. Unnecessary, but it finished the job.

As for Rouvière, he had been running away. He had probably witnessed the attack on Le Roux, realized he was next, and made a run for it through the deep snow. A single shot from a high-powered rifle had brought him down but not killed him. Creed found three spent shells from a .44 calibre rifle beside the sled. He assumed the first two had missed the priest. A Copper Eskimo murderer was probably not too familiar with the workings of the high-powered rifle. But by the third shot he found his mark.

Unless it was Hornby.

Hornby. This was a thought Creed had considered more than once after the Englishman's confessions about his feelings for Le Roux. But on reflection that seemed improbable. And it was doubtful Hornby would have needed three shots.

Creed followed the course of the bullet, which had entered the back, passed through the lung, bounced off a rib, and exited through the chest. Father Rouvière would have been knocked to the ground by the force of the gunshot, but then somehow he had turned around. Creed speculated that after his initial flight through the deep snow Rouvière knew he was finished. There was no escape. But he still had the strength to stand, turn, and face his killers. He might even have tried to reason with them. And their response? They put a knife deep into his stomach and then clubbed him with something hard enough to cleave his skull.

There was one final mystery. On both bodies the skin of the torso had been well enough preserved to permit observation of a large crescent-shaped incision to the right of the stomach. These were not kill wounds, more like the cuts a surgeon might make to perform an appendectomy. They had been inflicted after death, after the heart had stopped pumping blood; the fabric around the wounds was bloodless.

THE GROUND SQUIRREL was surprisingly good and the boy was pleased that Creed was satisfied. Above them, though the glow of the sun on the horizon would stay with them through most of the night at this time of year, the northern lights put on an impressive show, pinging and sighing and whispering above Bloody Falls. *Maybe the Catholics have some kind of connection to the heavens after all,* Creed mused, studying the luminescent green curtains that draped the sky.

The boy looked up at Creed from time to time, and then nervously into the dusk that separated them by only thirty yards from the sled. The Corporal had left the bodies where they lay, just on the far side. Angituk's people had always dealt with the dead very quickly, taking them to a place away from the living—a hilltop, into the ocean, onto an ice floe. The Corporal seemed intent on keeping the bodies close, studying them, poking at them with an irreverence Angituk didn't understand. More than anything, the boy just wanted to leave this place.

When Creed had finished the ground squirrel, he licked his fingers, wiped them on some heather, and took out Rouvière's notebook. "Do you want to hear?"

"Yes," the boy said, though he didn't.

Creed's translation of the French was far from perfect, but the gist of the entry was clear. "Father Le Roux arrived in Fort Norman, and I am travelling up the Great Bear River once more," the text began in Creed's translation. "It is such a relief to have company as we head into the far north, and already we have enjoyed some great talks. Father Le Roux is in excellent physical shape. He is a very confident man and quite opinionated and likes to take the lead on things. It is a relief to have someone else of strong will, for without it the Arctic could gobble you up! I hope to teach him Wisk and to instruct him on the sensitive diplomacy that is the best way to approach the Eskimos. He seems like he might be quite receptive to my experience."

Creed stopped reading and looked into the tiny fire for a moment, remembering what John Hornby had said of Le Roux and reading between the kindly lines of Rouvière's journal. The temperament of this new priest did not sound suited to life in the Arctic. Creed's mind drifted back to his examination of the bodies. He glanced up at the boy, who was lost in his own thoughts.

"Angituk." The boy looked up, startled. "There are strange circular cuts in the stomachs of both these men, made after they were dead. Do you know what they would be for?"

The boy hesitated, worried he would anger the Corporal. He spoke quietly. "Yes. Do you remember the caribou you shot on the Dismal Lakes, and what I did? It is the custom of the Copper people. It is a sign of respect."

"What is?"

"After a kill. To eat the liver."

Creed stared at him with growing revulsion.

"While it is warm. You eat some and toss some to the spirits as a sacrifice."

"You are saying they ate their goddamn livers?"

Angituk was warned by the disgust in Creed's tone.

"It is out of respect for the animal you have killed, and it also makes sure their spirit will not rise against you."

"All right! Enough about bloody spirits!" Creed snarled at him.

Angituk looked at the ground.

Then Creed thought of Begley smoking Ross's leg over the smudge fire at the cabin in the Caribou Mountains. No one civilization had the patent on barbarity. But with the war in Europe escalating, that was a whole different discussion. He was about to tell the boy he was sorry for raising his voice, but Angituk suddenly stood and headed for the tent.

"I'll sleep now."

CREED SAT UP in the small tent writing his report by the light of the oil lamp. Angituk slept beside him, but the boy was restless and dreaming. He moaned and cried out once. Creed put a reassuring hand on his shoulder.

"Shhhhh. It's all right," Creed whispered.

Angituk settled again and Creed went back to his report. A fearful little moan escaped Angituk's lips once more and he rolled over against Creed's side. He tossed an arm around Creed's waist and hugged him in a somnambulant embrace. Creed pulled up the boy's sleeping bag and placed a comforting hand on his thin, bony back, and stroked him a little to ease him back to deep sleep.

Creed felt the boy's arm around his waist, the long, thin fingers holding him with determination. He looked down at the long black hair fallen across the boy's face, the gentle arc of his neck, his full lips parted, and suddenly Creed was startled by a strange burning in the skin of his face and a flush that went up and down his body. Creed took the boy's tattooed hand from his side and folded it down between them, pushing the boy gently but firmly away. Angituk rolled over and within seconds was sleeping soundly again, but to Creed's mortification the response by his body continued. Creed threw his report book to one side, unpeeled himself from his sleeping bag, and launched himself out of the tent.

AS THE GREEN AURORA flickered above him, Creed stood naked, waist-deep, in the quiet pool at the bottom of the falls under a full moon, arms crossed, confused and disgusted with himself. As his lower body went numb, he reasoned that the aberration had some acceptable explanation to do with diet or exertion or exhaustion. Whatever it was, thank God the boy hadn't seen. He would put this embarrassment behind him and simply carry on with his duty. This would never happen again.

Five

The next morning, Creed and Angituk buried the remains of the two priests. Creed kept Father Rouvière's damaged skull for evidence, placing it respectfully in a small leather bag. The two distinct graves were shallow in the permafrost but well fortified by layers of rocks to prevent any more disturbance by animals. Creed broke apart the old sled and lashed together the runners to build and erect a large wooden cross between the graves. Though raised a Presbyterian, Creed appreciated what the priests had been trying to do. He said the Lord's Prayer over them, putting in the Protestant ending, "For Thine is the Kingdom, the Power, and the Glory, forever and ever," just for good measure. He prayed to God to have mercy on their souls. He and Angituk sang two verses of "Rock of Ages," which, to Creed's surprise, the boy knew well. Creed spoke what he remembered of the "dust to dust" passage and tossed some granite sand onto the graves. Then they walked down through the tumble of big rocks to the bottom of the falls, where they had loaded and secured the gear in the canoe, and set off downstream to find the murderers.

IT WAS LATE NOW in the brief Arctic summer and the heat of the sun on their backs reminded them to enjoy it while they could. The broad surface of the Coppermine was sparkling merrily, and Angituk was visibly relieved to be away from Bloody Falls with its violent history, old and new, and its ominous spirits. He paddled with enthusiasm, though the current did most of the work. They both looked up to watch a dozen northern pintails fly like artillery shells just above the surface of the water. At high altitude, a long V formation of Canada geese was heading south to warmer climes while Creed and Angituk pushed north into the Arctic.

THE RIVER MAINTAINED its slowly weaving course between high sandy bluffs rising up on both sides of the riverbed, and the current moved them along easily. Rounding a bend, Creed could see downstream to where a headland on each side squeezed the river through a rocky narrows. He began to look for a place to land and portage. He said as much to Angituk, who was silent for a moment and then asked a one-word question Creed could not hear over the rushing drone of the river.

"What was that?"

Angituk said the word again. "Scared?"

The boy turned and gave Creed a teasing grin through his long hair. Creed glared at him, irritated by the challenge, studying the intimidating rapids up ahead. All right. Several mammoth rocks, but he thought he could see a reasonable line to take. It would save time, and the headland didn't offer much of a path onshore.

"Okay, my friend. You're on!"

The boy looked at him, tying back the hair from his eyes and smiling with excitement.

They were swept into the first of the moving water with an acceleration so abrupt Creed was unprepared. It was all he could do to keep the Peterborough's stern from pulling them broadside, and he suddenly realized it was much worse ahead than he had thought. They should have scouted it first. Huge boulders loomed up. Standing troughs and a few ominous recirculating holes sought to pull them in and flip them over. Angituk drawed and cross-drawed like a madman, up on his knees, plunging his paddle into the churning ferment, his hands white-knuckled on the paddle's shaft, guiding the bow away from granite outcroppings. They struck the first rock off the starboard bow and the cedar ribs protested with a sickening crack. Bouncing off, they continued straight and tried to regain control. The biggest boulder yet, a monolith, stood in the centre of their line. Heavy current boiled up in front of it, spreading out and back. Their strokes did nothing against the surge of water carrying them into the vacuum, and as they hit, the canoe turned broadside, riding the boils and slamming again and again onto the face of the boulder. The entire force of the Coppermine hammered against them. Creed was sure the Peterborough would either cave in or dump upstream but though the ribs cracked and water splashed over the gunnels, they braced against the boulder with all their weight and presented the river with the wide underbelly of the canoe.

Creed levered hard with his paddle against the rock and suddenly the canoe's stern slid around the rocky face backwards and down into the boulder's opposing eddy, which for a moment held the canoe still. Creed wedged his paddle in a cleft in the rock on the downstream side and held on as the force of the current moved the bow around in a 180-degree turn. Creed pulled the paddle blade free of the rock just in time, and they were headed downstream once more, bow first. Creed couldn't believe it.

For a moment they were safe in deep water. They could see ahead one more set of rapids, as always the work of disgruntled spirits, before the Coppermine flattened out and became calm again. Angituk turned around, pushing his loose hair out of his eyes, and grinned at Creed, exhilarated.

"My friend," Creed gasped, "we are two lucky bastards!"

"The spirits like us, Corporal!"

"I guess they must."

Angituk let out a high-pitched whoop as the canoe dipped into the last of the rapids. They were swept, yelling and laughing, into the white water, paddling with a cocky confidence over the huge standing waves. They could see the calm water ahead. They were fifty yards out. Angituk looked back at Creed with a goofy grin.

"Want to do it again?"

"For God's sake, keep paddling!" Creed commanded, spotting disaster ahead, but it was too late. The canoe slid over a massive submerged rock and into the frothing, bubbling hole on the other side of it, turning them broadside and dumping them upstream of the canoe into the ice-cold maelstrom. It happened so fast both paddlers came up sputtering and were held for a few moments in the hole with their betrayed vessel, one on each side, before being spit out into the main current. The overturned canoe and paddlers were swept along in the outwash of the set, feet bumping against the smooth-worn rocks on the bottom and deposited quite suddenly in the calm shallows of a wide basin. They were both still laughing, despite themselves, choking and spitting out water.

"Why did you stop paddling?"

"Why did you stop steering?"

Angituk's fedora floated by upside down.

"Hey, you forgot something." Creed grabbed the wide-brimmed hat, dumped the water inside it over Angituk, and placed it firmly on the boy's head. They laughed again at this.

"Life sure is wet with you, Corporal Creed."

If the water were any colder it would have been ice, and they were both shivering, teeth chattering. Creed turned the canoe right-side up and surveyed the food and equipment tied securely under the thwarts. It was all there. Creed tilted the canoe over and drained some of the water out, and they stumbled toward shore, pulling the Peterborough with them. Onshore, they tilted her again, pouring most of the water out, and carefully dragged her up onto the pebble beach.

"It was your bright idea to run the damn thing."

"You could have said no."

Creed found the sealed bags and pulled out dry clothing and towels for both of them. Though he was in great spirits, Angituk's lips had turned vermilion and the trembling of his thin body was causing Creed concern.

"Here, get into some dry clothes before you catch pneumonia. We'll spread things out on the rocks to dry and camp here tonight."

They stood on the pebble beach in the Arctic sun and peeled their wet clothes off. As always, they discreetly faced away from each other. Creed shook his head in amusement, climbing out of his corduroy trousers and long underwear.

"Our *isuma*'s still working," Angituk declared.

"More luck than wisdom," Creed concluded. "So. You still want to try those rapids again?"

"No. Thank you. I guess that was enough," the boy said.

"When we were caught against that big rock, I was sure that was us gone. I mean, it should have crushed us. I'm amazed it didn't. Then what'd we do without a boat?"

"Going backwards was the worst for me. Like a bad dream," Angituk exclaimed.

Creed laughed, turned toward Angituk, and glanced at him. "I still remember your face just as we were—"

Creed suddenly stopped speaking. Angituk still had his back to him. Creed stared at the boy, his mouth open in mid-phrase. They were both naked now in the thin but vital sun, and Angituk was drying off with the towel, his back to Creed. It took a moment or two for what Creed was seeing to fully register with him. At first he believed his eyes were playing tricks. But there could be no doubt. The narrow waist, the curved hips.

Angituk noticed the pause in Creed's speech and half turned toward him, casually askance. "What about my face?"

Creed noticed then under her arm as she towel-dried her hair the small, firm breast, nipple erect from the cold water. *It can't be,* he thought.

In that second of silence Angituk saw him staring at her and realized her clumsy indiscretion. "Oh, no," she said under her breath.

She had done so well until now. She had simply forgotten. Ashamed, she covered her body with her towel, turned fully toward him, looked at the ground, and waited for his reaction. Creed could think of nothing to say but the obvious.

"You're a girl."

Angituk had nothing to add. Creed became aware of his nakedness and grabbed his towel to cover up. Then the anger and embarrassment hit him. He had been fooled.

"What do you have to say for yourself?"

Angituk didn't answer.

"Why did you agree to come with me?"

"I wanted the work."

"Why did you lie to me?"

"I never lied."

"Well, deceived then! It is absolutely unacceptable for me, a police officer investigating a murder case, to be travelling alone out here with a ... with a young girl."

"I don't bite."

"This is not funny! It could compromise the whole investigation. I'm after one or more dangerous killers. I can't be looking after you."

It was then Angituk's turn to be indignant. "You don't look after me. I have done my job well, feeding you and translating for you. You didn't complain before. This is my home and these are, as you say, 'my people.' But ... if you want me to go, I'll go."

Creed calmed himself, studying her for a moment, distracted by this new reality as she pushed her hair back out of her blue eyes, tightening the towel around herself and glaring at him defiantly, still shivering a little.

"I can't let you go. I need you for translation." He looked at her for a moment. "You can't go. Well ... turn around and let's get dressed."

They turned their backs to each other again in their usual manner, both silent with their thoughts. They quickly put on their dry clothes and did not speak again until well after dark.

ANGITUK FOUND two nice pieces of driftwood swept north on the river from below the treeline and enough twigs and bushes to build a small fire. Creed repaired three holes in the poor battered canoe with a melted bar of resin and patches of canvas he had for the job. The night was a freezing contrast to the sunny day and Angituk stretched out a tarp behind the small fire to reflect all the warmth toward them and the tent. She also managed to snare a fat Arctic hare, one of the last of the season, and roast it to Creed's pleasure. Frankly, she found it a relief to be a girl once more. Although they had not spoken again about her deception, Creed's manner had softened a little toward her and she wanted to talk to him about it. They sat by the remnants of the tiny fire after their meal.

"It was my mother's idea before she died. I was thirteen years old. I would pretend to be a boy and in that way I could get work in the white man's world and men would not try to have sex with me. And it's also a custom of our people, if we've had bad luck, we will dress in the way of the opposite sex. It confuses the bad spirits. They don't know who you are and they leave you alone."

"You understand with my people it is not appropriate for a man and a woman who are not married to be travelling alone together."

"Yes." She paused, thinking. "Why?"

"Because they might be tempted to become ... intimate."

"Intimate?"

"To have sexual relations without being married, and that is not allowed. So, what I'd like to do is carry on the way we were, as if you were a boy. You'll continue to dress like a boy and pretend to be one in the presence of any others we encounter. Okay?"

"Do you see any dresses around here?"

"Don't be smart. We'll just both pretend this never happened and go on as we were. Okay?"

"Is this for what others think? Or is it for you?"

"It is for others! We are on official business here."

"I want to understand. It is not boys that you prefer?"

"No! I don't want to talk about this anymore. Just continue as we were. Okay?"

"Okay."

LATER THAT NIGHT, Creed lay outside the tent in his sleeping bag. Angituk was asleep inside. The fire was dead, the meagre fuel used up, but Creed felt it appropriate to sleep outside. His breath came out in clouds of vapour in the moonlight of the cold, still night. The temperature had dropped dramatically and he was curled up to retain warmth, but he could not stop shivering.

Then it began to snow. Very quickly a soft white layer covered the bag and chilled him deeper still. He heard Angituk's voice at the fly of the tent.

"Corporal Creed. Come inside."

"I'm all right."

"No, you're not. You are cold, I am cold. Come inside."

"I'll be fine."

"If you get sick, then who will protect me?"

Creed noted the faint sarcasm in her tone. Still he didn't move. She crawled out of the tent, over to him, and poked his shoulder. The snow was coming down heavily now, filling in and softening the landscape all around them. Had he not been so cold, he would have appreciated the beauty of it.

"This is stupid," Angituk continued. "I am freezing and we need to keep each other warm. And I am a boy again, so you shouldn't be scared."

"I'm fine here," he said through chattering teeth.

"Okay. Go ahead. Freeze out here for all I care. But in the morning I'm just going to cover your body with snow and go home."

She went back inside the tent.

Creed lay there for a moment, the shivering uncontrollable now, thinking of what she'd said. He crawled from his bag and shook the snow off it. Then he climbed thankfully into the tent, dragging the bag after him. In the little tent, they lay chastely back to back in their bags, and it was in fact much warmer for both of them. As she fell asleep, Angituk smiled at Creed's prudishness. No question, the ways of these white men were strange.

Six

By morning, the violent seasonal shift to winter had dropped on them like a roof caving in. Two and a half feet of snow blanketed the land, crushing down on the little tent and covering the canoe. Along the shoreline in calm eddies and bays, a membrane of ice stretched just short of the strong current. The river was quickly freezing up. They would soon have to abandon the canoe altogether. For the first day since leaving Fort Norman, Creed didn't shave and they each wore every piece of clothing they had, including their heavy moosehide coats. When they stopped moving, the chill still cut through everything, deep into their bones. They turned the Peterborough over, loaded and launched her, and paddled north on the diminishing liquid path of the river.

NINE MILES DOWNSTREAM from Bloody Falls, the Coppermine widened suddenly and was swallowed up by the vast Coronation Gulf, a wide channel of the Arctic Ocean. At the mouth there were not even bushes or tall grass for fuel. They would be eating most things uncooked and even unwarmed. Their own bodies would be their primary source of heat.

At the mouth of the Coppermine there were a few small, flat islands, and in the distance, across the Gulf to the north, loomed larger, flat-topped islands with rugged cliff faces. Creed took out his binoculars to scan the distant islands and as he did so, a beautifully sculpted hill of ice came drifting into the foreground. An iceberg! It was moving to the east, mammoth, a cool opaque blue.

Creed and Angituk beached on the east side of the river mouth. A mile away on the west bank Creed could see movement, tiny figures against the vast white expanse of the Arctic shoreline.

"There's the camp. But I don't see tents."

"They live in snow now."

She was right. He could make out white bumps, the outlines of several snow houses, through the glasses. He had seen pictures of them in books. The Eskimos had no watch set up; no defences or guards were visible. There were children playing hide-and-seek. He could see one with a hoop and stick, making it roll along on the packed snow near the shore.

Creed put the binoculars away and they set off paddling across the great expanse of the churning river mouth where it contacted the deeper gulf water, toward the west bank and the camp. Halfway across, Creed slid the .38-55 out of the leather sheath, levered a bullet into the chamber, put on the safety, and laid the rifle across the gunnels in front of him.

Angituk, in the bow, heard this action and turned to look at him. "You will scare them, if they know what it is. Put it away, please."

Creed hesitated, then slid the rifle back into its sheath, leaving the flap open.

A moment later the Eskimos began to move down to the shore—men, women, and children. They seemed a healthy and energetic people. They wore heavier skin clothing than the Eskimos Creed and Angituk had met south on the river and it gave them all a round, short, childlike profile. Creed could see their open faces, free of fear or hostility, until he paddled closer and they took in his white face. There were a few expressions of vague apprehension, then a young woman cried out and grabbed her child. *"Kabloona!"* They backed away in fear, and a few ran.

Angituk waved an arm in the air. "We are friendly to you and in a good mood! We have no weapons."

Creed tried to repeat her phrases, missing the accents, hoping he wasn't making it worse or appearing a fool, and held up his mittened hands in a passive, saluting gesture.

Angituk continued. "The *Kabloona* means no harm! Don't run away. He wants to talk to Koeha. Is Koeha here?"

Her question had the desired effect. The people stopped their withdrawal at the name of their best hunter. A boy ran up toward the biggest snow house.

The bow of the canoe cracked through the thickening layer of ice on the shallow water as Creed and Angituk paddled up onto the beach. They stepped out onshore. Several men came up to them, while the women and children remained at a distance. Angituk made small talk with them while they stared at Creed. The hunters had known Angituk's grandfather and also her mother, before they moved away to the west. They greeted her with smiles, but they remained wary of Creed. One man moved close to them and touched the skin of Creed's cheek with his fingertips and peered into his eyes.

"I reassured them you are not a demon. They say you are only the third white man they have ever seen." She exchanged a look with him.

"The first two must have been the priests. Ask them about the priests."

"It might scare them. Maybe we should wait and talk to Koeha about the priests."

"All right."

As he had with the Eskimo hunting party farther up the Coppermine, Creed began a thorough survey of their primitive but resourceful way of life, noting the absence of any metals in their camp, save the copper implements they hammered into blades. Angituk told him that the people had been fishing in the rivers before the heavy snow and had lots of char to share. They would stay at this camp until the ocean froze and then move far out to the ice edge to hunt seal and narwhal.

As they stood among the Eskimos, a short older woman with a broad smile approached them, calling out Angituk's name. The two embraced joyfully and laughed and talked at length. Angituk finally introduced her. Creed noted the warmth of their greeting and the tears in their eyes.

"This is Kingagolik, who was a good friend of my mother's and was like an aunt to me when I was a child. She was married to Koeha's cousin and hunting partner, who was killed by a walrus three winters ago many miles west of here. She thinks you're my husband."

The women laughed and talked some more. A group of young children in hide clothing, looking like a litter of friendly puppies, surrounded Creed. They pulled at his coat and pleaded in their language.

"What do you want?" Creed asked them. They all growled in response. "A bear? I'm not a bear." He noted the subtle disappointment on the round, eager faces of the young ones, then suddenly raised his arms over his head and growled as loud as he could, baring his teeth for them to see. They screamed in terror and delight and raced away from him, but only so far. From a short distance they dropped to their knees and pelted him with a vicious barrage of snowballs.

"Little bastards," he mumbled, and raising his arms again he roared after them. Again they all ran squealing. He chased them in wide circles through the snow, but some doubled back on him just like wolves on a deer and he would find two or three at his heels, waiting for an opportunity to strike. One managed to leap on his back and hang on; he heard giggling at his ear. Another smaller one latched on to his belt and dug his heels into the snow. Others poked sticks at his feet to bring him down, and still the rain of snowballs continued, all thrown at his head with a sniper's accuracy.

Angituk and Kingagolik were laughing and cheering on the children hanging from Creed's body to bring him down. He felt slightly betrayed by this. He had tossed some of them clear, and was getting better at dodging the missiles and scaring them with his fearsome growls, when suddenly he came face to face with an old hunter. One last snowball hit Creed's cheek as Koeha greeted him: *"Aatituuq."*

"Aatituuq," repeated Creed.

Koeha was a tall man by Eskimo standards, dignified, with long grey hair to his shoulders and a wispy beard. He studied Creed's white face with curiosity and a little suspicion. There were several hunters with him. His short sealskin jacket with a long tail was beautifully embroidered and inlaid with Arctic fox and marten fur, festooned with amulets, claws, and teeth. Kingagolik told Koeha that Angituk, daughter of her once-close friend Kunee, had returned. Koeha turned to her, smiled, and held her hand, giving her arrival his blessing.

Creed had Angituk explain that he was a representative from the white world in the South where thousands of people lived.

"He has come with their greetings for Koeha—who is well known as a great hunter—and his people."

This pleased the tall man and he invited them to dinner in his home. With this invitation the people became excited, talking and laughing as they escorted Creed and Angituk up to Koeha's big dance house. Creed watched with concern as the people unpacked the canoe, running their hands over the uniform ribs and gunnels, and carried the bags and wanigans and the canoe itself up with them. Angituk reassured him nothing would be stolen.

"There will be a celebration and dance tonight in our honour."

"That's very kind, Angituk, but I do have to get on with the investigation."

She looked at him impatiently. "The murders were three years ago. Can it not wait a few more hours?"

Jack was taken aback by this impudent questioning of his authority, but if ever he needed her on his side, it was now.

IN THE BIG SNOW DANCE HOUSE, which was attached to Koeha's private dwelling, Creed and Angituk were given the seat of honour in the centre of the wide sleeping platform covered in thick muskox hides. Koeha sat beside them, with Kingagolik next to Angituk. Forty-eight men, women, and children crammed into the big igloo, leaving a small space in the centre for dancing. The women cut up and distributed several raw caribou haunches on meat plates made from the skulls of muskoxen and bear. Most of the men and a few of the women had stripped down to their waists because of the body heat. The smell of sweat was overpowering, but Creed soon grew accustomed to it in the atmosphere of warmth and welcome. He handed out chocolate and watched with delight as dubious faces broke into wide grins.

Creed and Angituk dined on raw seal meat, half-roasted fish, and a warm caribou broth in the polished horn of a muskox, which was quite good. So many were asking questions of Angituk that she had little time to put food in her mouth. Most of them knew members of her mother's people, who lived farther west along the shore of the Coronation Gulf. Who was alive? Who was dead? What babies had been born? What was life like in the South among the Cree and white men? Did they really have igloos built of trees? She did her best to answer the questions.

An old woman by the name of Utugauk, Koeha's first and oldest wife, took measurements of Creed's feet with a leather string.

"She will make you sealskin boots tonight that are watertight and much warmer than your boots for walking on snow."

"That's very nice of her but not necessary," Creed protested. The truth was that his rubber boots and three pairs of socks left his toes on the edge of frostbite every day.

Creed watched as three women tended several soapstone oil lamps, long bowls of fat and oil with a row of wicks that gave light and heat to the snow house and slowly cooked the meat. Creed noticed Angi's face in the golden oil light. She glowed with happiness to be here with her people, speaking in her own language.

"Angituk, I have a question about Kingagolik's husband. How does a walrus kill a man?"

Angituk consulted the widow, who was happy to tell the story while she translated. "It was several days' travel west of here, near Paulatuk. He was standing on the ice edge with his spear, looking for walrus. He was an excellent hunter for seal and caribou but not well experienced with walrus, for there were very few around the Coppermine. A big bull walrus saw his shadow from below and smashed up through the ice, knocking him into the water. Then it killed him with its tusks and dragged him down. Two other hunters saw this and it is a famous story. They never found the body."

"Does this happen often?"

"I have heard of other times. Walruses get angry and hunt men."

Two girls and a boy sat beside them on the sleeping platform, playing with two puppies. Angituk told him they were Koeha's grandchildren. Creed roughed up the puppies and they tried to bite him with their little milk teeth. He grabbed their throats, growling softly in mock attack, and they racked his forearm with their back paws. The children laughed. Angituk gave him a smile.

"You know, it's my people's belief that human beings are the product"—she hesitated self-consciously—"the product of a woman spirit mating with a dog. Long ago, all animals were good friends to human beings—the caribou, seal and wolf, fish and raven—all living and hunting together. They were smarter than us and guided us in our lives. We all spoke the same language. But we fell from grace with the animals. We did not honour them as we should have and so we are no longer friends. Now, speaking to them is difficult. The only animal friend left for us is the dog. They have been faithful because they are where we came from."

Two of the grandchildren rolled off the platform and began to fight. One hit the other in the eye with a closed fist and the screaming began. The combat escalated and Creed looked around to see if any adults would put an end to it, but the wild, scratching, screaming children were ignored. Finally, Creed bent down and pulled the two ruffians apart and gave them both a good shake.

"Stop that. Someone's going to get hurt."

For a moment the house fell silent. Everyone stared at Creed in shock. He let go of the boys and looked to Angituk. She spoke a few words of conciliation to the assembly and the two boys began playing again, peacefully.

"Have I offended somehow?" he asked Angituk.

Angituk asked two questions of Utugauk and then explained. "The two boys, Tuugak and Tavlo, Koeha's grandsons, have been given the *attiaq* of Koeha's father and uncle."

"What is an *attiaq*?"

"A spirit from a family member who has died, or someone in the community who was very wise, or very loved, or a good hunter."

"Is that like your spirit guide? Like the bear?"

"No. That's an animal helper. An *attiaq* is your soul. Who you were. Who you are. Pay attention." She chided him gently and smiled. "After children are born, they are examined for signs— shape of ears or nose, a type of behaviour—to see who they were in an earlier life, usually a dead grandparent or great-grandparent, uncle or so on. The mother chooses the Spirit of the Dead, summons it, and presents the child. The child becomes that person again."

"So all souls have been used before."

"Oh, yes. The good ones many times. This belief is strong."

"How about you?"

"I was assigned my great-grandmother's spirit and became her. She was very clever and beautiful, of course." She slipped in another smile.

"Of course."

"My mother used to call me Grandmother and I would call her Granddaughter, because I became my mother's grandmother. You understand?"

"I think so. So you are your own great-grandmother."

"Exactly." She beamed at his understanding.

The boys were quiet now, playing a stick game together on the muskox hide.

"And the boys are their great-grandfather and grand-uncle.

When you grabbed them and scolded them, you were interfering with two very wise and esteemed men. It was disrespectful," she reproved gently.

"Maybe they should spank me?"

Angituk laughed. "No one spanks anyone."

"So the kids are never punished for bad behaviour?"

"Oh, no! Good behaviour comes naturally. It would be like shouting at a bald man to make his hair grow."

Creed smiled at this analogy, but he was sure this convention wasn't going to be adopted in white society any time soon.

A communal bowl of *akutuq-akutaq* was served for dessert, consisting of caribou fat mixed with berries and small chunks of meat. Creed found it even more appealing than the broth. He noted that in the cold climate his body craved fat, and a dish that would have turned his stomach only weeks ago became a much-desired treat.

The leader, Koeha, stood to sing a song of welcome. He was accompanied by two young women who did a rhythmical, in-and-out vocal breathing from the throat unlike anything Creed had ever heard. In a high singing voice, with Angituk translating, the leader welcomed the white man from the South, who was handsome and strong, and hoped he would be good to the Copper people (which translated as "real human beings"). Koeha apologized for the poor food and cold accommodation and Creed made much of shaking his head to protest this assessment. There was a chorus and everyone joined in.

"Ai, yai, ya, ya ... Ai, ya, ya, ya!"

Koeha danced a short jig back and forth on his feet to the rhythm and everyone clapped and moaned their appreciation at his spritely expressions. He then recommended the best foods to make Creed get fat and suggested that if there was a woman he wanted to help keep him warm, that could be arranged. A plump woman with facial tattoos and beautiful teeth who had stripped to the waist touched his arm.

"She is highly prized as a lover," Angituk informed him, smiling.

Creed experienced a moment of panic. "I'm fine, thanks," he said, and Angituk laughed out loud.

Then another woman, elderly but spry, in a beautifully embroidered dress, stood and the people were respectfully quiet. She had a wide, thin hoop in her hand with skin pulled tightly across it and she hammered the drum and danced with her thick legs, each step a drama, all the while pounding in an essential rhythm that increased and quickened as she chanted the story of her life.

As Creed watched the singing and drumming and dancing, he felt as if he were travelling back in time. Eskimo celebrations like this had taken place five thousand years ago. Before the British Empire and Mozart and Shakespeare and Columbus. Before Zarathustra and Aristotle and the pyramids. He was awed.

The old woman ended with a triumphant flourish of drumming and the audience shouted their approval. She almost collapsed on him and Creed took her arm to help steady her. Then Angituk faced him, a smile on her lips.

"Your turn."

Creed hesitated. He had come not to dance but to investigate a murder, and he should get on with it. However, under the encouraging gaze of Angituk and the others, he supposed it would be rude not to accept the invitation. Then the questioning could begin.

Reluctantly, Creed tried out a simple beat on the drum placed before him. Then he essayed a shuffling jig and the people grunted with hearty approval. Warming to the task, Creed offered a few jig-type moves. His tired legs responded well and his audience cheered his efforts. Next he crafted several cakewalk kicks, tossed in a Chaplin shuffle, and as a finale negotiated a graceful pirouette, almost falling into the enthusiastic and welcoming arms of the plump, tattooed lover. Angituk laughed, as pleasantly surprised by his impressive efforts as his hosts. Led by Koeha, they clapped and cheered the *Kabloona*.

Creed was enjoying himself so much, he had almost forgotten his duty. The murderers could be in the camp. It suddenly occurred to him they could be here in this snow house, armed. It was time to ask questions. Creed turned to Koeha, who seemed slightly alarmed and disappointed at Creed's serious turn of mood.

"Are you sure you want to do this now?" Angituk asked before translating anything.

"Yes. I think now is the perfect time ... Koeha, you are a fine host and your food is excellent ..." Creed began, with Angituk translating. "But I do have some questions to ask."

As Angituk spoke, all drumming, dancing, and singing stopped. Everyone listened attentively.

"You and your people and this land are all part of a bigger country called Canada. We have laws for the country that must be obeyed by everyone, including your people."

Koeha thought about this and his expression darkened. "No. You have a country in the South that you come from and we have this land, which is ours. They cannot be the same thing."

Creed decided to sidestep this larger discussion and take a more direct approach. "Two white priests—white shamans— were murdered at Bloody Falls three winters ago. Do you know anything about this?"

When the question was translated, people's eyes grew wide in fear and there was complete silence. Koeha stared at him as if he had been slapped. Kingagolik and the tattooed lover covered their faces. Some were visibly trembling. Two began to weep.

Creed turned to Angituk. "So they knew the priests?"

Angituk asked Koeha and he explained.

"They have heard John Hornby's story. If an Eskimo kills a white man, more white men will come and kill them all. They want to know if you plan to kill them."

The weeping of the women grew in volume.

"Tell them they will not be harmed. I only want the man or men that killed the priests."

The women slowly stopped crying but stared at Creed anxiously.

Creed showed Koeha the two photographs of Rouvière. The hunter was amazed at the compact image. He recognized the white man immediately.

"So the white priests were here?"

"Yes. This is the one we called Kuleavik."

Angituk then translated Koeha's longer response, which was encouraged and added to by the others, men and women alike.

"Yes, two years ago, the two white men lived with us at this camp. We called the friendly one Kuleavik and the tall one Ilogoak."

Creed began taking notes in his journal.

"They told us about the good place in the sky and the bad fiery place under the ice. They showed pictures of these places, with creatures like us in the fiery place and white humans with wings in the place above in the sky. They gave us pictures of a white man with long hair and a thick beard and pictures of his mother. They showed us how to use our hands." Koeha placed his hands together as if in prayer. "And how to do this." Koeha crossed himself. "They taught us to sing songs in their language."

Koeha suddenly broke into song. To Creed's surprise, everyone joined in with "Silent Night."

> *Douce nuit, sainte nuit!*
> *Dans les cieux, l'astre luit.*
> *Le mystère annoncé s'accomplit.*
> *Cet enfant sur la paille endormi,*
> *C'est l'amour infini,*
> *C'est l'amour infini!*

Koeha put up a hand so he could go on. "They put tiny bits of food in our mouths and then they chanted. We let them do it. It made them happy." Koeha paused. "It was a very bad season for food when they were with us. The camp was hungry. "

Many of the other men in the snow house were nodding at the memory. Koeha gestured to a short, powerful man across the snow house with a wide face, dark eyes, and elaborately braided hair.

"This man, Kormik, brought them north to us. Tell the story."

Kormik spoke to Creed, and Angituk translated.

"I found the white men between the Dismal Lakes and the Coppermine when we hunted late-summer caribou. They made signs to me and I believed that they would trade me their rifle in exchange for taking them here to the mouth. So I took them."

Koeha continued: "They stayed in our camp for several days, as I said. It was a time of hunger for us. The fish and caribou were gone, but the sea ice was not yet in, so we could not go out after seal. We were all very hungry and many were weak and sick. After a few days we had no more food for them and the white men decided to go back south. We gave them two weak dogs to help them pull their qamutik. I went with them and helped them pull the sled until they were away from camp. Then I came back.

"There was an *angatkuk* named Uluksuk that we knew, staying near our camp with his family and his friend, a hunter named Sinnisiak, and his family."

"What is an *angatkuk*?" Creed asked Angituk.

"A shaman."

"Okay. Ask him to go on."

"Two days after the white men left, Uluksuk and Sinnisiak went up toward Bloody Falls to fish. When they returned three days later, they had the white men's rifles, their clothing, pictures and books, and my two dogs, which they gave back. They told everyone they felt badly but they had to kill the white men."

"They admitted it?"

"Yes."

"Did they say why?"

"They said the white men scared them. They had never seen white men before. They thought the white men were going to kill them. We didn't ask more questions, but we went to see for ourselves."

"You went to Bloody Falls?"

"Yes. We saw the dead white men and took some of the belongings that were left."

Creed's rising voice revealed his ire. "You took their belongings?"

The people looked very worried again.

"The white men would not need them anymore."

"We put flat rocks on the bodies to protect them and smaller rocks around them, but then we had fear of the spirits and ran."

Koeha took out a children's picture book of Bible stories and a rosary. "Here. You can take these back if you want."

Creed took the articles for evidence. "Do you know where this shaman Uluksuk is now? And the hunter Sinnisiak?"

"Oh yes. They are both just up the coast near the Rae River. Only a few miles."

Creed felt a new excitement at the prospect of apprehending the suspects. He read his notes aloud to Koeha, had Angituk do a quick translation for him, and asked him to sign them with an X as being the truth. He then thanked Koeha again for his hospitality.

"The shaman Uluksuk is powerful. He has been good to us, bringing back the seals twice, and once the caribou. However, I do not know him well. Be careful."

"Do they have the priests' rifles?"

"Yes."

Seven

Creed and Angituk walked across the windswept sea ice of the bay on the way to the shaman's camp. The daytime moon came into view between ragged, cruising clouds. Far out on the ocean they could see churning ice packs. It would not be long before freeze-up, and the seal hunt could begin.

The snowfall was increasing, whipped by an intermittent west wind that would conceal their approach. Creed used his compass to maintain a straight line on their heading. The new boots that Koeha's wife had made for him were remarkably comfortable, light and watertight. They had said a sad goodbye to the pretty Peterborough canoe and left her in Koeha's camp as a gift, along with the heavy tent. They carried the wanigans with food, clothing, and sleeping bags through two feet of snow. Creed had the twelve-pound .38-55 in one hand and the Colt in his holster. He was exhausted, but they were about to confront the men he had come more than a thousand miles to find, and he quickened his pace.

He looked back at Angituk, making her confident way through the growing snowstorm with no difficulty. She carried sixty pounds on her back and he smiled thinking of her. She gave him heart.

Angituk had become quiet and concerned since they left

Koeha's camp. She came up to walk beside Creed and spoke during a brief lull in the wind.

"I remember the shaman Uluksuk. He is well known. My people were usually west of here near the Dolphin Strait, but he visited us once when I was a little girl. It is known he can turn himself into a wolf or a bear. Some people have seen this. And others say that he spent two days under the sea ice to meet with Kannokapfaluk, the goddess of all animals, and ask her to send the seals one year when there were none. You see, that year Kannokapfaluk had been depressed by the people breaking taboos and she stopped combing her hair and it became matted, so the seals got tangled and couldn't get to the surface. We were starving. He fixed that. He convinced her we would be good and keep the taboos and she should release the seals from her hair. It is also well reported he has flown up to the moon."

Creed glared at her impatiently. "Angituk, people don't become animals or fly to the moon or stay two days under the sea. You're just scaring yourself. This is a man. That's all."

Angituk fell back behind him, chastened. He didn't have to be rude, she thought. She only wanted to prepare him. Maybe save his life. He doesn't know all things. No one is wise enough to know everything. The world is full of a thousand mysteries that even a white man can't know. Especially a white man.

CREED AND ANGITUK approached Uluksuk's camp on the shore of the Coronation Gulf from downwind. They hid behind snow-covered shore rocks and watched for several minutes as two men forty yards away skinned an early seal beside a snow house. One wore a black, close-fitting garment. As Creed studied it, he was shocked to realize it was a priest's cassock. The long cloak had been hacked off just above the knees for ease of movement.

There were two light qamutiks beside the house and five scruffy dogs. The men, intent on their butchering, tossed bits of seal to the dogs from time to time. The snow was lighter now, the wind had dropped, and the air was still.

Creed put his mouth to Angituk's ear. "I need you to interpret, but stay safe, well behind me. If anything happens I want you to run."

Angituk nodded. Creed took out two pairs of handcuffs and hung them on his belt. It felt like a trench raid. He withdrew the rifle from the soft sheath and opened the flap of his holster. "You ready?"

Angituk nodded and Creed stood up and walked toward the two men. He held the rifle in his hands but pointed to one side. Angituk followed cautiously.

"YOU! Are you Uluksuk?"

Angituk translated.

The two men let go of the seal and turned to stare at Creed in complete wonder, their mouths open. The one wearing the cassock was the older man, the shaman.

"I am Corporal Creed of the Royal North West Mounted Police. Are you Uluksuk ... and you are Sinnisiak?"

The two men stared for another moment as Angituk translated, then both nodded. The shaman recovered first. "I am Uluksuk. This is Sinnisiak. Are you a spirit?"

"No."

"What do you want?"

"I am looking for the two men who killed the white priests at Bloody Falls."

Angituk translated and the men's surprise became fear. Uluksuk turned and grabbed what Creed had not seen leaning in a cleft of the snow house: the priests' .44 calibre Winchester rifle. Creed threw off his mitten, levered a bullet into the chamber, and swung his rifle, drawing a bead on the shaman. Uluksuk turned back toward him, holding the priests' rifle out at arm's length, as an offering. Creed relaxed his trigger finger but kept the rifle trained on the shaman, and spoke to Angituk.

"Take the rifle and cover them with it."

Angituk did as she was told. Creed put his own rifle to one side and took possession of a second rifle leaning near the younger hunter, then pulled out the handcuffs.

"You are under arrest."

He demonstrated how they should hold out their hands and they did. They looked down at the handcuffs with alarm and curiosity. They gently tried to pull them apart, testing their bonds. Creed checked the back collar of the shaman's cassock and found the embroidered name *Père Rouvière*.

"Did you kill the priests?" Angituk translated.

Uluksuk answered without hesitation. "Yes, we did."

Then, for his own personal curiosity, Creed asked, "And did you eat some of their livers?"

Uluksuk answered, "Yes, we did."

"Okay. You don't have to tell me any more until you have a lawyer present to represent you."

Angituk stumbled in the translation. "There is no word for 'lawyer.'"

"Spokesman? Friend?"

"Maybe ... older brother. *Angak*," she translated.

Three women, several children of varying ages, and three old people who had heard the voices came out of the two igloos and stood staring fearfully at Creed. The women looked at the handcuffs and began to cry. Creed was somehow surprised to see them. Koeha had said there was a family, but Creed had forgotten.

"Who are they?" he asked.

Angituk determined that two of the women, one young and pregnant and one older, were Uluksuk's wives. Another, who seemed very young, was the wife of Sinnisiak. She was the most upset and fearful of all.

Uluksuk spoke for a moment.

"What did he say?"

"He said he knew you were coming. He has carried this thing a long time in his head and is glad you've come. He wants to know if you will kill them now."

The younger man, Sinnisiak, began to cry.

"Tell them I will not kill them," Creed said. Angituk translated.

"Will you hit us with sticks?" Sinnisiak asked through his tears.

"Tell them I will not hurt them unless they try to escape. I will take them to the place I come from in the South, where other white men will decide what to do with them."

"Will you harm our families?"

"No, we will leave your families alone."

Uluksuk and Sinnisiak, showing relief, spoke to each other, then to Angituk.

"They will co-operate and go with you if you promise not to hurt their families."

"I promise."

The two spoke again.

"They want to know if they can take their wives and children with them."

"No."

One of the older women spoke up.

"This is Uluksuk's first wife. She wants us to stay overnight so she can finish new mukluks for Uluksuk to take with him."

All looked to Creed. It was pretty late now to start out, but it seemed almost suicidal to stay in this camp. He looked at Angituk. "Do you think they mean us harm?"

"No. I believe they are sincere."

"Tell them if anything happens to me many more white men will come to get them."

"They know this."

For the first time Creed appreciated Hornby's dictum.

"We can take shifts watching them."

Angituk nodded and told Uluksuk's wife they would stay.

THROUGH THE EVENING, Creed watched his two suspects warily, his revolver resting in his lap, his rifle beside him, his back to the snow wall. The gathering was a quiet, tense contrast to the house of Koeha. The family ate raw seal, and caribou partially cooked over the soapstone oil lamp. The women and children watched Creed. At first Creed refused any food. Angituk hungrily ate seal and some caribou.

"It is good, Corporal. Eat some." And finally he did, served by Uluksuk's sombre, pregnant second wife.

Creed studied the younger man, the handsome Sinnisiak. Uluksuk was his mentor and he sensed their relationship was close. These close hunting partnerships were common, Angituk had told him, like brothers, or fathers and sons. Sinnisiak's young wife was braiding her husband's hair, expressing a deep sadness at the impending departure. Creed realized she was also pregnant. He looked around at the five children to try to guess who belonged to whom. Uluksuk's first wife worked quickly to finish the mukluks, folding over the top lip with an embroidered stitch, holding the material in her leathery fingers three inches from her nose in the dim light, using an ivory needle and thimble to push through the tough caribou hide.

Uluksuk helped his older son, a boy of twelve, create a short, delicately curved hunting bow from spruce twigs reinforced by a dense braid of sinew and a handle made of muskox horn with leaves of horn extending up and down to give the shaft strength. They tested the tautness of the gut. Uluksuk advised another boy, about eight years old, who looked more like Sinnisiak, on the setting and baiting of a snare. Angituk joined in this casual discussion and laughed once at something Uluksuk said.

In this quiet domestic scene, Creed had to remind himself that these men were murderers. They could jump him and cut his throat in an instant. He had heard their confession and only now, after the exhilaration of finding them and making the arrests, did the full responsibility of the task ahead strike him. It would take months to reach Edmonton. Two hundred nights on guard against attack. If they found Hornby again, he could travel with them and give Creed some relief with the prisoners, but Dease Bay was still many weeks away. Though she was certainly able, he could not depend too heavily on Angituk. It was dangerous and he was not compensating her enough to ask her to be an armed guard. If they killed him, they would think nothing of doing the same to her, though she was of their blood. The risk was deeply troubling to him.

Uluksuk's second wife was talking loudly and becoming more upset, and the wives and older children were agreeing with her. Creed looked to Angituk.

"She is worried that their shaman is going away. The families have relied on him and his spirit helpers to change bad weather and find animals to hunt, to cure the sick and kill evil spirits. She believes there is an evil spirit among them now."

The other women began to moan and Creed recalled Angituk's advice: make a sound with each breath in the presence of a bad spirit so it cannot enter you.

Then Uluksuk spoke and Angituk translated again. "With your permission, he would like to drive away the bad spirit from the families before he goes."

Jack studied the old shaman for a moment, then nodded for him to go ahead.

Uluksuk took out a small wooden oval disc. There were notches cut into the sides. On a sinew cord he twirled the disc over his head, showing great skill and accuracy in the confined space even with his hands bound by the handcuffs. To Creed's surprise it created a low, thrumming moan that built to a deep-throated, mumbling roar. It seemed to come from everywhere, both inside and outside the snow house. Creed imagined a surly host of invisible spirits surrounding them. The family was spellbound and Uluksuk called out to them to scare any malevolent spirits away. He counted one, two, three and everyone let loose a fearsome howl. As captivated as the others, Angituk joined in. After three such shouts, suddenly the whirling disc was deftly caught and it disappeared and Uluksuk shushed everyone to silence.

Listening and looking in each corner of the igloo, the shaman assured them that all the bad spirits were gone, and the people cheered. All, he continued, except one. The worst one. It was the hardest to get rid of. It was *Hílaq*, the white bear who made himself invisible.

"There he is!" said the shaman, gesturing to a space against the wall near the doorway, close to Creed. The women scrambled away from it, terrified, to the far side of the igloo. Uluksuk chanted magic words and Creed heard a rumbling growl from the open space. *Very impressive how the old man can throw his voice,* he thought. Suddenly the shaman leapt. As the women and children pulled back and cowered, he wrestled with the invisible spirit, and his efforts contorted his face. Creed held his pistol under one arm, prepared for an escape attempt, but he too was quite taken with the conviction of the performance.

It began to appear that Uluksuk was losing. He was on the floor with the spirit on top of him, pushing him down on his knees. His shackled hands went out to the cooking table and grasped a copper blade. Creed withdrew the pistol a little, ready in case he made a move toward him. As the spirit drove Uluksuk down, he brought the knife up in a desperate lunge into the air. An inhuman scream raised the hair on the back of Creed's neck and echoed through the igloo. Fresh blood splattered across the snow floor of the house. The caribou skin over the doorway flew open, untouched by any human hand, and the invisible monster fled into the night. Uluksuk scrambled after him out the exit tunnel. For a second Creed thought he might be escaping, but he could hear, as the people huddled together inside, a battle raging beyond the snow walls. Uluksuk shouted angry words and was answered by the growls and screams of the evil spirit bear surely receiving mortal wounds. Creed listened closely, amazed to find that the voices overlapped. *How does he do that?* He was tempted to follow Uluksuk outside to see what was going on, but the expression of alarm in Angituk's eyes gave him pause.

The night grew quiet but for the wind spirits outside. A moment later the caribou skin flew back and Uluksuk tumbled into their midst, clutching the bloody copper knife. Again Creed's hand had the pistol ready, but the old shaman lay down exhausted on the floor.

"He is dead. You will be safe now."

Sinnisiak went to him, looking for any wounds. Uluksuk was weak but unhurt. His family congratulated him on his victory over the evil spirit. Uluksuk accepted the praise graciously. His first wife brought him broth and touched his face with affection. Angituk too offered Uluksuk praise and thanks, no less impressed than the others.

Creed had to admit it was a skilled performance. He reached down and touched the spirit blood staining the packed-snow floor. He sniffed it. It was in fact blood. *The old man is very clever,* he said to himself.

THE SINGLE WICK of an oil lamp illuminated the glacial interior of the igloo, its subtle undulations creating phantom shadows that throbbed across the ice walls. Uluksuk, Sinnisiak, and their wives and children slept naked together beneath furs on the floor. Angituk lay fast asleep beside him, though she was fully clothed. Creed's eyes were heavy. His hand rested gently on the pistol. He slapped his own face twice to wake himself up. He moved to rouse Angituk to spell him, but she was sleeping so deeply he decided to wait another hour.

He slipped into waking dreams. He ran across the churning ice floes of a black ocean. He leapt from one tiny island to the next, tempting the bottomless waters below. He awoke with a start. He felt the pistol in his hand and his eyes passed over to where the prisoners slept. All was still. All secure.

His eyes settled on the little guttering flame and became heavy again. This time there was rushing water, but it was warm. There were rocks, but they did not threaten. He was naked, but he did not mind. And she was with him too. Angituk. Her full mouth open in teasing laughter. He stretched out a hand to her and she pulled it slowly to her face. She bit down hard, twisting, drawing blood like a wild animal. He startled and woke. He looked at Angituk, in peaceful repose, her full lips parted, breasts rising and falling with each breath, almond eyes lightly closed in dreamlessness. He gazed at her for a long moment, astonished he had once thought her a boy.

Movement across the gloom of the igloo caught his eye. His hand closed on the pistol, but as his eyes cleared he realized it was a man and woman moving beneath a muskox fur. Sinnisiak had mounted his young wife, who knelt underneath him, face down on the skins. They moved against each other, their urgent panting visible in the cool air, their thrusts growing deeper and more vigorous. Creed was an embarrassed witness to their intimacy; he could almost have touched the woman's splayed fingers with his foot.

The muskox skin slipped back off their shoulders and then off their flanks as the woman rose up on her elbows. She arched her back to better countervail her husband's determined strokes. Her full breasts swung above her pregnant belly and her brown skin shone with sweat in the cold air. Panting quickly, she spread her knees slightly and reached back with her right hand to grab her hunter's buttock and guide his efforts. The skins had fallen away completely now and Creed could not take his eyes from the naked coupling bodies so close to him. Sinnisiak raised himself upright and shuddered as he climaxed.

Their breathing slowed and they rolled to one side, still united. When Sinnisiak pulled the muskox skins over them, he looked up to meet Creed's eyes. The hunter nodded to him with no more self-consciousness than if he were greeting a neighbour on the street. The act was no more private than eating, dancing, or hunting. Thirty seconds later the lovers were asleep and the only sounds in the warm igloo were the gentle rhythms of breathing, moaning, snoring, and the wind howling again outside. Creed experienced a sudden deep pang of loneliness and longed for the warmth of a sleeping lover. He listened to the wind and his leaden eyes settled again on the single flame of the oil lamp.

A HAND ON HIS SHOULDER roused him. He awoke with a start and raised the pistol in defence. It was Uluksuk's first wife, the older one who had finished the mukluks. She took the pistol from his hand—it meant nothing to her, she had never seen one—put it on the ground, and replaced it with a soapstone bowl of warm caribou broth.

Creed looked around. Everyone was awake and moving except Angituk. Uluksuk and Sinnisiak had started packing. Creed put a hand on Angituk's arm and saw the mild panic come and go as she awakened. When her eyes turned to him, he smiled to reassure her. The first wife brought her a bowl. The broth tasted wonderful.

IT WAS A SMALL, sad gathering outside the snow buildings. Uluksuk instructed his twelve-year-old son and the old man, Sinnisiak's father, on where to move camp and what animals to hunt in the following year. Uluksuk's second wife and the younger children were crying. Sinnisiak was crying too. Angituk explained to Creed.

"Uluksuk and Sinnisiak are the strongest hunters in the family. There is great concern they will not find the animals without them. If they don't, the others die."

Uluksuk and Sinnisiak gave their spears, bows, and hunting tools to the old man and the boy and quietly continued with more advice on where they might find animals. They both listened attentively.

"We have to go," Creed said quietly, and Angituk gave him a sharp look.

"These instructions could save the lives of the entire family."

"Please ask them to say goodbye."

"There is no such word. It would be bad luck."

Angituk's eyes flashed at him, but she told them what he

wanted. Uluksuk put his shackled hands around each of his young children and hugged them. He embraced his wives. His second wife was crying; his older first wife remained stoic. Sinnisiak rubbed and licked noses with his pretty young wife and sucked back his tears to show courage. He also, as Uluksuk watched, licked the face of Uluksuk's younger wife in a way that left no doubt they too were lovers.

"I thought she was Uluksuk's wife."

"She is, but her last child is from Sinnisiak."

Suddenly Sinnisiak was talking quickly, very upset, appealing to Creed with tears in his eyes.

"He does not want to go. He wants you to kill him here."

"No one's going to kill him."

"He doesn't want to go. He wants to bring his wife."

"No. I'm sorry. No wives."

Sinnisiak was desperate and tearful and angry all at once, but it was Uluksuk who calmed him down and reassured him.

"He has no choice," Creed said quietly, but Angituk ignored this statement.

Uluksuk's words were having a positive effect on the younger hunter, who eventually began to nod slowly.

"All right. He will come."

"What did the old one tell him?"

"He said they must show courage for the others. It will be an adventure going south. They will have stories to bring back."

"I'd say so."

Creed took gentle hold of Sinnisiak's arm to guide him south from the camp and the young man complied. Uluksuk joined them. The final leavetaking was strangely abrupt and without conversation or words of farewell. The hunters simply turned away and did not look back.

Angituk kept up a brisk pace in front, followed by Sinnisiak,

Uluksuk, and Creed. Creed carried his rifle and guided a qamutik pulled by two of Uluksuk's dogs. No one spoke. The only sounds were the soft hiss of the runners and the crunch of boots on firm snow. The small sled carried the two wanigans, several caribou skins, cooking utensils, and the priests' rifles. The suspects each had a bag over one shoulder filled mostly with food that Uluksuk's wives had packed.

They passed by Koeha's camp early that afternoon to pick up the tent. Koeha's people quietly watched them go by, marvelling at the capture of the great shaman. Why does he not turn into a bird or a bear, they asked among themselves. The white shaman from the South must be powerful indeed. Uluksuk did not look at them, only at the ground behind Angituk's heels. Creed realized this was the very message of his mission: if you commit a crime in the Dominion of Canada, you will be caught and brought to trial. You must answer for your behaviour. This story would travel quickly among the Copper Eskimos. Of this, Creed was sure.

Creed stopped to thank Koeha again for his help and hospitality. Angituk taught him the word *quanaqqutit*. He bought some seal oil in a skin bag and three caribou hides from the old hunter, paying him the tidy sum of four silver dollars, though both knew there was no place for Koeha to spend it. Creed wrote the transaction down in his book; careful accounts were demanded by the force. He also gave him several cans of corned beef and sardines and a small package of Sweet Cap tobacco, which pleased Koeha more. *"Quanaqqutit."*

Kingagolik came out to see Angituk and they embraced and rubbed faces. Angituk shared tears with her old auntie and the woman made her promise to return to them. Angituk turned away from her and did not look back.

THEY WALKED SOUTH for several hours along the high banks of the Coppermine with Angituk leading and Creed behind, the rifle under his arm. The snow was compact and the walking not too difficult. Despite the constant need to unravel the tangled traces, the sled and the two dogs were a big asset for transporting the heavier gear. Creed's mukluks, with their three layers of pelt and dry grasses, continued to be comfortable and watertight. His beard had grown to a respectable thickness and gave needed protection against the wind.

That night, at a flat spot up on the high banks overlooking the Coppermine, they put up the tent and fortified it with a little wall of snow. Angituk laid the caribou skins fur-side down against the ground. The untanned skins put up a stink, but the others were used to it and the protection from the cold ground was substantial. Once the shelter was complete, they cooked some meat and fish inside over Creed's little oil stove with some of the seal oil he had bought from Koeha. Uluksuk and Sinnisiak were just as happy eating the meat raw.

The first night passed like the one in Uluksuk's igloo, Creed falling in and out of sleep, his hand on his pistol, his prisoners compliant and then snoring with the clear consciences of two babies. The dogs stayed outside in the snow, their muzzles buried under their tails to keep warm.

Eight

As they headed south day by day, the big river continued to freeze up. The days were becoming dramatically shorter; there were only a few hours between dawn and dusk, and for much of that the sun skimmed low along the horizon, their long shadows stretching out behind them to an almost infinite distance.

In these first days, the prisoners were very quiet. Even Angituk could get little out of them. They seemed resigned to their fate. Yet Creed continued his vigilance. He had been over the scene of the murders many times in his mind. It was not just his own life at stake but Angituk's too, if he let down his guard. If they so chose, the hunters could kill them as quickly as they had the priests, return home with impressive weapons and gear, and not expect to answer for either crime for at least a year. Creed kept his pistol close, and when Angituk could spell him with the pistol he took short, deep sleeps two or three times a day.

On the last night before they left the picturesque, barren valley of the Coppermine, Creed sat up on the ridge in the last precious moments of sunset. Angituk said her goodbyes to the land and left him to go prepare dinner before darkness fell. He noted again that the Eskimos did not make extended goodbyes. The white custom was considered crass, Angi had told him, demonstrating self-importance and unnecessary elaboration.

A few minutes after she left he was joined by Uluksuk in his shackles, who sat with him to enjoy the swift interplay of fiery colours that swept the sky in the last moments of sunset. The Eskimo murmured his appreciation as they watched, and it came as a surprise to Creed that not only could his prisoner savour a thing as simple as beauty but they could share it intimately. They were from such vastly different worlds, existing on such different planes, communicating not a word to each other, and yet they both understood perfectly the aesthetic message of the setting sun.

They smiled at each other in appreciation of both the beauty and the sharing as the last bit of solar gold disappeared behind the curved horizon.

WINTER HAD CLOSED IN completely by the time they got to the turbulent, unfrozen confluence of the Kendall River and headed west. His feet were warm in the mukluks, but Creed's woollen trousers, even with two sets of long underwear, had him shivering. He remembered Hornby's observation that a sheep wouldn't last a day in the Arctic winter. The ice on the river above the initial sets of rapids was two feet thick and the smooth surface made for easy travelling, but they would soon have to find a place to winter.

The countenance and demeanour of the Dismal Lakes was not improved by a thick cloak of snow. The travellers were four tiny figures in an enormous flat landscape without trees. Creed considered how the lack of foliage seemed to remove any sense of perspective or progress. Were they tiny figures in an enormous land? Or were they great giants hulking across the flat, featureless terrain, crushing tiny trees under the snow? The looming figure of an *inukshuk* on their path, a stone man with old moss for hair, banished Creed's maudlin thoughts. For the first time he realized how important these figures were to relieve the traveller of his loneliness. The stone man represented perspective and history and humanity. It was not simply a stylized pile of stones but the sum of the hopes and fears of the artist who had created it. His character and spirit lingered in the wind-worn chunks of granite, offering comfort and reassurance and company.

Angituk had been rationing their food now for several days, and their dwindling supplies had Creed worried. They had not seen one living creature since they entered the Dismal Lakes, and it was his responsibility to feed four people. They were still ten days from the meat cache Angituk had made at the headwaters of the Dease, and the Arctic hares and ground squirrels were now deep in hibernation. The last three nights Angituk had laid careful snares, even baiting them, and come up empty. They had few tools to break through the ice, and no nets to fish with if they did. They had enough food for only another day or two, and everyone in the party knew it. But there were always the dogs.

That night, as they divided the meagre servings of fish and caribou meat, Uluksuk spoke to Angituk in low tones, and Angituk turned to Creed.

"He says we are out of food. Even tonight we are still hungry. He would like to talk to the animal spirits on our behalf and explain our need."

Creed tried to hide his skepticism as much as possible. "Okay. How does he do that?"

"It is simple. He burns grasses. He says prayers."

"All right."

"But he needs to have the handcuffs off."

Creed's first impulse was to say no. This sounded like the trick he'd been waiting for. Uluksuk spoke again.

"He promises he will not try to escape. Sinnisiak will assist him."

Creed looked at Angituk and the two prisoners. If nothing else, he realized it would make them feel better if he allowed it.

"All right. He can go ahead. But Sinnisiak's cuffs stay on."

Angituk translated and Sinnisiak nodded. Creed reached into his pocket for the key and made brief contact with the loaded pistol.

SINNISIAK ROOTED AROUND under the snow for the long grasses that the caribou fed on. He returned with a small sheaf of them. Uluksuk sat outside the tent, cross-legged before Creed's stove, the flame high. Angituk and Creed crouched in the snow a few yards away. Uluksuk stripped to the waist. Creed was impressed that the old man's bare skin could stand such cold for more than a second. Uluksuk put the sheaf of grasses to the flame of the stove. The damp grass smouldered and the shaman, sitting downwind, guided the billowing smoke to blow across his body. He began to chant.

Angituk explained in a whisper, "He is purifying himself, body and mind. No bad thoughts."

When his upper body was fully engulfed in the acrid green smoke and the grass had almost burned down to his hand, Uluksuk extinguished the flame in the snow. Sinnisiak brought out a small, shallow hand drum and began to keep a slow, solemn rhythm. When the beat was well established, Uluksuk spread his arms wide, closed his eyes, and began to speak loudly to the night.

"He is talking to the animal spirits," Angituk whispered, translating carefully. "He greets them with respect. He tells them he has come purified and with true thoughts. He reminds them of the time humans and animals were close friends. He tells them we have need. We are hungry. He asks them to send help. He says, 'Please come to us. We have need.' He will repeat it all two more times."

Uluksuk did as Angituk said he would, repeating his request to the spirits and thanking them for their generosity.

After a moment of calm, Uluksuk suddenly awoke with a dramatic gasp and a flailing of arms. For the first time Creed saw him shiver. Sinnisiak helped him put on his layered shirts again. The performance had exhausted him.

Uluksuk told them, "It is good. The animals have agreed to be killed."

Creed chuckled quietly at this, then fell silent at Angituk's censoring glare. Creed went to him, cautiously but respectfully. "Okay. That was very entertaining, Uluksuk, but let's get these back on you."

Creed put the handcuffs firmly on his wrists. The old man did not resist.

They all crowded back into the shelter, bringing with them the little oil stove. Koeha's oil was almost gone. Angituk had stretched it out as long as she could, leaving their meat almost completely raw, but they were still a long way from the treeline and fuel. Creed would extinguish the flame in a moment, after the old man was warm; the last thing he needed was a prisoner with pneumonia. Uluksuk's eyes closed and soon his shallow, regular breathing indicated he was fast asleep. Sinnisiak too was asleep in minutes. Creed mused again that if he had committed their crimes, his conscience would never let him go to sleep so quickly. As it was, sleep periodically eluded him.

Creed supposed Uluksuk's performance couldn't hurt. In an Eskimo camp it would have raised the spirits of a starving people. They would actually believe the animal spirits had been contacted, giving them hope again that the uncontrollable was controllable. But he had to be more pragmatic. They would be in a bit of trouble if they didn't get practical and actually find food. He could send Angituk west over the watershed to the meat cache, but that would take days. Better to stay together.

A sleepy Angituk turned and smiled at him and rubbed her belly. "We'll be fine now. There'll be food."

"Oh, you think so? Any minute a big fat ground squirrel will come and jump into our pot?"

Angituk looked at him, now awake and irritated. "You don't believe. The animals will sense you don't believe and not come," she admonished.

"And then I suppose it'll all be my fault when we starve. Look, what other options do we have? This is your land. What can we eat? Are there nuts or frozen berries we could find? Or roots? Is there any way to get at the fish? Animals hibernating under the snow? Must be something."

"You should believe."

"You can believe anything you want, but tomorrow, if there's nothing else, we'll be eating one of the dogs."

"It is dishonourable to eat a dog!"

Just before Creed blew out the lamp, he saw the hostile look she gave him. In the complete darkness her look stayed with him. He couldn't get it out of his mind. He knew the dwindling food was his own fault. He had cached too much caribou and given too much canned food to Koeha. He had made mistakes, but tomorrow he would make sure they had meat.

BY DAWN, storm clouds had rolled in. Snow had not yet begun to fall. Creed was the first up and exited the shelter to relieve himself. He took the rifle with him. Outside, ravens circled in the sky. He hadn't seen a raven in days. In a small clump of dwarf willows he noticed a scrawny white fox eyeing him.

Creed chose the bigger dog, a mixed husky/coyote bitch who laid back her ears when he approached. Her name was Ubluruaq, he recalled, or, in English, Star, and her eyes were a disquieting turquoise. He had patted her a few times in the past, her disposition friendly. Unfortunately for her, she would provide the best fillets. He grabbed the rawhide leash around her neck and took her some distance from the shelter. She whimpered a little and looked at the gun as if she knew what was coming. He stood on the leash and levered a round into the chamber of the .38-55. A head shot was best and quickest if she didn't move. It occurred to him that the blunt, heavy bullet was meant for something much bigger, and at this close range a substantial part of her head would be gone. But it had to be done.

With his foot on the leash, he tossed a snowball so she would look toward it for a moment and give him a clean shot. But Star ignored the snowball. Her turquoise eyes were fixed on something behind Creed, and she gave a quiet, excited woof. No, this was the wrong angle, he realized, exasperated. With the long barrel of the .38-55 he needed a side shot. As unfortunate as killing the dog was, it'd be worse if he messed it up and left her wounded and howling. He could go back for the pistol, but he might wake the others, and he didn't want to review his decision.

Creed took his foot off the rawhide leash, knelt down, and placed a heavy rock on it to hold her. Then he took a couple of steps back and raised the rifle again. Much better. If the damn dog would just stop staring at him and move around for a side shot. Star ignored a second snowball and woofed again. He could get a clean head shot now. But something made him stop. He released his finger from the trigger, lifted his face from the rifle stock, and turned his head. Just behind him stretched a herd of caribou.

There were at least a hundred of the damn things, a winter herd, all nuzzling under the snow for the tender grass beside the lake. A big doe was standing nearby, separate from the others, so close he could hit her with a rock. He swung the rifle up to his shoulder, half emptied his lungs, lined the sights across her heart, and pulled the trigger. She was dead before she hit the ground.

His companions came out of the shelter, rubbing the sleep from their eyes, as the shot echoed across the lake. They laughed and smiled excitedly. Angituk took particular pleasure in the sight. "Better than a ground squirrel in your pot!"

Uluksuk went over to inspect the doe and said a few words to Angituk and Sinnisiak. Angituk smiled at Creed.

"He says this is good. This was the one chosen for us to have. Too old for breeding but the meat still tender."

"It was the closest one."

"Exactly." Angituk smiled at him.

"It was just good *isuma*," Creed told her.

"No," Angituk countered. "This was Uluksuk."

Creed decided to concede the point. However it had come to them, they had meat.

With Angituk's encouragement, Creed shot three more caribou. They needed the pelts, she told him, and could cache the meat. Uluksuk helped him choose the best animals for their needs, surveying the herd, the long-distance shots delighting him. So much farther than a bow. Creed always had a good eye. He had scored nine kills as a sniper at Ypres. Until his heart would not allow it anymore and he quit. It haunted him still, even more than what happened later. Creed killed each caribou with a respectful single shot and the shaman was satisfied.

Angituk gave Sinnisiak a knife and the hunter dropped to his knees by the first big doe and cut a careful crescent-shaped incision above the stomach. Two quick circular strokes and he held half the steaming liver in his hand. He cut it into four pieces and Uluksuk and Angituk took and ate theirs without hesitation. Creed looked at the crescent-shaped cut and at the knife in Sinnisiak's hand and refused the offer. Angituk saw Creed's face and understood why. She took Creed's portion from Sinnisiak's hand.

"For the spirits."

She tossed it toward the shore of the lake where in a few months the spring grasses would grow.

WORKING TOGETHER, Angituk and Sinnisiak cut up the first caribou, reducing the meat and leg bones to a tidy package for the sled in a matter of minutes. The sinew and intestine they kept for thread and braiding rope. They cut down the belly and around the legs, carefully pulling off the hide, then chopped through the neck at the base of the skull and cut out the entrails. Avoiding the bowels, they liberated the succulent organs. Sinnisiak had a particular interest in the stomach contents, which looked like a fine coleslaw, the hard winter grasses within softened for him by the digestive acids. They would eat well that night, and for many beyond.

They finished butchering the three other caribou in like manner, preserving the hides and sinew for future use, and cached almost three hundred pounds of the best meat. They gave the last of the old provisions to the dogs, but not the caribou legs; the spirits of the caribou would be offended by such an act. They packed up the tent, the skins, and the sleeping bags and set off. The dogs strained hard to pull the extra weight, but Creed noted a higher degree of enthusiasm in Star. The dog licked his hand in gratitude, much happier to be pulling than to be pulled.

Before them spread the last and highest of the Dismal

Lakes. Beyond that they could make out the gentle rise to the watershed they would have to cross, miles in the distance; it would be downhill after that. Creed's goal was to get over that high divide before nightfall or perhaps the day after. As things turned out, they would not cross it for many weeks.

Even as they approached the source of the Dismal Lakes system, snow began to fall and the view of the far ridge quickly disappeared. Creed's binoculars were useless. The snow was remarkable for its density: huge snowflakes, more flake than air, almost smothered them. They could hardly see three feet in front of them. The north wind rose quickly, and the big flakes that once fell in a gentle vertical descent now came at them in an aggressive horizontal trajectory, hitting their eyes and teeth. Creed's heavy beard saved his face from frostbite.

They made slow progress along the north shore of the lake, battling the snowstorm until the snow and the darkness became impossible. They needed to find shelter. Creed hoped that the eastern lee of the watershed might provide protection from the wind, but it was still far away. He had them stop and he began to pull out his heavy canvas tent, the snow swirling around him. Angituk came close to be heard.

"Corporal Creed. They want to build a snow house."

Creed looked to where Uluksuk and Sinnisiak had gone ahead and found several deep snowdrifts formed in the lee of a pile of rocks. Uluksuk turned toward Creed, pointed to the deep snow, and shouted, *"Iglukhaq!"*

"I've got the tent," he told Angituk.

Uluksuk called out again, *"Iglukhaq!"* This was one of thirty-two Copper Eskimo words for "snow," and it meant "deep, packed snow suitable for igloo building."

"They will build a snow house," Angituk told Creed again. "Better than a tent."

Uluksuk pulled from his pack a long, broad wooden knife. Creed's hand went instinctively to his pistol. How the hell had he missed that knife when he inspected the pack?

Angituk came between them, shouting over the wind. "He will build it here. There is good snow and it is almost dark. The storm will get worse."

Uluksuk made sawing gestures with the snow knife. Creed looked up through the snow at the darkly dramatic sky.

"All right, good. We stop here."

"They'll need their hands."

Creed hesitated a moment at this, but it was true. He dug out the keys and freed them both, keeping his rifle under his arm.

THE OLD MAN chose a flat place near the shore of the lake but far enough back to ensure that there would be grass underneath and not large stones. He walked in a circle, and he and Sinnisiak began to cut and shape square blocks from within the circle, using the wooden cleaver. These blocks they set where Uluksuk had paced, creating the first layer of wall. They worked quickly, almost cheerfully, in the snowstorm. Uluksuk's knife flew as if in the hands of an inspired sculptor.

Uluksuk had begun with a long, thin triangular block, and as his first circle came back to this, the blocks of the second row slanted upward so succeeding rows formed a continuous spiral. They progressed to the third and fourth rows, each bevelled at the top and bottom and canted slightly in so each layer had one or two fewer blocks and took less time. This was good, because they were now in almost complete darkness. By the fourth layer they had used up the snow inside the circle and Uluksuk began to cut blocks on the outside, creating a moat around the house and passing the blocks in to Sinnisiak, whose shoulders and head were just visible above the rising wall. Finally all that could be seen of him were his mittens reaching up with another block in the thin air and swirling snow.

They were working more by feel than by sight now. And when the final block, sculpted with great care by Uluksuk, was set in place at the top of the dome, Creed and Angituk cheered. Sinnisiak filled in a few gaps on the outside with snow while Uluksuk fashioned the little tunnel entrance. A caribou hide to cover the opening and the house was complete. It had taken perhaps forty-five minutes. Creed's two prisoners stood proudly at the entrance and gestured for his inspection.

Creed lit his little stove to see their handiwork. It was big inside, almost as big as Uluksuk's family igloo at his camp. Uluksuk had left two raised snow platforms for sitting and sleeping. They passed in their baggage. They left the caribou meat and bones in a depression to one side of the entrance, where they would remain frozen.

Sinnisiak took out a long, shallow soapstone dish and fashioned a series of wicks from dried grass. He had cut several strips of yellow fat from the doe and he began to melt them over Creed's stove, dripping the liquid into the dish. When he had enough to wet the wicks, he lit them, six flames in all. They drew from the liquid fat and quickly warmed up the igloo. Creed turned off his coal-oil stove.

Sinnisiak continued to feed his little soapstone dish with chips of fat. Then he suspended a caribou haunch sideways over the flames on moistened gut strings suspended from the roof, looped so he could turn the meat, and soon the pleasure of a warm house was followed by the tantalizing aroma of roasting caribou. Creed noted, as his mouth began to water, that patience was the order of the day. Six small flames would manage only a very slow roast. As it cooked, the haunch dripped its fat into the soapstone dish and replenished the fuel. Creed marvelled at the simple efficiency of the system. He demonstrated the thumbs-up sign to his prisoners.

"This means 'good,'" he told them, and Angituk translated.

"Isuma!"

They all tried it, thumbs up, with a little thrust forward. The prisoners did it to Creed and then to themselves and then to Angituk. Creed gestured to the fine snow house and the meat cooking and gave them another emphatic thumbs-up, which they clearly understood and returned. Then they both put their hands forward and Creed reinstalled the handcuffs.

AS THE WIND HOWLED outside and the cozy igloo warmed with their body heat, Creed took out Rouvière's tattered journal. He could not directly ask his prisoners for the details of their actions and motivations without a lawyer present, but he knew the journal held clues. The priest had written:

> The people who returned are very good-natured to us and well disposed. A whole brigade of them came to visit! I was delighted that the Eskimos of last summer that I taught to make the sign of the Cross remembered and made it for me and had even taught it to others! So they do have a notion of God and don't seem to be rebellious to the spirit. And they have a real interest in singing. God seems to want to bless us.

The priests continued to try to teach them about Christ. Again Rouvière wrote of how they struggled with the "incomprehensible" language and how even a fine linguist such as Le Roux was challenged by it. And he wrote too of how Le Roux struggled with his moods.

The Father is aware of his own quick temper and is striving valiantly to subdue it. He has never tried to hurt my feelings. I like to think that our good relations will not be disturbed. After all the reports I was given by Hornby, I was afraid there would be some difficulties, but God has taken everything in hand and nothing has come about to disturb our good understanding.

I have learned some skills here. I can drive the dogs pulling the sled. I have netted a few small trout through the ice. And I've learned to shake a little of the sacramental wine into the skillet for flavour, God forgive my indulgence. It is the small comforts that help us go on.

We have decided we will find some Eskimos to take us north to the mouth of the Coppermine and the Gulf. We will reconnoitre that place because it is a gathering place that would be the ideal spot for a mission church. We will win over the people to the one true faith. Then we have big plans. We will travel south again before the worst of the winter, make our way back to Fort Norman, take the riverboat to the Mackenzie delta, and hire a ship in the spring with building materials to take us down the coast to arrive at the mouth again, this time from the west. It is a good plan, may Mother Mary protect us. Let us say our prayers to see what the good God thinks about it.

IN THE WARM IGLOO, Creed's thoughts were turning to dinner. There were some impressive hors d'oeuvres: a finely sliced raw kidney, cups of blood, and chunks of tongue. Creed especially enjoyed the bones broiled over the oil lamps until they cracked and released their long jellylike marrows. He did not like the highly prized fat behind the eye sockets simply because he knew where it came from, and he also avoided the liver for different reasons; but beyond that, he loved all the caribou meat.

After they finished their meal, Uluksuk spoke to Creed at length and Creed listened patiently, looking into his eyes but understanding nothing. When he had finished, Angituk began her translation.

"When we kill animals, we must do so with respect. As you did this morning, you must avoid needless pain. We believe the spirit of the animal we kill goes into the next animal we hunt. We will meet him again, so we must treat him with respect and maybe he will give himself to us again. This is why after we kill a seal we give it a drink of fresh water. A bird gets a drop of oil on its head and feet. We do not give caribou leg bones to the dogs for this is disrespectful. And when a boy makes his first kill, his mother will weep over the animal and apologize to it for what her son has done."

Despite himself, there were cracks forming in Creed's skepticism about the Copper beliefs. Here on the land they made as much sense as the tenets of any religion he knew. More than most.

Nine

The snowstorms continued for days, but they stayed warm and well fed in the snow house. They had entered total winter night now. They would not see the sun again for many weeks, and even on the rare nights of a full moon's illumination, travel through the disorienting winds and the heart-stoppingly low temperatures would be too dangerous. Three or four tiny flames in the little soapstone lamp provided their only light and heat. Each day the two hunters would stuff themselves with caribou until their bellies were stretched, sleep for a few hours while more cooked, wake up, and stuff themselves again. They were building up their protein and fat stores so that when the caribou was gone and they had to move, they could go for days without eating. They relieved themselves in a bowl inside, or outside if temperatures permitted, but always close to the igloo. Disorientation in the winter darkness was not uncommon, and many a lost, frozen body had been discovered a few yards from an invisible snow house door.

Creed spent hours with his sharp steel knife, thinly slicing the *nipku*, the meat that would be dried for future use. Every part of the caribou they could not eat, they used elsewhere. Angituk had scraped and dried the new caribou skins. She emptied the forty-foot intestine of each caribou and now patiently cut sixty lengths of gut cord with Creed's knife.

Sinnisiak went out and returned with a small bundle of long willow saplings he found by feel under the deep snow. With these and the cords and other parts from the caribou, the hunters began to take pleasure in creating things: miniature but functioning bows and arrows—which they presented to Creed for safekeeping—a small, delicate fishnet, a ring-toss game. A carrying sack from the stomach. A bowl from the skull.

Creed's prisoners worked quickly, apparently unencumbered by their handcuffs. Angituk continued to process the caribou skins, chewing the hide over and over to make it supple. She told Creed she was making something as a surprise for him to wear and he was not to look. As the snow piled up outside in the darkness, Creed learned that the most essential project was yet to come.

Uluksuk started by fashioning a large oval of woven twigs bound together by moistened gut. Then he wove a pattern of open netting back and forth and used some of the caribou hide for straps. Creed was asking fewer questions these days. He had taken up the Eskimo custom of waiting and watching and learning, and so he knew without asking what Uluksuk laboured over: snowshoes. He inspected Uluksuk's impressive craftsmanship and without discussion fell to making his own. Creed quickly fell behind the progress of the others, but the storms were still howling and the sun was weeks away. There was no rush.

As they worked, Angituk told him stories of her childhood, including the great caribou hunts.

"When a herd came near, we would figure out where to drive them to for the best advantage to kill them. Wind direction was considered. And convenience. We would find a place, a shallow river or, once, I remember, a little walled-in valley. We would all work to build *inukshuks* on either side of a pathway to keep the caribou moving straight when they came. Then all the women and children would very quietly travel around to the far side of the herd and spread out and stretch out our arms and slowly, quietly begin to move the herd down the path to the place. And the *inukshuks* scared them, especially the ones with grass hair, and made them stay in the path. And as they got closer and started crowding, we would begin to yell and howl—kids and mothers with babies on their backs—and the herd would go faster and faster. And we would start to run to keep them going so when they got to the shallow river they could not stop. They would go straight in.

"Then the hunters would come out from their hiding places. In the water two legs move faster than four, and our hunters would run them down and kill them with their spears or arrows. If the river was deep, some hunters even used kayaks to paddle up and spear them, one after the other. And the river would be red, and the women and children would sing and cheer the hunters. And when the killing was done, we'd drag the animals into the shallows. The shaman would give thanks and make sacrifice to the caribou spirits. Then we would all be happy with full bellies for a long, long time."

"It's fine meat. Lean and tasty. Better than the meat from the cows we have in the South. And the southern cow hunt isn't nearly as interesting."

"But my favourite thing to eat is *uviluit*—mussels."

"Shellfish? Where do you get them up here?"

Angituk's eyes shone at the memory. "The ocean, of course. West along the coast. You can gather them on the seabed under the ice at low tide. There are places at Cape Parry where high tides make caves. We dig a big hole through the ice and when the tide goes out we light lanterns and slip down into these caves, these caverns under the ice, and walk through the tide pools to gather the *uviluit*. We would eat them out of the shell, all salty. My *amaamak*—my mother—could find lots of them to fill her bags. We'd stuff ourselves. It was scary and beautiful with only the glow of the lantern for light. We'd collect bull kelp and dulse to eat too. And we'd look up high to the ceiling with a thousand icicles hanging from it, through the green ice to the sun, all dim and distant.

"You know, Father Ducot had picture books on the churches in Rome. Cathedrals. Beautiful big rooms, but I don't think the tide caves at Cape Parry are any less beautiful. But all the time there was the groaning of the sea at low tide way back in the caves like something alive and dangerous, about to rise and come after us."

"It sounds dangerous."

"Yes, it was! My mother told me some children were caught by the tide rising too fast and trapping them deep in the chambers, and they drowned. We were warned. We stayed very close to my mother."

He had never seen Angituk so animated as by this breathless telling of the childhood memory of the caves and her mother.

"I'd very much like to see that," Creed responded.

"Sure ..." she said. Her voice trailed off, the silence swelling between them as they both realized this was unlikely.

WHILE WRITING IN HIS JOURNAL one morning, Creed made the calculations and discovered it was Christmas Day. Angituk was excited by the announcement, for she remembered it as one of the few occasions of pleasure at the mission school. She told Creed how the children secretly—for it was forbidden to speak their language—called it *Quviahugvik*, "the occasion of happiness." They were all given oranges as gifts. She could still remember her first incredible bite of that tangy, sweet fruit on Christmas morning.

Childhood Christmas mornings for Creed began with jumping on his sleeping brother, Charlie, to wake him up before dawn to go and see what Santa had brought. Charlie took a lot of waking up and would groan and push him away, even on Christmas morning. But then Charlie would finally give Creed his big smile and whisper, "Let's go see," and they would creep downstairs to find their stockings stuffed with walnuts, tangerines and candies. Gifts of new hockey skates or a rugby ball or a punching bag would await them, and there would be more wrapped presents under the tree. And there, near the fireplace, would be convincing indications of the visit by Santa Claus—sooty footprints leading from the hearth to the tree, an empty glass of milk, a half-eaten cookie, teeth marks on a carrot for Rudolph—signs that had Creed believing in the existence of the old saint until the embarrassing age of eleven. Creed told Angituk all of this. Her knowledge of Santa Claus was vague, but she understood him to be a most generous spirit and was stricken to hear Creed no longer believed.

CREED OFFERED TO TELL the hunters the story of Bethlehem and the birth of Jesus Christ. They had heard of this Jesus Christ fellow from the priests, but not of the circumstances of his birth. To the Copper people, birth, as Angituk had explained, strongly influenced the life ahead. The prisoners listened with great interest as Angituk translated.

"When Jesus was born, his parents, Mary and Joseph, were travelling."

"To new hunting grounds?"

"Well, yes, sort of."

"What season? Caribou or seal?"

"It was winter, so seal. And the baby was coming and there was no room in the inn, or ... the big igloo, so they had to go to the stable ... or a little igloo, and have the baby there, surrounded by cows and sheep."

"Tell us, what are cows and sheep?"

Creed was beginning to warm to the telling. "Actually, they were caribou and husky dogs, and they all loved the baby. And three wise men came, who had seen a star that marked the birth of Jesus."

"Wise men?"

"Shamans," Angituk ventured.

"Absolutely. Powerful shamans who saw the star, and they brought gifts."

"Which star?"

"It was a new star then. It was ... Polaris."

"Of course. *Ubluriaq*, the North Star."

"That's right."

"What gifts did they bring?"

Angituk prompted him. "Walrus oil. Narwhal tusk. Hard wood."

They passed those on to the hunters, who were impressed.

"And then the shepherds came," Jack continued.

"What are shepherds?"

"Seal hunters," Angi suggested quietly.

"Did I say shepherds? I meant seal hunters. A bunch of seal hunters came in from the ice edge to see the baby, because good spirits had come to them and told them that Jesus was born. But then there were enemies."

Creed now had the hunters fully engaged in his narrative. Angituk too.

"There was a king, an evil shaman named Herod, who was jealous and sent hunters to kill the child."

"Probably Cree," Sinnisiak ventured, looking at Uluksuk, who nodded.

"Could be. But the seal hunters and the shamans protected the baby and the bad hunters didn't find him, so there is a happy ending to the story of Jesus's birth. He went on to be a great man. A teacher and the best hunter of all."

Uluksuk and Sinnisiak were very interested in the story. Uluksuk offered, "Before we killed them, the priests showed us pictures of this Jesus, both as a child with his mother and as a man, but we had no idea what he had done."

Angituk took it upon herself to fill in the details of the life of Jesus. Uluksuk listened very carefully to the description of the miracles: the casting out of demons, restoring the blind to sight and the dead to life, walking on water.

Uluksuk casually assured them, "I have done all these things myself except for the loaves and fishes. That was a good one. I will try that one sometime soon. Go on with the story."

So when Angituk told the rest of the story, about the Crucifixion, she could not explain why some people had wanted to kill Jesus. Creed, too, was hard put to come up with a translatable explanation. Jealousy on the part of the bad shamans was as close as he got. The hunters found this troubling. Uluksuk brought out a small, very worn coloured card with a painting of Christ in agony on the Cross. Father Rouvière had given it to him the night before he died.

"Is this what will happen to us in the South?"

"No. They do not crucify people anymore."

But he could see neither of them was convinced.

THAT NIGHT, Creed and Angituk sang Christmas carols. She remembered every word of every verse of "O Come All Ye Faithful" and "Silent Night" in English as she had learned them at the mission school. Then she sang the latter in her own language, her voice clear and beautiful, bringing tears to Creed's eyes:

Unuak naguyuk,
Talvani nunami,
Uilagahuk nutaganikpaktuk,
Angutinuak ataniuyuk,
Negiyutikagvingmi-ituk,
 Anilihaktuk Jesus,
Anilihaktuk Jesus.

At midnight, they shook hands all around, an unusual white custom the Eskimos enjoyed, and wished each other a Merry Christmas. The two prisoners heard the words and enthusiastically repeated them with surprising accuracy.

"Merry Christmas! ... Happy New Year!" Sinnisiak revealed a real talent for pronunciation.

Creed had a small silver penknife his father had given him before he went overseas, and this he gave to Angituk as a Christmas gift. She was surprised and delighted.

Sinnisiak began to tell stories. They were jokes, really. Though Creed was only the third white man Sinnisiak had met, he liked to talk about white men and the strange things the Eskimos had heard about them.

"What did you hear we were like?"

Angituk laughed at Sinnisiak's ideas as she translated them for Creed. "They knew white men were very tall and big and pale-skinned and hairy."

Sinnisiak had enjoyed watching Creed's beard grow, inspecting it from time to time. It was so thick compared to his own, like a wolf pelt.

"Some said white men had no chin," Sinnisiak continued in Angituk's translation. "Some said you only had one eye. And others ..." Angituk was really laughing now. "Others said you had a mouth in the middle of your stomach!

"The people heard stories that the white man could be very generous with food and tools and then suddenly could be very selfish and dangerous. Even kill," Angituk went on to explain. "These changes in mood are rare in Eskimo society. Only the spirits are allowed such indulgences."

"What else do you know about white men's religion?"

Sinnisiak spoke up. *"Gratias ago vos! Deus beatus vos! In nomine Patris, et Filii, et Spiritus Sancti!"*

Creed smiled at his perfect pronunciation, his surprising proclivity for remembering language memorized more than two years earlier.

"Does he know what any of that means?" Creed asked Angituk.

"No," Sinnisiak responded, and they all laughed.

"They know nothing of the white religion except for the one day the priests showed them pictures, and what you've told them now," Angituk said.

"How would you describe the Copper Eskimo religion?" Creed asked her. "What do they believe? Do they have a supreme being? Do they believe in an afterlife? Do they agree with our creation story?"

"You mean Adam and Eve and the Garden of Eden?"

"Yes."

She paused. Creed seldom asked her such a direct question and she began to tell her tale slowly, as if laying the groundwork for a long story and knowing a skeptical audience when she saw one. "My people believe that the Earth has four corners with pillars holding up the sky. Storms come out of holes cut in the sky by unhappy Spirits of the Dead. The stars are dead people or animals. We don't know why they go up there."

"Where did humans come from?"

She thought about her response for a moment. "In the

beginning, when the world was new, there was a woman ..."
Angituk smiled. "A single woman. It was Kannokapfaluk. She
needed a husband, but there were no men, so finally she met
a strong, charming, and handsome dog and mated with him.
This worked out very well and they had many, many litters of
children together. In fact there were so many children, they
could not feed or look after them. So Kannokapfaluk took off
her two great mukluks. She divided the children into three
groups. She put some of the children in one mukluk and some
of the children in the other and set them off afloat on the ocean.
One mukluk landed not too far south, and those people became
the Cree and Chipewyans. One mukluk floated for a long time
on a current and landed much farther south, and those people
became the *Kabloona*, the white men. You are the hairiest and
most like the dog. But the children that Kannokapfaluk loved
best, who were most beautiful like her, she kept with her and
gave them the best land on the Coronation Gulf, and that is us.
There you are. Do you like our creation story?"

"Yes, I do."

"Like the Christian Bible."

"Well, your stories are not quite like the Bible. The Bible is
based on real people and things that actually happened."

"Oh, you mean like the seven days to create the world or the
parting of the Red Sea or the virgin birth? Or, for that matter,
Christ's miracles and his resurrection?"

Creed heard the teasing in her voice. Despite his own doubts
about the Christian Church, Creed felt a hypocritical pang of
offence. He was up for a good fight. "The Bible is a historical record."

"No more than our beliefs. They are based on everyday
life," she explained. "Animals, weather, landscape. They are
to connect and explain what we can see and what we can't.
We have taboos with food, as you do. At the mission school I

enjoyed your Bible stories, like David and Goliath. They are almost as good as ours."

Creed smiled at her, and she continued.

"We believe in the old days there were monsters roaming the land, hunting humans for food. A young hunter named Swan was given special powers, and he travelled all over the Coppermine valley turning these monsters into animals men could hunt. And there was a race of nasty giants, the *Tornrin*, that we had to chase away. And a gang of female giants with sharp teeth to eat our hunters who were finally defeated by our women. We still have Paija, who plays tricks but not dangerous ones, and Nighihk, who knocks down igloos if he doesn't like you. We have the hairy hunter dwarfs called *inyourligat*, so short their bows drag on the ground as they walk. And then we have the evil *Wenigo*, which lives at the treeline, waiting for when we go to get wood, to catch us and eat us."

"So let me understand. The *Wenigo* eats human flesh and is considered evil, yes? But Uluksuk and Sinnisiak ate human flesh too. Are they evil?"

Angituk's eyes flashed in anger. He was trying to trick her. "It is two different things. The *Wenigo* has a lust for human meat. Uluksuk and Sinnisiak ate the livers out of respect."

"You call that respect?"

"Yes. Respect for the spirits of the priests. As they have for the spirits of the caribou they kill."

"They killed harmless white men."

"Are any white men harmless?"

Creed stopped for a moment. She had taken this in a direction he didn't want to go. "What about an afterlife? Do your people believe in heaven and hell?"

"I have told you about the *attiaq*. If you are wise or loved or a good hunter, your spirit may be invited to enter a new-born child, and he becomes you. And, don't laugh"—her eyes flashed defiantly against anticipated disbelief—"but I remember events and people and feasts at certain camps that my great-grandmother experienced that I did not. I was never at certain places, certain camps, and yet I remember them clearly."

She paused for a moment, thinking. "But heaven? No. The afterlife for us is not a good place. We do not like to think about it. We think about surviving each day. Our beliefs are about life now, while your religion seems to be about death and what comes after. I've never understood that."

Creed did not know how to respond. *Maybe that's what allows us to fight the wars,* he thought. *It allows mindless, wholesale slaughter. The belief in life after death. Our arrogant preservation of the ego.*

"You were a soldier in the war, weren't you."

Creed looked up at her, startled. "How did you know?"

"Some of the men in Norman told me about the war. Do you think the 'harmless white men' were killed there with respect?"

For a second Creed felt anger at her sarcasm, but it quickly left him. "No. The men were not killed there with respect."

The shaman had been listening to them, and when Angituk translated for him she had no word for "war" and used the English word. Uluksuk asked what it meant.

"It is a fight between people, only much bigger." Creed considered for a moment how to explain it and then began to tell him, with Angituk translating every few lines in a comfortable rhythm. "Far away, across the land and then beyond a very wide ocean, two large bands of white people are fighting each other. They face each other every day in a field and dig holes to live in and they fight sometimes in the day but usually at night. They fight with rifles and bigger guns, twenty times as big as a rifle. A barrel this wide"—Creed held his hands as if around an artillery shell—"where one shot can kill many." Uluksuk and

Sinnisiak now listened closely, amazed. "And many are dying and continue to die, and this has been going on every day for three years."

"This is really true?"

"Yes, it is true. We call it war."

"They continue to kill each other every day?"

"Yes. Every day."

Uluksuk was bewildered. "But why? Is it over hunting rights, or respect, or revenge, or fear?"

Creed thought about the question. "I don't know, Uluksuk. It started over some of those things, but then it changed. I don't think anyone knows what it's about anymore. It just keeps going on."

"How many people have been killed?" Uluksuk stopped his work and held up his hand, fingers splayed. He made a fist and then opened his hand two more times to indicate fifteen people. "This many?"

Creed looked at him sadly. "If you did that with your fingers over and over for as long as it takes to build an igloo, the number of dead would still be many more."

When Angituk translated, Uluksuk's and Sinnisiak's eyes widened trying to fathom that number. Outside, the wind was full of howling, muttering voices.

"Can no one stop it?"

"No. It goes on and on. It is like *perleromeq*, winter madness."

They all worked in silence for a few moments, thinking about so many restless, angry spirits. It was good they were so far away.

"I remember a time of death when I was little," Angituk began. "We were hunting over near Paulatuk on the Horton River but the caribou didn't come at all. Then the seals didn't come. No walrus. No fish in the rivers. And there was nothing else. We ate our dogs and then we ate our boots."

She translated for Uluksuk and Sinnisiak. They knew the place and remembered the year of hunger. She continued. "Any extra scraps of food found had to go to the hunters so they could continue to look for animals, so the old began to die. There was one night I was in pain from no food and could not sleep and I remember my grandmother gave me a last bit of meat she had saved and talked to me. She told me the stories of her life again. She called me *Amaamak*—Mother—because my *attiaq* was my great-grandmother, and I called her Daughter. I slept then and dreamed about her all night. Her spirit was in me. The next morning we found her dead out on the ice with no clothing.

"Her death was near the beginning. Afterwards the mothers' milk went dry and the babies began to die. And I think some were smothered to spare them the pain of a starvation death. I think that's what happened to my baby brother. My mother had had a second child with a man named Akuluk who treated us well and was a good hunter. I remember the night he died out on the ice, kneeling beside a seal hole. He froze to death. He knew if he came back empty-handed he would not have the strength to go out again. The next day my little brother died.

"There were stories from the camps of other people like the Kanghir y uarmuit, stories of people eating the old ones and even the babies, but that didn't happen in our camp. Such things turn people into *Wenigos*."

"What finally saved you?"

"My mother's cousin's camp up the river killed a muskox. They brought some down to us. We could not get up—they had to feed us in our beds. Then there were more muskox and finally some caribou and we were okay then. But we lost three babies, four old ones, and Akuluk. It was the next year they took me away to the mission school."

"That was a terrible thing to live through."

"I never heard my mother laugh again. But pain is part of being alive."

Creed watched her as she went back to her work and there was silence for a long while. He was still struggling with his first snowshoe, trying to weave the strips of gut evenly over the frame without pulling too hard and distorting the oval shape. Uluksuk eyed his work and made a joke. Angituk laughed.

"What did he say?"

"He said if you are this slow with all the chores in your life, you will have to live a long time to get them all done."

Angituk moved over against Creed and took his hand in hers, guiding him through the special whipstitch to secure the gut to the frame. "See, you loop it around ... a tight hitch will make sure it won't slip on the frame, then back across, nice and straight and tight, well spaced, not too tight ... that's it."

She pressed her shoulder against his chest and her forearm rested on his and their fingers touched as she guided him through another weave. She sprinkled some meltwater on the gut.

"Keep it wet. It's important to keep it wet so it will dry and shrink tight and hard. That was a good stitch. Okay, then back across again like this."

Creed breathed in her warm aroma—sweet, a little musky, like freshly baked bread—and felt the weight of her thin, muscular body against his. She had tied her hair up on her head—it was quite long now—and he found himself staring at the soft nape of her slender neck, exposed and presented by the slight bow of her head to the left. The delicate blue tattoo lines on her strong, slender hand as she worked had never seemed so sensuous.

There was a sudden rise in the wind and Angituk stopped her work to listen and then spoke quietly to him. "We believe it is the Spirits of the Dead that cause blizzards. Sometimes ... I think I can hear the voice of my mother in the storm. But I'm not sure of the words. Of what she wants to tell me."

She turned and looked up into his eyes, their faces close, her lips parted, brown skin so smooth, blue eyes inquiring. "Do you ever feel that some spirit is anxious to tell you something but you're just not sure what it is?"

Creed felt a very sudden, intense urge to kiss her. And he knew without doubt if he did so, she would welcome it. But instead he turned and moved away from her and aggressively focused all of his attention on the snowshoe.

"No. Well, maybe sometimes. I don't really know. Anyway, thanks for your help on this. I can finish it up now."

Angituk looked at him for a moment askance, a thin smile and a ghost of disappointment revealed only in the set of her eyebrows. Then she resumed her work on her second snowshoe.

IN THE FOLLOWING WEEKS, life continued in much the same way. It was a strange existence with no day or night. No dusk or dawn. The construct of time dissolved into a continuum with no future or past. The entire world existed here in this snow house. They ate and slept and made things and told stories and played games and ate and slept some more as they felt like it. Creed and Angituk read their novels again. Creed stopped bothering to wind his watch.

He exercised daily, doing push-ups and sit-ups and squats to keep his muscles firm. The others had never heard of this before and treated it like a strange dance and joined in with him. All found that the exertion did limber up their muscles and free their stiffening joints.

Angituk had finished her surprise: caribou trousers and a hooded shell for Creed that fit him beautifully. He was touched by the many hours of work she had put into them, and he had nothing for her in return. Sinnisiak had fashioned an intricate model kayak frame about eighteen inches long for his new baby. Uluksuk asked Creed's permission to make a small hunting bow and Creed allowed it. With a long length of thin caribou sinew Angituk created cat's cradle–like images between her slender thumbs and forefingers, for the entertainment of the prisoners. She made the network of sinew form two polar bears that came together and fought elaborately; one was killed and then they disappeared. With a few deft finger moves she fashioned a man carrying a kayak, and a walrus swimming through the sea. They all murmured their pleasure and Creed applauded her as they recognized each image. For his part Creed became quite adept at shadow puppetry, his hands close to the flames, the images of his fingers huge against the dome of the igloo, forming a rearing bear or a dancing fox.

Creed was quite taken with a game of skill called *nugluak*, consisting of tossing an egg-sized piece of soapstone with ten holes drilled in the side up in the air and trying to catch it on a wooden pin. The stone and pin were attached by a length of sinew. Creed spent days aiming for ten successful catches in a row. His fellows clapped their hands, though Angituk teased him: she was sure he had only managed nine. The hunters became a little confused after counting past six or seven, but they believed him. Occasionally they would venture out of the snow house when the stars or the moon came out to illuminate the world. Creed was anxious to continue their journey after these weeks of inactivity. They could travel by moon and starlight, he thought, but Uluksuk advised against it. It was the season of bad spirits in the darkness. Be patient a while longer, he advised him; the sun would soon return to them.

Quite uncharacteristically, Creed had fallen behind in his daily journal, missing a few days' entries over the weeks of their seclusion and losing all track of time. But he calculated that it was about February 21 or 23 when the horizon first brightened with the return of the sun. Less than a week later they saw it, the top of the orb's light refracting over the curvature of the earth. It stirred the blood to feel its weak rays, if only for a few minutes, and everyone left the snow house to stand in the light, smiling. Creed remembered some obscure quote in Ecclesiastes and spoke it aloud: "The light is sweet; and it is delightful for the eyes to see the sun."

Angituk heard him and smiled and said to him, "I haven't told you yet where the sun came from. You want to know?"

She had told him so many stories. Their eyes devoured the last seconds of the divine illumination before night closed in.

"Of course."

"Pay attention," she told him sternly in an impersonation of one of the teachers at her mission school. "In the beginning ... there was no light. Everyone on Earth hunted in the dark. The wolf, Amaguq, and the wolverine, Kalvik, were digging in a cave. In those days all creatures spoke the same language. They were all brothers and sisters. Suddenly they uncovered part of the sun. It scared them both to see something so bright, and they covered it up again! The wolverine ran away in fear, but the wolf remained. He realized the sun would help him become a better hunter, so he dug it up and brought it out to illuminate the world. The goddess Kakivak was furious the sun had been released, but she could not convince the sun to hide again after he had been given his freedom. Through negotiations, she and the sun determined that he would hide for part of the day and part of the year. And as punishment for his impudence, the wolf had to do most of his hunting at night. There. You like that one?"

"Yes. So Kakivak has allowed the sun to come out for us."

"Very good. You are learning. Give thanks."

Ten

A week later, on a morning that dawned very cold and sunny, the party broke camp to continue south. The inside walls of the snow house had begun to rot, turning increasingly to ice and undermining the insulative effect of snow. They packed quickly. Sinnisiak took care with the miniature kayak he had made for his son. Uluksuk packed his little hunting bow made of spruce seedlings bound by tight-braided sinew backing with a muskox-horn handle, a quiver with four arrows, and a repair kit in a skin bag.

As they bade farewell to their snow house and set off, their long shadows extended to the right, behind them. The storms had deposited several feet of snow and Creed realized how helpless they would have been, floundering around without snowshoes. The frames proved light and very efficient compared with the heavy wooden versions Creed had used in the South. He was heavier than the others and occasionally one or the other foot would break through the thin crust and he'd go down in snow up to his crotch and they'd have to wait for him, but if he kept his feet spread and his weight distributed evenly and kept moving, he was okay. The other three never once broke through. Creed expressed his thanks to Uluksuk with a thumbs-up, and the prisoner returned the gesture.

The two dogs pulling the sled also seemed to float over the deep snow, and Angituk explained about their webbed toes. "They were our inspiration for snowshoes."

That night, Creed made a good inspection of Star's paws, and it was true, there was a wide webbing between the toes that kept them on top of the fragile crust.

Even better than the snowshoes, though, were the caribou trousers and jacket Angituk had made for him. They were so light and warm. There was a shell of fur next to his skin absorbing moisture and then a second layer of fur facing in, for additional insulation. She had added ermine trim and decorative panels of lemming pelt and lynx that she had traded for at Koeha's camp. The clothing was miraculous compared with his heavy, porous old fur jacket. Creed had not been this comfortably warm outside in almost a year. And Angituk knew it.

"If you ever had to, you could simply curl up in a snowstorm, let it bury you, go to sleep, and you would live. That is what they are made for."

THE LIGHT SNOWSHOES lasted well as they finally crossed over the divide of land Creed had first seen weeks before. That accomplished, they made their way down to the headwaters of the Dease. They found Angituk's cache of frozen meat near the river. Half of it had been taken by others in need. A doll-sized sealskin coat and a copper knife had been left as compensation. They still had more than enough meat for several weeks, and so they left a substantial amount at the cache for other, less fortunate travellers.

As the days passed and grew incrementally longer, they walked on the surface of the frozen river and drew closer to Great Bear Lake. Creed noticed for the first time the tops of a few tiny black spruce and willows poking through the snow in a sheltered gully. They were approaching the treeline. The appearance of trees seemed so foreign to him after all this time, he had to smile to himself. He had learned to live in a world without them.

He saw nothing more than the odd stunted copse for days before the saplings multiplied into anything resembling a forest. But soon the travellers were enjoying roaring fires at night, and then he realized how much he had missed the trees. To Uluksuk and Sinnisiak they were a curiosity, and the campfires were impressive but indulgent. The hunters had never been this far south. Of course, they had seen trees before. There were a few famous little oases of trees in the southern Arctic where the people could travel to find wood for qamutiks and spears, but as the trees multiplied and grew in size and began to dominate the bare land, Creed noticed that the hunters' mood had changed. They studied the increasingly taller trees around them, finding the vegetation disconcertingly oppressive.

They reached Imaerink Lake late in the winter and camped two nights by the burned-out remnants of the priests' cabin. The hunters were impressed by the design even as a ruin. They had heard of log cabins before but had never seen one. Uluksuk found it shameful that it had been burned.

"Eskimos would not do this. This was done by the Cree or Dene. Both are wasteful and unwise."

It was at this forlorn camp that Uluksuk and Sinnisiak first expressed regret for killing the priests. Sinnisiak was eager to explain how it had happened and why they had to do it, but Creed cautioned them. Anything they said he would have to report, and they should first speak to a lawyer, or "older brother," when they got to Edmonton. Even after Angituk translated this, they did not understand. They looked around at the strange trees that seemed to be closing in on them and became silent with worry.

Creed took out Rouvière's tattered journal again and by the light of a roaring fire read the description of the priests' impressions of their final objective: the mouth of the Coppermine. It had taken Rouvière so long to get there:

> We have arrived at our destination. It has been a hard trip with the Eskimo Kormik and his band. We slowed him down and there have been disagreements over food. Now we look out on the gloomy expanse of the Coronation Gulf, flat treeless hills behind us, a gravel beach extending east and west. A cold wind is blowing. It would be the Catholic Church's most northerly post! We have taken the word of God to the farthest shores, the very edge of the world. We are the pioneers of the Lord! But yet ... my good Lord, how would we live here? Through the months of killing cold and darkness? So incredibly far from home. Like a distant planet. Good God, forgive my doubts. Mother Mary, be our protector and make us worthy of this mission that you have entrusted to us.

Father Rouvière's journal went on to tell the story. Kormik's band had been greeted by some other Eskimos who had arrived for the winter hunting season, and they all set up camp on the little islands in the mouth of the Coppermine. They gave the priests a small hide tent to sleep in. Rouvière's journal described how they stayed together for five nights with the sun very low on the horizon. The ice on the sea was still too thin to hunt seals and food was scarce. The Eskimos gave what food they could spare to the priests, and the women fixed the holes in the priests' boots and mended their mittens and clothing. Rouvière's apprehensions remained:

I ask myself if we can truly teach these people. Could there really be a time when they would help to build a church and come to hear my Mass? Could they incorporate our beliefs into theirs? Could they ever accept the idea that animals are our inferiors when for thousands of years they have believed animals are all-knowing? This I don't know.

Creed closed the little journal and felt sadness at the fate of the passionate young priest, and again the sense of loss that they would never share a conversation.

CREED AND HIS PARTY arrived on the shore of Dease Bay at the north end of Great Bear Lake and were surprised by the sight. The enormous lake was a clear sheet of ice! Whatever forces of weather had conspired, perhaps a windstorm that had blown the snow clear or an unseasonable melt and refreezing, it was a flawless, dazzling skating rink. At first Creed thought this a good thing for them, until he ventured out on the surface and fell promptly on his backside. The others laughed and he glared at them. This was serious. They were facing three hundred miles of a route—two or three weeks of travel—too slippery to walk on. The snowshoes wouldn't work and Uluksuk and Sinnisiak could provide no solutions. These conditions were rare. The hunters would normally choose to go around such a lake, but with the massive bays of the Great Bear to the east and west, such a detour through stunted, dense forest would add weeks to the journey. Frustrated, Creed decided they would make camp here and consider their options.

Angituk and Sinnisiak set up camp near the frozen shore while Creed walked very carefully out onto the slippery ice. This was amazing. He remembered a winter with ice like this when he was a young boy living at Rice Lake. Clear, perfect ice for miles. They had played hockey from dawn to dusk, unlimited by boards or blue lines. They could skate with the puck and make a breakaway, undertaking a battle for possession that could last a mile until the goalies left in their wake shouted for them to come back. And when the wind rose, they had put down their sticks, unbuttoned their coats, and opened them wide to let the wind blow them on their skates, faster and faster, skimming across the pristine black mirror, their only destination the setting sun.

Creed scanned the horizon to the south and returned to his problem. They could not walk on this surface. He often found that solutions would present themselves in obtuse ways, when he wasn't thinking about them, so he resolved to put the problem out of his mind for a while. He returned to shore, toward the pebbly beach. He found scattered lengths of sapling spruce, driftwood, their surfaces smoothed by the water. He chose one with a sharp curve on the upright end. He examined it and then flipped it end for end and laid the curve on the ice. Next he chose a small stone, the size of a fist, flat and smooth, and tossed it onto the ice. The little puck travelled a few feet. He smiled.

He decided to keep the rules of the game simple for the two new recruits. He placed two big rocks ten feet apart on the ice. He provided suitable sticks for his opponents from the spruce driftwood and he told them all they had to do was slide the puck past him through the two rocks. Their shackles would not limit them too much. Angituk had come to watch and translate. Uluksuk and Sinnisiak were interested to learn a white man's game, but even with the support of the sticks they slipped and fell before even touching the puck. When they reached it, Creed called to them, "Spread out and pass it back and forth to each other to warm up."

The puck went everywhere but stick to stick. Uluksuk fell hard a couple of times and was in a bad mood. He fanned at the stone, once, twice, three times. He went down on his knees, grabbed the puck with his hand, and slid it toward the goal. Creed stopped it easily.

"You have to use the stick."

"Why?" The shaman scowled at him. Creed slid it back to him. Both men could shoot an arrow through the heart of a caribou, or spear a seal with speed and accuracy, but propelling a small object toward a target with a stick on a slippery surface held no relevance in their world.

Uluksuk, now on his feet, hit the stone with his stick and made a reasonable pass to Sinnisiak.

"Good. Good work," Creed called out. And Sinnisiak passed it back. All right. They were getting the idea!

They moved toward him, focused and determined. They passed the stone between them, two, three times, sliding along the ice with one foot pushing.

"That's good, that's good. Get ready for your shot. Okay. Let her go."

Sinnisiak was in possession at the sweet spot and he wound up, his backswing high and ready. Before he could follow through, his feet went out from under him again, his windmilling stick came around in a powerful arc, and the end made contact with the little stone. It rocketed between Creed's legs and slid a hundred feet behind him on the perfect ice along the western shoreline.

"You did it! That was a beautiful goal!"

But Creed's opposition had abandoned him. The two hunters limped unsteadily for the shore.

"Don't you want to try it again? We'll play to five!"

Their speed of retreat increased.

"I think they've had enough," Angituk told him, amused. "I better go make dinner."

CREED WAS LEFT STANDING in his goal. He turned and looked to where the puck had stopped, well down the shore. And like a thousand times before in his childhood after a score on an open goal, he went to retrieve the puck. Though there were a thousand stones on the shore to replace the puck, it was the puck, and he had to go and get it. He could almost hear Charlie's command on the wind.

He walked carefully, slipping and sliding, trying to stay on his feet. He arrived and bent down and picked up the stone puck. He glanced back toward the goal and the empty path to their camp. He would have liked to play a little more. He hadn't played since Charlie left for the war. Charlie had been a beautiful hockey player. While Creed managed a scrambling, physical game, Charlie floated across the ice, untouched by the opposition, his stick blade guiding the puck with the grace of a rapier, a smile on his face, as if the puck in the net was a foregone conclusion. *God, that was a lifetime ago,* Creed thought.

His tentative, slippery walk to retrieve the stone had brought him around the shore of the bay not far from the old wrecked York boat they had passed on the trip in, its mast still standing. Creed put the puck in his pocket and made his careful way to the derelict hull. A drift of snow provided a solid path to the abandoned craft. He climbed aboard, sat on the wide, weathered thwart, mused about the men who had sailed her this far, and looked south again across the broad expanse of ice.

Sometime later, he heard a voice. Angituk had come out to him with a stone bowl of hot caribou broth. How she had not spilled it on the ice was a mystery. She had found some wild leeks, she told him, under the snow, and the addition tasted wonderful. She smiled with her perfect teeth when he complimented her. Her hair was braided up on her head again. The light of the late day gave her skin a tawny golden glow and illuminated her blue eyes, and in the interest of remaining faithful to their understanding, Creed had to quickly look away from her and concentrate on the current problem. Also, he was starting to have an idea.

She broke the short silence. "They are worried about crossing the lake."

"I know. So am I."

"No. They are worried about what's on the other side."

"The trees make them nervous."

"No. It's not the trees. It's the Indians. The Dene, the Cree, and the Chipewyans are their sworn enemies."

"They're under my authority. I'll protect them."

"We are still a long way from other white people."

"Fort Norman is not that far from the south side of the lake. They are my prisoners and my responsibility. The Indians will respect that."

This seemed to satisfy her. "I will tell them. But what are we going to do?"

Creed got up and went to a long metal reinforcing bracket on the gunnels of the *Jupiter* just below the oar pins. He ran his hand along the three-foot strip of flat steel, three inches wide, half an inch thick. The heads of the iron bolts had rusted through and he was surprised to be able to pull much of the steel free of the wood. There were six of the heavy strips on the boat. He'd only need three. He picked up and inspected one of several long, straight, three-by-eight-inch planks loose in the bottom of the boat. Finally he looked at the still-erect mast and horizontal boom. The sails were long gone, but the weathered wood of the mast and boom had not rotted and the brass hardware was still functional.

Creed licked his finger and held it up into the breeze that came from behind him, and he mumbled out loud. "Northwest. Excellent. We have to hurry. It'll clock to full north by tomorrow if we're lucky." He turned to Angituk, who still awaited patiently for an answer to her question. She would have it soon. "Ask Sinnisiak to come. I'll need some help."

THAT NIGHT, by the light of a roaring shore fire, as the others looked on and helped where they could, Creed constructed his ice boat. He and his father had built a simple version of one when Creed was a boy, and they had taken turns roaring across the wide frozen surface of Rice Lake. Why couldn't it work here?

With the boards from the ruined York vessel he constructed the basic frame of a Christian cross about sixteen feet long and twelve feet wide. He sandwiched the steel strips from the boat between blocks of wood to make runners, crimping the iron nails securely. The runners were then lashed with cords of gut to each end of the forward crossbeam. Under the stern section, where he would sit, he bolted a similar swivelling rudder blade with a long tiller for steering. The mast and boom he took complete from the old boat, used nails and cords of gut to secure the base at the cross point, and reinforced it using support members lashed together with more gut cords. They offered terrific strength and yet enough give to the joints to sustain the structure against vibrations. Three strands of the gut were woven together to create each of the two cablelike stays, attached from the masthead to the port and starboard runners, which served as outriggers. Angituk wove the heaviest stay from five strands, and it was was secured to the stern behind the rudder to support the old mast in the freshening northerly, for their course would be southwest. Finally Creed bound twelve-inch secondary boards at forty-five-degree angles from the cross member to the main beam on each side for strength and to hold passengers.

Angituk finished coarse-stitching together the light, dry caribou bedding hides for the roughly triangular sail. Uluksuk and Sinnisiak were fascinated by the craft. They'd never seen anything like it. A huge sled without dogs. They knew about sails for boats, but nothing like this, on ice.

Creed proudly announced to them all that they should catch some sleep. They would "weigh anchor" at sunrise.

THE NORTH WIND rose with the sun and the promise of a bright day, the lake a mirror of shimmering mirages before them. They tethered the ice boat to a scrub tree onshore, sails down, and, slipping and sliding, the passengers made their way aboard. There was little room for anything but their bodies. They packed their belongings, tent, sleeping bags, and the food they had saved on the sled towed behind. The two apprehensive sled dogs would ride on the frame with them, held by Uluksuk and Sinnisiak. In this sober morning light Creed had no idea if it would work, but what the hell.

When all were on board and settled on the triangular frame— Sinnisiak and Uluksuk positioned themselves on their bellies well forward on the outriggers, holding a sled dog each, Angituk crouched on her knees on the main beam in front of Creed, who sat upright on the helm at the back with the aft stay under his left arm and the tiller under his right—Creed ordered Sinnisiak to raise the caribou-hide sail. Sinnisiak did as he was told, hauling the heavy sail up to the top of the mast. It bent alarmingly in the steady wind, but it held. The craft strained at the tether. Creed smiled at Angituk, who looked back at him with excitement.

"Will it work?"

"Who knows? But I wish we had a bottle of champagne."

"What's champagne?"

"Never mind. Can I borrow your knife?"

Angituk gave him the little penknife that was her Christmas present. He opened it and held it above the tether. Angituk stared at him.

"Come on. Go! Why are you waiting?"

"It's an important moment. I want to remember it." He felt the north wind blow quite strong through his beard.

"Just GO!"

A sudden gust embraced the big hide sail, bent the mast, and strained the aft stay to the breaking point. Angituk took the little knife from Creed's fingers, leaned past him over the stern, and quickly cut the tether. The craft bolted out across Dease Bay in the stiff wind toward the wide ice of Great Bear Lake dragging the qamutik behind them like a rag doll. Everyone scrambled to hang on to something. Angituk moved forward to find her place behind the mast. They were under way.

Creed was amazed by the speed. They must be doing thirty-five miles an hour in this old rig! The oscillating qamutik finally settled on its frozen rails and now rode smoothly behind. He hoped the hunters were enjoying the ride. They would never have experienced this speed. Luckily, the surface was smooth, for the craft had no suspension at all, and they rumbled along feeling every bump and imperfection in the ice. With the constant and intense vibration, each word Creed tried to say was a stutter. "How do you like it?" he shouted into the wind.

Uluksuk and Sinnisiak both turned back toward him. Their faces were masks of terror with tears streaming down. They were shouting something in Coppertuk that could only mean "Slow down!" The dogs too had caught their fears and their eyes were wild, jowls blown back, exposing teeth clamped shut as the wind unfurled their black lips.

"This is where the big lake breathes," she called to him. "It is a living thing and needs oxygen like you and me."

Creed looked out over the frigid water, watching the lake breathe as his primitive vessel rumbled past toward thick ice.

As the day wore on, Creed's buttocks and tiller arm grew completely numb. His back was stiff and eyes red and sore, but he was happy. The sun was on its descent now and they were approaching a mass of land to their right, another peninsula jutting out from the west shore. If he followed this shoreline to the southwest, he would find the mouth of the river. Couldn't be more than a couple of hours. They would make it before darkness fell. Almost three hundred miles in a day! If there were spirits out there, they were smiling on them.

AN HOUR LATER, Creed squinted up at the distant horizon and saw the south shore. His idea had worked beautifully, but he was very tired and sore. They all were. They had gone over two pressure cracks that could have torn the runners off and ripped the boat apart if they were not descending. As it was, the drop had rattled their bones and severely tested the structure, but it somehow stayed together. The initial exhilaration of the voyage was long gone. He could see his weary passengers just wanted to get to land.

Creed studied the approaching shoreline. He could see the river mouth and looked for a place there to camp. It was late in the day and he was having trouble seeing. His eyes were painfully irritated. How far was the shore? And how was he supposed to stop this thing? The wind was still high and if he tried to turn into it they would topple and crash for sure. Damn, his eyes were hurting. He had to figure this out. The others were looking back at him apprehensively through their eye slits. How close were they to shore? He could hardly see. *Is that it right there?* he asked himself, staring through the blur.

The shore was quite flat and treeless near the river mouth where, at full sail, they left the ice and ploughed into a five-foot snowdrift. It was like being hit by an avalanche, but the snow was soft. The mast cracked in two and the sails came down on top of them. They all remained still for a moment as the snow settled around them. They had made it to the south shore. They clambered out of the wreckage, spitting out snow and testing their land legs. The dogs barked madly and wagged their tails.

Creed stumbled out of the drift holding snow against his burning, scratchy eyes. He was in pain.

Angituk noticed the eye protectors around his neck. "You wore the eye protectors, didn't you?"

"No."

"Not all day?"

"I was going to ..."

The others looked at Creed and at each other with concern. Creed took the snow away from his eyes and tried to focus on them. All he saw was a red haze and blurry figures.

"I can't see."

"You are snow-blind." She knew it would get worse before it got better.

His eyes felt like a hundred needles were embedded in them. "DAMN IT!"

He crouched down on his knees to find more snow. Star tried to lick him and he pushed her away. Breathing in between his clamped teeth, he scooped two handfuls and held it against his burning eyes again.

Angituk knelt down beside him. "We will make a shelter here. We'll have to stay for a while."

"When will I see again?" She didn't answer. "Will I see again?"

"Maybe."

"Maybe? Damn it! Look." Creed grabbed her arm, upset and breathing hard. He took his Colt revolver out of the holster and put it in her hand. "You'll have to guard them. You know how to fire this?"

"No."

"Put your hand here." She did so. "There's the trigger. This is the safety."

"Yes. Like a rifle."

"Okay. You can't let them go. Let me hear you fire it once."

"Why?"

"Pick a tree. Shoot."

Angituk pointed at a Jack pine twenty feet away and pulled the trigger.

Sinnisiak and Uluksuk jumped as the revolver fired. It kicked Angituk's shoulder and put a dime-sized hole in the centre of the tree.

"Okay. Now you know how to fire it and they know you know. Don't let them go."

"I won't," she said defensively, rubbing her wrist.

"I'm sorry about this."

"I told you—"

"I was stupid, I know."

"Yes, but never mind—"

"No, I really was. Goddamnit, I'm sorry."

Angituk held fresh snow up to his eyes and looked to where Uluksuk and Sinnisiak were already building a shelter for him from saplings and the caribou hides that had been the sail.

The first few hours of the night were the worst for Creed. He lay on his back in agony exacerbated by his feelings of stupidity. They had given him the protectors and told him to wear them, and he had ignored them. Now fire roared inside his eyeballs. He was furious with himself. Angituk continued to bathe his eyes with snow.

"Where are they?" he asked through gritted teeth.

"They've made their own house.".

"You're sure they're there?"

"Yes."

It was long after midnight before Creed found his way to a restless sleep. Angituk put their sleeping bags together and lay down beside him to keep him warm. She had seen snow blindness before and she knew the extent to which the pain could cripple the sufferer. It was good he slept, for tomorrow the pain would be even worse. And for a couple of hours she slept too.

It was well before dawn when his bad dreams started. He was talking to someone and trying to get up.

"It's coming from the box. The pillbox. No use till we blow it. Well, DELAY THE GODDAMN ADVANCE! Give me two good men and half an hour ..."

Angituk stroked his face. He settled for a moment.

"WHAT! Is he trying to kill us all? Where is the idiot?"

Creed was sweating and feverish. Angituk wiped his face.

"Get your masks out. Everyone get out your masks! COOPER! WHERE THE HELL'S YOUR GODDAMN MASK? Well, take Riley's—he doesn't need it anymore."

She spoke to him. "Corporal? It's all right. You're safe. It will be okay."

"No. No, I've got to do the night patrol. Go get Hedley and Turkstra for me."

"All right," she said, stroking his face. "Okay."

He settled again and his breathing became shallow and relaxed.

It was after sunrise when Creed suddenly sat up. He was blind.

"Where are they?" He was wide awake, his voice cold and hard.

"Who?"

"What do you mean 'who'? The prisoners. What are you doing here? You're supposed to be guarding them!"

Feeling around, Creed grabbed the pistol on the floor and then slipped the .38-55 out of its long sheath and stumbled out of the shelter. He opened his eyes and the faint sunlight daggered them. All he could see was a red wash with hazy images beyond. He pulled on his boots and groped his way to the other shelter.

"Sinnisiak! Uluksuk! Where are they?"

The other shelter was abandoned. Creed felt around for his prisoners and their belongings. The shelter was empty.

"WHERE ARE THE PRISONERS?!"

Creed stormed and stumbled around the camp, waving the rifle left and right, tripping over some cut firewood and raging at his bad luck.

"Goddamnit! How could I let this happen?"

Angituk had followed him out of the shelter. He turned and confronted her, seeing only a vague image through the red.

"You let them escape! I told you!"

Angituk looked at the empty shelter and the smouldering fire, confused and upset. They did seem to be gone.

"Maybe they're around."

"Of course they're not around! Now what are we going to do? They could be anywhere! They could be on their way back to the Coppermine. I found them and brought them all this goddamn way. And then you lose them! I just asked you for one thing! ONE THING! So goddamn stupid!"

Angituk stood there shivering without her coat on in the

morning chill. Creed could not see the tears that pooled in her blue eyes.

"I'm sorry."

"Lot of good that does."

"I never thought they'd run away."

"Well, they did!"

"Maybe we can find them."

"With me half blind?"

"I can go. I'm a good tracker."

"Right," he said with a seething sarcasm driven by the pain. "I should never have trusted—"

And then they heard his voice.

"Angituk?"

It was Uluksuk. Creed could not see him, but Angituk smiled with relief at the old man. Uluksuk and Sinnisiak had returned. Sinnisiak held up two fresh hares he had snared. And Uluksuk showed her a skin full of special mosses.

"I found the 'mother moss' for his eyes, under the snow. Didn't know if it grew down here. This will be the best for him."

"Quanaqqutit," the girl said to both of them as she took the rabbits and examined the moss.

Creed turned toward Angituk. "What did he say?"

She looked at him with disdain, her voice acid.

"Figure it out for yourself."

Eleven

Uluksuk had Creed lie down again in the shelter and carefully prepared and applied the special paste from the mosses he had collected. Then he put a blindfold around Creed's head.

"That's incredible. The pain is almost gone. Thank you."

But Angituk was not there to translate. Creed gave him a blind thumbs-up and the old shaman did it back against Creed's thumb. Sinnisiak brought in the rabbits he had roasted over the wood fire. Angituk came then and ate with the hunters, but did not say a word to Creed. Creed accepted this. He deserved it. It would work out in time. The rabbit was excellent and cooked through for him. Though he was blindfolded, Creed heard the sound of the chain on Sinnisiak's handcuffs against his tin mug.

"Stick out your hands."

The hunter was unsure what Creed wanted. Creed found Sinnisiak's hands, pulled them toward him, and fished the key out of his jacket pocket. He undid the shackles first of Sinnisiak and then of Uluksuk. He shook their unencumbered hands and told them they were good men, and then he stood and threw the cuffs as far away as he could into the bushes.

BY THE TIME CREED regained some of his sight and was ready to travel again, the days had grown longer. The Great Bear River had begun to open up and the first subtle signs of spring were all around them. Creed still had pain and could not see details well, but he wore the eye protectors through the day and his eyes slowly healed. They walked along an old path on the riverbank, Creed with his hand on Uluksuk's shoulder. Uluksuk took an interest in Creed's compass and now kept it in his pocket and consulted it on a regular basis. But his attraction to it had nothing to do with determining direction; he knew the precise direction he was travelling at any given moment as unfailingly as a river runs its course. He was trying to fool it. He would turn around one way and then quickly the other, turn it upside down, hide it in his coat and spin round again, but the compass would not be confounded—it always pointed to where Uluksuk knew north to be. Home.

The shaman had also taken over Creed's binoculars and he looked through them from either end. When Creed first showed the glasses to Sinnisiak, the young hunter told him: "Yes, with this you can see a long way, but can you see into the future like Uluksuk?"

Creed's rapport with the hunters deepened, but Angituk was still not speaking to him. She had not forgiven him for his accusations. She never looked at him now or initiated conversation, and her responses were monosyllabic.

"They behave like they are married. Do you think they're married?" Sinnisiak asked Uluksuk one morning when Angituk was out of earshot.

"I don't know. You're right, but it would be rude to ask."

Creed had tried once to apologize and Angituk had not answered. In the meantime she had become great friends with Sinnisiak and Uluksuk, chatting away all day, telling jokes and stories without translating, leaving Creed on the outside. Twice he had heard her say to them in reference to him, *"Kabloona ayortok."* He was sure it meant, "The white man knows nothing."

ULUKSUK ONCE TOLD a long, entertaining story and the others listened with interest and amusement. They laughed for a long time when he was done.

"What was his story about, Angituk?"

She didn't reply.

"Angituk? What was the joke?"

She tossed a cold look in his direction. "He called down the northern lights one time to help him trap a caribou." And that was all he could get out of her.

ONE MID-AFTERNOON only a few days away from Fort Norman, they had the encounter with the Cree. Uluksuk led and Creed took up the rear, watching the path ahead of him through his eye protectors. Silence except for a few bickering crows. Suddenly Uluksuk was grabbed and thrown up against a tree with a knife pressed to his throat. Creed's pistol and rifle were yanked from his hands. Angituk struggled against two men who held her. Star bit the leg of one of the men who held Angituk and he swung a club against the dog's head, knocking her unconscious. The leader had Sinnisiak against a tree with two men holding him. He slapped Sinnisiak across the face.

"Ejaka! What you do here? WHAT YOU DO HERE ON MY LAND?"

Creed got one hand free from the men who held him and took off his eye protectors. He squinted at the leader and spoke in Oji-Cree. "Leave him alone. He's with me. I am Corporal Creed of the Royal North West Mounted Police."

The leader glanced at Creed, unimpressed. "Police. What you doing with filthy *Ejaka?"*

"These two men are my prisoners. They're expecting us in Fort Norman."

"Why you in filthy Eskimo clothes?"

"They're warm."

The leader studied him. "Prisoners? So what they do?"

Creed hesitated. "They're accused of murder."

"Murder? Filthy murdering Eskimos."

The leader put his knife up to Sinnisiak's terrified face, the point making an indentation in his cheek. It broke the skin. A drop of blood. Sinnisiak was trembling.

"Why go to Fort Norman? We kill them here for you. Free service."

"If you do that, you will be charged with murder and arrested too."

With a quick movement, as Sinnisiak cried out, the leader sliced open the front of Sinnisiak's hide trousers. "Let's see what he got down there. Maybe I want an Eskimo cock," he said, brandishing his knife.

"I'm warning you. Leave him alone!"

Sinnisiak was crying. The leader turned and came slowly over to Creed with the knife, and smiled at him.

"You long way from white friends. Many people, even white men, even police ... many people disappear in the bush. You can disappear too."

One of the other Cree who was holding Angituk now spoke up. He was feeling her breast with one hand. "Look! This one's a woman!"

Angituk spat in his face and tried to break free from the two men holding her. The leader stepped over to her, opened her coat, tore open her flannel shirt, and looked at her small breasts. The men forced her down on her knees.

An icy calm came over Creed and he spoke with all the authority he could summon.

"Listen to me. I am under direct orders of the King to safely bring in these three people. If you harm them, you will have to kill me. And if you kill me, the King will send one hundred officers just like me to track you down, arrest you, and hang you. All of you. Do you understand?"

He was realizing the usefulness of Hornby's crass threat. The Cree were listening but not yet convinced on a course of action. Uluksuk suddenly gave a wild, ear-splitting yell. He opened his eyes wide and stared maniacally at his captors and shouted words they did not understand. After a moment Creed took the cue.

"He is an *Ejaka* shaman," he told them in Oji-Cree. "He has powerful magic. He has sucked the souls of many men to take them to the place of the dead. Why do you think I am taking him to Fort Norman?"

The men holding Uluksuk let go of him then and stepped back. The shaman began to dance, his hands raised, eyes wild and intense, hands rotating in a conjuring motion as if to possess them, a sinister smile on his face.

"This is a trick," said the Cree leader, but his voice betrayed a deep sense of apprehension.

Creed continued: "Release us. NOW!"

The men holding Creed, Angituk, and Sinnisiak let go and backed away. Uluksuk kept up his dancing and leering as the Cree stared at him, mesmerized.

"Drop the weapons!" Creed commanded.

His pistol and rifle fell to the ground.

"Now save yourselves! Save your souls! Go!" Creed warned them, and the leader backed away from the crazed Uluksuk. "And tell any other Cree you meet, we are not to be bothered. RUN!"

A moment later, they were gone.

Angituk scrambled to her feet and, wrapping her shirt around herself, stood beside Creed. He put an arm around her and she leaned into him, trembling.

"You all right?" Creed asked.

She nodded.

TWICE MORE in the next few days they passed parties of Indians on the river, but there was no more trouble. The Cree avoided them, and they felt safer the closer they got to Fort Norman.

At a widening of the path on a slight decline, Creed came alongside Uluksuk.

"Uluksuk. How do you get to be a shaman? Are you born to it?"

Angi was close enough to translate. "It is determined during pregnancy. A shaman came to examine my mother and determined I would be one. So when I was born, I was shown my afterbirth, and I examined it. And as soon as I was able, I was fed large amounts of caribou brains. My mother would chew them for me. Then, when I had been through a few winters, the old shaman came back to instruct me for a time. And since then I am guided by the spirits."

"Do you feel them now?"

"No. They are busy with their attention on others. They have no interest in us right now. And that is a very good thing. Believe me, you do not want their attention. Enjoy this time. Let it be a time of healing for you."

"My eyes are almost as good as new."

"I don't mean your eyes."

He paused. Creed looked up at the old man with surprise.

"Enjoy this healing time," the shaman repeated to him.

THE SNOW MELTED QUICKLY now and the qamutik was no longer practical. They cached it near the river, still forty miles from Fort Norman, and built a simple travois for the dogs to pull, two poles they dragged behind them with a small woven platform that could take thirty pounds of gear and food. Creed decided to shave again and Angituk laughed at his clean baby face and felt his smooth cheek for a long moment.

Spring had come upon them with a startling, almost violent suddenness. The days were sunny and warm, and the snow had all but melted into the swollen river. The cells of plants and trees attuned to their short growing season had already begun their vigorous photosynthetic multiplication, and the ducks and geese and other wildlife were engaged in a flourish of activity. Creed's eyes were almost completely recovered now, so he could enjoy both the rich odours of the earth and water and the visual performance of the greening forest full of creatures and the blue sky full of birds.

The ravens were most numerous and entertaining, with their mystical connotations shared in the mythologies of hundreds of cultures. They would pass overhead and call out their distinctive, almost human croak. Creed found he had a talent for duplicating the raven's guttural speech and he would call it out in reply, much to the amusement of Sinnisiak.

"Do it again," the hunter would ask, and Creed would oblige with a long, croaking raven phrase, and Sinnisiak would laugh again. "Uluksuk! The white man is turning into a raven."

"Good choice."

As they walked in these spring days, Uluksuk sometimes sang a song and Angituk translated it:

There is joy in feeling the warmth!
Come to the great world,

And seeing the sun,
Follow its old footprints in the summer night,
And rejoice for the life you are given.
Iy-alya-ya-ya-ya!

IN THE INTOXICATING FREEDOM of the warm weather, and with the slightly melancholy anticipation of the end of his mission, Creed felt no huge impulse to hurry into Fort Norman. At a particularly pleasant spot on the river where a series of calm pools had formed in bays out of the main current, he declared a rest stop for a day or two. They built two shelters from saplings and skins and found themselves surrounded by wildflowers. Creed was amazed: the buds had matured and blossomed in a matter of days. Sinnisiak murmured, "The spirits are in a good mood."

Angituk had been more civil to Creed since the Cree episode, translating their conversations freely, but there was still a distance between them. It occurred to him that she might be doing it out of self-defence. In Fort Norman they would have to separate, and that realization saddened him. He watched her talking and laughing with the hunters, combing out her long hair with a wide comb of walrus tusk. The warm spring sunshine—the sparkling clarity of Arctic air intensifying the sun's extravagant rays—made her playful and he found himself preoccupied by her beauty. He was astounded again that she had ever convinced him she was a boy. As he watched her, he became aware of the deep ache that entered him whenever he thought of leaving her.

Early in the afternoon, the sun was so luxuriously hot that Creed told himself it could counteract the numbing effect of the river. He was determined to take a bath. He walked along the riverbank with a towel and a handful of sweet-smelling leaves

Uluksuk had found, in search of a particular pool. It was out of the stronger current and just waist-deep. He was amazed at the flowers blooming along the path that had not been there the day before: pink saxifrage, white Arctic poppy, and blue Arctic heather. He would never have known or cared about the names of any of these but for the little handbook Cowperthwaite had slipped into his pack with sketches of Arctic wildflowers. How it had not been used for fuel these past months, he had no idea.

Multicoloured butterflies flitted from flower to flower. He recalled with amusement a version of purgatory that Angi had described to him where the meat-obsessed Eskimos—those who had offended the spirits—were doomed to an eternity of eating nothing but butterflies.

Before he reached the pond, he noticed a slender figure bent double in the frigid river, feet apart for stability, studying the bottom. It was Angituk. Her hands hovered just above the surface of the water like a fortune teller's above a crystal ball.

Creed stopped on the bank, curious, to watch her. He noticed she had built a primitive weir of rocks to direct the fish into the shallows near the bank where she stood. Suddenly her hands moved, broke through the surface, and clutched at something, but they came up empty.

"It's impossible to catch a fish with your bare hands," he called out to her.

Angituk studiously ignored him. Creed sat down on the bank to watch.

"You know, you've told me many things about your childhood and your people, but I feel, after all this time, I don't really know that much about you."

Angituk's eyes followed a movement in the pool below, her hands poised, thumb and fingers spread.

"I'd like to know more about your mother."

"*Shhhhhh*. I'm busy."

"And the mission school. What was the mission school like? And who was your father?"

She did not respond. Her hands were still, and then they plunged. She was fast, but not nearly fast enough.

"You are ruining my fishing."

"I told you, it's impossible."

Angituk stood up straight, arching her slender, curved back into a stretch. She put her hands on her hips and faced him.

"My *amaamak* was a Copper Eskimo woman, as I told you. Her name was Kunee. My father's name was Angus McAndrew. He was a Scottish fur trader whom I never met. My mother was very beautiful, with pretty tattoos, and they loved each other very much, but he had to go away. I grew up in hunt camps with my mother and my uncles in the Coppermine and each year we travelled to the west as far as Tuktoyaktuk and the Mackenzie River."

"Where did you learn to say 'whom'?"

"I learned to read, write, and speak English at the mission school, the Mission of Notre Dame at Fort Good Hope on the Mackenzie River. Most of the teachers told us we were a backward people and God was punishing us. They beat us for speaking our language. Many of us got sick and some died. But there was one special teacher there, Miss Calhoun, and we read Shakespeare and Robert Burns and Balzac together every night. She taught me to say 'whom.' Anything else?"

"How did your mother die?"

"Consumption. Tuberculosis they call it now. Five years ago. In Fort Norman. I ran away from the school to be with her at the end and they didn't make me go back. I stayed with her for three weeks before she died. I sang the songs to her. I told her back the stories she had told me about the green ice caves. And I told her back the stories of my handsome father just before she died. Then I worked for the priest at Saint Theresa's who buried her there—Father Ducot. He was kind to me. He had books. Kipling and Conrad. Have you ever read Joseph Conrad?"

"Yes, of course. He's a favourite."

"English was his second language too."

"I know."

"So that was good for two years, until another priest came to visit Father Ducot and he tried to touch me. He thought I was a boy. I threatened him with a knife. So I had to leave there." She saw a movement below the surface. "Now excuse me, because I made a promise to Uluksuk, for *whom* I will catch dinner."

"Impossible."

Angituk bent over again, hands poised, back arched, breasts almost touching the smooth surface of the water. She would never pass for a male in her undershirt, Creed thought. She remained motionless for several moments. She waited. Then she plunged. With two hands she raised the struggling fish up in the air in triumph, to Creed's amazed expression.

"I'll be damned."

"My mother said nothing in the world is impossible."

She waded over to the bank, her forefinger deep under the gill flap so it couldn't struggle free. She disengaged her finger and threw the struggling char in Creed's lap. It was big, maybe eight pounds. Creed almost lost it and let it slide back into the river. Angituk giggled at his attempts to secure it. He found a fist-sized rock and killed it with two blows. He laid it on the grass, tail toward the river.

"No! Don't you know anything?" Angituk turned the fish sideways, parallel to the river. "You have to lay it in the direction it was swimming so the spirit can continue on its way and be happy."

"We just killed it. I can't imagine the spirit is very happy."

"It *is* happy. There is an understanding. It moves on."

Creed looked at her as she took the knife from her belt and quickly began to skin and fillet the char. "Angi ... It was a long time ago, I know, but I'm very sorry for how I behaved when I thought Uluksuk and Sinnisiak had escaped. I treated you badly, and I am sorry."

Angituk listened to what he said very seriously.

"Okay."

"Will you accept my apology?"

"Yes."

"Good, then." Creed left her thoughtfully filleting the fish.

THE SHALLOW, CALM POOL he was looking for was an eddy off the river, and though it was surrounded by pine trees, at this time of day the high sun shone down intensely, warming the smooth surface. The water travelled in a gentle circle in this shallow pool removed from the icy river and was several degrees warmer. Creed stripped off his clothing and swam out to the centre. After crouching on the bottom for a full minute, Creed blasted up through the water to the welcome sunlight above. He broke the surface gasping and immediately began to scrub his naked body with the sudsing leaves Uluksuk had provided. It took a little work to establish a lather, but with them he thoroughly addressed all his neglected parts until he felt pristine, almost pure.

He realized in this moment how much he had enjoyed this journey. His desire for solitude had been replaced by a renewed joy in companionship. Maybe he should give up the long patrols and settle down. Edmonton was as good a place as any. Maybe with Nicole, if she would still have him, though the thought of a future with her did not stir the excitement it might in other men. He dipped himself into the water to his shoulders to rinse the thin lather from his body.

Suddenly he became aware he was not alone and turned to find Angituk making her way along the bank. Her movements were slow, slightly self-conscious. Though it was obvious she knew he was there, she did not look at him at first but found a flat rock at the water's edge and knelt down to wash. She dipped her long hair into the cool water current and rubbed mosses into the tresses, giving them a silvery sheen, and then worked it all through with her tattooed fingers. Creed watched her, his arms around himself to help keep warm.

Her movements became even more languid, sensuous. Their eyes made contact once. Then she pulled the tail of her flannel shirt out of her trousers and undid the buttons, then the buttons of her long underwear underneath to her waist. Slowly, she lathered the cloth again and began to wash her underarms and breasts in a slightly dreamlike slow motion. Creed tried to look away but could not. She wanted him to watch her; there was no doubt in his mind. She had never behaved like this before in front of him, at least knowingly, and he wanted her to stop. She undid her belt next and the buttons of her jean trousers, loosening them on her thighs, and then the rest of the buttons of her long underwear as far as they would go. She lathered her belly well, then much deeper between her legs. She looked up at him again as she continued her intimate ablutions, and he tried to assess her. He stared back at her, his breath quickening, body shivering.

She smiled. "Are you coming out?"

Creed glanced down, embarrassed at the physical effect she had had on him even in the cold river. "Ah, no. You go ahead back to camp. I'll be along shortly."

Angituk looked down and laughed a little. Then she took off her shirt and slid out of her jean trousers and long underwear and slipped naked into the water. She swam out to him where he was standing waist-deep in the Great Bear River, her body a shimmering flash beneath the sun-dappled surface coming very quickly toward him. He found himself backing away a few steps, his bare feet negotiating the slippery shale on the river bottom, stubbing a heel.

She stopped short and stood up suddenly before him less than an arm's length away. Her blue eyes looked into his. He watched the water flowing from her hair down along the contours of her body, licked his lips once, and tried to speak.

"Angituk, I ... we ..."

She stepped forward, their bodies not quite touching, and put her nose against his neck and cheek, smelled the sweet scent of the leaves on his skin, and nuzzled him. He put his hands on her shoulders, at first to hold her back. He looked deeply into her eyes. She desired him.

"Angi ..."

He found his hands moving gently to her face and he drew it close to him. He kissed her mouth. He knew he had a strong affection for the girl, but when he kissed her it was with a passion he did not know was there. It was deep and mysterious, like an ocean tide rising suddenly in green caves of ice.

"I love you," he told her, catching himself completely by surprise. But then he realized it was true. It had come to him in this moment, when his heart was about to burst, and he knew it was forever.

He touched his tongue to hers and she responded quickly and with enthusiasm, licking his lips and nose and plunging her tongue into his mouth. She arched her back and pressed herself against him. Her strong legs encircled his waist, and together they guided him into her. The cold river lapped against the heat of their bodies working together and they lost themselves in their eagerness to give each other pleasure. The girl began a faint chanting under her breath that matched their rhythm, and though Creed had long forbidden himself this day, there was no hesitancy now to his lovemaking.

When finally they were both spent, they slid down into the cold water of the Great Bear to cool their lust. They looked at each other, wet and shivering, and Angituk laughed out loud at what had just happened between them. Here they were again in cold water together. She stroked the furrows of his frowning brow and made him laugh too. Her eyes had the intense glow of the aurora.

"Let's do it again."

"Okay."

"Now?"

"Soon."

Twelve

They lay beside the roaring fire that night as the green lights crackled and pinged in the sky overhead. Creed had never seen them this active; a glorious rainbow of colours grew and radiated in spirals and long silver threads. Uluksuk and Sinnisiak snored in their makeshift shelter nearby. Creed was exhausted. Angituk was insatiable. She lay in his arms and watched him with gentle wonderment as he dozed between lovemaking, and touched his lips with her tattooed fingers as if she thought he might disappear.

"What does your great-grandmother's spirit think of all this?" he asked her.

"She is my spirit. My great-grandmother outlived three husbands. She wondered if there was something wrong with us that we did not do this before." Angituk snuggled against him, looked into the fire, and spoke a word. *"Quvianaqpiaqtuq."*

"What does that mean?" he asked, his eyes closed.

"It means like a ... an indulgent enjoyment of something. It is the joy you feel looking up at the lights, or coming into a warm igloo, or seeing a fresh blanket of snow—or when I put my lips against yours."

"Quv-ianaq-piaq-tuq," he repeated, leaving his lips open. He opened his eyes and went to kiss her, but she pulled away, teasing.

"No. Now it is time you were educated," she told him. "The word for earth: *nuna*." She patted the ground.

"*Nuna*."

"Good. The word for sea: *tarjuq*."

"*Tarjuq*."

"Good. The word for sky: *qilak*."

"*Qilak*."

"Good. We call the weather spirit Hila, so if the weather is fine we say *Hilaqijuq*, or 'Hila is absent.' If it is stormy, *Hiladlutuq*: 'Hila is upset.'"

"*Hiladlutuq*."

"Good. Okay, now in Eskimo language *inuk* means one real person. *Inuuk* means two. *Inuit* means three or more. The language is Inuktitut ... *titut* means 'in the manner of.' Our Copper dialect is called Inuinnaqtun. It is very precise. For instance, there is no one word for 'fish.' There is a word for a char going upstream, another for one going downstream, one for one resting in a pool. Three separate words. And for 'snow,' in any Eskimo dialect, the list of specific words goes on forever, as you know. Wet snow, dry snow, blowing snow, snow with a crust, snow with ice below, snow accumulated behind a rock ..."

"The most important thing in Arctic life."

"Yes. It's important to be precise. And our words can be very similar. This will be hard for you. For instance, *ugjuk* is a bearded seal, *uqhuq* is fat from a seal or walrus, *uuttuq* means a seal sleeping on the ice, *uujuq* means boiled meat, *utsuk* is a vagina, *usuk* is a penis."

"I would not want to get all of those mixed up."

"No." They laughed together. "What else can I teach you today? As I told you, we have no words for hello or goodbye. We feel to make such a big moment of things is posturing, arrogant ... intrusive. It 'implicates'—all of these are Miss Calhoun's words—it implicates others unnecessarily. So when white men needed some kind of greeting, we came up with *guanuippit*, which means 'What has gone wrong for you today?'"

Creed grinned at this. "Not very optimistic."

"The world is an uncertain place. We don't even have simple words for yes and no. We would say *qu-immaqa*, which means 'probably yes,' or *immaqa*, 'probably not.'"

Creed tried the words and Angituk became distracted a little by his mouth.

"To say simply yes or no would be rude. It would challenge the spirits. Now you can be the teacher. Teach me about kissing again. Am I doing it all right?"

"*Qu-immaqa.*"

"Probably yes?"

"Nothing is certain."

She laughed and kissed him hard.

"You are already a master—a mistress. You kiss very well," he told her.

"As good as white girls?"

"Much better."

"Did you know I was born on a stormy day?"

"Doesn't surprise me."

She was pleased. "The weather on the day you are born is very important. It was a terrible storm. It raged for hours! It made me strong and—here's another Miss Calhoun word—*perseverant*. My grandmother massaged me the first day and pulled on my legs and arms to make them grow long and strong, and she sang a magic blessing to me and gave me gifts: a raven skin to be invisible, some of her hair for a long life, and my umbilical cord to connect me to my past lives."

"And did it?"

"Yes, it did." She looked at him for any sign of skepticism before she continued. "Even here, in this camp, I wanted to tell you. I have never camped here in this life. When I was little, we never travelled on this river. But I have been here before, long ago. I was a man and I speared fish where I caught them today by that weir. That's how I knew. I think it was before my grandfather's time. An earlier life. I had two wives and four children, three boys and a girl. I bet my mother could tell me who I was."

"You're certainly not a man anymore."

She turned to him. "You don't believe me, do you?"

"I didn't believe you could catch a fish with your hands."

She smiled at this deflection. The lights in the sky separated into two ethereal curtains and they watched for a few moments.

"It is a good sign," Angituk hoped.

"Let's try and whistle them closer," Creed suggested.

"No! It would anger the Spirits of the Dead. They are very jealous of us. Especially today. They could make a storm to drive the lights away. Let's just enjoy them quietly."

Creed was amused by her fears. She studied his smile.

"I wonder if my father looks like you."

"What do you know about him?"

"My mother loved him. And he loved her. He was a trapper and trader. A tall man with a beard, and very good-looking, very kind. And a good hunter. He had a pretty mermaid tattoo on his left arm. They lived together on the land for a year. But then he had to go south to his camp ... a big village called Edmonton. He could not take her there."

"Edmonton is where I live."

"Really! You must know him. His name is Angus McAndrew. Do you know him?"

"No. It's a very big village."

"I was told that. They say it's even bigger than Fort Norman. He said he'd come back to my mother, but he was never able to. I always wanted to go and find him. He could be hurt or sick and I could help him. His enemies could have stopped him. Maybe he has other wives. Maybe I have brothers and sisters! That's what I always wanted, to be part of a big family. Except for my baby brother who died, it was always only me."

Creed's heart turned at her innocence, her naïveté. "Angi, I would like to take you to Edmonton with me, but I can't. I have orders to escort the prisoners there, and there will be a trial. It will take some time. After the trial I can apply for leave. That means I can come back to Norman and see you."

Her eyes searched his face. "Yes? You'll come back to me?"

"Yes."

"You told me you love me. Is it true? Do you love me?"

"Yes. I love you, Angituk."

She smiled her flawless, trusting smile. "Good."

And suddenly Creed knew it was true. He knew it more clearly than he had known anything in his life. Here in her arms he felt that his heart was about to burst. They kissed again and Creed held her body tightly against his, and then tighter still, to remember.

ON THE FINAL NIGHT, Uluksuk conducted a meeting with the spirits of his land. Perhaps some would follow them farther south, but he was not optimistic. They would stay here and wait for him. There would be new ones in the South. The shaman went a little way out of the camp to be alone, and burned sweet-grasses and purified himself as he had done to conjure the caribou spirits months before on the Dismal Lakes. As Creed and Angituk watched from a discreet distance, the shaman chanted for some time and then spoke in greetings to the invisible host. Angituk explained to Creed as they watched that Uluksuk was speaking to them of his hopes and fears, asking their advice, and answering any questions they might have. Creed could hear him talking, followed by periods of silence. Then Uluksuk would speak again as if carefully answering a question.

The rhythm of this communication with the spirits seemed somehow familiar, and Creed realized it echoed a courtroom examination of questions and answers. He thought then of the trial and what they were about to face. He listened to the sound of Uluksuk's earnest answers to the spirits, carried to him on the warm wind.

Angituk studied Creed's pensive expression as he watched Uluksuk and asked what he was thinking.

"I was wondering how to prepare them for all of this. Tomorrow in Fort Norman they'll see their first white community. They've never seen a complete log cabin or a horse or a combustion engine. Edmonton will be like no world they've ever imagined. What can I tell them? Where do I start?"

"They aren't going to hurt them, are they?"

"No."

"They'll have food and a bed to sleep in?"

"Yes."

"Then they'll be all right," Angituk told him. "Remember, my people adapt. Just don't lie to them. Don't do that. Tell them the truth and they will find their way."

That night, Creed took out Rouvière's journal once more and turned to the relevant passages:

> The important thing in our dealings with these people from the very beginning is to stress the importance of truth—that we are truthful in our day-to-day dealings and in the values of our greater society and also, and most important, that we bring to them the one true God. In a relationship that we hope will go

on for hundreds of years, we must demonstrate that
of all the virtues of the white man's society, we cherish
truth above all.

Creed thought about this. Rouvière had been two years
older than he was now, had travelled in Europe and worked
within the same society as Creed, worked with people and with
governments and within the Church. How could he be so naive?

THE FIRST SIGN OF FORT NORMAN appeared as a wisp of
smoke on the horizon still some twenty miles west of their
final camp. Creed was back in his field uniform, wool trousers
with the yellow stripe and high boots. Creed and Angituk had
discussed the good sense in reaffirming her male presentation
in Fort Norman for a number of reasons. So she had dressed in
her flannel shirt, wool trousers with suspenders, and fedora hat,
and had rubbed ashes on her face to simulate the shadow of a
beard.

Creed had been watching her as she turned into a boy again
and she smiled and went to kiss him with a sudden, rekindled
passion. But this last kiss of his was subdued, a gentle warning,
and her eyes revealed her subtle disappointment, though it was
what she had expected. Reunited with his own people, he would
now have to distance himself.

She stepped back from him and took off her hat. She raised
her sharpened skinning knife, looked at him, and began to cut
off handfuls of her long black hair, the beautiful tresses falling to
the ground.

A YOUNG RNWMP CONSTABLE smoked and chatted with
Oberly on the veranda outside the log detachment at Fort
Norman, watching the swirling confluence of the Great Bear

and Mackenzie rivers. They speculated on spring leave to Edmonton. Over Oberly's shoulder the young constable noticed four figures approaching along the muddy main street.

"Who's this, then?"

Oberly turned and squinted for a long time against the sun, low in the sky, as Creed, Angituk, Uluksuk, and Sinnisiak approached.

"My God." The cigarette fell from his lips. "It's Creed!"

Creed came up to them, the others trailing behind.

"Creed! Good Lord! We all thought you were dead!"

"Not to my knowledge."

"Let me find the Sergeant."

Oberly hurried to the Hudson's Bay post a hundred yards away. Creed looked back at his three companions, all hesitant to go inside.

"Come on. There'll be food."

Uluksuk and Sinnisiak entered the detachment apprehensively. They'd never been inside a wooden building before.

Creed led Angituk and his two prisoners into the mess. Sinnisiak and Uluksuk looked around at the inside of the structure, their eyes wide. They stared at the huge mirror, staying close together and talking quietly.

"Look at that little pond hanging sideways."

"Why doesn't the water spill out?"

"They must have strong magic."

Two other officers were having a drink, and they looked up at the Eskimos with surprise and distaste. Then they saw who accompanied them.

"Creed? Jesus, Creed. You're back! We heard you were dead."

"Nope. Still here."

Creed walked up and addressed the man who was bartender and cook, a burly, moustached civilian drying dishes behind the bar. "What's on for lunch? You have some stew back there? Four bowls of stew, my good man."

The cook didn't move. He looked at Sinnisiak and Uluksuk as they stared around in fascination. "It's the rules, Corporal. Can't serve Indians. Same applies for Eskimos, I figure."

With a strained smile, Creed leaned over the bar toward him as if to whisper. When the cook leaned toward him to hear, Creed grabbed him firmly with both hands by his flannel shirt, popping a button. He held the cook's grizzled face close to his own. "I said four bowls of stew. Now. You understand?"

The man glanced over at his two patrons, who were watching with interest and amusement. "But ... but there are white men in here."

Creed let him go and the cook stumbled backwards. "That's all right. My friends aren't that particular."

The cook hesitated, then went back into the kitchen to get the stew.

Creed turned around and leaned against the bar. "Welcome to Fort Norman, my friends."

One of the two officers moved closer to him. "So how far did you get, Creed? You see the Coppermine?"

"I did. All the way to the Arctic Ocean."

"Really? You got that far? And you still got your scalp?"

The other officer laughed at this. The cook returned with four bowls of stew with spoons and set them loudly on the bar. They had not yet eaten that day and Sinnisiak, Uluksuk, and Angituk quickly addressed the stew, the hunters shovelling it into their mouths with moaning enthusiasm. Sinnisiak gave Creed a thumbs-up.

"They like your stew," Creed told the cook.

Sergeant Farrell came in then with Oberly and several other officers.

"Creed! I am very happy to see you. We heard you were dead. I was about to send some men out to see. But anyway, you can't have those Eskimos in here."

Uluksuk and Sinnisiak had finished and were licking the bottoms of their bowls. More officers arrived to see Creed.

"Let me give you my preliminary report."

"Your friends can step outside."

"I'd like them to stay."

"Come on, Creed."

"They are my guests."

"They'll have fleas."

"Then so will I."

The Sergeant looked at the other officers. They wanted to hear the story. Farrell prudently decided to ignore the issue. "So, what happened?"

"In my investigation in search of Fathers Rouvière and Le Roux, I interviewed several people on the Coppermine River and was directed to a place known as Bloody Falls. There I discovered the partial remains of the two priests and determined by a study of the bodies that they had in fact been murdered. I buried them in a Christian manner and continued north to a large hunt camp at the mouth of the Coppermine on the Arctic Ocean to interview witnesses. I proceeded to the hunt camp of the two accused, confronted them, and they confessed to killing the priests and eating their livers. Whereupon I arrested them. And"—he gestured in gracious introduction—"here they are: Uluksuk and Sinnisiak."

The officers looked at the two Eskimos in shock. Uluksuk and Sinnisiak nodded and smiled congenially at the officers.

"Merry Christmas!" Sinnisiak told them loudly.

The Sergeant withdrew his revolver and pointed it at the two prisoners. "Take them to the cells!"

Four officers grabbed hold of Sinnisiak and Uluksuk, who, in sudden fear at the touch of the white men, began to resist and struggle against them. Jack was frustrated by the sudden brutality.

"They're all right! You don't need to—"

More officers joined the scuffle as they dragged them toward the cells in the back. Sinnisiak howled in fear. Creed couldn't get close.

"They'll do as they're told, damn it! Don't hurt them! Angituk, go and tell them it's all right, please."

Angituk hurried to follow the scrum of officers surrounding Sinnisiak and Uluksuk back to the cells.

Creed turned to face the Sergeant. "You can put that away, Sergeant. They're quite docile."

The Sergeant put the pistol back in his holster. "They ate the livers?" he asked.

Creed looked at him and nodded.

Just then three more officers came inside and the others returned from the cells. They all gathered around, looking at Creed, and there was a moment of silence before the Sergeant began in an almost accusing tone.

"Let me get this straight, Corporal Creed. You expect us to believe you went into a barren, unmapped territory of one hundred thousand square miles to look for the priests. You found and buried their bodies, then you conducted an investigation, identified the murderers and arrested them, extracted a confession, and single-handedly through the middle of winter brought the accused five hundred miles south to stand trial?"

"Yes, Sergeant."

"Any thoughts regarding how you managed this?"

"*Isuma*, Sergeant. Good luck."

"Luck? Well, you know what I believe? I believe this calls for a fucking round of drinks!"

Suddenly the men were laughing and talking and clapping Creed on the back.

"Bloody marvellous!"

"Amazing effort!"

"How did you ever find them?"

"And they admitted it, just like that?"

"Weren't you worried they'd just cut your throat?"

"How did you ever sleep?"

And dozens of questions they didn't give him time to answer.

A jar of whiskey was put in his hand and he was encouraged to drink. Oberly raised his glass in a broad gesture.

"Here's to Jack Creed! A hero! A friend ... and one hell of a Royal North West Mounted Police officer!"

Creed looked at the whiskey. He had gone for a year without a drink. There was a time he could barely get through an hour without one. Someone gave him a lit cigar, and in a little while he was telling his colleagues stories of the dances at Koeha's camp, the weeks in total darkness, and the ice boat on the perfect skating rink of the Great Bear Lake.

Angituk sat in the far corner of the room and watched and listened to him. He was making the other men laugh. She felt invisible there, but that was what she expected and desired. She was pleased at the respect he was enjoying from his people. They liked good stories too. Angituk had made enough money from this job that she could properly outfit herself with a good rifle and gas stove, a good tent, even a canoe. She could order a canoe all the way from that village called Peterborough, where Creed was born. She'd like that, she thought, watching him, to have a canoe from there.

She rose to say good night to Uluksuk and Sinnisiak in their cell and go back to her little cabin near the tannery, but still she lingered, watching and listening. In a day, when the boat came, Creed would be gone. And she believed in her heart that, like her father, she would never see him again.

THEY MET OUTSIDE the log detachment building under a full moon. The party inside continued with boisterous conversation, and someone merrily played a squeezebox. She yearned to kiss him and touch him as before, but felt the new distance now. She accepted it. He was with his own and had developed a level of formality toward her. She had expected this and knew it was necessary, but it still made her sad.

"The boat comes in tonight. Our timing was lucky. It leaves in the morning."

Angituk nodded, making an attempt to smile. "Lucky."

He glanced toward the door and then took her hand in his. "I'll miss you, Angi. I'll be back as soon as I can. Okay?"

Angituk nodded again, and the gesture caused a tear to slide down her cheek in the moonlight.

"Oh, no. Don't be sad. After the trial we'll have time together. I could take you across the mountains on the train to Vancouver. The winter there is very short. Flowers begin to bloom in late February. Would you like that?"

"Yes. That would be nice."

"Good, then. We'll have a great time. Angi?"

Just then a voice from the veranda called his name and Creed dropped her hand.

"Here."

The duty officer approached them. "There's a telegram for you, Corporal. From your Super in Edmonton."

The moon was so bright he could easily read it:

HEARTFELT CONGRATULATIONS ON YOUR SUC-
CESS STOP HAPPILY ANTICIPATING YOUR RETURN
WITH PRISONERS STOP REQUIRE SERVICES OF
ADDITIONAL INTERPRETER COPPER DIALECT FOR
TRIAL STOP PLEASE BRING WITH YOU.
SUPERINTENDENT G.S. WORSLEY

He turned to her, a mixture of emotions behind his smile. His life had just become much more complicated.

"They want you to come with us, Angituk." Creed looked at the officer. "Reply to them that the message is received and I will do as ordered."

"Yes, Corporal."

The officer went back inside the detachment and Creed looked at her with excitement. "You're coming to Edmonton!" he told her.

But her initial response was clouded in doubt. "Am I?"

"Of course! They need an interpreter. I should have known that. Of course they do."

"But do you really want me to come, Creed? Won't it be difficult for you?"

"Why would it be difficult? I want you with me, Angi."

These last words pushed her doubts away and she kissed him. Creed glanced up nervously toward the door of the detachment to make sure no one saw them.

She touched his face and looked into his eyes. "I'll stay as a boy so you won't have to worry," she teased him. "And I promise I'll never embarrass you. You just go about your duties and I will be happy just to be near you, even if we can never ..."

Creed held her for a moment and smiled into her eyes. "You're incredible."

NICOLE HARVEY STOOD on the veranda of her uncle's house holding in her white-gloved hand a copy of the telegram Corporal Cowperthwaite had sent over for her. She read it again, though there was not much to it. It gave the time of Creed's arrival by train the week after next and stated that he was bringing the two prisoners with him. Creed had sent it to his commanding officer. She was a little irritated he had not sent her a telegram too, but she forgave him.

"Funny old Jack, his head in the clouds," she said aloud.

Her love for him had survived a year of waiting. There had been other opportunities, other young men who sought her company, but love had triumphed. Her heart belonged to Jack, wherever he was, and it beat in giddy anticipation of seeing him and holding him again.

She would be at the station all smiles and embraces ready to greet her returning hero. It was so exciting. The papers were full of it, and everyone was talking about it. How Jack had made it all the way to the Arctic Ocean only to discover the priests had been brutally murdered. Probably tortured, the paper said. How he had single-handedly subdued his suspects and brought them home in chains! Speculation was rampant as to the vicious nature of these murderers. There were whispers on the street that they were cannibals.

Whatever the case, Nicole was delighted. She had already started to accept interviews with magazines on his behalf and invitations to dinner parties for them. It had been a long wait for him, but it had been worth it. Love had prevailed. And this time, when she had him back, she would be so good to him he would never imagine leaving her again. So what if he forgot to send her a telegram. She knew he loved her. He must. As much as any man can love with his head in the clouds all the time.

She looked at the train's arrival time again and smiled. This was going to be fun.

LOCKED DEEP IN THE HOLD of the steamboat *Mackenzie River*, Uluksuk and Sinnisiak sat in a storage area outfitted with wooden bars and two small cots. Angituk had a third cot in an open space outside. They were surrounded by bales of fur, barrels of salted fish and whale meat, crates of geological samples, several drums of benzoline fuel, and two heavy internal combustion engines in crates addressed to the Hay River Corporation. Uluksuk was softly chanting to the throb of the ship's engine.

"Bad spirits in this land," the shaman sang. "I am an innocent traveller in this dream world and mean you no harm. I wish you well. Please leave me and Sinnisiak in peace."

Sinnisiak was nervous and agitated by his confinement. Those white men in Fort Norman were bad enough, but there would be even more where they were going. When Uluksuk paused in his chanting, Sinnisiak spoke his mind.

"We should have escaped. The time he was blind."

"Are you talking about that still? They would have found us again. We had to go with him to face this thing."

"We should escape now."

The old shaman revealed his impatience at his student's imprudence. "How?"

"Angituk will open that door. Then use your powers to sink the boat."

"I can't swim. Neither can you."

Sinnisiak realized this was true. Outside their cell, Angituk had been listening to them.

"Stop talking about things sinking, you two. This is a good boat. And most of the whites are good people. They won't hurt us."

"What if we meet the bad ones?"

"You're going to be okay. Don't worry. You know that Creed will look after us."

This made them all feel better, and they settled down to sleep as the *Mackenzie River* pushed its way upstream toward the big village of the white men.

THAT NIGHT, Creed stood under the stars on the deck of the sturdy little steamboat again, its iron heart thumping away below as they headed south, upstream, against the current, a slower journey back toward civilization, or "outside" as Hornby had called it. Angituk was sleeping down in the hold with the hunters. He looked out over the moonlit surface of the water and went back again to the vivid memory of her making love to him in the sun-warmed waters of the Great Bear River. He could not get the event out of his head. But what about Nicole? His thoughts were returning to her as he drew nearer to Edmonton. He could not live a lie with her. He had to be honest. If he was lucky, she would have found someone else. That would be best. That could have already solved the problem, he thought hopefully.

The prospect of Edmonton did offer its share of apprehensions. Only now was it truly hitting him that his friends Uluksuk and Sinnisiak were facing murder charges. As the investigating officer, his role in this drama would be crucial. He had a responsibility to be clear, accurate, and professional in all of his conduct. He knew the prosecution would sniff out and illuminate any personal bias on his part. Yet his testimony could send them to prison for a long time. He had to stay focused on the trial. As he looked out at the rounded peaks of the Franklins, backlit by a deep, starry sky, he knew both he and Angituk would have to be strong.

He thought then of the simpler time before the "revelation," when somehow she had convinced him she was a boy. It was with amazement again that he remembered it. How she had faced up to the Cree on the Great Bear River, how she spoke to the huge bear she called her spirit guide at the mouth, how she saved Creed's life in the middle of the big lake. And he remembered her face at the top of the high ridge when they first looked down on the valley of the Coppermine that was her home. And how she had taught him to listen to the Earth and contemplate its question: *"Il-viunna-hugi-vit?"* Are you who you appear to be? All that time she was hiding herself from him. She was a woman, and the most amazing woman he had ever encountered. And now it was his turn to answer the Earth's question, and the Earth would want the truth, the whole truth, and nothing but.

PART TWO

Thirteen

The train from Peace River slowed like a toboggan after a good downhill run. It passed brick-walled factories and rows of little clapboard houses, unpainted in the haste to accommodate the ballooning workforce. It slowed to a crawl as it approached the Canadian National North Station in the city of Edmonton.

Creed took a deep breath to calm himself, focus, and prepare for his re-entry into civilization. He realized he was dreading this on many levels: living for weeks in a crowded city, resisting the temptations of any intimacy with Angituk, sorting out his relationship with Nicole, carrying out his job properly as a peace officer while trying to protect Uluksuk and Sinnisiak. The latter worried him the most. He had almost blocked from his mind the potential outcome of this case, but now, as the train neared their destination, he knew that the full weight of the judicial system, not to mention the Catholic Church, would be brought to bear on his two prisoners. How could he think it would end any way but badly?

As he spoke to Angituk and the hunters, he could not keep

the sarcasm out of his voice. "Welcome to Edmonton, 'Gateway to the North,'" he announced.

"Don't you mean 'Gateway to the South'?" Angituk corrected him.

"You're absolutely right."

Sinnisiak stared with amazement at the size of the white man's village, on the verge of outright panic. Before Fort Norman he had never seen large wooden buildings or horses, or even wheels. The houses appeared like long, uniform rows of little square mountains. So many white people, and the noisy motor cars and trams, possessed of malevolent spirits. Edmonton was overwhelming to him, a fearful, magical land. "Are all of these people our enemies?" he asked. "When we go outside, will they all fall upon us like the men in Fort Norman? How will we ever get home? Where will I relieve myself with all these people around?" He paused. "Do you think they have seal meat here?" Sinnisiak turned to Angituk for answers.

"I don't know," she responded.

"Will we have to shake hands with everyone?"

"I don't think so."

Sinnisiak stared out at the baffling, congested village, his heart pounding. "I'm hot. Does it get even hotter here?"

"Maybe. I'm not really sure."

Uluksuk gave Sinnisiak a look that told him to stop asking questions and observe and learn. Uluksuk took in the sights of the white world with a detached interest. He had, after all, experienced exotic travel before, to the moon and the bottom of the sea. But this was no less interesting to him as he gazed out the window.

"We must remember, this is only a dream," he told his nervous companion. "I sense there will be just as many evil spirits here as in the North—probably more, so we'll have to be careful. I will use my charms and chants often. I hope they will work here. But what will be will be, and in the face of it we must retain our dignity and perspective."

Angituk had been to enough white settlements to have seen multi-storey buildings before—though never ones nearly so high or so numerous—and the vehicles that moved without dog teams, using engines like the one that powered the riverboat, but it was the sheer number of people in the streets and railway yards that amazed her. Far too many to count. How could anyone ever find a particular person here? Where would she start looking?

Creed spoke to Uluksuk with affection and reassurance and Angituk translated.

"Are you ready for this?"

"Yes."

"They will not hurt you."

"I am prepared for this adventure," Uluksuk told him.

"Good." Jack smiled sadly at him as the train came to a slow, shrieking stop.

A FINAL TELEGRAM had told Creed to expect a small welcoming contingent and to have his prisoners ready with him, dressed in their "Native garb." Still, Creed wasn't prepared for the fanfare that greeted them. As they appeared at the door, a company of twenty-five Royal North West Mounted Police officers in formal dress came to crisp attention and a military band struck up a rousing version of "The Maple Leaf Forever."

Creed studied the prisoners, who were overwhelmed by the crowd, the noise, and the intimidating vastness of the city beyond. Angituk too was in awe, but she smiled at Creed under her fedora. He quelled the impulse to take her hand.

When the verse was finished, the band fell silent and

Superintendent Worsley came forward. Creed descended the two steps and returned his salute.

"Corporal Creed reporting, sir!"

Worsley gave him an enthusiastic handshake. "Welcome home, Creed. Well done! Bloody well done, indeed."

"Thank you, sir."

Angituk, Sinnisiak, and Uluksuk all stepped down, staying as close to Creed as possible. Worsley assessed the prisoners for a moment, then gestured to four officers behind him, who began clapping manacles and shackles on their hands and feet.

"That's really not necessary, sir."

The Super replied quietly, "Orders from above, Creed."

One officer was trying to put handcuffs on Angituk, who, though dismayed, held out her hands as ordered.

"Not him, Constable. He's the translator," Creed told him.

When the prisoners were suitably restrained, Worsley himself positioned Creed between Uluksuk and Sinnisiak in front of the train, then gestured to the press that this was their moment. Six cameramen rushed forward and flash powder began to explode. Creed tried to turn away, but finally Worsley ordered him into a posed shot and he obeyed. Sinnisiak cringed at the flashes as if he'd been shot.

Sinnisiak looked to Jack, who gave him silent reassurance. Sinnisiak stood still, though he continued to look worried.

The officers tried to hold the crowd back as it surged forward to see Creed and the primitive murderers.

There were press from the *Toronto Star*, the Montreal *Gazette*, and of course the Alberta papers, both the *Edmonton Journal* and the *Calgary Herald*. The *Chicago Tribune* had a man and there was another from the *San Francisco Chronicle*. A New York reporter, E.K. Mainprize, whose train had just come in that morning, was delighted to be there for the arrival. A friend had telegraphed him about this strange little murder case. He would see to it that it made headlines in *The New York Times*. He had already interviewed Worsley and called out to him now.

"You should be in this, Superintendent."

"Don't mind if I do."

The Superintendent stepped into the frame, taking Creed's place beside Uluksuk. Creed stepped out, relieved, but Worsley ordered him back in. Uluksuk studied the Superintendent for a moment, then duplicated his stance and expansive smile. The Superintendent noticed Angituk off to one side.

"There's the translator. Come in, Mr. McAndrew. Into the picture."

Showing fear for the first time, Angituk shook her head.

"Come on, man. You're an important part of this."

Reluctantly, Angituk stepped in beside Sinnisiak, hat in hand, her chopped hair shadowing her downcast face, which was turned slightly sideways from the camera. There was another round of photos taken of the five of them.

A short distance away in the crowd, Nicole Harvey surveyed it all. Her gorgeous face was bright with a proud smile. Her hair was bobbed and curled in the most recent Paris style in solidarity with that war, and she wore a long silk dress and jacket with heels. She held back, waiting for the right moment.

"Jack!"

Creed only had a moment to glimpse her before she ran to embrace him, and kissed him on the lips. Creed was startled, first by the public kiss and then by how natural she felt in his arms.

She spoke intimately, her throaty voice in his ear. "This is so exciting, Jack. Look what you've done! I'm so proud of you, darling."

The camera flashes were going off like artillery and all Creed could do was smile.

"Thank you, Nicole."

Angituk had watched as the attractive white woman made her way through the crowd with her eyes so intent on Creed, like a wolf after a young caribou. Creed talked closely to the woman and they shared a smile and a kiss. Suddenly Angituk felt a thousand miles away from him.

Mainprize had taken out his little notebook. "Pardon me, Miss Harvey. Corporal Creed? E.K. Mainprize of *The New York Times*. Did these cogmollocks give you any trouble?"

"They realized they had little choice and came along quietly."

"Would you call them Stone Age men?"

"They have no forged metals." The other reporters were scribbling notes.

"Is it true they are cannibals?"

"Well, I ... I think you'll have to wait for the trial on that."

"From the place of arrest, how far is it to Edmonton?"

"Maybe ... fifteen hundred miles."

"Fifteen hundred miles! And were there times you feared for your life—not to mention your limbs?"

This garnered some laughter. Suddenly a dozen reporters were shouting out queries and the Superintendent stepped in.

"All right, gentlemen. Corporal Creed and I have to debrief."

Worsley gestured to the attentive bandleader, who had been looking over his shoulder at the Superintendent, arms and baton raised. They started up with "It's a Long Way to Tipperary."

Lyle Cowperthwaite pushed his way through the crowd to Creed, grabbed his hand, and pumped it. He needed to shout over the enthusiastic music. "We're so proud of you, Creed! So proud!"

"We'll walk to the detachment," Worsley instructed.

With an arm gesturing in the air and the band continuing to play, Worsley led Creed and the others south along 105th Street.

The municipal police officers struggled to maintain an open route for them down the crowded street. Worsley walked with a determined step, his face set and serious. Creed followed, with Nicole smiling and proudly clutching his arm. Behind them walked Uluksuk and Sinnisiak, both shuffling along in their shackles with an officer on either side. Angituk brought up the rear. The crowds fell back to make room and stared at what the papers had called "Stone Age Cannibals" with absolute fascination.

Sinnisiak and Uluksuk stared out at their surroundings: the tall buildings with faces at the high windows, an electric tram, a Clydesdale pulling a heavy wagon.

"How do they grow those dogs so big?"

"I don't know."

Sinnisiak peered back at the faces in the crowd. "They're not going to grab us again, are they?"

"I don't think so," Uluksuk reassured him. "They would have done so by now. But don't show them you have fear. Pretend they are bears or walruses. Stick out your chest and raise your hands."

The two hunters put their shackled hands in the air to show their courage and intimidate the crowd. The crowd was delighted. The cannibals were waving! Two hundred arms waved back at them in welcome.

Sinnisiak was amazed. "I never dreamed anything like this place could exist."

"Maybe it doesn't."

The procession made a left onto Jasper and continued east. The band marched behind them in the street, now playing "Pack Up Your Troubles in Your Old Kit Bag."

Angituk, walking alone, was trying to get a glimpse of Creed up ahead and didn't immediately notice that a young reporter had fallen in step beside her.

"You speak English?"

"Yes."

"You're the interpreter, right? You went with Creed?"

"Yes."

"Did you see the bodies of the priests and everything?"

Angituk was intent on keeping watch on Creed and the question didn't register.

"What do you think of Edmonton?"

"It's very big. So many people," she answered distractedly.

Angituk decided not to try to see what Creed was doing. She didn't want to think about Creed or the woman. She had another idea now and suddenly looked the young man in the eye and asked him, "Do you know Angus McAndrew?"

"No."

Angituk picked out certain faces in the crowd as she walked along and asked them, "Do you know Angus McAndrew? Do any of you know Angus McAndrew?"

Blank, white, slack-jawed faces stared at the half-Eskimo boy. Angituk tried a few more times, shouting over the music, but no one responded to her question. They were passing Wellington Terrace now, overlooking the wide brown river. Straight ahead of them, the police barracks waited like a castle fortress.

As they approached the detachment, Superintendent Worsley, Creed, and Nicole continued toward the front entrance to the building while other officers grabbed the arms of Uluksuk and Sinnisiak and directed them around to the holding cells. Angituk followed. They looked to Creed for reassurance, when suddenly he turned back to them for a moment, raised an arm, and shouted out over the crowd, "It's okay. Go with the officers."

Angituk translated this for the prisoners while she watched Creed and the blond woman enter the detachment together. Then they were gone.

CREED SAT in the walnut-panelled mess with the Superintendent, his friend Lyle Cowperthwaite, and several officers, drinking whiskey. As a woman, Nicole was banned from the mess, but she had cheerily ordered Creed to meet her later that night for dinner at the Macdonald, kissed his cheek, and left him to his colleagues. After a toast to Creed, Cowperthwaite brought in several copies of the afternoon *Herald*. The headline read STONE AGE MAN MEETS BRITISH LAW!

"It's a huge story, Creed. There are journalists and law professors from all over North America coming into town to observe the trial. England, too. And a couple of Frenchmen. It's something other than the war. Who is that fellow ... Edwin Keedy? From the Harvard Law School in Boston. He's brought twelve postgraduate students to observe."

Creed smiled at Cowperthwaite's enthusiasm. "I had no idea."

"You're a hero, Creed. A real hero."

"I was lucky."

Superintendent Worsley interjected. "What you did represents the basic tenet of the force, Creed: to maintain order and prosecute the laws of the Dominion throughout our country, even unto the North Pole!"

"So you're saying if Santa Claus started stealing toys—"

The other officers laughed. Creed had to make light of the accolades. In truth, he found them irritating. Any man here could have done what he did. He was lucky, that's all. Creed took a long drink from his whiskey and his thoughts drifted again to Angituk.

ULUKSUK AND SINNISIAK stood naked and shivering in the shower stalls of the detachment as two officers, stripped to their undershirts, roughly turned the hunters around and sprinkled them liberally with powdered insecticide.

"They don't seem hostile. Mine is even smiling a little," Uluksuk commented.

"That is good in our culture, but as you have told me, the Cree smile before they kill you."

"I do not think they mean to kill us. Why would they have brought us all this way? Creed would not let them."

"Let us see what they do."

The two RNWMP officers were firm with them, giving orders in a language they didn't understand. The showers were a shock, but the warm water felt good on their skin. The officers held them still at first and then released them when they did not resist.

Sinnisiak turned to Uluksuk. "Look how they control the rain to make it fall in this small spot."

"They are very smart."

"And so nice and warm. It must come from the sun."

The officers handed each of them a bar of soap, but they both found it tasted terrible.

"This isn't caribou fat!"

The officers gestured impatiently for them to rub the soap on their bodies and the hunters understood and did so with enthusiasm.

"You smell so good, like spring flowers."

"I am going to do what they want so I can stay a long time in the warm rain."

"Good idea."

A new man in a white coat came to see them, and he didn't smile at all at first. He put his hands on them in different places, and examined their eyes and teeth. Uluksuk warned Sinnisiak when he pulled back.

"It's all right. Let him. He is a shaman checking for bad spirits."

The white shaman placed on their chests a cold metal circle that was attached to his ears.

"Very interesting, giving sounds he hears to our hearts," Uluksuk said aloud. "I must make one of those."

The doctor announced to no one in particular, "Excellent specimens. Fine physical shape." And though they did not understand, Sinnisiak and Uluksuk were pleased to see him happy. They smiled and nodded back to him.

They were given plaid shirts and blue denim trousers. The material felt scratchy compared with the silky deer and caribou hide they were used to, but the officers gave them candies to compensate and the prisoners felt that was a good deal. The candies gave them little bursts of pleasure they'd never experienced before.

Sinnisiak felt the light material of the shirt between his fingers. "I wouldn't want to go into snow wearing this."

"Don't worry. I don't think we'll be going into snow any time soon."

The final transition was the hair. Two men sat them in chairs with blankets around their shoulders and used scissors to cut their long hair and beards. The hair fell to the ground. Uluksuk admired the tools as he sucked another humbug.

"Look at that. Two knives, hinged. The blades opposing each other to cut. It is so simple. These white men are not stupid. We should have thought of that."

The white men were still not satisfied and went at them again with other very sharp knives that trimmed off the hair on their faces and heads. Sinnisiak panicked for a second when the man came at his neck with the knife. But the officer made reassuring noises, and Uluksuk told Sinnisiak again to be calm.

"We are at their mercy, and they seem merciful."

When the white men were finished, the hunters' heads

looked like big clean rocks and they laughed at each other, but then wondered what was next.

TWO ENTHUSIASTIC OFFICERS at first tried to process Angituk in a similar way. She held them off with her knife as she explained in fluent English who she was and that she could do her own ablutions. Angituk had expected to stay with Uluksuk and Sinnisiak beside their cell until a representative from the prosecutor's office, named Mr. Ainsley, explained that as an official interpreter they needed her together with the other members of the court in the hotel.

"Will Corporal Creed be in the hotel?"

Ainsley checked his list. "Yes, he is. You can eat in the dining room and charge your meals to your room. Just sign the bill they bring you," Ainsley told her. "Let me know if there's anything I can do."

Even though the Hotel Macdonald was only a few blocks from the barracks, Angituk had to ask people on the street three times for directions to it. There were no bushes or big rocks or streams to identify the place. Carrying her knapsack past the bowing doorman, she found her way, in accordance with Ainsley's directions, through the three-storey lobby. It caught her breath for a moment as she looked up at the ceiling and turned completely around. It reminded her of the pictures of cathedrals in Father Ducot's book. Then she went on to the "check-in." Ainsley had underlined "check-in."

The assistant manager gave her a reserved smile. "What can I do for you?"

She wondered where to start, and after a moment of verbal stumbling under his inquiring gaze she finally thrust the letter toward him. His smile expanded and he told her, "Welcome to the Hotel Macdonald, Mr. McAndrew. We're pleased to have you."

An enthusiastic young man in a dark red uniform insisted on carrying her knapsack down the long hallway and around the corner. He talked very fast. He unlocked a door and welcomed her in, spreading curtains, turning on lights, and opening doors with such familiarity that at first she thought it might be his own room, but he insisted it was hers alone. The young man pointed out the bath salts, ran the water in the bath until it became steaming hot, then turned it off, and headed for the door.

"There's always a good supply of hot water if you care for a bath. You can have extra towels if you like. Just ask. Dinner's served between five-thirty and eight o'clock. Oh, and you have to press the door lock down hard in this room or it will flip up and open." He showed her, tapping the lever with his finger. "Press down hard and it will stay. Any laundry or shoes to shine can be left outside your door before six a.m. And there is wake-up service if you need it."

He stood in the doorway and smiled and put out his palm. She reached out and shook his hand enthusiastically in the way white people do. He looked slightly disappointed but smiled again cheerily.

"Good night and enjoy your stay with us."

Angituk wandered around the room in awe for several minutes. It was more beautiful than any place she had ever been in her life. There were flower-print bedsheets on a bed easily big enough for four people, and a bathroom right through the door with running hot water and a dressing table with a big mirror. It was even nicer than Father Ducot's house in Fort Norman. She tried switching the lights on and off a few times. She turned on the tap to fill the bath with hot water and threw in a handful of the granules that smelled like flowers, marvelling to see bubbles emerge; and while the tub filled, the slim girl spent her time bouncing up and down on the springy bed.

Fourteen

Early the next morning, Angituk sat beside the cells in the detachment reading a magazine from a pile beside her. She was not quite used to the isolation of her beautiful hotel room, and though she had enjoyed the bath and the soft bed she couldn't shake the suspicion that someone would come and claim the room back. She still felt more at home with the prisoners.

She had never seen anything quite like the magazine she was inspecting. But she found the pictures fascinating. All the long thin women wore long thin dresses with their chins high and some with round hats pulled down to their eyes. This was beautiful, she guessed, to white people. Just like the yellow-haired woman on Creed's arm. Angituk shook away the dark thoughts she had about the blond woman and continued leafing through the fashion magazine.

Uluksuk and Sinnisiak sat quietly in their cell. Uluksuk's stomach had been giving him trouble for two days. The white food was not agreeing with him and he had thrown up twice that morning, feeling terrible embarrassment. It was the first time in his life food had come up. Angituk had given him wet towels to clean himself and water to drink. Overheated and restless, they had both had trouble sleeping through the night. Uluksuk's eyes were closed and he seemed to be sleeping now. Sinnisiak was looking at one of the magazines too. It was called *Harper's,* and he also marvelled at the skinny white women.

"Uluksuk. Look at this." The old man opened his eyes, his stomach still giving him pain, and surveyed with disapproval the slender woman in the picture. "This one is obviously starving," Sinnisiak continued. "Their men must be poor hunters."

Uluksuk nodded and closed his eyes.

"They would be so cold and bony to sleep with. I can't see them pulling a qamutik very far. I doubt they could even set a snare."

Uluksuk nodded again without opening his eyes.

"Maybe good for a rich man."

There were other compelling pictures in a different magazine. There were men with guns in the mud. Angituk showed them to Sinnisiak.

"Look. This is what Creed told us about. The war across the ocean."

There were pictures of guns so big it took four men to load the bullets and fire them. There wouldn't be much left of a caribou with that firepower, Sinnisiak thought. Other photos showed long holes in the earth where men lived like ground squirrels and where the mud was so deep that wagons and horses and men became stuck in it. There were pictures of dead bodies, men without arms or legs or even faces. This was how white men made a war. Angituk and Sinnisiak studied the pictures in silence. It occurred to Angituk that this was the source of the deep sadness she sensed in Creed.

She leafed back to pictures of things to buy: clothes and motor cars, and machines that could be hot or cold by pressing a button. One item that caught her eye was a woman riding something called a bicycle. Two round wheels. She would like that. A bicycle to ride along the road. But why didn't it fall over?

So many mysteries. She looked at the woman in the picture, who appeared quite confident. If she could do it, Angituk could. But the woman reminded her again of the yellow-haired woman and her mood darkened, just as Creed came in.

"Hello. How are you doing?"

Uluksuk woke up and he and Sinnisiak were very relieved to see him.

"Hello, Creed! Hello!" Sinnisiak spoke the English words well.

Creed took Uluksuk's hand in his through the bars and smiled at the old man sadly.

"How are you doing?" Creed asked again.

Angituk's response revealed more irritation than she wished, but she couldn't help it. "You can see. They have cut off all their hair. And they put them in those white men's clothes. Uluksuk is sick. He doesn't like the overcooked white food. It's mushy. They have taken away their dignity. And they don't sleep well on the wool blankets. It is too hot. You have not cared for them very well."

Creed turned toward Angituk, surprised by this attack. "Well, I can get cotton sheets and maybe a small fan and raw fish."

"Maybe they should have run away from you after all."

Creed looked down, studying her for a moment. "What's wrong, Angi?"

"Nothing. You just went and left us alone."

"Look, why don't we go for a walk?" Creed suggested.

"No. Thank you. I don't like Edmonton."

"Come and see more of the city."

"I have seen enough."

"Come and see the river. There's a beautiful new bridge."

"I've seen plenty of rivers."

"How do you like your hotel room?"

"It's too hot and dark and smells like soap."

"There's a park you could see with pathways and gardens in bloom."

"Then why don't you take your yellow-haired friend?"

Creed was taken aback. "Oh. I see."

Angituk would not look into his eyes.

"Angi? Look at me." She did not. "Nicole is just a friend."

"Does she know that? You say Uluksuk is your friend. I never see you kiss him like that." Angituk sniffed away an angry tear with irritation.

"Well, you're right. Once we were more than friends, but not now." Creed caressed her cheek with his hand. "Angi, I do love you. That hasn't changed."

"No? I thought maybe it was a dream."

"It's real, Angi."

Angituk looked up at him then for the first time, wanting so much to believe. "Yes?"

"I do have to make things clear to Nicole. And I will. I just haven't had a chance. Things are complicated. She is the niece of the Justice, the *Ishumatok* who will be the judge of Sinnisiak and Uluksuk. She has a lot of influence on him. Just give me a little time."

"All right."

"Will you come for the walk?"

She looked at him pointedly. "Yes. After you make things clear to her."

Creed didn't hide his disappointment, or a whiff of irritation. "Okay, fine. Probably for the best."

CHIEF JUSTICE HORACE HARVEY threw a small dinner party for Creed at his mansion just off Saskatchewan Drive, overlooking the North Saskatchewan River. Nicole had helped her uncle through his grief for his wife and now looked after him like a daughter, filling the house with a warm and festive feeling. Harvey adored her.

He sat at the head of the table with Creed on one side and Nicole on the other. Harvey's son, Harold, was a captain on leave from Edmonton's Princess Patricia's Canadian Light Infantry. He was friendly and pleasant with Creed, a good-looking young man. He had been stationed at headquarters in London, England, and Creed hid his disappointment on hearing that after his leave he was set to assume a command for the first time on the Belgian front.

"I can't wait to get there, Jack. I've been training for more than a year. I want my chance to teach the Boche a lesson."

Creed nodded and smiled sadly. He had spoken those same words a lifetime ago.

Next to Harold was an English friend, Lieutenant Richard Wilkerson, who frequently played with his thin moustache and eyed Nicole's cleavage too often. He had seen a bit of action the summer before at the Somme and would make the most of it with any encouragement at all.

When the staff had cleared away the dishes, the Chief Justice held up a glass, his eyes shining. His affection for Creed was obvious. "Let's have a toast. To Jack Creed! For demonstrating courage, endurance, and fine police work. I hear there's already a promotion to inspector in the works. And only fitting. To Jack!"

Nicole reached out and patted his hand as they all raised small stemmed crystal glasses that reflected the light from the huge chandelier above, reminding Creed of fresh, still Arctic snow at noon.

He lowered his eyes and smiled. "Thank you, sir, for your complimentary words, for this esteemed company you've gathered here, and for this excellent claret. But let me say again, the element most at work in my travels was blind luck."

"Too modest, Jack!" Harold insisted good-naturedly. "You must have had at least one eye open."

"Maybe one," he said over the laughter.

The most recent newspapers were brought in and distributed.

"Have a look at these," the magistrate directed them.

There were copies of the *Edmonton Journal*, the *Toronto Star*, the Montreal *Gazette*, the *Chicago Tribune* and *The New York Times*. The headlines read: THE MOUNTIES—RED-COATED GUARDIANS OF THE LAW—GET THEIR MEN, and from the *Times*: CANADIAN LAWS ENFORCED IN ARCTIC DOUBLE MURDER.

"There's the important one," the Chief Justice declared. "We have enforced our laws in our land. And that's what will resonate in Moscow and Washington when we begin to tax and regulate the whalers and lumber companies up there."

"Yes, but the public doesn't care about that, Father," Harold said. "The press is covering it because of the murder investigation and the Eskimo and the sort of people they are."

"And that they ate the livers," his English friend, Wilkerson, added. "My God. That's outstanding."

"You know," the Justice continued, "what makes the case fascinating is that the brutes seem so docile, so amenable— yet the crime reveals their duplicity. They have confessed to actions—and you yourself have seen the grisly results, Jack— that prove they are nothing less than savages!"

Creed calmed his angry reaction. "One thing I can say, sir, is they are not savages. I think you will find it interesting as an educated man, when all the facts are presented, how morally intact they are."

"But we must send a message to their kind: you can't get away with murder," said the Justice.

"They are here to face judgment. With all due respect, sir, I hope you will keep an open mind."

There was silence at the table at Creed's remark, which verged on impudence.

"Do you actually think them anything more than primitive Neanderthals?" Wilkerson asked Creed.

"They are certainly more than that. They live a simple life, true, but they think and feel, show kindness, affection to their wives and children, have a very complex and subtle language, they tell jokes, appreciate beauty, are sometimes worried ..."

"As well they should be, charged with murder," said Harold.

"Surely they'll hang," Wilkerson asserted.

Creed gave him a sharp look. "We shouldn't assume any conclusion before the facts are heard."

Harold spoke up. "What was it like, living with them?"

"After the first few days with them I began to feel secure. They had resigned themselves to going to Edmonton. They hunted and cooked for us. They once cared for me when I was ill."

"Maybe they were just fattening you up, Corporal." Wilkerson smirked, and everyone laughed.

"So you became quite chummy with these men?" Harold asked.

"Impossible not to be when you eat and sleep and travel with them for almost a year."

"Are you concerned your 'relationship' might bias your testimony?" the Justice asked, turning Creed's earlier comment back on him.

"That is a true concern for me, sir, but no greater a concern than that these men be written off by the jury as vicious animals."

"Let me get this straight, Corporal." Wilkerson gave him a thin smile. "You would like us to see these two men as fine, civilized chaps when they knifed, shot, cut the throats of these poor priests, and then ate their—"

Nicole spoke up. "Enough, Lieutenant. Not at the dinner table, please."

"My apologies, Miss Harvey. Truly." Wilkerson looked grave. "It was thoughtless of me."

Creed glared at the pandering Wilkerson. "Lieutenant, you consider England a civilized nation, don't you? And yet isn't what you've just described exactly what's going on in the battlefields of France? Ten thousand times over?"

"What a ridiculous comparison!"

"Don't we all knife and shoot and cut the throats of the enemy, machine-gun them down, blow them up, gas them, burn them out, in order to ... in order to what? What are we doing over there?"

There was a moment of shocked silence.

"Are you a pacifist, Jack?" the Justice inquired with a note of concern.

"I believe in peace, sir."

"But you were in the war, Nicole told me."

"Yes. I served."

"What unit?" Wilkerson asked with sudden interest.

"Second Canadian Battalion."

"What regiment?" Harold now asked the question.

"Fourth Princess Louise."

"So what are you doing here?"

"Discharge. I was wounded a short time after the second battle of Ypres."

Harold was excited, speaking for everyone's benefit. "You were at Ypres number two!" Creed nodded and Harold continued. "The first time the Germans used gas. Opened a gap four miles wide in the French lines. Killed every soldier that didn't run. If the

Second Canadian Battalion hadn't moved in and held fast against them, filled the gap, and then counterattacked, the square-heads would have broken through and taken the Channel ports. Cut our supply lines. They would have won the war!"

"Possibly," Creed agreed. At least he was proud of that.

Nicole's eyes were shining at Creed and she reached across the table to take his hand. "You've never told me any of this. You were wounded?"

"Minor. Recovered now. My shoulder is restricted. I was lucky."

"I never heard the Fourth Princess Louise were at Ypres," Wilkerson suddenly ventured, creating an abrupt silence.

"Well, the English have never done well keeping track of the success of their colonials. The Canadians retook the French trenches and then, when the British failed, we took the German ones too."

Wilkerson looked at him coldly. "As I recall, the Germans made a strategic withdrawal."

Creed laughed sincerely. "They did, did they? I think we might have helped them make that decision, just a little."

Harold broke the cold silence. "That's marvellous, Jack. To think what you've been through."

Creed was saddened again to think of this handsome boy leading an assault into German guns.

"A hero twice over!" the Chief Justice declared, and downed the rest of his claret.

OUT ON THE EXPANSIVE WRAPAROUND porch framed in delicate gingerbread, Creed and Nicole strolled alone, his hand a little tentative in both of hers. A wind chime tinkled pleasantly in the warm, gentle wind off the river.

"I'm so proud of you."

He smiled gently. "You'll have to stop saying that."

"Not at all! Almost single-handedly bringing the rule of law and civilization to the High Arctic! That's what my uncle said. And it's true. All because of you."

"I did my job," he said lamely.

"It's just all so clever of you, Jack. No one will underestimate you again. You're going to go a long way. I'm going to see to it."

"What do you mean?"

"Oh, just something we'll talk about later. Give me a kiss."

Nicole raised her face to his, and he couldn't bring himself to do it. He had decided to break off their relationship that night, but he now understood that to lose her as an ally in the trial could be disastrous. For a second her face held a look of concern, then as a compromise he kissed her cheek, gave her an enthusiastic hug, smiled, and the awkward moment passed.

"Jack, what shall we do?" she asked, now lightly.

"About what?"

"About us, silly. I waited for you. All this time apart. I was angry at you at first for going off on your adventure, but then I realized how much I loved you. I will always believe that love trumps everything. Don't you?"

"Yes. Love is the important thing."

"I thought perhaps we could talk about the engagement. Even make an announcement. If you want."

"We've been apart a long time, Nicole."

"You haven't gone and fallen in love with some Eskimo princess, have you?" she asked with a note of playfulness.

Jack studied her for a moment. "I just need a little time to sort myself out."

"It's true—the trial would eclipse the engagement announcement in the newspaper. Can't have that."

"No."

"All right, then, after the trial. Right after the trial, we'll make the announcement. Because the executions might not be for weeks or months after."

"The executions?" he said with sudden alarm.

"Well, it's possible they could hang them, darling. That's what my uncle said."

This was what he was afraid of. "I don't want to see them hanged, Nicole."

"Well, I appreciate you've grown attached to them. You've been very kind to them. Very fair. But my uncle says we have to send a message. And you've provided the perfect opportunity with their capture. That's why he's so pleased with you. You're his golden boy."

Creed wondered how he might countervail the bias this trial was promising without showing his own. One thing was certain: breaking off his relationship with the Justice's favourite niece would not strengthen any influence he might have with the court. He hated living this lie. But then, it was only one more.

He took her hand as an idea came to him. "Nicole, why don't you come with me. Come and meet them."

"Really? Now?"

"Yes, now. Why not? Tonight. Before the trial. Just for a minute."

"What about the guests?"

"No need to tell them. The detachment's only ten minutes away. We'll be back in no time. It would mean a lot to me."

"All right. I would love to!"

CREED TOOK NICOLE through the back door of the detachment and down to the cells. He turned up the new electric lights and found the two hunters sleeping in their cell.

"Uluksuk, Sinnisiak," he said quietly. "I have someone for you to meet."

They began to stir slowly.

"Do they speak English?"

"No, not a word, but the interpreter is around here somewhere ..."

Angituk had sat up in her cot in the corner of the open area and stared at the interlopers. Was this a bad dream? It was Creed and his yellow-haired woman. What could they be doing here? Angi wondered.

Creed turned to her. "Angituk? I'd like to introduce a friend to them. Could you translate?"

Angi felt no need to give an answer as Creed and the woman were looking intently at the hunters, who rose sleepily from their beds and then stood up straight behind the bars. The woman smiled at them and nodded.

"We're sorry to get you up," Nicole offered.

Creed continued more formally, gently. "Uluksuk, Sinnisiak, this is Nicole. She wanted to meet you before the trial."

There was silence and Creed said to Angi, "Can you translate, please?"

Angi hesitated, then spoke in Inuinnaqtun to the hunters. "The bitch's name is Nicole."

Uluksuk and Sinnisiak both glanced at Angi in surprise at her harsh assessment but then turned back and smiled at Creed's woman.

"Is good to meet you. May you have good digestion for many days," Uluksuk offered, and Sinnisiak nodded and they put out their hands as the white men liked to do.

"It's okay," Creed assured her.

Nicole, at Creed's urging, tentatively shook hands with each of them in turn through the bars, the sentiment needing no translation.

"She is the niece of the man who will judge you. The *Ishumatok*."

Creed looked to Angi to translate, and she did. "Apparently she's the niece of the *Ishumatok* who will decide what to do with you, so you should be nice to her, even if she is ugly."

The hunters politely moaned their understanding and appreciation and nodded to Nicole, who turned to Creed, delighted.

"They're really quite charming, aren't they?"

"I told you."

Nicole studied their expectant faces for a moment. "Well, I'm glad you have come to visit us and we are happy to have you in our town and I hope things ... work out for the best."

Nods and smiles all around.

"Angi?"

"She is pretending she cares about you. So you better smile and be nice to her because she can help you or she can really ruin your lives."

Uluksuk and Sinnisiak did not miss a beat in their warm smiles, their ingratiating nods and then, at the end, in unison, their thumbs-up. Nicole laughed at the thumbs-up and offered her own.

"Good night, then," Creed offered, and guided Nicole out of the cells area.

"Good night," the hunters said, their pronunciation good.

Creed looked back to give a smile of thanks. "That was very good, Angituk. Just wanted her to meet them." But what he caught was the icy cold gaze of Angituk just before the door closed behind him.

"What do you think?" Uluksuk asked her when Creed and the woman were gone, noting her caustic mood.

"I think Creed's choice in women improved on the Great Bear River."

And that was a good reason for them all to laugh.

A SHORT TIME LATER, Angituk left the cells for the front office where Corporal Cowperthwaite was on night duty. Though she was free to come and go, she stayed close to the cells for Uluksuk and Sinnisiak's sake. She was also there because the thought of going out into the city with all those people was intimidating.

She had given herself an encouraging talk. She had a job now and money and a position at the court. She could handle herself with white people. Furthermore, she had an important quest here in Edmonton.

Angituk went up to Cowperthwaite. He had an open face. "Sir?"

"Your name is Angituk, correct?" he said cheerily.

"Correct."

"You can call me Lyle, lad." He smiled.

"Lyle. There is someone living in Edmonton I want to find but don't know where to start."

"Do you know the name?"

"Yes. Angus McAndrew."

"Ah! Chinese!"

"Pardon me?"

"Just kidding. He's Scottish, then. Like ninety percent in this town."

"Yes. That's right. Scottish."

Cowperthwaite lifted up a thick book and placed it on the counter. "Here are the municipal lists. Let us see ... let us see ... let us see ... Mac ..." He leafed through to the appropriate pages. "McAndrew, McAndrew ... a few hundred. Angus, you say?"

"Yes, please."

He ran his finger down until it slowed and stopped. "Here you are. Angus McAndrew. There's three of them. I'll write their addresses down."

"What are 'addresses'?"

Cowperthwaite looked at her blankly for a moment then realized. "Ah, yes. Well, they are the street names or numbers where the house is, and then the number of the house."

"How do you know the street names?"

"Well, there are street signs posted ... up on poles ... with the names, and then on maps ..." Cowperthwaite brought out a folding map to show her. He opened it up and they bent over it to examine the streets of Edmonton together. "See, there's the streets and most of them are numbers, some names, like ... see, Jasper or 106th Street."

"What is that long blue thing?"

"That's the river."

"But it's brown. I saw it."

"True. Quite true, but never mind. It's blue here. And here—look here—these are the avenues."

"Why is there an 'NW' after the number?"

"Oh, that means North West ... or here, South East. It's the southeast part of the city. Get it?"

"I ... get it. And the houses have numbers too?"

"Yes. On the outside. So the first address is 106 Avenue NW, which is here"—he ran his finger down the line—"and the house number is 651, which is probably about ... here. You have to go and look."

"It's complicated, eh?"

Two officers came in with a drunken suspect and Cowperthwaite turned away from her to deal with them for a moment. Angituk quickly folded up the map and hid it under her shirt. She made her way inconspicuously toward the door.

"Good luck, Angituk," Cowperthwaite called out to her. "And when you're finished, bring back my map."

She gave him a big smile, acknowledging the theft. "Thank you."

"By the way, who is this fella McAndrew?"

"Just a man my mother knew."

ANGITUK WENT BACK to the cells where the prisoners were sleeping and laid out the map of Edmonton on the floor under the hanging electric bulb. She stared at it until she had found and circled in pencil the streets where each of the three Angus McAndrews lived. She considered each location with excitement and fear. He was so close to her. Now all she needed was the courage to find him.

Fifteen

Just after dawn at the pillared brick courthouse on 102nd Avenue, the crowd began to queue up for the trial of the Eskimo cannibals. An enterprising merchant selling peanuts and lemonade from a cart gave a carnival atmosphere to the gathering. The municipal police were on hand to keep order, stop queue jumpers, discourage pickpockets, and guide the line of spectators in an orderly fashion into the courtroom. They had to limit the overflowing numbers, leaving the disappointed and disgruntled outside. The officers chased young men and boys off the high outer windowsills and away from the crowded doorways. It was widely known the trial would be an event to see.

The courtroom was packed, with three rows of spectators standing at the back and some sitting up on the deep ledges of the banks of tall windows on both sides. The temperature rose with the sun, and although there were two brass electrical fans overhead in the high corniced ceiling to stir the hot, laden air, they offered little respite from the rapid rise in body heat.

Creed sat in the front row in his dress uniform, a dark blue tunic and light blue breeches with a gold stripe down the leg, his stetson on his lap. He looked up to the empty ornate leather chair behind the bench set high on the dais. Chief Justice Harvey had yet to arrive. He was referred to as *Ishumatok* ("the Thinker") to the defendants by the interpreter Ilavinik, an older Copper Eskimo the defendants had never met, dressed in a baggy tweed suit and white shirt buttoned to the neck without a tie. This word caught on among the journalists. It was their first Inuktitut word. They tried it out on each other.

On the evidence table before Creed was Le Roux's rusted .44 Winchester octagonal-barrelled rifle, a blood-encrusted cassock and a torn surplice, the damaged skull of Father Rouvière, a crucifix, a silver paten for serving the Eucharist, a bible, a weathered journal, and letters and pictures Creed had brought back.

Over to his right, facing the bench and the witness box, the jury of six—all Edmonton businessmen in expensive, conservative wool suits of brown and blue, long ties, one bow, one winged collar, three with pocket watches, three with watches on their wrists, Creed noticed—sat with expressions committed to the determined pursuit of justice. Creed recognized W.H. Martin, a city alderman, and Alfred F. Fugl, district manager of the Hudson's Bay Company.

To the left, at the defence desk where most eyes in the courtroom were directed, sat the defendants, Sinnisiak and Uluksuk. They were dressed in their Native clothes: the brown caribou-skin summer shells, the necks trimmed with a strip of white fox. These had been fumigated and washed. Creed had argued that the defendants would roast in these clothes, but the prosecutor, C.C. McCaul, had insisted on "authentic garb" so the jury might see them as they were when they were arrested.

McCaul was disappointed that their hair and beards had been closely cropped. As a concession to their sensitivity to the summer heat, beside each defendant was a small electric fan and a large tub of water containing big chunks of ice so, according to the court staff, they "will not be disoriented by their surroundings in the courtroom and can cool off." Into these tubs they could dip their hands and feet as necessary. They both spoke with Angituk, who was beside them to offer translation, but they turned every once in a while to get a reassuring smile from Creed. Creed realized that in this strange world he and Angi were the only links between their past and their present.

Sinnisiak munched the little candies he had developed quite a fondness for and gazed around at the people. He leaned toward Uluksuk and whispered, "This is an impressive dance house. Look at these people. Are they all here for us?"

"I think so."

"Who feeds them all?"

"*Ishumatok*. Angituk says he's the Best Hunter. Probably out hunting now. This must be his tribe."

"There can't be many caribou around here."

"That's probably why he's late."

"He would need eight or ten just to feed all of these people once!"

Sitting in the front row to Creed's left were Bishop Breynat and an assisting priest, both of them in long black robes almost to the floor. The Bishop was a good-natured, energetic man who Creed was surprised to find had made several Arctic journeys, mostly along the Mackenzie. He and Jack had spoken of Father Rouvière. Breynat's affection for the young priest was apparent and the grief at his passing intense.

Creed turned with one arm over the back of the bench to look around the courtroom. Nicole, who sat three rows behind, gave him a little wave and repressed a giddy smile and he smiled back. No question she was stunning. Radiant. He might be a fool, but his life was running on instinct now. He looked beyond her.

Cowperthwaite had briefed him about the surprising variety of attendees. There was a press section on the left rear side with earnest, note-taking journalists from across Canada and the United States, including the eager E.K. Mainprize from *The New York Times*. The *Edmonton Journal* had two reporters on the story. There were European representatives from the London *Times* and French-Canadians from *La Presse*, and a very unpopular but determined gentleman from the *Deutsche Zeitung*. No one knew why he hadn't been detained. "Germans love Indians," was all he would say. There were several professors and scholars of law from Osgoode Hall in Toronto and McGill University in Montreal, and, remarkably, the twelve postgraduate students from Harvard Law School brought to observe the trial by their famous mentor, Dr. Edwin Keedy. Finally, a small group of ethnologists had reserved seats, including New Zealander Diamond Jenness, one of the few white men in the world to have travelled and lived with the Copper Eskimos west of where Creed had been. He was writing a book on his travels. Creed had met him a few days before and shared some Arctic stories. They raised a hand to each other.

Prosecutor C.C. McCaul was a large, handsome man in his fifties with a thick moustache waxed and tweaked at the ends like exclamation marks. His long black robes added to his air of authority. McCaul had been a cowboy, a prospector, a businessman, and an explorer in his youth before turning to law at Osgoode Hall in Toronto. He had come back west, dabbled in politics, and settled into law, on the side of the Crown. Sitting motionless, turned in his chair to face the courtroom, his eyes half closed as if conserving his energies for the battle ahead, he exuded the complete confidence that a long, distinguished career afforded him. His powerful aura unsettled Creed. McCaul was renowned for his photographic memory and Creed noted that the table before him was bare of notes.

In contrast to McCaul, at the defence table to his left sat a thin man with a pronounced Adam's apple and several piles of notes he shuffled nervously. He seemed lost in his black robes. James Wallbridge was the defence counsel for Sinnisiak and Uluksuk, and this was his first murder case. His long, bony nose and spectacles were downturned in contemplation of the notes before him.

Angituk sat beside Wallbridge as a secondary translator, to ensure "fair play" and to interpret for the two defendants. She was dressed in a dark, baggy man's suit Mr. Ainsley had found her and a white shirt buttoned to the neck like the old translator Ilavinik. Creed watched her as she studied the people around her with a mixture of intimidation and excitement. An ache came over him again as he imagined the confident woman's body under the man's clothes. And when her blue eyes suddenly shifted to his with a tentative smile, there was no doubt—he was helplessly in love with the girl. But, he reminded himself, that would have to be put very carefully aside for now.

The private side door of the court opened. "All rise!" Justice Harvey seemed to float in his long black robes up the three steps to the chair high on the dais behind the bench.

"Court is in session!" announced the clerk.

"Let the charges be read," the Justice instructed.

Mr. McCaul stood up. "Your Lordship, the Crown is proposing to try the two accused on the murder of Father Rouvière alone at this time."

"I object!" The skinny, furtive Wallbridge was on his feet.

"Your indulgence, Mr. Wallbridge." Justice Harvey registered his impatience. "Mr. McCaul, are you suggesting then a second trial for the murder of Father Le Roux? I am deeply concerned this will unduly lengthen the proceedings."

"If I may explain, your Lordship, on the contrary, I hope to save time. This is owing to the fact that at the time of his murder Father Rouvière was unarmed and actually running away. We are confident of a conviction here and if we get the sentence we seek, the second trial will be unnecessary."

The Bishop stood up. "I object! You are saying you will not try them for the murder of Father Le Roux?"

"No, Bishop Breynat. We will certainly try them if we have to. We are saying there is no use in trying ... condemned men."

A surly voice came from the rear of the courtroom. "Can't hang 'em twice!"

There was laughter and Harvey banged his gavel three times. "That's enough of that! I'm warning you once: there will be no such outbursts in my courtroom or I promise you the penalty will be severe."

The courtroom was silent.

"Good, then. Bishop Breynat, please sit down and, with respect, please don't interrupt again. Mr. Wallbridge, I am overruling your objection. Clerk, read the new charges."

Wallbridge sat down. Bishop Breynat was still troubled by the ruling but offered no further comments.

The clerk began: "Sinnisiak and Uluksuk, you stand charged that in November of 1913, at a place near Bloody Falls on the Coppermine River in the Northwestern Territories, you did murder one Kuleavik, alias Father Jean-Baptiste Rouvière, a Roman Catholic missionary."

"How do you plead?" Harvey looked down at them.

The interpreter Ilavinik asked them if they had killed the priest. Sinnisiak and Uluksuk looked at each other for a moment and began to nod.

"Yes, we killed the priest. Oh, yes, we killed them both," Ilavinik translated, and a loud murmur filled the court.

Wallbridge was on his feet. "May I have a moment, your Lordship?"

"Go ahead, Counsel."

Wallbridge spoke quietly to Uluksuk and Sinnisiak. Creed watched them, numbly realizing again that it was possible they would be hanged. He had done his duty as an officer. What had he expected the court to do—award them a medal?

Sinnisiak turned and whispered to Uluksuk. "But we did kill them."

"I know, but Older Brother is saying we should say no."

"We should lie?"

"I guess so. It is complicated. Anyway, Creed said to trust him."

"Okay, but will you explain it to the spirits tonight so they won't be angry at us for lying?"

"Yes."

Uluksuk and Sinnisiak finally nodded that they understood and Wallbridge returned to his table.

"Shall we try this again, Mr. Wallbridge?"

"At your pleasure, your Lordship."

"How do you plead?"

This time, in perfect unison, they spoke in English the words: "Not guilty."

"Very well," Justice Harvey declared. "Let's proceed."

CROWN PROSECUTOR Charles Coursolles McCaul did not spout rhetoric. He spoke from deeply held convictions. A cloud drifted across the bright sun as he began, lending a sombre and dramatic element to his opening statements.

"Gentlemen of the jury, you should consider yourselves lucky.

Lucky, because you are to witness a trial absolutely unique in the history of North America: the murder trial by a modern court of what are essentially two Stone Age men. You will have before you a thrilling story of travel and adventure in lands forlorn, and I am quite sure that after you have heard all the story you will agree with me that too much credit cannot be given to the young police officer who is here, Inspector Creed, for his discretion and for his splendid courage in effecting their arrest. It is extraordinary in that this one police officer, Creed—not a soldier, mind you, a 'peace' officer—investigated, located, and arrested these two individuals out of a whole tribe of Eskimos with whom the priests were working and living. Contrast this, I ask you, with what would have happened elsewhere if white men had been killed by a tribe of savages—in central Africa, Borneo, the Philippines, Mexico, or even our neighbour to the south. Let me tell you: a retributive military force—a punitive force—would have been sent against the tribe and the tribe would have been decimated, possibly even exterminated. I offer Wounded Knee, South Dakota, as an example—December 29, 1890, only a scant few years ago. A white man killed somehow, and Hotchkiss machine guns were turned on three hundred men, women, and children.

"But here in Canada, instead of these warlike measures, British law—Canadian law—reaches a strong hand out to the distant shore of the Arctic Ocean in the person of one Corporal Jack Valentine Creed, and says, 'We have found the two men we hold responsible for these murders. We have no quarrel with the rest of the tribe.' And here, gentlemen of the jury, is the essential thing! British justice is not about retribution. It is not a justice of vengeance! There is not a bit of vengeance in it. These two men will receive a fair and impartial trial. We have educated the Blackfoot and the Cree and the Stoneys and the Sarcees and the

Chipewyans that our justice is a fair and impartial justice, and we must spread that message to the Eskimos, the message that they are under the law. They must regulate their lives and dealings with their fellow man accordingly. They must respect the principles of justice, not just submit to it. They can take advantage of it, be protected by it. And this message must be heard out on the barren lands of North America, on the shores of the Arctic Ocean, on the ice of the polar seas—even as far as the Pole itself!"

McCaul paused to pull the handkerchief from his sleeve and wipe the perspiration from his face. He was pleased by the vacuum of silence in the courtroom. Every ear strained for his next word.

"Hard on the footsteps of the explorers in North America have always followed the Roman Catholic missionaries. Canadian history furnishes us with many, many examples of their courage, their fortitude, and their martyrdom, braving hardships, starvation, and death to spread the word of God. Gentlemen of the jury, whether we agree or not with the dogmas and tenets of the Roman Catholic Church, all good Christians must acknowledge and respect the zeal and fervour, the courage and fortitude of the Catholic missionaries who sought to bring a knowledge of God and the divinity of Christ to these human beings. The very God in whose name we have here sworn today to render justice!"

McCaul was in full flight now, demonstrating all his talents of oratory. He paced the courtroom floor, commanded the stage, and the audience went with him willingly.

"Bloody Falls. The irony would be amusing were the crimes not so cruel and dreadful. They sought only to bring enlightenment to these people, and what happened?" Here McCaul's deep voice broke for the first time. "The murderers stabbed them, several times, shot them, cut their throats, mutilated them, and then went back to their tribe, bragging of their deed!"

Creed listened, deeply alarmed. This was the tangent he feared most. McCaul's eyes filled with tears of sorrow and fury. His voice cracked again with emotion as he continued.

"They told the whole of the revolting details to the assembled crowd. They told, gentlemen of the jury, how, after they had killed these men, they ripped them open, tore out their livers, and each ate a portion." He whispered the word: "Cannibalism!"

Two women in the middle of the courtroom had their handkerchiefs out, sniffing back tears. McCaul pulled out his own handkerchief again to address both the perspiration and his own hot tears. He paused for a moment, staring down at the floor, overcome with emotion.

Creed had found the opening comments both inspired and entertaining, but now McCaul finished with a dark new message.

"The lesson we must teach these people is that a life is sacred. Murder cannot be tolerated. And if they commit it, they will be caught and arrested, they will be tried, and if they are found guilty of murder, they will be made to pay the required penalty. We must render justice, swift and sure, and send this message north: not justice done but justice taught! I expect you to do your duty. Nothing less than a guilty verdict and the ultimate penalty are acceptable in this case. Thank you, gentlemen."

Jack sat there stunned. They were in fact going to try to hang them.

As McCaul sat down, Wallbridge stood up. "I object!"

Harvey took a deep breath to summon his patience and Creed's heart sank a little deeper. There was a flurry of muted conversation in the courtroom. The ultimate penalty was on everyone's lips: death. "They're going to hang 'em."

Uluksuk looked askance at Angituk, who moved over to sit beside him.

"What did that man say?" Uluksuk asked her.

"He thinks you should be killed," Angituk told them without hesitation. The defendants exchanged a look of shock.

Mainprize and his colleagues hurriedly made notes. Two ran for the telephones. The Bishop and his priest seemed satisfied as they smoothed out their long black cassocks and adjusted the crucifixes in their sashes. The jury remained stone-faced. Harvey called the room to order.

Wallbridge continued. "I object, your Lordship, to my learned colleague's pointed statements calculated to prejudice the jury by unfair and inflammatory remarks! Such an epic display of rhetoric leaves little chance for a fair trial. It seems to me it would hardly be right to proceed unless you empanel a new jury."

McCaul responded as if personally insulted and stood again to reply. "I believe I put the case quite simply, your Lordship, but you must admit that with a case of such importance we must expand the context beyond merely outlining evidence. But again, I leave myself in your Lordship's hands."

Justice Harvey cleared his throat. He wanted to get on with it. "I am of the opinion this jury can be trusted, Mr. Wallbridge. Therefore, your request is denied. The court would now like to hear your opening remarks."

Wallbridge rose and faced the jury. He swallowed deeply, his Adam's apple bobbing, and consulted his notes for a moment. "I submit that by the time you have heard all the evidence, you members of the jury will conclude that the killings were justified. Thank you."

Wallbridge sat down and there was a moment of shocked silence. Creed stared at Wallbridge. Justice Harvey was as shocked as anyone.

"Is that all you have to say, Mr. Wallbridge?"

"It is at this time, your Lordship."

Creed glared at him and leaned forward to whisper, "That's it? What are you doing?"

"The jury doesn't want another earful right now. They want to get on with the trial."

Creed bit his tongue.

Justice Harvey addressed the court. "It is almost noon. This court is adjourned. We will resume at two o'clock to hear the Crown's case." Justice Harvey rose and disappeared through the side door.

Everyone in the courtroom stood but Creed. He had no impulse to join in the cacophony of conversation around him. Creed looked over at Sinnisiak and was amazed to see the Eskimo propped comfortably in his seat in a deep, blissful sleep.

WITH THE NEW RANK OF INSPECTOR, and the title of Chief Investigating Officer in the case, Creed was the first witness to be examined by Crown counsel McCaul. His black eyes peered into Creed's.

"Now, Inspector Creed, you are a distinguished veteran and survivor of the war that still rages across the ocean in Europe?" The black eyes prompted him to respond to the rhetorical question.

"Yes."

"You have seen a lot in your young life."

"It has been my privilege."

Creed wondered why he had made that pompously humble statement. It was no privilege. He wished he'd never seen Europe. McCaul was manipulating him already.

"You travelled many months across uncharted lands enduring these hardships of isolation to investigate and make arrests in this remarkable case."

"I enjoy the land and the travel, sir. It was no hardship for me."

McCaul recognized this direction of questioning was gaining no points.

"Tell us what you found at Bloody Falls."

"There is a high granite hill that the Coppermine River dissects at the falls, and to the west, down a slope, I located the qamutik sled that belonged to the priests. On the far side I located the remains of Father Le Roux."

"How did you know it was the priest?"

"There was a hand-sewn tag on the scrap of shirt: *Père Le Roux.*"

"Can you describe the remains?"

"They had been dead almost three years. They had had protection under flat rocks. The cold had dried them. Mummified them, in fact. Wolves or foxes had been at them and some of the limbs had been scattered, but I was able to study parts of the torso and determine the cause of death."

"What did you determine?"

"Father Le Roux had been stabbed, several times. And there was trauma to the skull."

"Did you locate Father Rouvière?"

"I did. He was some fifty yards away. His body was in a similar condition. Animals had taken much of him away, but I determined in the mummified torso and the splintered rib bones that there was a gunshot wound in the upper back and several knife wounds to the skin of the torso. The head had been cleaved, halving the skull, I assume by an axe."

"In both cases you could assess the stomach skin of the torso. What did you see there?"

"In both cases there were identical crescent-shaped incisions in the right abdomen."

"And what did these indicate to you, Inspector Creed?"

"Similar incisions are made by the Eskimos in a caribou

they have killed. It would indicate that the livers had been removed."

"And presumably consumed immediately, do you think?"

"That is custom, so I think that not unlikely."

One of the women who had been sobbing earlier that morning tried to stand up and collapsed in a faint in the aisle. Harvey declared a ten-minute recess and disappeared into his chambers while the clerks and several men in the audience attempted to revive the woman. She was gently carried out by two men, semi-conscious.

"INSPECTOR CREED, after leaving the scene of the crime, in your search for the murderers you arrived at the mouth of the Coppermine on November 2, 1916, according to your notes, and met with a community of Eskimos there. The leader's name was Koeha."

"That's correct."

"What did he tell you?"

"He told me the two priests had lived with them for a few days three years before. At that time food was scarce at the mouth of the Coppermine and the priests had decided to return to the South. They set off up the river with a sled and two dogs. Two days after the priests left, two hunters from a neighbouring camp passed through on their way up the Coppermine allegedly to meet relatives on their way down."

"And what were their names?"

"Uluksuk and Sinnisiak."

"The defendants."

"Yes, the defendants."

"Please continue."

"These two hunters passed through the camp and headed south, following the priests. Three days later they returned with many of the belongings of the priests, including their rifles, cartridges, and clothing. They told Koeha they had killed the white men."

"Objection." Wallbridge stood up. "This is hearsay."

"Sustained. The jury will ignore the last statement."

"All right," McCaul continued. "Koeha saw they had the belongings of the priests."

"Yes."

"And that was almost three years ago now."

"Correct."

"And when you arrived there last year, did Koeha tell you where these murderers could be found?"

"Yes. They were camped just up the coast."

"And you risked life and limb to apprehend them."

"I went after them. Located them in their camp ... with their families."

"And did you ask them if they had killed the priests?"

"I did. They informed me that they had, and inquired as to whether I would kill them on the spot."

"They asked if you were going to kill them! So they knew retribution was on the way?"

Wallbridge had been waiting for an opportunity to slow the Crown's momentum. "I object to that statement of conjecture."

"Sustained."

"Did they fear you?"

"I'm not sure. I think probably. But they were very co-operative."

"No further questions."

"I believe they felt very badly about the deaths of the priests."

"That'll be all, Inspector. Thank you."

WALLBRIDGE STOOD UP to cross-examine Creed. He sensed fertile ground for his clients' defence in the sentiments of Creed.

"I would like to ask you, Inspector Creed, about your impressions of the Copper Eskimo."

McCaul rolled his eyes but offered no objection.

"They are living in what we would call a very primitive state," Creed told the court. "They have had little or no exposure to the white man. They are a simple people, kindly as a rule."

"What about their intelligence?"

"Well, they are very clever in their work. They adapt brilliantly to conditions. They are inquisitive ... curious. But their minds don't work like ours."

"They compare more with children, don't you think?"

"That's a hard question to answer."

"But you've said they are a simple people."

"Yes. Simple. But in no way helpless or dependent. They want to examine everything and see how it's made, how it works."

"But they are what you would call primitive."

"Yes. Relative to us, they are primitive."

Creed avoided the glare he was getting from Angituk.

"And what do you know of their religion?"

On this one, McCaul objected. "The witness is not a trained ethnologist. His comments will be subjective and speculative."

Justice Harvey gave Creed a gruff smile. "Still, I'm going to allow it for my curiosity. Please answer the question, Inspector."

"My understanding is they believe in many gods or spirits, who have the potential to be good or bad. Probably the most powerful is Hila, who controls the weather. They neither love her nor hate her. She just is. And they try not to offend her. I believe they find their world full of magic, with marvels happening around them every day. There is no heaven and hell as we know it. Their mythologies are often about fantastic transformation: a boy becomes a fish becomes a bird becomes a tree that becomes a man. Fantastic, but not unlike many of our Christian beliefs."

This caused an uneasy whispering in the courtroom that McCaul picked up on and interrupted. "May I have a point of clarification, your Lordship. Is the witness comparing Christianity to these simple pagan beliefs?"

"I'm thinking how plausible all our beliefs sound to them: the virgin birth, the loaves and the fishes, water into wine. But their religion is more centred on a philosophy of rituals and taboos."

"Things they should do and they should not do?" Wallbridge prompted.

"Yes. They do not cook land animals on the ice, or vice versa, or the spirits would be angry. Certain foods are forbidden. They do not sew on a full moon. They do not carve tools near their tents or during lightning storms. They never allow an animal to suffer. There is a time and season for each activity. They weave virtually everything in the natural world into a spiritual pattern of life."

"Governed by good spirits and bad spirits?"

"Correct."

"You would call them, then, superstitious?"

"No more than us. It was not that long ago we burned the last witch in England. They fear the unknown. Rightly so. Up there any day could be their last, and so the act of living each day brings them ... joy, I guess."

"Can you tell us about their custom when they kill a caribou?"

"Before skinning and butchering, they cut off some meat, often organ meat, some to eat and a little to give to the spirits."

"The spirits from the caribou."

"Yes. They want to keep them happy or the caribou may not come again."

"Very well. Now, at the time of the arrest you were forced to stay in their igloo for the night. In fact you shared sleeping quarters with these accused murderers for months on the return trip to Edmonton. Were you not in fear for your life? They could have slit your throat and put you under the ice."

"They wouldn't do that. I wasn't a threat and I wasn't food."

"So, you feel safe among the Eskimos?"

"As safe as anywhere in the world."

McCaul objected again to these subjective and irrelevant details that were "muddying the waters." Justice Harvey agreed. Wallbridge set off on a new line of questioning.

"Inspector, you spoke at length with Koeha, the leader of the people at the mouth of the Coppermine, and you copied down a statement from him about the events at the camp before and after the deaths of the priests and had him sign it. I would like you to read from that statement—"

C.C. McCaul interrupted. "I am sorry, but surely my learned colleague realizes the witness cannot swear to the testimony of someone who is not in the courtroom. It is nothing but hearsay, as my colleague challenged me on the statements of Mr. Koeha during Inspector Creed's testimony. He can't have it both ways. Mr. Koeha could have been telling the Inspector a complete fantasy story. If you wish to offer this evidence, you'll have to produce the witness and swear him in."

"But your Lordship, this evidence pertains to the physical and mental state of the priests, to events leading up to the killings and afterwards that clearly help explain—"

"I'm sorry, Mr. Wallbridge. I agree with Mr. McCaul. With all due respect to the accuracy of Inspector Creed's notes, Koeha's statements are hearsay and not admissible without Koeha."

Wallbridge was visibly deflated. "No further questions, your Lordship, but I do wish to retain the right for future cross-examination of this witness."

"Very well, Mr. Wallbridge."

Wallbridge sat down. He looked at Angituk and shook his head.

Sixteen

The Crown's next witness, Father Duchaussois, a short and heavy-set man with large brown eyes, had been a college roommate of Father Rouvière. He was having difficulty controlling his brimming emotions. He identified Father Rouvière from a photograph taken by Father Ducot in Fort Norman just before Rouvière went up the Great Bear River for the first time. McCaul asked Father Duchaussois to translate from Father Rouvière's writings. He began reading from an old and faded letter to Father Ducot, one of the ones Creed had brought back. Creed remembered it was written just as the priest began his first trip north. Duchaussois translated the letter's conclusion:

> So far the Good God has kept me healthy and I pray each day to preserve me so I will be able to complete this difficult mission which has been entrusted to me, to teach these people of the one true God. No one knows how many there are or what sort of people they are. There may be some difficult ones—some "tough nuts," up there, but I trust they are too good-hearted to put up much of a fight against grace. I rely upon your prayers.

C.C. McCaul approached the evidence table and picked up the mutilated and weathered diary that Creed had found beside the sled. He placed it in Father Duchaussois's hesitant hands. The battered little journal, an artifact of and witness to the final massacre, held an aura not lost on anyone in the courtroom. McCaul asked the priest to read from the first marked entry. Father Duchaussois took a moment to gather himself before translating the excerpt, dated four years earlier:

> October 8, 1913. We have started on our way north to the mouth with an Eskimo guide, Kormik, and his people. We have started very late in the season. Hornby was to take us in June, but he disappeared. So now we travel with Kormik, one of the last Eskimos to return north. Though this summer we have met with many of the Copper Eskimos, not knowing their difficult language has been a source of much frustration. How can we explain Jesus' parables of the farmer when these people have never planted seed or taken a harvest? How can we explain "breaking bread" and giving Communion when the people have never tasted bread? Even explaining the Crucifixion in a land with no trees. It is so difficult. We feel we have failed to make the Eskimo understand anything of Christianity. And Father Le Roux's impatience with these people doesn't help us. He has already made an enemy of our guide, Kormik.

McCaul gently encouraged the priest to turn to the next marked place, and he began again:

Tomorrow we arrive at the mouth of the Coppermine, the centre of the Copper Eskimos' hunting grounds— and the chance that I have been waiting for, for three years. This is where I dreamed of building a church, welcoming a congregation, "sending a few specimens to paradise," as the Bishop had challenged. We have made it here. But not without cost. We are both ill and severely malnourished. The language has almost defeated us. Something as simple as "Be good and you'll go to heaven" is impossible to translate. The only word we can determine for "good" means "an effective hunter." But "morally good"? We have no idea. And Father Le Roux has been little help. He is not the linguist I was led to believe, among other things. But the Father is aware of his own quick temper and is trying to subdue it. Soon we will make our way south again—such a long trip—back to the cabin. The snow is heavy. We don't have much food. We are tired. Mother Mary grant that I survive to further your work.

The priest took a deep breath and steadied his voice.

"And now the short, final entry in the journal, Father, the last thing Father Rouvière would write," McCaul gently directed, and the priest bowed his head to the text:

We are at the mouth of the Coppermine. We have become disillusioned by the Eskimos here. Many families have already left. We are threatened with starvation. Also ... *nous ne savons que faire.*

At this point Father Duchaussois broke down and could not

manage a translation of the final line. Creed looked at the jury and found sympathetic faces.

McCaul eyed the clerk in expectation. "The last line translates: 'Also, we don't know what to do.'" McCaul's voice was hushed and empathetic. "Thank you, Father. *Je connais qu'il est très difficile pour vous.* You are free to go."

THE EMOTION OF THAT FINAL LINE in Rouvière's journal resonated with Creed. "We don't know what to do." After studying the murder site, determining the events that led to his death, and hearing Rouvière's voice in the lines of his journal, Creed was perhaps the only person in the courtroom who could truly know what Father Jean-Baptiste Rouvière had experienced.

The two priests had been in retreat, and Rouvière's thoughts, Creed was sure, would have turned to the man who walked in front of him.

Creed knew that Rouvière had had such high expectations for Father Le Roux: a young companion and brother in faith to share the joys and disappointments of his important ministry. A philosopher to encourage, stimulate, and keep it all in perspective during the three months of constant, oppressive night that approached. A young, fit shoulder to share the crushing physical burden of travel and survival in the High Arctic. A linguist to help unlock the mysteries of the Copper dialect. Rouvière had tried to give him time to adapt and settle in, he made excuses and blamed himself, he had sent encouraging letters to the Bishop about Le Roux's attempts to curb his temper when working amongst the people, but in all honesty, Father Le Roux was an arrogant, insolent, domineering racist.

Father Le Roux had been a toxic influence from the beginning. He had driven away the guide Hornby. He had complained about the lack of good food and wine and creature comforts, of the weather, of the tedious landscape, of the smell of the people and the small numbers of souls to save. He had carried a stick and actually used it on a few of them when he grew impatient—an outrage! Though fluent in Latin, Greek, Spanish, and Mandarin, Le Roux had declared the Copper language indecipherable. Creed wondered if, and surely Father Rouvière suspected that, Le Roux had been sent to this posting as a penalty or at least a lesson in humility. In learning this lesson, Rouvière's colleague had failed completely.

From what Koeha had told Creed, one of their most fundamental disagreements had to do with tolerance for the pagan beliefs. Father Rouvière had been convinced he could introduce the Christian belief structure slowly into the pagan one. These people already understood the importance of taboos in bringing prosperity and good health; concepts of sin and salvation would fit in nicely. Slowly the truth of the Christ would take over and the pagan beliefs would die. Death was to the Eskimo nothing but a gloomy end, but the priests could give them the gift of the Kingdom of Heaven after death! Father Le Roux, on the other hand, according to Koeha, was set to immediately forbid the Eskimos' pagan beliefs—a belief system so closely intertwined with almost every daily act and decision in an Eskimo's life—as sinful nonsense, even "devil worship"! He had knocked down the *inukshuks*, believing them idols, thrown handfuls of the amulets and dried animal parts he had taken from the people into the fire, and angrily put his hands over their mouths if Eskimos tried to sing spirit songs.

Creed believed Rouvière, on that final day, would have told himself it was not hopeless. He would winter at Imaerink, resupply from Fort Norman, and return alone here in the spring to the Coppermine to pick up the pieces of his alienated congregation. He would beat those Anglicans coming in by ship from the Mackenzie delta to poach in his land.

WITH THE READINGS of Rouvière's letters and journal, McCaul had finished the presentation of the case for the Crown. It was Wallbridge's turn to bring out the only witnesses for the defence: Sinnisiak and Uluksuk.

Sinnisiak came to the stand first, sweating and terrified. He looked around at the alien faces staring at him and was on the verge of panic. Because Sinnisiak was not a Christian, the clerk dispensed with the bible and spoke the words that Justice Harvey, McCaul, and Wallbridge had agreed upon for Eskimo witnesses: "Whatever you speak now, you speak straight; do not speak with two tongues. Do you so promise?"

At the aggressive tone of the clerk, Sinnisiak looked desperately toward Creed, on the verge of losing control. Creed wondered what he could do to somehow put him at ease. He needed something to ground him, something familiar— and the idea came to him. Creed croaked like a raven. He started with a great squawk and descended into a muttering monologue like those they had heard on spring mornings on the Great Bear.

The Justice glared at Creed. "Inspector! Have you lost your mind?"

But Sinnisiak's stricken face had relaxed. The hunter laughed out loud. "That's good!" Sinnisiak told the judge, speaking in Inuinnaqtun. "Creed does that really well!" And the tension was broken.

Again Justice Harvey summoned his patience, gave a cautionary glance at Creed, and addressed his remarks to Wallbridge. "Let us proceed."

The clerk repeated the instructions, "... do not speak with two

tongues. Do you so promise?" and Sinnisiak thought of ravens
and relaxed.

"Yes," he said in English.

Wallbridge turned to the interpreter, Ilavinik. "I want
you to tell Sinnisiak he has to speak to the big hunter and
thinker: *Ishumatok*. Tell him I want him not to be afraid and to
say everything. I don't want him to be afraid because all these
people are here. Just talk as if he is talking to me alone."

When Ilavinik gave this message to Sinnisiak, the young
hunter thought a moment and nodded. "I am not afraid."

Sinnisiak took his place in the witness box. Creed nodded
encouragingly to him. It would be all right.

"Mr. Sinnisiak, can you tell us your age? How many summers
old are you?"

Sinnisiak thought hard about this and began to count on his
fingers. "I'm not sure. I think I am maybe ... eight."

The courtroom filled with laughter when this was translated
and people exchanged amused glances. The sound of the gavel
brought a speedy silence.

"You are eight years old?"

Sinnisiak surveyed the audience suspiciously. "Maybe ten. I
am not sure."

Wallbridge was pleased with his response. He showed
Sinnisiak a photograph of Father Rouvière at Fort Norman and
he identified it.

"That is Kuleavik."

"Let the record show he has identified Father Rouvière.
Please tell us what happened at the mouth of the Coppermine."

Sinnisiak spoke slowly and clearly, allowing Ilavinik to
translate, but the old man did his job very laboriously and
deliberately. Everyone in the courtroom realized this testimony
was going to take ages.

"I was at the mouth of the Coppermine River with Uluksuk. We were fishing there, but the fishing was poor. Our tent was near the camp of Koeha, where the two white men were staying."

"The two white men: Kuleavik and Ilogoak?"

"Yes. We heard they were going back south up the river. Uluksuk and I were planning to go up the river to fish at the falls and to meet my cousin who was coming down, but we didn't want to travel with the white men, so we waited."

E.K. Mainprize checked his watch. The word-by-word translation dragged on in a numbing monotone.

"Were you afraid of the priests?" This question took a full minute to hear and translate.

"Yes. They were the first white men we had ever seen."

"What was your impression of the white men?"

"They were strange. Big and pale, with the features of their faces gathered around sharp noses like a marten or weasel, or demons the shamans told stories about. So we waited two days at the mouth."

Suddenly, Ilavinik spoke angrily in Inuinnaqtun to Sinnisiak. The old interpreter appeared to be accusing Sinnisiak, who tried to defend himself, arguing with him. The young hunter looked to Creed for help. Angituk turned angrily to Wallbridge and explained: "He's telling Sinnisiak to confess! He accuses them of going after the priests to steal their guns. That they planned to murder them all along!"

Wallbridge was on his feet. "Your Lordship, my interpreter Angituk McAndrew informs me that apparently this interpreter is putting Sinnisiak through the third degree, accusing him of lying and trying to get him to give an answer which the Eskimo clearly does not want to give."

Ilavinik defended himself. "But it is true."

Harvey looked weary. "We are all here to discover what is true, Mr. Ilavinik. Not your opinion."

Seizing an opportunity, McCaul interjected, "Still, I feel it my duty to point out, your Lordship, that even their own people believe them guilty."

Harvey was furious. "Mr. McCaul, that has nothing to do with anything, and I strongly suggest you restrict yourself from such cheap, unprofessional snipes in my courtroom! Clerk, strike Mr. McCaul's last statement from the record. And jury members, you will ignore that last comment by Mr. McCaul."

McCaul looked sheepish.

"So where does that leave us?" the Justice mused.

In the moment of silence that followed, Creed summed up their prospects as rather bleak. McCaul was running roughshod over Wallbridge, they had no defence witnesses who had met the priests, and the Eskimo interpreter had made it clear he believed the defendants were lying. The whole thing was going exceedingly poorly. He looked over at Angituk and the two worried hunters.

Just then, three men brusquely entered the courtroom. Creed and Angituk both stared at the new arrivals with surprise and relief. It was John Hornby and Koeha from the mouth of the Coppermine! They were accompanied by Corporal Oberly from Fort Norman, in field uniform. Koeha was wearing his light summer sealskins, while the diminutive Hornby sported an old wool coat with an astrakhan collar and was holding a fox-fur hat in his hands. Angituk smiled at Wallbridge and told him loudly enough for everyone in the courtroom to hear, "It's Koeha!"

Wallbridge could not believe his ears: the one witness who could turn this trial around. A murmur of excitement passed through the courtroom and every head turned to see the new faces. Wallbridge asked for the court's indulgence and gestured the men up to the front. Koeha stared around the room in awe at the number of people and the impressive structure of the court. Creed stood and shook hands with Koeha, Hornby, and Oberly.

"They just showed up in Norman one day," Oberly explained. "We thought you could use them."

"You thought right."

Koeha gave Angituk a friendly wave and smile.

"I decided to come and see how they live down here and what goes on with Uluksuk and Sinnisiak," Angituk translated for Koeha, as happy as Creed to see him.

Creed then introduced Koeha and Hornby to a delighted Wallbridge. Both men could prove huge assets to the defence. Koeha was pleased to see Creed, but he and Hornby were intimidated by the crowded courtroom.

Justice Harvey banged his gavel and they all jumped. "Mr. Wallbridge, I can see this is a happy reunion, but may we please get on with the business of the court."

"Of course, your Lordship. As you may have heard, this is Koeha, the leader of the Coppermine camp where the priests ministered. And this is John Hornby, who guided for Father Rouvière. If it pleases the court, my next witness."

McCaul objected to the unforeseen introduction of these defence witnesses, but Justice Harvey overruled him. "I'd like to hear what they have to say. They have come all this way for our benefit, Mr. McCaul. So I will agree, Mr. Wallbridge, as long as we can proceed in a timely manner."

"Then I'd like Mr. Sinnisiak to stand down temporarily, your Lordship, and I will examine Misters Hornby and Koeha to establish a context before the critical portion of Sinnisiak's testimony."

Justice Harvey allowed it.

"Finally, your Lordship, I must object to continuing with the present interpreter," Wallbridge came out forcefully. "Mr. Ilavinik has proven himself biased against my clients and must be replaced."

"Well, then, what about your interpreter, Mr. Wallbridge? Let us have your boy take his place, shall we? If he's capable."

"Oh, he's capable, your Lordship."

"Very well, then. Mr. Ilavinik, you may go."

Wallbridge looked at Angituk with a nod of encouragement. Ilavinik stood up with a hostile glare at Sinnisiak and another at Angituk, then exited the courtroom. Angituk looked at the vacant chair she was about to fill. John Hornby took the stand, a little unnerved by the hundreds of faces.

"Mr. Hornby, can you start by telling us about when you first met Father Rouvière," Wallbridge inquired, "and your impressions of him?"

"Yes, I can."

The court sat in silence, waiting.

"So will you do that for us, please?"

"Oh! Yes, of course."

In his halting, slightly confused manner Hornby spoke about Rouvière with affection. "Very good-natured. Always cheerful. Never complained. Not the most skilled in living in the North, mind you. He'd make an awful mess of skinning a squirrel. You know, it's harder to skin a squirrel than a caribou. I once skinned nine caribou in a single day. It was at Thelon River in nineteen hundred and twelve. Or was it the Calder River in eleven?"

"Yes, Mr. Hornby, but what about Father Rouvière?"

"Father Rouvière wasn't on the Calder River."

"No, I mean ... the Dease and the Dismal Lakes."

"The hunting season is early there. After the first of November there's nothing."

"No, we want to know about Father Rouvière when you guided him on the Dease. How did you get along?"

"Oh, very well. He was a very good man. Good heart. He'd make jokes. And he sure loved the Huskies. The Eskimos."

"Did he feel his ministry was progressing among them?"

"Well, we only met them the once, for a few days. He was frustrated he couldn't speak their lingo. He was hoping this new priest would learn to communicate with them."

"You mean Father Guillaume Le Roux."

"Yeah, that one."

"You met Father Le Roux in Fort Norman."

"Yes. I like to go into Norman. There's an Indian woman there makes a great bear stew."

"But what about Father Le Roux?"

"I don't know if he liked the stew or not. I don't even know if he tried it. You have to cook it long and slow or the meat is tough and oily."

"Yes, Mr. Hornby, but please tell us your impressions of Father Le Roux."

Hornby thought about this a moment and then unleashed an uncharacteristic flood of clear comment and description.

"Le Roux was a first-class, grade A horse's ass, ordering people around. Especially the Cree in Norman. Can only imagine how he acted among the Huskies. And they're a sensitive bunch. Right away he started in on me about my sins. Didn't like my girl, Arimo. Then he takes half my supplies, 'for the glory of God,' he said. I'll give him glory. But the worst thing was how he treated Father Rouvière, ordering him around, speaking to him like his superior. I felt badly for him, but I wasn't going to stay and guide them if Le Roux was there. So that was it. I quit them in Norman. And that was the last time I laid eyes on them. I do feel badly for what happened."

When Koeha was called to the stand, Justice Harvey gestured to Angituk. "Mr. McAndrew? Please take your seat."

She looked at Creed, proud in this new responsibility. She stood and went to sit in the interpreter's chair beside Koeha.

Koeha was sworn in, in a similar manner to Sinnisiak: "Whatever you speak now, you speak straight; do not speak with two tongues."

After his initial apprehension, Koeha quickly warmed to his task. Wallbridge wisely chose a question or two to break the ice.

"Mr. Koeha, how do you like Edmonton?"

"It is like a magic dream. How do you grow your dogs so big?"

"The dogs?"

"The dogs that pull the big sled with the round things."

Angituk helped here. "He means the horses pulling wagons."

There was cautious chuckling in the courtroom and Harvey let it go. Wallbridge engaged nicely in the discussion.

"They are not dogs. They are horses, a different animal, like a caribou without horns."

Koeha nodded thoughtfully, thankful for the clarification. He seemed to assume his testimony was a casual give-and-take conversation. Looking around at the expansive courtroom, he asked Justice Harvey, "And did you carve this igloo of yours out of a mountain?"

Harvey responded quickly to the question, and Angituk translated, telling Koeha, "No. They built this from wood and stone blocks, like an ice house is built."

"This is some big ice house."

Angituk explained these impressions to the amusement of the courtroom. After the ponderous, heavy-footed translations of Ilavinik, the interpretations by "Mr." McAndrew were deft and vivid. The new interpreter had suddenly given, so the newspapers would report, a whole new life and immediacy to the trial. E.K. Mainprize made notes that would appear in *The New York Times*:

> With the replacement interpreter, at once a new personality is felt. A slight, dark-haired boy of about sixteen, Angituk McAndrew has a face that is almost aristocratic. He is alert and catches instantly what he is asked to transmit. There is a gleam of mischief in his oddly blue eyes. His answers, promptly and clearly rendered, have a humorous twist. The struggle with translation ends.

Wallbridge pressed on. "So you are enjoying your visit here?"

"Yes. It is very nice to visit the land of the *Kabloona* and will be very nice to get home."

Justice Harvey's patience was nearing an end. "Mr. Wallbridge, would you care to get on with pertinent questions."

"Of course, your Lordship. Mr. Koeha, can you tell us about the two white men? When did you first see them?"

"It was Kormik that brought them. He was hunting summer caribou down at the trees and they came back with him. We had never seen *Kabloona* before. With their big eyes, they looked like beluga whales."

There was stifled laughter at the back of the courtroom.

"We called the one man Kuleavik, because he always smiled. We called the second man Ilogoak, because he wore the long black gown. We did not know they were shamans. We thought at first they were there to trade, but they had no goods. Then we thought they were there to hunt caribou, but they were poor hunters and missed, even with their guns. Once they shot a rabbit but didn't kill it, and it suffered. Finally they chopped off its head and tried to skin it. They made an awful mess of it and so we saw few rabbits for two summers because of this disrespect.

"We found it odd that they had no women partners to make them clothing and prepare food. We had no idea what these white men wanted. They showed pictures of the good place up in the sky and the bad place of fire down under the earth or the ice, things to do with our hands." Koeha put his hands together in prayer then crossed himself. "They put tiny pieces of food in our mouths and chanted. We let them do it. It made them happy. Our women sewed up new boots for them. Their clothing was no good."

Angituk translated these long statements in an efficient rhythm and Koeha needed only to pause slightly to accommodate her.

"We liked Kuleavik. He could make jokes in sign language and we'd all laugh. But Ilogoak did not laugh. He would shout at us and threaten us with a stick. They stayed with us for a few days. It was a time of no food. The fish were gone from the rivers and the caribou from the land, but the sea ice was not yet strong enough to hunt seal or walrus. Many of us thought the two white men had caused the animals to be gone. That was very serious.

"Ilogoak had promised the hunter Kormik that he would give his rifle to him if Kormik got them to the mouth of the Coppermine. But he lied, so Kormik took the rifle and put it in his tent. Ilogoak saw it was gone and was very angry."

Wallbridge interrupted him. "Mr. Koeha, tell us how your people view the expression of anger. Is it normal? A common thing?"

"No, to show anger is immature ... indulgent. And if it continues, it can mean a bad spirit has entered a man."

"And how, Mr. Koeha, is a bad spirit dealt with?"

"We send them away or, if they won't go, we pack up and leave."

"What if you can't go away and they won't go either?"

"If such a man threatens lives, the others will consider killing him. It will be discussed among the elders."

"Murder, for the good of the community?"

"Yes. It is a terrible thing, but it frees the soul of the man from the bad spirit. Afterwards, forgiveness is asked from the ghost."

"All right, so Father Le Roux—Ilogoak—was angry. What did he do then?"

"He took the second rifle and pointed it at Kormik and demanded he give the rifle back. Kormik refused. They argued until Kormik's mother was afraid and got the rifle and gave it back to Ilogoak. Then Kormik was angry. We had never seen him like this. Maybe the bad spirit was in him too. We were worried Kormik and the white man might kill one another. The white men had to go. I gave the *Kabloona* a little food and two dogs to help pull their qamutik. I helped them get safely out of the camp on their way south. They were very weak and hungry, but I thought they'd be all right when they got to the land of the trees.

"The shaman Uluksuk was staying near our camp with his friend Sinnisiak. We knew these men and were friendly with them. Two days after the *Kabloona* left, Uluksuk and Sinnisiak went up toward Bloody Falls to fish. When they returned three days later, they had the white men's rifles, their clothing, pictures, and books. They told everyone they had to kill the *Kabloona*."

"Do you think they followed them up the river to kill them and steal their rifles?"

"I don't think so. They went to fish, and meet Sinnisiak's cousin."

"Did they tell you why they killed them?"

"They told us when they met the white men they were starving. They had not made much distance. They were angry. They asked the hunters to pull their qamutik. Uluksuk and Sinnisiak pulled for a day, but on the second day the priests were acting strange and the hunters wanted to leave them and go home."

"What did they mean by 'acting strange'?"

"They said that one man, Ilogoak, pointed his gun at them and said he would kill them if they didn't pull the sled. But they believed the priests were possessed by evil spirits. So near Bloody Falls the hunters killed them instead."

"Did they describe how they killed them?"

"No. We didn't ask questions."

"But you did go to Bloody Falls to see them."

"Yes. We went to see them for ourselves. They had bindings on their hands and feet put on after they were dead."

"What were the bindings for?"

"To hold the spirits in. We were scared of them, but after two days the spirits had to be released. We cut the bindings on their hands and feet to allow the spirits to leave. Then we placed stones on top of them and around them to mark their place, and then we ran away."

"In the world you believe there are many spirits."

"Yes, there are spirits everywhere."

"Do you feel them here in this room?"

"No. Here in this village I do not feel them anywhere."

"You feel them strongly where you live, in the North, beyond the trees."

"Yes. The North is full of spirits."

"Are they good spirits?"

"There are some good ones. Some animal spirits can be good and give you food. And some spirits of dead people can help you if you respect them. But there are many bad spirits out there to avoid. Especially at Bloody Falls, where many were killed even before these white men came. Often the spirits of dead people are jealous of the living. They want us to join them. That is why we ran."

"Are the spirits invisible?"

"Usually."

"Do they ever appear in human form?"

"Yes. Sometimes."

"And when the priests were staying with you, did you ever wonder if they were bad spirits?"

"Not Kuleavik, but we did wonder about Ilogoak. When he was angry, we could see an evil spirit in his eyes."

MCCAUL'S CROSS-EXAMINATION was brief.

"Mr. Koeha, you've described the misunderstanding between Father Le Roux and Kormik about the rifle. Kormik thought he had been promised the rifle and so he went and took it."

"Yes."

McCaul turned toward the jury. "One can easily picture the scene at Koeha's camp: the two white men suspicious and alarmed but determined, surrounded by a crowd of excited Eskimos. Kormik, angry and disgruntled, sulks in his tent. Some of the Eskimos encourage him to keep the rifle, others urge him to give it up. Father Le Roux, with loaded rifle, stands at the tent door ready to shoot—a horrible position for a missionary—and finally the old mother comes out and hands over the disputed rifle. But this has little to do with the murders. The absent Kormik is not on trial here. It is the two accused who followed the weak and ailing priests up the river and killed them."

Justice Harvey interrupted him. "Mr. McCaul, please save this for your summation. Do you have more questions for this man?"

"Yes, your Lordship. Mr. Koeha, can you please describe the day after the murders, when you went to see the bodies at Bloody Falls."

"There were six of us: myself, Kormik, Toopek, Kallun, Agbrunna, and Kingagolik. Three men and three women. I was very, very sorry the two white men were dead. When we got to the place, I saw one man lying dead by the sled. It was Ilogoak. He was lying on his back with his head up. The snow had covered his face, all but his nose. The man that had killed him had cut him up inside with a knife."

"And where was the other priest?"

"The other priest was far away from the sled."

"Do you think he was running away?"

"Maybe. I don't know. He had been shot and then his head was opened with an axe. We cried when we saw him."

"Was his belly cut open?"

"Yes, it was cut open."

"As you do with caribou."

"Yes. As we do with caribou."

"No further questions, your Lordship."

Seventeen

Wallbridge recalled Sinnisiak to the stand to resume his story. Uluksuk was taken out of the courtroom so Sinnisiak's testimony would not bias his own. Sinnisiak looked again to Creed for encouragement and he nodded for the young hunter to go ahead.

"I was camped at the mouth of the Coppermine River with Uluksuk, beside the camp of Koeha where the two white men were staying. We were fishing there."

"The two white men were the priests, Ilogoak and Kuleavik?"

"Yes. The fishing was very poor. We were hungry. We decided to go south, upriver to the falls, and try the fishing there. Also to meet my cousin who was coming north, down the river. But the two priests had left camp to go back south to their home in the trees. We didn't want to travel with the priests, so we waited two days then started out.

"We found the priests' trail and met them on the river. They had not got very far in three days with their sled. When we found the white men on the trail they were very weak and their sled was stuck in the deep snow. Ilogoak, the big man, asked if we had food. We did not. Ilogoak told us that if we pulled their sled he would pay us in steel traps when we got to their cabin in the place of the trees. We did not want to go that far, but we agreed to help them for a while. We and the dogs pulled the sled for the rest of the day—it was hard work. On the first day the priests were not angry and we made camp and stayed with them. We were still a long way from the trees. Uluksuk caught one fish through the ice and we ate it. We made a small snow house and slept there. Kuleavik showed us again the pictures of the place above the skies and tried to tell us what it was all about. It was then Ilogoak was first angry and spoke hot words to Kuleavik, but we didn't understand them."

Creed considered sadly the already desperate plight of the priests in that harsh land where the margin for error was so dangerously narrow. The personal conflict only added to it.

Sinnisiak continued. "The next day we started off again. It was stormy and snowing and very tough going. We had a hard time staying on the trail. Uluksuk and I were ahead, pulling the sled, and the two white men were behind. The *Kabloona* were sick and weak. Ilogoak was saying angry things to Kuleavik, but I could not understand his talk. I wanted to turn around and go home. Then, on the edge of the riverbank near Bloody Falls, the dogs smelled something and we stopped. It was a cache that the priests had left and we all looked to see if there was food. But there was no food, only an axe and boxes of rifle cartridges. The cache had not been built very well and the food left there had probably been stolen by a wolverine. This made Ilogoak even angrier. He began to throw the cartridges into the river and yell at Kuleavik. Kuleavik tried to stop him and they pushed each other. Ilogoak had gone crazy, and that is the sign of an evil spirit."

Le Roux had lost control, Creed thought. It all seemed so suddenly, overwhelmingly familiar to him. He now understood why it had happened. Why the priests had been killed. He understood the contagious nature of losing control, of having nothing left to hold on to. Of reacting violently. Of having no choice.

"Uluksuk and I were scared and wanted to go back home. We began to walk away from them, but Ilogoak had the rifle in his hand. He was mad at us and he pointed the rifle at us to stop. I asked him, I said, "Are you going to kill us?" and he nodded his head. He made us go back to the sled and get into the harness. We were scared, but we began to pull. Ilogoak put his rifle on the sled and walked beside it. We went a little way and Uluksuk and I talked about what to do. They were going to kill us. They said so. Every time I tried to talk, Ilogoak came to me and put his hand over my mouth. He was mad and pushing us with his hand and pointing the rifle at us. I was thinking hard and crying and very scared and the frost was in my boots and I was cold. I wanted to go back home, but I was afraid. I got hot inside my body, and every time Ilogoak put his hand on the rifle or on his knife I was very much afraid. I spoke to Uluksuk and said, 'I think we have to kill him before he kills us. We have to be strong or we will never see our families again.'"

In the courtroom, everyone strained to hear Angituk's translation of Sinnisiak's testimony. A squeak from one of the electric ceiling fans broke the silence. Angituk took a breath and continued her translation.

"We came to a small hill close to the falls and we stopped there. I took off the harness and went to one side. Ilogoak ran after me and pushed me back to the sled, but I said I was going to relieve myself and he let me go. I did not want to relieve myself. I went around behind him. I looked at Uluksuk, then I stabbed Ilogoak in the back with my knife. Ilogoak tried to get the rifle and Uluksuk went after him. The other white man wanted to come back to the sled. I had a knife in my hand and he went away again.

"Uluksuk and Ilogoak wrestled for the rifle and it fell in the snow. Uluksuk had to finish up Ilogoak with a knife. He stabbed him twice and he dropped down beside the sled. I asked Uluksuk, 'Is he dead?' and he said, 'Yes.' When Kuleavik saw Ilogoak die, he turned and ran away. I said to Uluksuk, 'Give me the rifle.' The first time I shot, I did not hit him. I put in a new bullet as I had seen them do and shot again, and missed. The third time I took my time and got him. The priest sat down after the bullet hit him.

"I dropped the rifle, picked up the axe and knife, and went after him. Uluksuk came too. The white man was sitting in a shallow creek. When I got close to him, he got up again. I had the knife in my hand. He looked at us and said something. Uluksuk told me, 'Go ahead and put the knife in him.' I said to Uluksuk, 'Go ahead you. I fixed the other man already.' Uluksuk tried to stab him but missed the first time. The second time he got him. The priest lay down on his back. He was breathing a little, lying there. I hit him across the face with the axe I was carrying. I killed him dead."

Sinnisiak looked to Creed for reassurance, but Creed was gazing up at the creaking ceiling fan. In his mind, having heard Sinnisiak's precise description of Rouvière's death, he was fifteen hundred miles away, imagining what the end had been like for Rouvière at the top of the world.

As they headed south, Rouvière would have been starving, ill, and terribly cold. His nose hairs would have been frozen, his lips cracked, and he would have felt the marrow in his bones congealing. For perhaps only the second time in years he would have been deeply, almost hopelessly depressed by his plight. He had failed his Church and his God. There was nothing else to call it. After three years he had finally made it to the mouth of the Coppermine. Then came the business with the rifle.

They had only been in Koeha's camp at the mouth of the Coppermine a few days. Their important work was only beginning. Why hadn't Le

Roux let Kormik, who had replaced Hornby as guide (because of Le Roux's imprudent actions), keep the rifle? They had a second one. Rouvière had not heard the promise of the rifle to Kormik, but it was not an unreasonable gift, as the hunter had guided them safely to the mouth. But no, on some arrogant point of principle Le Roux demanded the rifle back, and to Rouvière's horror he had pointed the second rifle at Kormik. From Kormik's point of view he had been lied to and humiliated in front of his people by a white man, and his life had been threatened at the point of a gun in his own tent. Rouvière could not believe that the hand of a Roman Catholic priest could do such a thing. He did not at first believe that Kormik was capable of killing Le Roux, but by the urgency in Koeha's insistence that they leave, Rouvière realized it was quite possible.

It had all been a terrible mistake. Rouvière had seen the hostility and disillusionment in those Eskimo faces as he and Le Roux left the camp. Banished. Three days after that, God provided. They chanced upon two hunters from Kormik's camp, Sinnisiak and Uluksuk. The hunters agreed to pull the sled in exchange for traps.

The hunters caught a char and built a snow house, providing them with food and shelter. The fish would get them through to the next day, when they would make it to a small cache of food they had left up the river. The two hunters had responded well to some Christian teaching that night, but when Rouvière had asked the taciturn Le Roux to help with a point of translation, Le Roux ignored him and then exploded in front of the hunters.

"Don't you realize it's a hopeless effort? How can we articulate the abstractions, teach the subtleties of the mysteries—the Immaculate Conception, the Holy Trinity, the Resurrection—with only hand gestures! But then, look at these two primitive, ignorant creatures. What use is it to offer them salvation? Even if we were fluent, they would still have no idea what we're talking about."

Rouvière could see that the hunters were upset by Le Roux's anger. They got as far from him as they could in the little snow house, and a tense *silence fell over them. In the morning Le Roux was adamant they continue south.*

The two hunters and the two dogs pulled the sled. Rouvière and Le Roux walked behind. One of the dogs was tending off the track, where something had his attention. The sled came to a stop.

"It must be the cache," Rouvière said, and they all went to find it through the swirling flakes. It was a pile of rocks Father Rouvière had built. When they pushed away the drift of snow, they found it had been disturbed, several rocks pushed aside. The packets of fish and caribou meat were gone. All that was left were several boxes of rifle cartridges and a small axe.

"Goddamnit, Rouvière. You can't even build a cache properly. Now what are we going to do?"

"I don't know. Keep going."

Le Roux grabbed a box of cartridges. "Maybe we can eat these! Should we eat these?"

Rouvière was startled by the subtle beginnings of hysteria in his companion's voice.

"Don't do this, Guillaume."

Le Roux opened the box and began to take handfuls of the shells, throwing them through the falling snow down into the river.

Rouvière tried to grab his arm to stop him. "Don't! We need them."

Le Roux pushed him back. "What for? You couldn't hit a caribou if it came up and bit you on the ear. You are hopeless, Rouvière! We're going to starve to death, don't you understand?"

Sinnisiak and Uluksuk were very upset by the fighting between the white men and began to back away from them.

Le Roux turned toward them. "Where do you think you're going? Get back to the sled!" He raised the gun and pointed it at them. They stopped. "Didn't you hear me? Get back to the sled!"

The hunters stared at him and the rifle, wide-eyed, until Le Roux pushed Sinnisiak hard toward the qamutik, gesturing to the traces. Sinnisiak and Uluksuk returned to the sled, put the rope harnesses over their shoulders, and began to pull again. Le Roux placed the rifle on the sled and walked beside it.

Father Rouvière heard the two hunters talking quietly to one another as they walked together through the deep snow, straining against the sled. Father Le Roux sprinted forward to Sinnisiak and put his hand over his mouth.

"Stop talking!"

Father Rouvière continued walking in the deep furrows left behind the sled. He had been shaken by the incident at the cache. Not only was the food gone, but Le Roux was beginning to lose control. The snowstorm was not letting up and it made him wonder how much longer the flesh could go on.

Up ahead, the sled stopped and the younger hunter took off his harness. Rouvière watched as Le Roux pushed the hunter back to it. The Eskimo made a gesture. Apparently he had to relieve himself. Rouvière leaned against a rock to the right of the qamutik to catch his breath, thankful for the stop. For the first time he noticed, over the wind, the distant roar of open rapids and realized they were very close to Bloody Falls. They should stop to fish.

Rouvière looked up to see the young hunter come around behind Le Roux. What was he doing? He brought up his fist as if he were punching the priest in the lower back, but then Rouvière saw the bloody copper blade. Rouvière froze in horror.

Le Roux grabbed for the rifle on the sled, but the older hunter wrestled him for its possession. The rifle fell into the snow. Le Roux grabbed a tent pole from the sled and hit him with it on the head and shoulder. Then Rouvière saw the old hunter stab Le Roux twice in the stomach with a copper blade. The priest fell to his knees, then over onto his back.

Rouvière ran to help Le Roux, but the younger hunter was there with his knife. The hunters now turned and directed their attention toward him. Rouvière looked into the eyes of these men who, the night before, had sung Christian songs with him. Now he could see their intent. He turned and in a panic ran back along the trail they had broken, back toward the mouth of the Coppermine. Despite the wind, he could hear the cartridge sliding into the chamber. He heard the shot and the whizzing bullet pass within inches of his head. He ran faster through the heavy snow, gasping for oxygen in the cold air, raising the skirts of his cassock, leaping over drifts with a desperate energy. Again a bullet passed him, pinging off a rock just to his left. He ran on, hoping the falling snow would obscure him, hoping the rifle's unfamiliar mechanism would confound the hunter, hoping that ...

He felt the punch before he heard the shot and looked down to see the bullet had passed through him, high and to the right. His hot blood glistened and steamed in the cold air. He slumped down in the snow, looking at the new opening in his body. He listened to the wind. He knew they would be coming. He mouthed the words under his faltering breath.

"The Lord is my shepherd; I shall not want. He maketh me to lie down in green pastures: he leadeth me beside the still waters. He restoreth my soul: he leadeth me in the paths of righteousness for his name's sake ..."

He could hear them coming for him, closer now, the muffled footfalls of their mukluks in the snow and their heavy breathing. But the words of the psalm calmed him and gave him strength. Rouvière rose slowly to his feet and turned away from the mouth of the Coppermine to face his killers. They stopped in front of him, the old and the young hunter. They watched him with wide eyes.

"Yea, though I walk through the valley of the shadow of death, I will fear no evil: for thou art with me; thy rod and thy staff they comfort me ..."

There was no evil in the hunters' eyes. They were as scared as he was. The old hunter stabbed deep into his stomach and the searing pain made Rouvière bend forward and scream. His lungs were filling with blood and no sound came out. He fell onto his back away from them in the deep, soft snow and looked up into the opaque sky where the wind had calmed *now. Fat snowflakes rushed toward him. He could hear water flowing. He continued to whisper the words:*

"Thou prepareth a table before me in the presence of mine enemies: thou anointest my head with oil; my cup runneth over ..."

The image of Sinnisiak appeared above him, his expression worried, fearful, looking down at him.

"Surely goodness and mercy shall follow me all the days of my life."

He saw the axe rise over the hunter's shoulder, the dark profile stark against the white sky.

"And I will dwell in the house of the Lord ..."

"I KILLED HIM DEAD," Sinnisiak repeated to the court sadly, and Creed awoke from his reverie with a shudder.

"I am sorry," Sinnisiak said with conviction, and then he fell silent after these last words of his testimony. There had been an eagerness to tell the story and a deep regret in his voice. Even after studying the site and imagining the climax of the murders, Creed was in mild shock at the brutality of the final moments. He looked over to see the stricken expression on Angituk's face and thought he saw her shiver.

After a moment Wallbridge shook himself as if from a trance. "All right. Mr. Sinnisiak? So Father Le Roux is dead beside the sled and Father Rouvière is in the creek. What did you do then?"

"We apologized to them for killing them. After they were dead, Uluksuk said to me, 'Once in my grandfather's time hostile white men came and killed some of us and we killed them and the people cut off some of them and ate it. We better open him up.' So Uluksuk cut into Kuleavik's belly as we did with caribou and he gave me some of his liver. I ate it and he ate it too. We gave some to the spirits. I licked the blood off the knife. Then we went back to the other man, Ilogoak, and I cut him open and we ate some of his liver also and shared with the spirits."

"And why did you eat the livers?"

"It was because Uluksuk's grandfather's people did it with white men once a long time ago."

"But do you know why? Was it to protect you?"

"I'm not sure. Out of respect for the spirits, I think. It is what we do after killing a creature. Uluksuk is the shaman. He knows why."

Eighteen

In the cross-examination, McCaul's chief aim was to show that Sinnisiak and Uluksuk had deliberately set out to trail the priests, kill them, and steal their rifles.

"So, Mr. Sinnisiak, after you had killed Father Le Roux and Father Rouvière and left their bodies lying in the snow, what did you take from them?"

"We each took a rifle and cartridges. I took one of their black coats and a book with pictures. That was all. It was the others who came with Koeha that took the other things, the shirts and other clothing and books and medals."

"But you took the rifles."

"Yes. And three boxes of cartridges."

"Because that's all you really wanted."

"Yes."

"You followed the priests because you wanted those rifles, right?"

"No."

"The priests had insulted your friend Kormik. And they had rifles."

"We were going fishing and also to meet my cousin."

"Then why didn't you go fishing? Why didn't you wait for your cousin?"

"We had killed the priests. Hornby said if white men were killed, more would come and kill us all. We had to warn the people. So we went back to the camp at the mouth of the river as soon as it was light. I went to Kormik's tent. Both Kormik and Koeha were sleeping. I woke them up and told them that we had killed those two white fellows."

"And what did they say to you? Did they tell you you had done a bad thing? Did they say it was very bad to kill two human beings?"

"I can't remember what they said. They went to get the rest of the priests' stuff. They started in the morning and came back the same night. I can't tell any more. If I knew more, I would tell you. I can't remember any more."

"No further questions."

ULUKSUK'S TESTIMONY was identical in every detail to Sinnisiak's. There was no tendency to make the other more culpable or even to mitigate the facts of the killings. The older man looked often to Creed or to Angituk for encouragement, and his speech was slower. He had lost weight; the lines of his face cut deep. His powerful shoulders drooped. It was apparent he was ill and weak. He still had trouble keeping down the unfamiliar food, and the old shaman was growing more depressed every day. But, with Angituk's affectionate encouragement, he did his best to rally enough to tell the story and answer questions. When he was finished, Wallbridge asked the question many had been waiting for.

"So, Mr. Uluksuk, we have heard that it was known that your grandfather once ate the livers of white men who had been killed."

"Yes. They told the story of one year, many years ago, two lifetimes ago, that white men came from a ship caught in the ice.

They were hostile and killed two of our people and so our people killed some of them. It was recommended by the shamans that their livers be eaten."

"Why did they do that?"

"We eat the caribou liver to show respect to the animal. This was the same for the white men—to say we are sorry we killed you, but it was necessary so that we would live. And we share some with the other spirits out of respect so they will not trouble us. The liver also gives us the strength of the caribou or, in this case, the white man. And finally, if we eat the liver it is protection so that the white men will not get up again and kill us."

"Thank you. No further questions."

MCCAUL'S CROSS-EXAMINATION began in an amiable way.

"Mr. Uluksuk, you are a shaman. You provide a link between the human world and the spirit world."

"Yes. That is true. I find out what the good spirits need to keep them happy."

"And what about bad spirits?"

"I find ways to avoid bad spirits or drive them away to protect the people."

"And you do other things. I hear you flew to the moon." McCaul actually winked at the jury.

Angituk glared at him for a moment before translating. "Yes. Once, I flew to the moon."

"How was that?"

"I found it much like the Earth, but no snow."

"And you dove down into the sea under the ice and stayed for two days."

"It was only overnight. I talked to Kannokapfaluk, the goddess of the animals, to convince her to let the seals come back to us so we could eat. And she let them, so all was well again."

"And you can fly through the air and swallow fire?"

"Oh, yes."

"And I am told you can transform yourself into other creatures—a wolf, a bear, a bird. Is this true?"

"Yes. Other creatures. I may even try to become a white man, but it is hard. A wolf is my favourite."

"You prefer being a wolf to a white man."

"Yes."

The courtroom murmured their amusement and again McCaul looked at the jury with an indulgent grin, having fun. Angituk resented this disrespect.

McCaul continued: "But dealing with spirits is what you do most. It is your stock-in-trade as a shaman, if you will."

Angituk hesitated over the translation of "stock-in-trade." She used "respected skill."

"That's true."

"If there were no spirits, you'd be without a job."

"A world without spirits—it would be very lonely."

"I'm saying you encourage your people to believe in evil spirits. It is in your personal interest to promote the belief in spirits, isn't it?"

"I object, your Lordship," Wallbridge responded. "I find the direction of questioning offensive and disrespectful. It is like suggesting a priest is in it for the personal gain, or that my learned colleague's declared belief in Christianity is solely to promote his commercial interests."

Harvey sustained the objection.

WALLBRIDGE RECALLED Jack Creed to complete his cross-examination. "Inspector Creed, when you stayed in Koeha's camp at the mouth of the Coppermine, did you carry a gun with you?"

"No. I didn't want to cause any fear among the people."

"Because they were scared of guns?"

"Yes. Few had ever seen one. They hunted with bows and arrows and spears, but they had heard the legends about guns and seen those of the priests, who had demonstrated how they worked. The people knew what a gun could do."

Wallbridge picked up a book from his table and showed it to Creed. "Inspector Creed, are you familiar with Vilhjalmur Stefansson's book *My Life with the Eskimo*, of 1912?"

"I am."

"In it, Stefansson states that the three things the Eskimo fears most are evil spirits, white men, and strangers. Is this true?"

"He is the authority. But I would say from my experience that is accurate."

"If a white man, a stranger, possibly possessed of an evil spirit, approaches an Eskimo, would he feel threatened?"

"Certainly."

"And if this white stranger were holding a gun, would he feel threatened?"

"Of course."

"And if this white stranger with the gun is pointing the gun at the Eskimo, does the Eskimo have any doubt it's going to be used?"

"No doubt whatsoever."

Young Wallbridge was satisfied with Creed's response. Creed caught a glare from C.C. McCaul, as he had expected, but he was concerned to find similar disapproval in the stern face of Justice Harvey.

As the Justice declared the court adjourned and left the courtroom, Nicole came up to Creed. "Darling ... I was just a little surprised at you playing into the hands of the defence. I know they are your friends and they're very charming—"

"I was just giving the facts."

"Of course you were, and facts are admirable things, but you have to be careful. They can be manipulated so easily."

"Yes, they can."

"Anyway ... no matter. Come over for dinner tonight. We have a fine leg of lamb and some friends from the Rotary Club who would love to meet you."

"I'd like to, Nicole, but duty calls. I have some people to see. Could we have dinner tomorrow?"

"Of course, Jack. I realize you have responsibilities."

There was a slight chill in the air as she kissed his cheek.

CREED VISITED ULUKSUK and Sinnisiak that night in their cell beneath the courtroom. He reassured them they were doing well, even though the jury's stone faces were quite unreadable. He had found the prisoners some frozen caribou and they ate and talked of home. Sinnisiak ate hungrily, but the old shaman remained depressed and taciturn and ate very little. His eyes were dull, his skin opaque, and Angituk explained to Creed:

"He misses his wives and children and grandchildren. He is worried that without him to hunt and interpret the spirits, they will not have enough food. They could be ill. Or, sensing they are defenceless, a bad spirit could be harassing them. I have been trying to tell him they are fine, but he doesn't know. He feels his powers are weak here."

Sinnisiak too was homesick, but he found this new world interesting. He was fond of the food, he liked the beef stew a lot, and he loved the candies. He was learning some English words: "Court ... rifle ... river ... priest ... food ... to hunt, to kill." But he was worried about Uluksuk. "I have never seen him like this. He is very unhappy."

"Uluksuk, you must eat and stay healthy," Creed told him. "You cannot give up. Stay strong. Try to get some sleep."

Uluksuk raised his eyes to him, and nodded slowly that he understood.

Creed said a quick goodbye to Angituk and then he left to have a talk with Wallbridge. When he had gone, Sinnisiak turned to Uluksuk.

"Why don't you change us into ravens and we can fly home? Or a bear. If you become a bear, you can break this cage, maybe."

"I cannot become a bear. Don't you understand? We are too far from home. I am weak here. I cannot find the power. There are no spirits here. I am sick."

"Have a candy."

The old man took one and licked it, but he didn't trust it and gave it back.

ANGITUK LEFT THE CELLS not long after Creed, giving a little wave to Cowperthwaite as she passed the front desk. She was sad Creed had gone in such a hurry and seemed so distracted. She had hoped they might have a few minutes alone together. She wanted to tell him about her search for her father.

Angituk went to find the first address on Cowperthwaite's map. Her excitement grew. The place was a big old mansion with added wings on the outskirts of town, where old people came to live in the care of the St. Mary's Anglican Order of Nuns. The nuns were friendly in a brisk way, but visiting hours were over. Angituk explained she was looking for her father. They didn't believe her at first, but finally, when Angituk said his name, the head nurse recognized it and allowed her inside.

The ward was set up like the sleeping room of Angi's mission school. The nun directed Angituk to locate bed B12; there she would find Angus McAndrew. It was after lights out. Most of the elderly men she passed were asleep. As she went by them, Angituk looked at their pale, unconscious faces and worried that if he was like them, he might not have much time left.

Her heart pounding, she approached bed B12 to discover a pleasant-looking man, clean-shaven, with pink cheeks and a full head of white hair. His eyes were closed. She watched him intently for a moment before she spoke his name. He immediately opened his blue eyes and turned to look at her with a kindly smile. When he spoke, his voice was frail.

"Who are you?"

"I am ... my name is Angituk. Are you Mr. Angus McAndrew?"

"Aye, lad. I am. What can I do for you?"

"I am looking for a man with your name. Were you ever on a ship that went up north to the Mackenzie delta many years ago?"

"Sure. She was called the *North Pole*. Fine vessel. I loved the ice and snow."

Her heart pounded faster. "Do you remember the village of Paulatuk, along the coast to the east?"

"Of course! Very nice people up there. Very friendly. I shot a polar bear. A big brute that almost ate me!"

Angituk's excitement grew. "Really? A bear? And ... and do you remember a young woman named Kunee?"

"Ach, beautiful she was. An Eskimo princess. I remember her face as if it were before me. Do you know her?"

"Yes! But she is gone. I ... I am her child. And you are ..."

Her lips trembling, eyes tearing up, Angituk took his limp hand in hers. He smiled again, but there was something vague and unfocused in the blue eyes and loose smile that she found unsettling.

"Yes ... yes, I loved those years in the Congo. Did I tell you about the lioness I shot there? Mean creature. Had killed two villagers."

She stared at him in sudden alarm. "No, we were talking about the North. The Mackenzie delta. Paulatuk. My mother, Kunee."

"Oh, yes. An African princess. Black as coal. What a temptress!"

"No. The North. Ice and snow. You were in the North. In *Canada*. The Arctic. Paulatuk!"

A female voice came from behind her, a note of amusement in it. "Angus was never in the Arctic, or Africa, or anywhere else, my dear." It was the nursing sister who had let her in. "He was a clerk in the Imperial Bank of Canada on 102nd Street for forty years. He married my cousin."

"But he said he knew my mother."

"He's dotty, love. He'll tell you anything. Quite sad, really."

Angituk turned back to the man she had for a long, deep moment thought was her father. "You never went to Paulatuk? You didn't know Kunee?"

"I knew her well indeed. The daughter of a warlord named Pan I supplied arms to outside Shanghai," the little old man told her. Then he fell silent.

"He loved books, you see, dear. All his spare time in the library. Especially after Ethel's death."

"Beautiful, she was. A Chinese princess. I remember her as if she were standing before me. As if she were standing before me ..."

Angus McAndrew's eyes unfocused and his lips continued to silently repeat the last sentence. Angituk looked up at the nursing sister, who then saw her brimming eyes. Her voice softened and she placed a hand on her shoulder.

"I'm sorry, my dear. He's not who you're looking for."

"My mother said he had a picture, a tattoo of a sea woman on his left forearm."

"Have a look."

Angituk hesitated, but now the nursing sister's curiosity was aroused and she leaned over and rolled up the sleeve of his bed shirt. Beneath the grey hairs the translucent skin of the forearm was clear and unmarked. Angi took a long, deep breath, wiped her eyes with her sleeve, then thanked the nurse and left.

That night she lay in the soft, warm bed of her hotel room and stared at the ceiling. She felt a horrible relief. Relief that the little man dying in the bed wasn't her father. The dream her mother had given to her of the tall, handsome white father remained intact. He was still out there. And she would continue to hunt for him.

THE NEXT MORNING, James Wallbridge stood before the jury to present his summation for the defence. Creed noted that Angituk seemed distracted, but when she saw him watching, she smiled and began to focus on Wallbridge's words, to translate them for the accused. He found himself thinking how proud he was of her, of how well she had adapted to this strange and bizarre new environment.

Wallbridge spoke first to the court of the laudable efforts of the priests. "These men had made it to their goal: the mouth of the Coppermine River. An impressive feat. And they had begun their ministry and everything was friendly with the Eskimo at first, but then ... then they got into trouble. The key is found in Father Rouvière's final entry in his journal: 'We are threatened with starvation. We do not know what to do.' Weak, starving, desperate, they had headed south through heavy snow to get to the treeline where there was fuel, where there might be animals to eat. It had taken three days to walk just a few miles. They were facing death when the two hunters found them. One way or another, they had to have their help."

It was Wallbridge's turn to wipe his face in the morning heat, leaving the jury for a moment to ponder the implications of these last words. Then he set off on a new tack.

"These Eskimos we are now asked to judge are men absolutely unlettered, knowing nothing of our civilization except what stories and rumours they have heard. They gaze around this fair city and what do they see? When they look at our buildings, they see mountains. To them our horses are big dogs. Our trains are not trains, but ships that run on land. They see things through different eyes. Their world and our world are not the same."

Murmured comments passed through the courtroom as Wallbridge caught his breath.

"They are not merely remnants of the Stone Age. They *are* the Stone Age, here and now. The great charter of English liberties, the Magna Carta, provides that each man must be judged not by his superiors but by his peers. *Peers*, according to the Oxford dictionary, meaning 'equals in their own land.' Unfortunately, this we cannot do. We are in violation here of one of the greatest principles of the Magna Carta! We have none of their peers here. It would take years to realize this fundamental tenet of our justice system, to find and transport a jury of Eskimos all the way down here to hear this case. It is regrettably ... just not possible."

Wallbridge cast his eyes to the floor as if taking a small part of the responsibility for this failure. Creed suddenly realized that the staid and sometimes fumbling Wallbridge had a certain talent for the dramatic. The courtroom all leaned forward to hear where he would now go.

"But ... what *is* possible ... what we *can* do, is try and approach in our minds something of the same by trying to understand the Eskimo point of view. In short, you members of the jury must think like an Eskimo. Think ... like an Eskimo."

E.K. Mainprize chuckled softly as he took notes. This defence tactic was brilliant. Justice Harvey glared at him. Wallbridge continued.

"You must descend to their point of view. When you judge if the conduct of these men was reasonable or unreasonable, you must put yourself in the position of these untutored savages and determine whether *in their minds* they were justified or not.

"From the Eskimo point of view, the three things they fear most are evil spirits, strangers, and white men. Exposure to the white man began in 1771 when Samuel Hearne brought a war party of Chipewyans that massacred their entire camp at Bloody Falls! It was an unfortunate start.

"The next contact with white men came, according to the testimony of Mr. Uluksuk, in his grandfather's time when hostile white men came from a ship and killed two Eskimos. Begging the court's patience, I offer an interesting aside. This reference to white men would have been, according to my math, around the year 1850. There were no records of white men travelling in the Coppermine area at that time, except ... except for the ill-fated Franklin Expedition of 1845. Could it be that this reference to 'hostile white men' referred to the desperate remnants of Franklin's crew stumbling south, crazed from lead poisoning and starvation, attacking and killing the first human beings they came across? And they in turn being killed. Perhaps a blessing under the circumstances. The history of encounters between the Copper Eskimo and the white man in this region has not been one of peace. It has been one of sudden violence and death."

Wallbridge paused a moment to let his message be considered. Justice Harvey finally prompted him. "Thank you, Mr. Wallbridge, for your interesting historical speculations. But please continue the summation."

"I submit again: the three things the Copper Eskimos fear

most are evil spirits, strangers, and white men. These two white priests were all three!

"Now, any man, whether he is white or black or red, civilized or uncivilized, is justified in killing another in his own defence. To preserve his own life. If he does kill in self-defence, that killing is what we call 'justifiable homicide.' As long as his belief that he is in danger of being killed is reasonable, he is justified in defending himself by taking another life. I respectfully submit that what these men did was nothing more than any of you would have done if the concern in your minds had been the same.

"Now I don't suggest that you would have come to their conclusion, knowing your fellow human beings as you do. But these Eskimos, these primitive men, these savage men of the Stone Age, were they not justified in the conclusions they came to? Were they not justified in believing that these men were going to kill them? Did the priests themselves, in their ravaged state, their desperation, become murderous? Were they stripped of all vestiges of their civilized training and reduced to their own brand of savagery?

"Was it not reasonable, considering the minds of the accused, the little knowledge they had of the white race, and the three great fears they had—strangers, evil spirits, and white men? In the Eskimo life, evil spirits are a fact of life, supernatural wonders swirling around them every day, appearing at any time in any guise. Were they not justified in believing their lives were in danger?"

Wallbridge took a moment to let this sink in before he set off on his final tack, reading briefly from notes.

"As for cannibalism, the *Encyclopaedia Britannica* recognizes 'the consumption of a small part of the body of the dead man in order that his ghost might not trouble the killer' as a definition.

It is an ancient tradition in many primitive countries. And then again, it is not so primitive, is it?" Wallbridge paused for effect. "It is a tradition practised, in fact, across the street, in the Catholic Church!"

The courtroom had followed Wallbridge's summation with interest, but with this statement he completely captivated them. Bishop Breynat and his priest stared at Wallbridge in shock.

"Is it not true that half the population of Canada believe at Communion they are eating, not a piece of bread and drops of wine, but through transubstantiation the actual flesh and blood of Christ? This widely accepted ritual of respect was endorsed by no one more than the priests themselves! In fact they taught the Coppermine Eskimos to say the Mass and consume the flesh and blood of Christ!"

Wallbridge's assertion garnered a welling up of protesting whispers. Justice Harvey let it rise for a few moments while he himself reflected on the implications. The Bishop crossed himself and spoke the word "blasphemy" under his breath.

McCaul disliked where all this had gone, but despite his experience and impressive memory he could think of no grounds on which to object. Harvey brought the courtroom to order and asked Wallbridge to stick to relevant facts.

Having made the points he wished, Wallbridge finished quickly, asserting at the end that the defendants were really like children. "They see the world much differently than we do. We must offer, as British and Canadian law dictates, a jury of their peers. We must judge them not by our standards but by theirs. Whether they believed the priests to be demons or just hostile, threatening white men, there is no question they were acting in self-defence."

When Wallbridge sat down, Creed gave him an appreciative nod. He had done very well. Creed wanted to applaud.

C.C. MCCAUL KNEW he had to calm things down to a rational, unemotional level. The "cannibalism as Communion" ploy by Wallbridge was a coarse, sensational red herring. He expected that the jury, men of his age and station, felt the same way.

"I have spoken on the peculiar and important significance of this case," McCaul began conversationally, "what makes this case so different from others. The advantage of British justice ... now Canadian justice ... and fair play is to make it known that if a white man travelling in the North is killed, the tribe will not be threatened. A punitive expedition will not come to exterminate the tribe, as has been the case in other countries. They will be given the same fair trial as any white man would get under similar circumstances.

"All that aside, it is my contention that the evidence proves that Sinnisiak and Uluksuk planned to kill the priests for their rifles. It was clearly a case of premeditated murder. But the civilized standards under which the defendants are tried must not be influenced in any way by the question of guilt. These men used a knife and a gun and an axe to kill these priests. Father Rouvière was completely unarmed and running away!" McCaul's voice rose steadily with his rhetoric. "He presented no threat to them when they shot him down, stabbed him, and finally finished him off with an axe. They cut his body open, ate his liver, stole the rifles and cartridges, and returned to their people, boasting of their deeds! You, gentlemen of the jury, have a duty to send the strongest message to the North that these actions will not be tolerated. I ask you ... I plead ... I demand of you, that you do your duty. Thank you."

AFTER A QUICK, late break for lunch, Justice Harvey addressed the jury. Like McCaul, he assumed a calm, reflective tone.

"I wish to point out, as has my colleague Mr. McCaul, that despite the fact that these defendants are poor, ignorant, benighted pagans who come from beyond the borders of our civilization, they still receive all the protection that our laws can give any person charged with such a crime. They have been furnished with a fine counsel"—Harvey shot a cold look at Wallbridge—"who has left no stone unturned to ensure no unfair advantage was taken of them and everything possible brought out in their favour.

"Now the defence has put forward the idea that the defendants acted in self-defence. Killing in self-defence is justified only when there is no question you are about to be killed. Killing that may prevent you being killed sometime in the future is something else entirely. For this I use the example of the war raging in Europe. Germany first made war with France—they attacked first—claiming it was for self-defence. But this was not self-defence. If you believe them, it was to prevent what Germans feared would be an attack. This is not true self-defence. And I suggest you compare that to the events that transpired on the banks of the Coppermine near Bloody Falls. This was not self-defence."

Harvey had locked eyes with each juryman over the course of his summation, but now he turned away dismissively, preparing to retire to his office and tossing his final order over his shoulder as he left.

"Gentlemen, I ask you to do what the law demands of you."

Nineteen

The jury retired to deliberate quite late in the afternoon. The people emptied the stifling courtroom, retreating to the lawns outside to fan themselves in the hot summer evening and speculate on how long the jury would take to reach a verdict. A young boy selling copies of the *Edmonton Journal* still warm from the presses emptied his bag in moments. E.K. Mainprize was at the centre of a gathering of reporters. One opened the pages and scanned Howard Fleishman's column from that morning. He read aloud:

"The Eskimos, half asleep during the proceedings, were dreaming perhaps of a place far away, less complicated, less hot, less full of people and more of caribou."

The reporters laughed. "You're a poet, Howie."

"Those Eskimos won't be seeing that place again." Fleishman was confident.

"I wouldn't be too hasty with your conclusion," Mainprize told him. "In fact I'd be willing to bet a dinner at the Empire Hotel they are acquitted."

The journalists responded in an uproar, not one among them supporting Mainprize's prediction.

"The Eskimos said they killed them."

"Rouvière was shot in the back running away!"

"Self-defence'll never fly."

Mainprize's bet was taken by Walter Fresson of the *Seattle Daily Times*. Mainprize just smiled as the debate continued against his position, and he moved away from his colleagues to another, more interesting circle that included Inspector Creed, Nicole Harvey, John Hornby, Koeha, Wallbridge, and the young translator, Angituk. He shook Wallbridge's hand.

"A beautifully directed defence, Mr. Wallbridge. 'A jury of their peers' as is guaranteed by British and Canadian law. You instructed them to 'think like Eskimos.' Brilliant!"

"Thank you, Mr. Mainprize." The young lawyer's expression betrayed a lack of optimism. "We'll see."

"Miss Harvey? Who are you rooting for?"

"This is hardly a cricket match, Mr. Mainprize. What I'm 'rooting for' is justice. I do hope there is a modicum of compassion in our justice system, but I think the gruesome facts of the murders speak for themselves."

Mainprize smiled at her then turned to Koeha, extending his hand. The hunter, who was growing accustomed to white rituals, took his hand and smiled.

"Mr. Koeha, you were an interesting and enlightening witness for the defence." Nearby, Angituk translated as he spoke. "It has taken many months for you to get here. Will you stay for a while or go back to the North?"

"I like it here. White people are not demons at all."

"High praise indeed."

Mainprize was subtly checking the time to calculate his deadline for the morning edition when Koeha took an interest in his silver pocket watch.

"That is very beautiful. What is that?"

"A watch. It tells the time."

"What is 'time'?"

"It is a point in the day, early or middle or late, or just before the sun goes down."

Angituk rose to the challenge of interpreting the concept of time. She listened carefully to the white man's choice of words and translated with accuracy and imagination, briefly adding references Koeha would understand: if you're building an igloo, the moment your knife breaks the snow to the moment of the last block installed—that amount of *time* is measured on the little instrument. It is called about one *hour*.

"Show me on the little machine," the hunter instructed.

Mainprize opened the watch to demonstrate. "You see? This hand tells when it is six o'clock a.m., when the sun comes up, and it turns around through the six numbers to twelve, when it is the middle of the day." He waited until Angituk nimbly translated this. "Then on to maybe seven o'clock, when the sun goes down. You see? When the little stick is there, the sun will go down. Here, it's a gift to you!"

Koeha took the watch with awe and held it carefully. Mainprize repeated his remarks so Koeha would understand.

"When that stick ... we call it a *hand* ... reaches the six ... right there ... tomorrow morning, then the sun will rise!"

"*Quanaqqutit,*" Koeha said with conviction. "This is a fine gift, but the responsibility for the sun is too great!"

The others laughed.

"No, it is easy. Just remember to wind it once a day. Here." And Mainprize showed him how as Angituk explained.

Koeha tentatively turned the winder and marvelled at the metallic clicking sound. "It scares me," Koeha told Mainprize, and the others laughed again.

A voice was heard on the steps of the courthouse and people stopped their chatter to hear. The clerk of the court repeated, "THE JURY HAS RETURNED! THE COURT RESUMES!"

Wallbridge appeared depressed by such a fast verdict. He spoke the obvious to no one in particular. "We better go in."

THE JURY FOREMAN rose. It was Alfred F. Fugl of the Hudson's Bay Company, in a smart blue pinstriped suit and long patterned tie.

"Mr. Foreman, have you reached a verdict?" Justice Harvey inquired.

"We have, your Lordship." The company man spoke out to the Justice and to the expectant audience in the packed courtroom. He was a businessman, a chairman of boards, not uncomfortable about addressing gatherings, but the weight of responsibility could be heard in the measure of his voice. "For the murder of Father Rouvière in the first degree we, the jury, find the defendants, Sinnisiak and Uluksuk, NOT GUILTY."

A murmur of disbelief reverberated through the courtroom. Creed tried to cover his relief and gave a discreet thumbs-up to Sinnisiak and Uluksuk. They only stared. Wallbridge was shocked but delighted. The Bishop and his priest stood up in open amazement. C.C. McCaul and Justice Harvey made no pretence of hiding their outrage as they glared at the jurymen. Creed looked at Angituk and they shared a subtle smile of triumph. Nicole watched him askance.

Justice Harvey hammered his gavel to settle them all and glared at the accused. "Mr. Sinnisiak and Mr. Uluksuk." The two defendants looked up at him. "The charges are dismissed. You are free to go." Next he turned to the jury, his tone an obvious rebuke. "Members of the jury, your duties as such are complete. You are dismissed."

The Justice rose and stormed from the courtroom. Released from Harvey's oppressive governance, the room erupted. C.C. McCaul stood for a moment, stunned. He watched as the

Bishop, badly shaken, turned, and walked out of the courtroom with the aid of his young priest.

"C.C.? Would you care to give a statement?"

Mainprize asked the question gently, sensing the furies raging within the counsel for the Crown. McCaul's bear-trap expression fixed on him.

"The obvious agenda of the jury was to pull down the mighty from their seats and to exalt the humble and the meek." Then he turned and followed the Justice into his chambers.

Creed went to Uluksuk and Sinnisiak and shook their hands. "Yes, you are free. It will be all right. You are going home."

Journalists had surrounded the defendants to offer congratulations and ask questions.

"What will you do now?"

"How many wives do you have?"

"What does human liver taste like?"

Angituk stopped translating halfway through this last one and refused to continue. E.K. Mainprize pushed his way in to join the interrogation.

"What are your favourite things that you've seen here in Edmonton?"

Sinnisiak thought for a moment and Angituk translated his response. "Candies ... magic lights ... sleds with no dogs in harness to get tangled ... how nice the women smell."

"Very astute choices." Mainprize thanked them.

Creed turned to find Nicole beside him. He tried to remove the smile that had been on his face since the verdict. She had to raise her voice over the din.

"Aren't you a little frustrated? You've wasted a year of your life bringing these men to justice. Did you see how upset my uncle was?"

"They are my friends, Nicole."

They looked at each other like strangers.

A distinguished man and his elegant wife were escorted over by Wallbridge to meet the exonerated Eskimos. Angituk translated.

"Sinnisiak and Uluksuk, I'd like you to meet the Honourable Mayor Henry, the Best Hunter in this city, and his wife, Mrs. Henry." Angituk explained to the mayor and his wife, "The closest I can come to explain the title of Mayor is 'the Best Hunter.'"

Though he rather enjoyed this unusual title, Mayor Henry exuded a detached air about it all. He had done well in business as a canny retailer, but he had no idea what to make of these Eskimos. His wife, on the other hand, made the most of the situation, laughing about being the wife of the Best Hunter: her husband hadn't fired a gun in years. She was fascinated by the exoticism of the Eskimos. Uluksuk bowed his head slightly in a courtly gesture and she was charmed by him. She held Uluksuk's hand in both of hers and told him, "Call me Ada." Uluksuk smiled and repeated her name with perfect inflection, to her great surprise and delight.

MAYOR HENRY AND HIS WIFE, with their guests, Sinnisiak and Uluksuk and the interpreter Angituk, led the parade slowly down Jasper Avenue in the mayor's shiny new 1917 Cadillac landaulet. The traffic officer at 109th stopped all cross traffic. Passengers from a line of backed-up streetcars heard news of the verdict and emptied the cars to come and see the exonerated Eskimos pass by.

The mayor whispered his perplexity to his wife. "I don't understand how they got off."

"It doesn't matter, darling. Just make the most of the publicity. They're so cute."

Somehow Mainprize had found a seat in the first car. "What do you think, Mayor Henry? You could declare this Eskimo Day."

"Eskimo Day," the mayor repeated. He liked the sound of it.

They were followed by Wallbridge's rented Model T, which held Creed, Koeha, and John Hornby. Nicole had refused Creed's offer to join him. A third car, a large Packard, held other reporters, and behind them were a mix of carriages and honking cars. A horse spooked and bolted down 113th Street, its empty buggy fishtailing behind it. The streets were crowded with people waving and even cheering for the Eskimos. Paper boys shouted out the news and sold papers with the headline NOT GUILTY! and Creed realized that the *Journal* must have printed two versions. A sea change of public opinion had attended the announcement of the verdict and turned the "murdering cannibals" into exotic celebrities, akin to ambassadors from a faraway nation. The hunter and the shaman sat in the open landaulet and looked out at all the people in amazement.

"So they like us now? They're not going to kill us anymore?"

"Yes, I think they like us. They treat us like special guests now. Just go along with it."

"Okay."

Uluksuk had rallied substantially from his depressed state and began to smile and even enjoy himself, waving back at the crowds. People ran up to the car and gave them candy bars and cigars. A young man handed them a newspaper with a photograph of the two of them on the front page. Sinnisiak and Uluksuk stared at it.

"That's you."

"No, that's you there."

Each could see the other, but neither could recognize himself in the photographs.

A pretty young girl jumped up on the running board and, in the emotion of the moment, threw her arms around Sinnisiak and kissed his cheek. He yelled in fear and pulled away from her. The girl hopped easily down from the car, holding her skirt up so she could run along, still smiling at Sinnisiak until she came up against the crowds and was lost.

"I thought she was biting my face!" Sinnisiak explained, and Angituk laughed out loud at this.

"It is called a *kiss*," she told them with authority, using the English word.

Uluksuk and Sinnisiak stared out at the horses and human beings going by like herds of caribou on a migration. What a strange world this was. Sinnisiak turned to look back and was reassured to find Creed in the car behind them. Mainprize stopped taking notes for a moment to ask Uluksuk what he was thinking. Angituk spoke from her own heart as she translated the old hunter's response.

"Never have I imagined or dreamed that such a place could exist, or so many people!"

Twenty

Uluksuk and Sinnisiak were offered a luxurious suite at the Hotel Macdonald, and Creed and Angituk were to escort them in and get them settled. The impressive "Mac" was a railway hotel and featured the town's first public elevators. Even Uluksuk was impressed by them. They stood in the little room and each time the doors opened there was a new place outside. The hunters could have ridden the elevator for hours.

Ada Henry insisted on coming with them to the room. She was planning all kinds of activities for them the next day. Ada stood observing them as Sinnisiak examined the light coming from a bedside lamp, assessing the heat with his open hand.

"This would take a long time to cook meat."

Uluksuk was turning the taps on, and off in the bathroom, scalding himself with the hot water. He looked at his red fingers and chuckled.

"What are you thinking, Uluksuk?" Creed asked him.

The old man laughed and pointed to the taps as if they were a private joke between them. Who could have imagined?

The mayor's wife watched them for a moment longer, fascinated. She didn't want to leave. "Is there anything else they need?"

Creed smiled, shook his head, and offered his hand.

"Thank you so much for all you've done, Mrs. Henry. They've really had quite an afternoon. If I know them, a nap will be in order."

"They really are like children, aren't they? All right. But I'll be back bright and early tomorrow morning at ten o'clock."

"Yes, ma'am. We'll be ready for you."

"Goodbye, Mr. Uluksuk ... Mr. Sinnisiak."

"Goodbye," they both said in English, still very distracted by their surroundings.

Just as she was leaving, the suits she had ordered were delivered from her husband's clothing store, Blowey & Henry, on 106th Street. They were dark brown pinstripe, three-button wool with cuffs, along with white shirts and brown spotted ties and black oxfords and checked, brimmed caps. The tailor had taken measurements from their old caribou skins.

"These are for dinner tomorrow night," Mrs. Henry explained before she left.

There was a suit for Angituk too. Blowey & Henry had asked that in return they be allowed to take photographs of the Eskimos to prove their motto, "Our clothes make the man." Sinnisiak and Uluksuk tried them on with Creed's help and they fit perfectly. They stared at themselves in the full-length mirrors and then laughed at each other. Angituk laughed at both of them.

"I knew you could become a raven or a wolf," Sinnisiak told Uluksuk, "but now you have become a white man!"

The hotel sent up barbers who shaved and trimmed them.

"I wish old Agalakti could see us. Can we bring this clothing home to show?"

Creed assured them they could.

"It would not be very warm," Uluksuk cautioned.

"That's true," Sinnisiak agreed. "But it would be okay for the summer caribou hunt."

Angituk laughed at them again. "That I would love to see—
you hunting caribou in those suits." She shared the joke with
Creed.

"The caribou would be laughing so hard they would be easy
to kill," Creed suggested.

They each tried one of the cigars they had been given. Creed
lit them, and after the initial coughing fits they both began to
enjoy the rich smoke, which they found much smoother than
the dried lichens and caribou grass Uluksuk usually smoked in
his pipe.

The photographer from the Blowey & Henry department
store arrived. He wanted to photograph them just as they
were, in the chairs with the barbers, only he gave Uluksuk a
newspaper and Sinnisiak a movie magazine to pretend to read.
Creed warned them about the flash powder so they wouldn't
think they were being shot, but they were used to photographs;
it was nothing to them. They relaxed and smiled. Uluksuk took
a deep draw on his cigar.

"You know, I think this is proof that what we dream is life
and what appears as life is really a dream."

They all agreed.

THE NEXT MORNING, the mayor's wife and her entourage of
press, photographers, and councillors' wives took them to the
museum to view the African exhibit. They stared in awe at the
stuffed elephant, the rhinoceros, and the lion. The hunters were
cautious in case the dangerous-looking creatures somehow
became reanimated.

"I thought the horse was impressive, but look at these ..."
Uluksuk said in a reverential whisper to Sinnisiak. "Are these
animals found around here?"

"I don't know."

"I would like to go hunting for them."

"Me too."

"Do they have any fresh ones we can eat?" Uluksuk inquired of Angituk, and was disappointed with her reply.

"No. Those animals do not come from around here. They come from other lands far away."

Uluksuk considered this for a moment. "Other lands? You mean there are other lands beyond our lands, the Cree lands, and the white men's lands right here?"

Angituk looked at him and nodded. "It is a big world."

ULUKSUK AND SINNISIAK posed for press photographs among the Neanderthals in the prehistoric exhibit with Mainprize quipping, "Stone Age Man Meets Stone Age Mannequin." They admired the fine quality of the bearskins the statues wore and the nicely made flint tools.

Next was the matinee at the Imperial Theatre, of a new movie called *Yankee Doodle in Berlin* that parodied the German Kaiser and his officers. The Eskimos stared at the world within a world. The close-ups scared them when an actor's disembodied head suddenly blew up large. They were relieved to be sitting on either side of Creed, who continued to reassure them. And then there was a short afterwards, a ballet sequence with women in tutus that appealed to Sinnisiak but Uluksuk found shocking.

"Those women are naked."

"They are too skinny for much comfort, but I like how they move," Sinnisiak offered.

The afternoon finished at the Funland at Borden Park, where Sinnisiak teased Uluksuk into riding the notorious roller coaster known as the Green Rattler. Uluksuk, convinced he was about to die, passed out and Creed had to hold on to him tightly for the rest of the ride so he would not slide down onto the floor of the car. When at the end the cars rolled into the loading area and stopped, Uluksuk pulled away from Creed, jumped out, and walked away unsteadily. He was very angry and it took Sinnisiak and Angituk and Creed to calm him down.

Their day ended at the calliope. Uluksuk loved the colourful wooden menagerie that rotated to the pretty organ music. It lifted the shaman's spirits and Creed and Angituk breathed a sigh of relief. Uluksuk rode a silver unicorn with a golden horn because it reminded him of the noble horn of a narwhal. The last photograph of the afternoon showed old Uluksuk riding the unicorn and Ada Henry's entourage all around him, smiling.

MAYOR HENRY HAD PROVISIONED and outfitted gold seekers headed to the Klondike in '98 and '99. With his profits he had opened two large department stores and acquired a beautiful home. The Henrys' large manor house overlooked the North Saskatchewan River. As Ada Henry's entourage approached, the house was so brightly lit by the electric lights inside that it appeared to Uluksuk to be on fire.

Sinnisiak and Uluksuk, in their new suits and trimmed hair, were shown to their seats near the head of the long table of twenty-five guests in the mahogany-panelled dining room. A large and dazzling electric crystal chandelier, all the way from Montreal, hung above them. Tridents of open candles were interspersed along the table, making the hunters feel at home, as much as they could in this foreign environment. Creed observed his former prisoners and was amazed to see how quickly they adapted to the observed table manners around them. Their napkins lay across their laps, and they ate with the knives and forks, cutting their meat into small pieces. They politely passed food plates to others and sipped their wine quietly. Sinnisiak had by observation and practise perfected lifting the wineglass with only three fingers, as if he'd been doing it all his life.

Creed sat across from them in his scarlet jacket with Nicole by his side in a lovely long white silk dress with matching scarf. Creed could feel Angi's eyes on him when Nicole put her hand on his or smiled playfully at him. He had decided, with the verdict in, he would have to have his talk with Nicole tonight.

He stole an amused, affectionate long look at Angituk in the pinstriped suit as she conversed with Koeha and Ada Henry. He wondered if the mayor's wife would appreciate the clever way she could gut a caribou or snare and cook a ground squirrel, or the fact that she was a girl. Angituk laughed at something Ada Henry said and pushed her cropped hair back from her eyes, and Jack's mind returned to the Great Bear River on that spring day, her skin a hot contrast to the cold water. Then Angi's eyes were on him and, as if reading his thoughts, she smiled.

The mayor was still a little awkward in the presence of his two guests, but his wife made up for it with a stream of chatty questions and observations.

"I say the time has come," Ada Henry declared with conviction to her dinner guests. "It's absurd we haven't had it before now in a progressive, modern world. Women were given the vote two years ago in Manitoba. Are we more backward than Manitoba? God help us."

"I entirely agree with you, Mrs. Henry. It's absurd," Nicole offered.

"What do you think, Inspector Creed?"

"I'm all for it, the women's vote, ma'am. Could make for a kinder, gentler world."

"There, you see, William? A progressive young man. Now, Mr. Uluksuk, do your women have a vote?"

Uluksuk had found the smoked salmon, the one white man's

food that pleased him and didn't upset his stomach. Somewhat putting aside the white manners he had perfected, he used both hands to make short work of an entire tray. Ada Henry was happy to see him so enjoying the dish. After Angituk translated the question about sexual politics in Copper Eskimo society, Uluksuk stopped eating and wiped his hands and mouth to better respond to his hostess's question. Angituk explained the dynamics of the inquiry to him and he responded.

"Our women always had the vote."

Creed went on to explain. "There does seem to be a relative sexual equality, a mutual support, where the man does the hunting, fishing, trapping, and the wife looks after the home—cooking, clothing, children. But sometimes they will trade jobs: the wife will fish and the man will sew clothes. And decisions are made by consensus of husband and wife. Oh, and wife beating is rare."

The mayor's interest was aroused. "But I thought Eskimos could take more than one wife. Doesn't the old one here have two or three?"

"That's true, but there are also some women who take two husbands. It is about what is practical. Uluksuk here, as you know, is a shaman or medicine man, but about one-third of the shamans are women. It's quite egalitarian. There are no real politics. Communal hunting and food sharing is the norm. The environment forces everyone to work together to survive."

"You see, William? Sexual equality, practicality, even socialism. It's almost like you've discovered a utopian society in the High Arctic, Inspector Creed. It's so exciting."

"That may be overstating it, ma'am, but I think we can learn a lot from these people. I've come to like and respect them very much."

Angituk smiled at Creed's coy compliment and felt an overwhelming desire to tease him, until she felt Nicole's gaze settle on her. Angituk lowered her eyes. She was asked to translate a question for Sinnisiak, directed to a pretty girl across the table. The girl, whose fashionable dress revealed a provocative bit of cleavage, had been drinking wine and was flirting with the handsome hunter, showing off a little, asking about the animals he hunted and if he sang songs and did dances. It was apparent, too, that she had attracted Sinnisiak's interest, and he was quite candid about sizing her up as possible wife number two. What he wanted to know now was her technique for butchering caribou. Did she possess a good knife, and were the sealskin boots she sewed soft and waterproof? She confessed to her inexperience in these things.

"But I'm a fast learner!" she exclaimed, and everyone laughed.

AFTER DINNER, they retired to the large parlour for brandy and champagne, and in keeping with the new sexual politics of Mrs. Henry, the women joined the men. Her two blond daughters, Elizabeth and Victoria, aged six and nine, were also permitted because they were fascinated by the strange little men they had seen in the newspapers.

Uluksuk was sitting in a large wing chair looking apprehensively at the pocket watch Koeha had given him. It had been a gift from the man named Mainprize, but Koeha was scared of it. Uluksuk studied it again, the second hand rotating in microscopic increments, controlled by the gears he could see in one corner through a tiny glass window inside. Koeha had explained carefully to him that he who held the watch held the power of the entire world in his hand. When the little black stick reached the bottom figure of 6, the sun would rise. And, as he understood it, of course the opposite was true too: if the stick failed to reach the bottom, the sun would not rise and there would be no day. It would be like the time before the wolf and wolverine digging in the cave discovered the sun. Koeha had transferred this huge responsibility to Uluksuk, and Uluksuk was having second thoughts. The stick on the watch still seemed to be moving. All should be well, but he was beginning to wish Koeha had not given it to him.

He put it safely, carefully, into his pocket just as young Victoria and Elizabeth arrived. They approached him without fear.

"Are you a magician?"

When Angituk explained, Uluksuk replied, "I am."

"What tricks do you know?"

"I can become a wolf or a raven."

"Can we see?"

"Not tonight. It takes a day or two."

"Are there unicorns where you live?"

Angituk explained the reference and mentioned the merry-go-round. Uluksuk smiled at them.

"Not a unicorn. Not a horse creature with a single horn, but we do have a fish with a single horn, and they are magic."

"Can you ride them?"

"Maybe. That I have never tried. But there are stories of young girls who do."

This image pleased the children.

"Do you really eat people?"

"No, not usually. But when we do, it is with great respect."

With Angituk's seamless translation, Uluksuk went on to tell the inquisitive girls about his own daughters and granddaughter, and what they liked to do, such as play tag and hide-and-seek, hunt for plover eggs, play rock houses, or search in the rocks and snowdrifts for *inyourligat*, the furry dwarfs, even though they feared them. Elizabeth, the younger, climbed up on his knee to listen to the stories of the spirits and creatures that lived in the North. Uluksuk loved telling the stories to these young ones, for he deeply missed his own children and grandchildren. And the best part was that this new audience had never heard any of his stories before.

A CIRCLE OF GUESTS had collected near the big bay window. Nicole's cousin Harold and his English friend, Lieutenant Wilkerson openly discussed the verdict.

"These men may have been found not guilty on a technicality, but they did kill the priests. With all due respect to our hosts, it is hardly a thing to celebrate," Wilkerson pronounced.

Nicole offered, "I know my uncle is very upset by the verdict. He said it may not stand."

Her words triggered an alarm in Creed. "Are you saying Justice Harvey is thinking this may not be the end of it?"

"That's what he said."

Wilkerson continued. "I can't see how the verdict could stand. The message would be: you kill a couple of white men and they bring you south and throw a party for you. Then you go home. It would mean open season on white men in the North." He turned to Creed. "Surely after all your efforts, Corporal—I mean Inspector—Inspector Creed, you don't think they should be released?"

"It is not my job to assess the actions of these men and what should be done. They are truly from a different world."

Wilkerson's voice hardened. "Their world is now our world, and they better damn well adapt to it just like the Indians have and like all the Aboriginals have in all the territories of the Empire. We made them."

"Often with tragic consequences."

Wilkerson was surprised by Creed's liberal sentiments. "The civilizing process is what the Empire does. It is the price Natives have to pay for peace, prosperity, and security."

"I think only the peace, prosperity, and security of whites."

"Would you have chaos?"

Creed wondered why Wilkerson had taken a dislike to him. "No. I've seen chaos, and I'm not partial to it. I'm only asking they be treated with tolerance and respect."

"'Tolerance and respect' gets you nowhere. They must be shown the new order. They must be taught who's boss!"

"But they really are just like children," Mrs. Henry offered in defence.

"Again, with respect, Mrs. Henry," Lieutenant Wilkerson continued, "I believe you're naturally far too kind."

It suddenly occurred to Creed that Lieutenant Wilkerson was interested in Nicole. He was playing to her by putting Creed in his place; with every other line his eyes glanced over to assess her reaction. But more perplexing, Creed noticed, was that Nicole seemed to be responding. Creed looked again at Wilkerson, finding the fashionable little moustache particularly irritating, and re-entered the fray.

"So you were saying, Lieutenant, the Empire's history of brutal repression is the ticket?"

ANGITUK CAREFULLY WATCHED Nicole in the circle by the window. She smiled at the men and blinked her eyes and held her glass of champagne up just so. Angituk plucked a glass from a tray and tried to hold it like Nicole. She blinked her eyes a few times and cocked her head and smiled with her mouth wide like Nicole. She took a swallow of champagne and then another. It was sweet and good. She took another, and soon the warmth was spreading through her. She had a sudden desire to be dressed like Nicole. Beautiful and elegant.

Angituk procured another full glass from a tray, hardly spilling a drop. She took a good swallow and sauntered over to join the gathering by the window. She came up quite close to Nicole and smelled her rich, flowery scent and examined her diamond earrings. She smiled at her.

"You have beautiful earrings, Miss Harvey."

Nicole glanced at the boy, distracted from the conversation, a little irritated. "Thank you."

Angituk gave her a smile. She finished the second glass and took a third, holding it high in her fingers as she had seen Nicole do. Nicole gave her an odd look then focused again on the men, who were engaged in a heated discussion. Wilkerson barely remained civil.

"You know, Inspector, there was something I was meaning to ask you. You said you were in the Second Canadian Battalion at the second battle of Ypres in '15 with the Fourth Princess Louise regiment. But Harold here has a friend in the Princess Louise, the quartermaster, so he knew everyone's name, and I asked him about you. He was quite sure there was no one with the name Creed in the regiment."

Angituk continued to admire Nicole's white dress. It was the most lovely thing she'd ever seen. She wondered again how she would look in such a dress. She leaned over toward Nicole.

"I think your dresh is beautiful."

"Thank you."

"It was a very large regiment," Creed told the lieutenant, trying to maintain his patience. "Many of us, myself included, went to the Princess Pats just before Ypres. What was the name of your friend? The quartermaster."

"It must have cost a king's ransom," Angituk continued.

"*Au contraire.* Quite reasonable, really," Nicole replied coolly.

"You don't say. How do you like that?" Angituk swayed unsteadily. She was using phrases from magazines she'd been reading. "I would give my eye teeth."

"Fitzgibbon. His name is Fitzgibbon."

Angituk did not register the woman's irritation with her and carried on. "Where might one get their hands on a shweet little number like that?"

"Montreal."

"Well I'll be a monkey's uncle."

Nicole's expression darkened.

"But what I'm curious about is just where you were wounded. What was the date of your discharge?"

"And your hair is so ..." Angituk put out her hand to touch Nicole's golden curls. "How do you get the curls sho big?"

"What exactly are you getting at, Wilkerson?"

Nicole pushed Angituk's hand away. "Don't touch me!" she said, sharply enough to draw the attention of those nearby.

Angituk staggered back a little, caught herself, and then lurched forward. To Nicole's horror half Angituk's glass of champagne slopped down the front of her dress. Nicole stepped away from her, furious.

"You stupid, drunken little half-breed! Get away from me!"

"I'm so sorry ..." Angituk took out her handkerchief to wipe off the front of the dress.

"Get away!" Looking down at the stain spreading across her bodice and waist, Nicole gasped in disgust. Creed and Wilkerson moved forward in unison with handkerchiefs ready, and glared at each other.

"Come to the powder room, dear," Mrs. Henry offered.

Nicole stormed out of the room.

"Let's have some lively music, shall we?" Mrs. Henry ordered over her shoulder, and followed Nicole.

Harold Harvey went quickly to the gramophone and with a hefty crank a symphonic version of the popular "The Sunshine of Your Smile" flooded the parlour. A young couple started dancing. The conversation between Creed and the English lieutenant was over. Creed turned and went after Nicole.

CREED STOOD ALONE in the dark hallway outside the locked door of the powder room. He could hear Nicole and Mrs. Henry speaking inside. After a moment Mrs. Henry came out and put a hand on his arm.

"She'll be all right, Inspector. It's coming out."

When Mrs. Henry had gone back into the parlour, Creed called through the door. "Do you need any help, Nicole?"

From beyond the door: "It's not polite to talk through powder room doors. Have you lost all your manners? I'll just be a minute." The voice was softer, less angry.

He was anxious to ask her more about what Justice Harvey had said concerning the trial verdict but decided not to push it. He felt a presence and turned to find Angituk standing in the shadows.

"She's not sho pretty when she's mad, ish she?"

"Shhhhh. You shouldn't drink any more champagne."

"*Au contraire.* I require more now I've spilled it all over your lady love."

Angituk walked up to him and gave him a goofy smile. She put her strong hands on either side of his face, pulled him toward her, and kissed him hard on the mouth. He hesitated and then for a moment he responded, pulling her to him, feeling the length of her body against his and matching the eagerness of her mouth and tongue. Just as suddenly, he stopped. He glanced toward the entrance to the parlour, where laughter and music could be heard. The door to the powder room was just a few feet from them and he gently, reluctantly, pushed her away.

"We can't do this. Not here."

"Then come with me." Angituk spoke in a breathless whisper. "I want you."

"For God's sake, Angi, *shhhhhhh*. Look, I think Uluksuk and Sinnisiak are still in danger, and a scandal won't help things. And Nicole could be the key to protecting them. When she comes out, you should apologize ... again."

Angituk looked at him, both hurt and amused. She reached up and touched his lips with her fingertips, then stood back from him a little unsteadily. "You really don't know what you want, do you?"

The door to the powder room opened and Nicole was surprised to find them both there. Angituk turned toward her.

"Miss Harvey, I am dreadfully sorry. That was very clumsy of me and I apologize."

"That's all right. Try to be more careful next time." She dismissed her. "Jack?"

She raised her white hand expectantly and Creed took it. They walked toward the parlour. When Creed glanced back, Angituk made a sour face at him. It covered the pain she was feeling. The champagne was wearing off. She watched them until they disappeared through the doorway. Enough of this, she thought.

She went into the cloakroom to find her light coat. She heard a shuffling and a sigh. She turned on the dim electric light to find Sinnisiak and the pretty girl from across the table lying on the coats. They looked at her, startled. The girl's hair was dishevelled and Sinnisiak had a happy expression. Angituk turned out the lights again. She put on her coat and old fedora and headed for the front door.

Twenty-One

Angituk crossed the river at the 106th Street Bridge and made her way north toward Jasper, the cool night air clearing her head. She tried to put Creed out of her mind and focus on her quest. It was late and the streets were quite deserted as she crossed Wellington Terrace and returned briefly to the hotel to change her clothes. She took off the pinstriped suit and slipped into her jean trousers, checkered shirt, and old fedora. She put a light patina of ash on her face and assumed the shoulders-up, eyes-down, slightly rolling gait of her male persona.

Standing on the narrow boardwalk, Angituk double-checked the address written in pencil on the little piece of paper in Cowperthwaite's meticulous hand. Dooley's Bar on 98th Street. A lamppost illuminated its dark green exterior and two drunks counting out their pennies. A third was relieving himself in a puddle in the middle of the unpaved street. No one gave her a glance as she went into the bar where she hoped to find her father.

It was loud and smoky and dark inside the bar, and Angituk stepped to one side to look around from under the brim of her hat. Miners and tradesmen, a few soldiers, and a couple of farmers sat at tables served by an elderly waiter. The only three women in the place wore bright dresses with old-fashioned

crinolines underneath and had faces heavily made up and lots
of curls in their hair. They sat with the men and laughed and
smiled and patted the men on their arms or knees. As Angituk
watched, one of the ladies took a shy farmer in overalls upstairs.
His face was red and he glanced around nervously, but he
followed her when she took his hand.

Her father—or at least a man named Angus McAndrew—
lived upstairs, and Cowperthwaite had made a phone call for
her to determine that he was the bartender on Thursday nights.
There was no one behind the bar when she first entered, but
then a big man came out from the kitchen. He was yelling back
at the cook.

"I said stew, not goddamn soup, you crazy Chink. Get me four
goddamn bowls of stew. And bread. *Now*, for Chrissake!"

Angus McAndrew stood behind the counter scratching the
few days' growth of beard on his chin. Angituk instinctively
lowered her brim and looked away. She could feel his eyes settle
on her for a moment and then move on. Then he was looking at
the piano player.

"Hey, Beethoven. Something faster. Let's hear some goddamn
ragtime. You're putting us all to sleep, you stupid wop."

Angituk's heart sank. She had hoped her father was a kind
man. She walked up to the bar.

Angus McAndrew fixed his angry eyes on Angituk as she
approached. "You a breed? We don't serve breeds in here, kid."

"I'm looking for Angus McAndrew."

"Oh, you are? And what's he to you?"

The Chinese cook came out with a tray of bowls of stew and
put it on the bar.

Angituk asked, "Are you Angus McAndrew?"

"Why? Did he win the Irish Sweepstakes?" The big man
laughed at his joke and slapped the cook too hard on the back,

but even he laughed a little. McAndrew's eyes narrowed. "What's this about? Who wants to know?"

"A friend."

"I've never seen you before in my life, you little shit. Now get out of my place."

"Were you ever up in the Arctic? The Mackenzie delta?"

"How'd you know that? Who are you?"

"Were you there?"

"I was a cook on a whaler."

Angituk's heart sank for the second time. Could this unhappy man be her father?

"What's it to you anyway?"

"Do you remember the village of Paulatuk? A woman named Kunee?"

"I don't remember any goddamn flat-face village or any Eskimo whore. Enough of this. Get out of my place! No, let me help you out of my goddamn place."

Angus McAndrew jumped over the bar with amazing agility for his size. Before Angituk knew what was happening, he grabbed her by the neck, lifted her off the ground, and began to drag her toward the door. The patrons clapped and cheered at the entertainment, but Angituk wasn't finished yet. She wasn't leaving without the answer. She wrapped her legs around his legs and tripped him. He fell hard with Angituk on top of him, his head bouncing off the dirty wood-plank floor with its spilled beer and cigarette butts. He was dazed for a moment, losing his grip, and Angituk twisted around onto her knees and grabbed for his unbuttoned left sleeve, tearing it as she forced it up his forearm. The skin was clear! There was no mermaid!

Angituk let go of his arm and slumped back with such a feeling of relief that she didn't see Angus McAndrew's right fist coming as it slammed into the side of her head. McAndrew dragged her through the door and dumped her face down in the mud and urine outside Dooley's Bar.

When she rose slowly, spitting blood and rubbing her chin, she struggled up onto her hands and knees. She saw her hat in the mud beside her. She smiled and then laughed. She thanked Kannokapfaluk and the small animal and bird spirits and especially her spirit guide, the bear, and even the Jesus and Mary spirits that she had learned about at the mission school— thanked all of them that this McAndrew was not the one she sought. Her good father was still out there somewhere.

THEY ARRIVED at the train station at dawn for the 7:28 to Fort McMurray. Once Sinnisiak and Uluksuk were on their way, they would be safe and Creed's life would be simple again. He could sort out the situation with Nicole in an honourable way.

It was a small and subdued gathering, with only E.K. Mainprize and surprisingly few other members of the press. Wallbridge was there, still amazed by his successful defence. He had developed an affection for his Eskimo clients and would miss them. John Hornby was also there to say goodbye. He was going to be heading east later that day on the train from South Station. He had decided to go and fight in the war in Europe for King and country. Creed was worried about him. Worried about what would become of him.

"You really shouldn't do this, John. The war is not what you think. You should stay here. We could find some guiding work for you with the police."

"I'm already outside. And the King has asked for me personally. That's what the sign said. You can't just ... just ignore your monarch. After all, he's the King."

Nothing Creed said could dissuade him.

Sinnisiak and Uluksuk were going home, accompanied by

Koeha, and also Angituk, at least as far as Fort Norman. She
had been contracted by the court to accompany them as
interpreter that far and ensure they had what they needed to
continue on to the Coppermine. Angituk did not mind leaving
the crowded city, but it saddened her to think of her father out
there somewhere. Her face was bruised from her encounter
at Dooley's and she had been evasive in her explanations to
Creed, but she was glad that she had gone to see. Glad her
father was not the old dying man in the cot or the bartender at
Dooley's. She had the address of one last Angus McAndrew in
her pocket, but Uluksuk was anxious to get home and they had
to go. Maybe it was for the best. Maybe they were not meant to
meet. Creed had explained to Angituk that after a few days of
administrative duties in Edmonton he would take some leave
and join her in Fort Norman. That would be the moment she
would work toward.

Uluksuk presented Creed with the small bow he had made
in the igloo the previous winter. The policemen who had taken
it when they first arrived had given it back to him. It was in its
leather case with three arrows and a small tool kit for repairs.
Creed inspected the spruce bow with the ornately braided sinew
that gave it strength and sighted the little copper-tipped arrows,
each straighter than a pool cue. With Angituk translating,
Uluksuk explained quietly that the bow and arrows were to be
given to their first son. Creed smiled at Angituk, took Uluksuk's
hand in both of his, and shook it warmly.

"*Quanaqqutit*, my friend."

Uluksuk paused and studied him seriously for a moment,
holding his hand. He spoke directly, looking Creed in the eyes.
"I had a vision last night. You must be careful. The dark spirits
that you fear are closer than you think. They mean you harm."

Creed stared at him. "I don't understand. Dark spirits?"

"I don't know. I don't know anything more. I would tell you more if I knew, but down here, you know, my powers are so weak. When I am home again and strong I will speak on your behalf to the spirits. They will help you if they can. But for now you must be careful."

Creed was shaken by the shaman's words.

The engineer blew the two-minute whistle. With Angituk's help, Uluksuk made a statement to the reporters.

"Thank you for your hospitality. I have found white society quite interesting, but it is not really what I like. There are too many people and the food is bad. I am in a good mood now, but I have to get back and feed my family."

A disruption farther down the platform captured the attention of the reporters. A small patrol of Mounties arrived, led by Corporal Cowperthwaite. Creed didn't like the look on Cowperthwaite's face as he came up to him.

"What is it, Lyle?"

Cowperthwaite took a deep breath. "I'm very sorry, Jack. They've come up with new charges. They're putting them on trial again. For the murder of the other priest."

"What are you talking about, Lyle?" he asked quietly. Ever since the verdict he had wondered if something like this could possibly happen. He had dismissed his premonition as improbable, and yet it was unfolding just as he had feared. "You can't do this, Lyle. You're going to kill them. This is going to kill them!"

"I'm so sorry. It's orders."

Creed turned away in frustration. "Goddamnit."

Mainprize was in Cowperthwaite's face. "What are the charges?"

"The murder of Father Le Roux this time."

Mainprize ran for the telephone inside the station.

Angituk looked at Creed. "How can they do this? Uluksuk won't survive."

"I know." Creed went to the old hunter, trying to stay calm. "This is bad news, Uluksuk. They are going to have another trial. You will be tried for killing the other priest. I'm very sorry."

Angituk translated for them, and the light in Uluksuk's eyes went dim. Quietly, Sinnisiak began to cry. Cowperthwaite put cuffs on them and helped the prisoners down off the train. Angituk turned angrily to Creed.

"This is all a lie! They were found innocent. They were free to go. The court is dishonest. Can't you do anything?"

"I don't know, Angi. I don't know. Let me think."

JUSTICE HORACE HARVEY and C.C. McCaul had met early that morning after the late-night phone call from the Attorney General, who told them another trial would be required. McCaul was very pleased with himself. He had decided in the first trial only to charge them for the murder of Father Rouvière just in case something like this happened. Now they could, with complete legitimacy, try the two again, for the murder of Father Le Roux.

According to the Attorney General, Archbishop Bruchési had visited the Prime Minister's office with a very clear message: the verdict in Edmonton was not acceptable. It would make it open season on all his northern missionaries. The verdict could not stand. They must be tried again.

Prime Minister Borden was anxious to give the Archbishop what he wanted. The Canadian Expeditionary Forces in Europe were stretched to the limit and the Prime Minister was preparing a bill for the conscription of soldiers. He knew Quebec would strongly oppose it. Only two weeks before, the multilingual Bruchési had made a stirring speech to French Canadians, insisting that they owed a debt to their mother country and that every able-bodied man should enlist. If the conscription bill was going to pass, he would need Archbishop Bruchési's continued support. So in return, the Archbishop would have his second trial.

"I'll hand-pick the jury myself," Justice Harvey had assured the Attorney General. "And it will be a more ... aggressive prosecution. Given the evidence against them, I was counting on a cut-and-dried guilty verdict. I thought we should be easy with them. I won't make that mistake again."

The Attorney General said he would let the Prime Minister know.

THE PRELIMINARIES of the second trial of the Eskimos began two mornings after their arrest, when jury selection was complete. Everyone was back in their seats, McCaul, Wallbridge, Justice Harvey, Bishop Breynat, and his assisting priest. And a new jury. The courtroom was as crowded as before, and just as warm, with the brass fans turning slowly, the familiar periodic squeak of one making it all as it was. Justice Harvey declared the court in session and immediately Wallbridge stood up before the bench.

"With all respect, Justice Harvey, given the fact that you have already expressed your opinions as to the guilt of the prisoners, I demand we secure a new presiding judge."

Justice Harvey replied in a tone that left no room for resistance. "I have made inquiries, Mr. Wallbridge, and all other judges are on summer recess. Therefore I shall be forced to preside. Now sit down."

In the presence of the same press and Keedy's intrepid law students, jury selection had taken place. Justice Harvey was anxious for a conclusion to this business and warned the court, "I would like matters dealt with as speedily as possible." He had compiled a list of jurists from Calgary, all Roman Catholics. They had taken the morning train to Edmonton. Wallbridge's objections to four of the particularly devout were systematically denied.

The two accused were brought in with Angituk. At the request of Justice Harvey, Bishop Breynat uttered a prayer, asking for wisdom and justice "in the name of the Father, Son, and Holy Ghost." The jurists all gave the "Amen" and Wallbridge's heart sank as everyone crossed themselves. Bishop Breynat and his colleagues were satisfied.

Uluksuk, his body thin, his step hesitant, seemed almost in a trance as a worried Sinnisiak helped him to walk to the prisoners' bench and sit down. To Creed he looked as if he had aged twenty years. Mainprize wrote in his column of his alarm over the shaman's failing health.

McCaul began his prosecution by telling the jury that it was their moral duty to find the accused guilty. Justice Harvey denied Wallbridge's objection to this statement almost before it was out of his mouth. McCaul continued.

"Canadians are determined to develop the North, and I urge you men of the jury to execute your judgment not merely to avenge the deaths of Fathers Rouvière and Le Roux, but to ensure a lesson will be taught to the Eskimos to respect the white man's laws, the laws of humanity, the laws of God. Only then will the North be safe."

Wallbridge flinched at the use of the word "avenge" because this was exactly the direction McCaul had denied he would take the prosecution in the first trial. He had said this was a system of impartial justice. But maybe not this time.

The trial proceeded much like the first one. Father Duchaussois read tearfully from the diaries of his friend Father Rouvière. Creed described finding the remains of the priests

and repeated the conclusions from his investigations. He began
to retrace his discussions with Koeha, but McCaul hurried him
past them, especially Koeha's recollections of Father Le Roux's
bad mood and of his confrontation with Kormik in the hunting
camp over the rifle. And when Creed told of the arrests, McCaul
interrupted Creed's description of how docile and co-operative
they had been for the months of the return journey.

However, in the cross-examination this was exactly what
Wallbridge encouraged him to talk about. He wanted to hear
the story that Koeha had told of Father Le Roux's altercation
and the hurried departure, but repeated objections slowed
Creed to a stop. Wallbridge wanted the court to hear the
details of how the accused saved Creed's life, but they were
deemed irrelevant: the episode did not have bearing on the case
at hand. As Creed revealed his frustration and talked over the
objections to state the remorse demonstrated by the accused,
McCaul came forward and asked the Justice to have a word
with his witness. Justice Harvey called Creed to the bench for
a private chat.

"Is it possible, Inspector Creed, you have forgotten you are
a police officer and witness for the Crown? Govern yourself
accordingly."

Before Creed stepped down, McCaul asked to be permitted
one last question. "As you look to the future, Inspector, don't you
realize we have an obligation to help these people, to bring them
into the twentieth century, to present them all the advantages
of our society, teach them justice and fair governance, and give
them all the benefits of modern civilization?"

In the moment of silence that followed, the pencils of
Mainprize and his colleagues could be heard scratching quickly.
Creed's eyes looked over at Uluksuk and Sinnisiak and then
settled on Angituk.

"Those of us with the good fortune to have seen these people living their strenuous, healthy lives"—he looked out over the courtroom—"couldn't wish them a better fate than having our civilization kept at arm's length from them for as long as possible."

WALLBRIDGE CALLED JOHN HORNBY, who had delayed his enlistment trip east to appear as a witness for the defence. Wallbridge asked him to speak of the irascible disposition of Father Le Roux, but Justice Harvey dismissed him, saying that his opinions had no bearing on the case. Wallbridge then called old Koeha, who had proven an invaluable witness for the defence in the first trial. But when his name was called, he did not appear. Corporal Oberly reported to the court his belief that the hunter had had enough and had left on the train the day before. Harvey ruled they would proceed without him. Wallbridge moved on to his final witnesses: the accused.

Sinnisiak could not keep it together on the stand, even with Angituk's encouragement as she translated. In tears, he told Justice Harvey that Uluksuk was dying and asked to be allowed to take him home. "We will never kill anybody again."

Harvey told Wallbridge to get his witness under control. Gently, Wallbridge calmed him and with Angituk's help walked the young hunter through the essential details of the story: meeting up with the priests, pulling their sled, the priests becoming impatient and angry with the reluctant helpers; Ilogoak forcing them at rifle point to continue pulling the sled; how they had indeed feared for their lives.

In the cross-examination, McCaul's questions were all about the rifles.

"The priests left the camp after the conflict with Kormik."

"Yes."

"They were weak and defenceless and they had rifles."

"I don't understand."

"Beautiful, powerful rifles."

"They were nice."

"Rifles would make you important if you had one."

"Everyone would like a rifle."

"And no one at the camp liked the white priests. They had insulted Kormik. No one would protect them or avenge them if they disappeared."

Angituk had to translate quickly to keep up.

"I don't understand."

"So you and Uluksuk followed them to steal the rifles."

"No! We were going fishing at Bloody Falls."

"You followed them and killed them so you could have the rifles."

"No!"

After these rhetorical questions Sinnisiak began to cry again and McCaul could get no more out of him. But McCaul had a new bit of evidence to present, and for this he needed Uluksuk. The old man replaced the whimpering Sinnisiak on the stand and was sworn in by the clerk: "Whatever you speak now, you speak straight; do not speak with two tongues."

Uluksuk promised what was asked and turned and looked out at the crowded courtroom, dreaming of a place far away, beyond the white men and the trees, a place where he could breathe, play with his children and grandchildren, and eat a freshly caught seal.

Creed watched the old shaman and remembered that first night when his magical illusion and stories of shamanistic wonders had so impressed him despite himself. As shaman, Uluksuk had performed a valuable service for his people: to seemingly control the uncontrollable, to keep despair at bay and give hope for the future, to enrich their simple lives with drama and colour, not unlike a Catholic priest. Now Uluksuk looked small, powerless, his once-strong frame emaciated, his formerly expressive eyes dull. Sunken, he sat there staring at the floor, deprived of magic and dignity. Creed would order the doctor to examine him again that night, but he was pessimistic anything could be done.

McCaul went through the sequence of events. Uluksuk gave slow, simplistic answers consistent with Sinnisiak's testimony.

"Now, Mr. Uluksuk, did you know that Ilogoak and Kuleavik were priests—shamans?"

He answered slowly. "No. I thought they were trappers or traders."

"But eventually you realized they were shamans?"

"Yes. They showed us rituals with eating and drinking, and chanted songs and spoke to the spirits as we do."

"So, there was a professional recognition there? A professional courtesy."

This caused a humorous stirring in the courtroom.

"Yes. The last night we finally understood they were white shamans."

"And you have been a shaman for many years near the mouth of the Coppermine. You have served the people there."

"Yes."

"It would not be good if new shamans came to the Coppermine, would it?"

"I don't understand."

"They were your competition. Your rivals. They could ruin your business. You had every reason to eliminate them!"

Wallbridge stood up. "Your Lordship, there is no evidence to support this. My learned colleague has pulled this idea out of his hat!"

"Nevertheless, Mr. Uluksuk, you will answer the question."

Uluksuk looked out the tall windows to the deep blue sky beyond and the cirrus clouds that were blowing north. "Yes. I did not want the white shamans in the Coppermine, so I killed them."

Shocked, Angituk heard his response but did not translate it. She asked him in an urgent whisper, "What are you saying, Uluksuk? That's not true."

The old man looked at her, defeated. "The white men are going to get their way. I will make it easy for them. Tell them it was my choice, not Sinnisiak's. I decided to kill the priests."

"No! It is a lie."

Justice Harvey was losing patience. "What is he saying, Mr. McAndrew?"

"Don't give up," Angituk urged Uluksuk.

"You know they will never let us go."

"Mr. McAndrew! Please translate."

Angituk hesitated.

"Tell them," Uluksuk commanded. "I want it to be finished. Please."

Angituk looked around at all the faces intent on her. She avoided Creed. "He said ... it's true. Sinnisiak was not involved in the decision. He, Uluksuk, wanted to get rid of the shamans, so he killed them."

It took several applications of Harvey's gavel to quell the noisy courtroom after the remarkable confession. Wallbridge sagged in his chair. McCaul could not keep the smile from his face.

"No further questions."

WALLBRIDGE HAD NOTHING LEFT. Runners had been sent and had confirmed that Koeha had returned north. Uluksuk's admission had sunk the defence. He would not withdraw his statement. Wallbridge in his summation tried to put it all in perspective.

"These men gather their food with the tools and weapons of the Stone Age, and think their primitive Stone Age thoughts and live their tense, insecure lives day to day. Men and women, very human, entirely friendly, who would welcome into their homes the very few white men who get that far north. First the priests and then Inspector Creed. They were treated with hospitality, fed, given a place to sleep, even though they were feared. And because the Eskimos fear them, those white visitors had to be very, very careful not to do anything that would trigger that fear.

"The accused, Sinnisiak, told the court he believed he was about eight years old, and that is a fair example of his knowledge. He doesn't know his age. He has no need to. He doesn't know what time it is. He gets up when it's light. Sleeps when it's dark. Age and time are 'white' conventions. I submit to you these men should be treated like children, like young children or imbeciles, and I say that because a young child or imbecile is incapable of committing a crime and these men are equally incapable of appreciating a crime." Angituk did not translate this last part for the defendants.

"These priests went to the mouth of the river to create a mission and look after the Eskimos, a very laudable purpose, but they got into trouble. When there developed a dispute over the rifle, instead of sitting down and reasoning with the Eskimos, Father Le Roux settled the matter by loading his other rifle and demanding the first rifle back at gunpoint. And this is how he later settled the business of pulling the sled south. When an Eskimo sees a gun pointed at him, as Inspector Creed has testified, he believes he's going to be shot. And I say any man, whether he is civilized or uncivilized, whether he is black or white or brown, if he truly believes he is about to be killed, is justified in killing another in his own defence.

"I submit that the Crown would have no case at all except for the naive and innocent confessions of these men. The Crown may tell you that whether these men are guilty or not, they must be made an example of to prevent other incidents of this kind occurring in the wilds. That is not in accordance with our ideas of justice and fair play. That is persecution and not justice.

"Now I think it is my duty to mention to the jury the reason they are here. There was a previous trial you should know about, and I want to explain what—"

Justice Harvey interrupted. "I think you had better confine yourself, Mr. Wallbridge, to the evidence."

"I think it is important for the jury to understand—"

"It is not necessary at all," Harvey said with a note of irritation. "In fact it is quite improper."

"I ought to be at liberty to tell them—"

"It is quite improper!" The Justice cut him off angrily. "It is out of the evidence."

The courtroom fell silent as Wallbridge considered defiance. Should he tell the jury of the first trial and risk professional penalties or even a mistrial? He took a deep breath and turned back to the jury.

"Then I bow to his Lordship's ruling. But let me just say it is your privilege as jurors to find these prisoners not guilty. It is the liberty gained by the people of England in the great Magna Carta that no one should dictate or influence you in your verdict. Not the agenda of my colleagues or the press or the heavy hand of Ottawa." Wallbridge glanced at both McCaul and Harvey. "I leave it to you with confidence that you will find in your wisdom they are not guilty."

C.C. MCCAUL BEGAN HIS SUMMATION standing very close to the railing, looking from one jury member to the next.

"My learned friend, while most eloquent and forcible, is asking you not to judge this case by the law of the land but by the law of the Eskimo. The law of the Stone Age! Their standards of vengeance and their value of human life. When white men go into that northern country, would such a ruling render it safe for them? Stone Age law says a man may kill if he is afraid of being killed. British law does not recognize this law. British law—Canadian law—says a man may kill only at the actual moment he is about to be killed and only as a last resort.

"Let's take an extreme case: suppose that one of you gentlemen and myself have been cast adrift from a sinking ship in a dinghy. Starvation threatens and you pull out your watch and put your revolver down in front of you and say to me, 'It is now a quarter to four. At four o'clock, unless we sight a vessel, I am going to kill you.' I would not be justified in killing you by virtue of that threat. I could not simply kill you even at four o'clock, without being guilty of murder. And if I did kill you, unless you were actually at that moment attempting to kill me, I would be guilty of murder. If a ship were to appear on the horizon a few minutes later and I was then rescued and afterwards charged with murder, my statement of your threat, if believed, would not avail as a defence in any British or Canadian court.

"Now, my learned friend submits that without their confessions the Crown would have no case in these murders. I disagree. I ask you to look at the circumstantial evidence before us. It is apparent that the time of the murders was a time of scarce food. Father Rouvière tells us himself in his diary, found on the spot where they were killed: 'We are menaced by starvation and we don't know what to do.' Menaced by starvation themselves, the Eskimos had evidently turned ugly. They were no longer the hospitable hosts putting the best of food before their guests and giving them open access to their houses. Again the good Father tells us, 'We have become disillusioned by the Eskimos.' The Eskimos did not want two extra mouths to feed. They wanted the priests to go. There was the argument over the priests' rifle. The priests' hasty departure. An escape, in effect. A return to the trees. And the two defendants followed.

"Why did the defendants go south on the Coppermine? They said to meet and help friends coming north. And they travelled light and with only two dogs. But there are no telephones or telegraphs at the mouth of the Coppermine. How did they know their friends were coming? And if they were, they could have been away one day or twenty days. Yet they took no food and only two dogs. Three days later they return to camp, and what do they have in their possession? The disputed rifle. But why didn't they wait for their friends? Unless ... there weren't any. I submit that on this evidence alone I would be completely justified in asking any reasonable jury to decide to find these men guilty of murder.

"For me, the most poignant and telling moment is after they have killed Father Le Roux. Father Rouvière is running away unarmed and Sinnisiak says to Uluksuk: 'Give me the rifle.' Was Father Rouvière at that moment threatening their lives? Was he in a position to kill them? He was running away! Why didn't they let the poor devil run?"

"Objection, your Lordship." Wallbridge's voice was strong, but McCaul pushed on.

"Why didn't they let him go off and starve to death in the wilds? Why didn't they let him have a sporting chance even of getting back to the village and receiving assistance?"

"Your Lordship, I object."

"No, my friend Mr. Wallbridge tells you they had to kill him too, 'in self-defence.'"

"This trial does not pertain to the murder of Father Rouvière." Wallbridge finally stated his objection.

"They killed this poor, unfortunate priest. They shot him down and then knifed him and then finished him off with the axe."

"The charges against my clients are for the murder of Father Le Roux, not Father Rouvière!"

"Sustained. Members of the jury, please disregard the comments concerning the murder of Father Rouvière."

McCaul, hardly missing a beat, continued. "My friend must admit, everyone must admit, that if it were a white man on trial under these circumstances, the jury could not possibly take five minutes to bring in a guilty verdict.

"And finally you heard the additional motive that the shaman, Uluksuk, admitted. He did not want the priests in his land. They were competition. Rivals to his business of negotiating with spirits and casting out demons. And so he eliminated that competition and gained a rifle in the bargain.

"The priests came to the Coppermine as innocents bringing the enlightenment of the teachings of our Saviour to the heathen. And what happened? They were murdered, mutilated, and their meagre possessions stolen. It is your responsibility to convict these men and thereby re-establish law and order in the Far North. Thank you."

Creed watched the dejected prisoners stare at the floor, wondering what would become of them. Justice Harvey told the jury they could now retire to consider their verdict. As the members moved slowly toward the exit, Creed noticed that Angituk's seat was empty. Where had she gone?

Twenty-Two

The shop was in a prestigious section of Jasper Avenue. The sign hanging outside, on a spearheaded pole over the glass-panelled door, was a deep green with gold letters: McANDREW'S FINE FURS. SINCE 1901. PROPRIETOR: ANGUS McANDREW. It was a very nice store, she thought as she tried to calm her pounding heart.

She was drawn toward the door of the shop but held back. She was wearing her brown suit from the court. A young, fashionably dressed couple went inside and the man turned and held the door open for Angituk. She hesitated a moment, and then entered behind him with a nod of thanks.

The store was all rich, dark colours and textures: oak panelling and racks of fur jackets and full-length coats reflected in long mirrors that gave the rooms the expansive illusion of infinity. She had never been in such a place, but the fine furs made her feel at home, safe and warm. She liked the good animal smell. Her father must have been a good hunter and trapper and therefore a good man, because the spirits would never help a cruel or selfish man. Angi did hear a man's voice near the back. It must be him. It all made sense. She moved closer and listened to the warm voice, deeply resonant, muted by the walls of fur, a soft Scottish rolling burr, and quiet, almost reverential in its tone as he discussed styles and cuts with a lady customer. Angituk could have stayed there all day among those beautiful furs listening to the kind voice.

Angituk peered around a rack of coats made from Arctic fox to try to see him. He stood only a few feet away. He was a tall man with red hair and bright blue eyes, slender and handsome with some grey in his trimmed beard. He was just as her mother had described him. He was coatless in a shirt and vest with a yellow measuring tape around his neck, and a warm smile crinkled the skin around his eyes. She moved close enough to him to enjoy the pleasant scent of his lavender and tobacco. His pinstriped shirt sleeves were rolled up, and it was then she saw it. On his left forearm. The mermaid tattoo! Just as her mother had described: the long hair, the smile, the full breasts, and the shell necklace. Angituk stared at her father, breathless with fear and excitement.

"May I help you?"

The sharp, disapproving voice seemed to come from among the furs. Angi turned to find a little woman staring expectantly at her. She had a wide face with all her features crowded into the middle. Angi looked back at her father to find he had not noticed her presence at all.

"Is there something you want here?"

"Yes. No. I was looking at the furs. They're very nice."

"I'm afraid we'll be closing soon."

"Oh, that's all right. I guess I should go."

"Yes."

The little woman gave her an unpleasant smile full of sharp little teeth like a marten. Angituk looked once more at the man with the red beard, still intent on his client. She yearned to have his smiling attention on her for even a moment, but she was too scared and the woman was gesturing with her guiding hand.

Angituk retreated toward the exit. The little bell on the door rang, announcing her departure as it closed behind her. Out on the street, she gazed back at the store. She had found her father. But now she must find the courage to speak to him.

ANGITUK RETURNED to the courthouse in a state of exhilaration. Maybe just to know he was there was enough, she thought. Maybe to introduce herself would somehow ruin it. The jury was still deliberating in the evening and the crowds were cooling themselves out on the commons. Angi found Creed with Wallbridge, Cowperthwaite, and John Hornby.

"Where have you been?" he asked her with a tone of accusation.

All breathless, she wanted to tell him the news about her father. She wanted to share her feelings and ask his advice. "Can I talk to you?" she asked, but Creed was distracted.

"Angi, they could be out any minute. Don't you realize how important this is?"

"Yes, I understand," she responded coolly.

Angituk turned and walked away from the court and from Creed and went back to the detachment.

ANGITUK REMAINED WITH ULUKSUK and Sinnisiak at the cells for a little while. A doctor came to examine Uluksuk. He was shocked at his physical state, but there was little he could do as Uluksuk would not eat. When the doctor left, Uluksuk turned to Angituk and smiled, his voice a thin reed in a swollen river.

"It's all right. I am ready to die."

"But they were going to send you home."

"They are still. A spirit can travel much faster."

"But a spirit cannot embrace your children."

"How do you know? Maybe it can. Whatever it is, it will be better than here. You go now, Angituk. Get something to eat. Go to your nice room in the hotel. Go to Creed."

Angituk's voice lowered and she came close to the bars. "Uluksuk, I have a secret." Uluksuk did not rush her and she savoured the moment before announcing the news. "I have found my father."

"Here in this camp?" Uluksuk asked with interest.

"Yes! He has a store of many fine furs and a house."

"He must have been happy to see you."

"He doesn't know I'm here."

Uluksuk studied her face for a moment. "You must go and see him. What are you sitting here for?"

"I am afraid. What if he does not want me?"

"He is your father. You will bring him great joy."

"Do you think so?"

"Of course! I would consider it a huge treasure if you were my child."

Angituk smiled at the old hunter. Uluksuk reached through the bars and gave her hand a squeeze.

"Go to him, Angituk."

THE CLERK OF THE COURT finally announced that the jury would not return a verdict until morning. Later, at the detachment, Cowperthwaite took Creed into Worsley's empty office and brought out a bottle of Hudson's Bay rum and two glasses. As Cowperthwaite told a long, funny story about a blind prostitute, they set about the task of finishing it.

ANGITUK STOOD UNNOTICED on a little rise behind a row of mature cedar shrubs and looked down through the expansive bank of windows to see into the McAndrew parlour. This was her father's home. Inside, an attractive woman, his present wife, she assumed, was telling two other women who wore cloth caps what she wanted done. They were cleaning and moving furniture. The present wife directed the other two around; she could hear her orders through the screen windows, and they obeyed—a little rude by Eskimo standards, but this was sometimes how white people talked to each other. Angituk counted three children in the room. A boy, perhaps nine years old, was lying on a sofa reading and two girls, about four and seven, were having a tea party on the floor. Angi was close enough to see their expressions clearly. These were her brother and sisters! This was her family!

The beautiful wife suddenly, with slight impatience, clapped her hands and the little girls began to put the toy cups and saucers away in a box. Angituk's father walked into the room. He wore a suit coat and tie as the white men in the city wore, and kissed his wife on the cheek. He went to the girls and, bending down, kissed their heads, then shook the hand of his son, who marked and closed his book. The boy stood up for the helpers to move the sofa. Angituk was enthralled as she watched all of this through the window.

Although she wore her jean trousers and plaid shirt again, Angi had brushed her hair and reddened her cheeks and lips just a little as the ladies did and left the fedora behind, determined to present herself as a daughter. It was a relief. Perhaps this was the beginning of never being a boy again.

Angituk heard a wagon pull up out front and also an automobile. The doorbell rang. The wife ordered an inspection in the parlour and the children lined up. She made a few adjustments to their clothing and hair and then, with a smile and kiss, sent them toward the front of the house to greet the guests. She followed them with an expression of pleasant anticipation.

Angituk made her way along behind the cedar row until she had a good perspective on the generous circular porch where guests were starting to arrive. The McAndrews were having a party. Some guests carried gifts in their hands. Maybe it was a celebration of some kind. And then, like a flash, it crossed Angi's mind. Perhaps they knew! Could Corporal Cowperthwaite have told them she was coming and these people had been invited to welcome her? She had made him promise not to, but he still might have told them. Could it be? Another automobile and a carriage had arrived.

Angituk took her position on the porch just behind the last family, who were waiting to be greeted and ushered inside. The father of this family gave Angituk the once-over. His teenage daughter with protruding teeth and tiny eyes did the same. Angi brushed her hair back from her face with her fingers and wiped her nose thoroughly with the back of her hand. She straightened her plaid shirt and brushed off the bits of cedar from her trousers.

Laughter and loud conversation drifted from the foyer ahead. The two maids were stationed at the door, the children just behind them, greeting the guests as they entered. The children were addressing the guests by name, the girls with curtsies, the boy with a smiling handshake and slight bow. When the family in front of her had gone through the rituals, Angituk presented herself with a huge, self-conscious smile. All three children and the maids stared at her for a silent moment in wonder. Finally the boy spoke, his question congenial.

"And whom may I say is calling?"

At this, Angituk looked at the younger of her sisters and went down on one knee in front of her. She held out her hand and the little girl squeezed it without hesitation. She took the second girl's hand in her other and smiled into the eyes of each of them.

"You are all very beautiful. I'm so happy to meet you finally. My name is Angituk McAndrew."

"That's our name too," said the seven-year-old.

"I know. You see ... I am your big sister."

"Sister?" was repeated in unison by the two little girls, with hesitation and then delight.

"Yes, I just dress as a boy for now."

The brother remained silent behind an expression of apprehension.

One of the maids repeated, "Sister?" with a tone that implied there were deep troubles ahead.

"Yes, yes, it's true." Angituk looked up and assured them, "Angus McAndrew is my father."

The younger girl embraced her and smiled into her face with open enthusiasm. "I'm Cleo and this is Portia and that's George."

Portia came close and looked at her in amazement, a smile coming slowly, breaking wide. "You look like Daddy!" Then she hugged her too. "I always wanted a big sister." There was joy in her expression too.

"But who was your mother?" George inquired, looking very unsettled by all this. The maids hovered in the foyer, having no idea what to do.

Before Angituk could answer, Cleo took her hand and drew her inside. "Let's go and show Daddy." Portia claimed her other hand to lead her forward and present her to the party.

George and the maids exchanged deeply alarmed glances, but they made no attempt to stop them. Holding her hands tight, the girls led Angituk proudly into the parlour, followed tentatively by the brother and the maids.

Cleo and Portia brought Angituk right up to Angus McAndrew, who was standing with his wife and speaking pleasantly with guests on either side. A maid called out to Mr. McAndrew gently but with enough note of warning to catch his attention. He looked up at her, smiling, then quizzical, and then at the stranger who was being presented to him by his daughters. Cleo made the announcement.

"Daddy! You didn't tell us we had a sister!"

The room fell into a profound silence.

"I beg your pardon?"

Angituk smiled and nodded first to Angus and then to Mrs. McAndrew. "Mr. McAndrew. Mrs. McAndrew. I'm sorry. I didn't mean to disturb your party. But it's true, sir. I am your daughter." Tears of love came to her eyes.

"What are you talking about?" Angus said tonelessly.

"My mother's name was Kunee. She was your friend during caribou season in our hunt camp east of the Mackenzie delta near Paulatuk. She died five years ago, but she told me all about you. Tall and thin with a red beard and hair."

"This is ridiculous." Angus McAndrew looked at his guests and his wife. "I was never in—"

"Paulatuk," Mrs. McAndrew said evenly. "I've heard you speak of Paulatuk."

"We passed through briefly. Just a trading post. We provisioned there. This was many years ago."

"Eighteen," Angituk told him helpfully. "You have a mermaid on your arm." McAndrew's hand went instinctively to his sleeved forearm. "My mother described the mermaid to me, with her smile and the shell necklace."

Mrs. McAndrew's expression hardened and there was frost in her tone. "Why don't you show her your mermaid, Angus?"

"This is ridiculous!" McAndrew insisted. "There was no woman in Paulatuk."

Portia repeated her earlier observation. "But she looks like you."

He turned toward the maid and pointed to the door. "How could you let her in here? Escort her out!"

"Father?" Angituk spoke the sacred word.

"How dare you!" He turned to the others. "Don't you see what she's doing? She found out some information, saw the tattoo, and is using it to make up a story. She wants money, that's all. She's a lying little half-breed gold digger. But it's not going to work. Now get out!"

"I don't want any money," Angituk told him, her voice breaking.

"Her eyes are blue like yours, Father," George said, hazarding, he knew, his father's wrath.

"Shut up, George!"

Angus McAndrew took Angituk by the arm and escorted her through the foyer and out the door. She tripped and fell on the porch and he pulled her to her feet. He walked her down the steps and out to the road, where he pushed her away.

She turned to face him. She wiped her eyes and studied the man whom she had dreamed of meeting. They looked at each other for a moment.

"I waited all my life for this," Angi told him quietly.

Her father's fury had dissipated. "It can't be true. You've made a mistake."

"Do you believe that?"

He stared at her but remained silent.

"Do you at least remember her? Her name was Kunee."

"No," he said too quickly. She could not tell if he was lying. His voice suddenly softened. "Where do you live? What will you do now?"

Angituk's eyes flashed at him, but she said nothing.

Angus McAndrew removed several bills from his wallet, took her hand, and placed the five folded twenty-dollar bills into it. She held them for a moment and then dropped them in the road.

Angituk looked back over her father's shoulder toward the house. Some of the guests stood in the open doorway, others at the windows in the parlour. In the bay window of the drawing room Cleo, Portia, and George were watching intently. Angituk raised a hand and the children all waved back, even George. Angus McAndrew made an angry gesture toward them and a maid came and directed them back, away from the window.

She turned to her father and looked into his blue eyes—her blue eyes—one last time.

"I'm sorry," he told her. "I will never recognize you."

She nodded, then turned and walked away.

McAndrew watched her for a moment, then bent down and picked up the money. When he stood again, he shouted for the benefit of those who might hear from the house.

"And don't come near my family again or I'll call the police!"

CREED DIDN'T REALLY KNOW what he was doing, but part of him thought it was worth a try. He had washed his face and drank water to clear Cowperthwaite's rum from his head, put on civilian clothing, and gone into the park to gather the dry grass he thought would work. He had found a solitary place to light the grass and sit downwind of it so the acrid smoke swirled around his shirtless body in purification. He slowed his breathing, and when he thought it was enough, he let the grass burn down and tried to clear and calm his mind of all of the troubles and worries he had about the trial, all the petty and selfish thoughts, and focus only on the welfare of Sinnisiak and Uluksuk. Then he called on the spirits. He explained that he was not a shaman and he knew they were not his spirits, and perhaps he had no right to address them, and maybe they couldn't hear him so far south, but he told them he was speaking to them on behalf of his friends who needed help. He avoided asking directly for the verdict he wanted, because that would be rude and demanding. He asked only that they help his friends find a way through these troubles. He made that sincere request three times.

When he was finished and had replaced his shirt and was making his way back to the hotel, he did not feel foolish at all about what he had done. In fact he felt somehow reassured, even hopeful, as if there had been something. As if he had been heard.

ANGITUK WALKED ALONG the bank of the broad, brown, powerful river out to the edge of town, the full moon bathing everything in a silvery negative version of midday, and thought of Angus McAndrew and his family. Was it her fault? Should she have put on a dress? Done her hair like Nicole? Would he have refused her if she had worn a dress?

Sitting by the river just before dawn, Angituk realized the truth. Angus McAndrew had not been the wonderful, loving man her mother had described to her when she was a little girl. She had always imagined her mother and Angus McAndrew living a full romantic summer season as husband and wife in the skin tents during the caribou run near Paulatuk. She thought of the tearful parting when he was ordered to return south and his promise to come back to her. It was all a pretty dream, Angituk knew now. It was all a lie.

Other things now made more sense. Her mother had hated alcohol and warned her it was poison to the men who drank it. As soon as she reached puberty, her mother dressed her as a boy when there were strangers around, especially white men. Later, when Angi grew interested in boys and wanted to redden her cheeks or lips with berry juice, she had to do it in secret or face her mother's anger. And once, shortly before her death, Kunee caught Angituk admiring her new breasts in her hand mirror. She spoke bitterly about men then, especially white men. The reason for all this, Angituk realized as she sat musing on the riverbank, was that Angituk was not the product of love. That was just a pretty fantasy her mother had created for her. Angituk now knew this as clearly as if her mother had confessed the truth that her father had forced himself on her. Angituk kept going over it all in her mind for most of the night.

Sometime before the first glow of dawn, she sensed movement, heard a rustle between the trees. A small brown bear came snuffling down to the river for a drink. Her spirit helper.

"It took a long time to find you. What are you doing down here, so far from home?" he asked.

"I'm looking for something."

"Do you know what it is?"

"No. Not quite. Not yet."

"Are you close to finding it?"

"I don't know. I hope so."

"It can take a long time. It is not easy or straightforward. Do you remember when you first found me and we wrestled to see if I was the right helper for you?"

"Yes."

"Who won?"

"I'm not sure. I don't really remember."

"Because, like in your life, the wrestling is not over yet. It is never over."

"The journey has been interesting."

"Yes. Keep moving every day. Keep wrestling. It gives you new possibilities."

"*Quanaqqutit* for your guidance."

The little bear finished scratching his belly with his right paw, gave a snort, and ambled away through the foliage along the bank.

Twenty-Three

At nine o'clock the next morning, a large crowd had gathered outside the courthouse. Was the verdict in yet? There had been no announcement, but it had been made known the jury was very close. Angituk arrived and Creed confronted her.

"Where have you been? Court's about to start."

Angituk stopped. She turned to look at him, angry and flushed, and was about to say something hurtful when the clerk appeared in the courthouse doorway.

"The jury is in! The jury is in!"

The crowds began to move like fish schooling toward the doors. Creed looked back at her once and then joined them. Angi stood still in the stream of people for a moment, and then she followed them inside.

JUSTICE HARVEY TURNED to face the foreman of the jury. "Gentlemen of the jury, have you reached a verdict?"

"We have, your Lordship. We find the prisoners guilty of murder."

In shock, Angituk stared first at Creed and then at the prisoners. She had been so concerned with her own affairs, she had given little thought to the possibility of a conviction.

But now it had happened. Sinnisiak and Uluksuk would not be going home. Creed too stared at the foreman. How had he thought it would come out otherwise? Of course they would need a conviction after all of this. Of course everyone must have expected this, except him.

Chief Justice Harvey replied, "Gentlemen, you have performed a very unpleasant duty and, I think, have come to the exact correct conclusion in all respects. I think the verdict is the only honest verdict that could be rendered on the evidence. The court thanks you." He paused for the translator. "Tell them, Mr. McAndrew," Harvey prompted her. "They've been found guilty of killing the priests, which they should not have done."

She did as she was told. Sinnisiak looked frightened, Uluksuk resigned. Sinnisiak asked his old mentor quietly, "They are not going to let us go home, are they?"

Uluksuk shook his head slowly.

Justice Harvey continued. "Tell them that under our law, when a man takes another man's life, he must give his own in return." He paused, gauging the prisoners' reactions. "Angituk, tell them to stand up. I will pass sentence."

Angituk told them and Sinnisiak jumped to his feet, but she had to take Uluksuk's arm and encourage him to stand.

"I am obliged by the laws of Canada to impose the sentence of death in the usual form of hanging, and I fix the fifteenth of September as the date of execution."

Gasps and murmurs issued from the crowd. Justice Harvey thanked the jury again, dismissed them, then stood and—robes flying behind him like a giant crow, Uluksuk noted—disappeared from the courtroom. E.K. Mainprize soon did the same, exiting out the back door, text in hand, headed for the telephones to file the verdict to New York. He did not run; he had paid off the operator to give him the first line out.

Angituk turned to Creed accusingly. "I thought you would protect them. You said you would protect them." Creed stared at her in silence as she moved to stand beside Sinnisiak and Uluksuk. He couldn't look at them as they were led away.

Nicole watched Creed for a moment then came up to him as he remained in the emptying courtroom. She sat down on the bench beside him. She moved closer to him and put a hand on his knee.

"I'm sorry, Jack. But you must have known it would go this way. What else could you expect?"

Creed turned and looked at her. "I don't know. Maybe a little humanity. Civilization, whatever that is. I had hoped your uncle would show more ... vision."

"My uncle gave the proper sentence. It's all he could do. I know you've had these travels and this special friendship with them, but they did kill the priests."

"Since when have you started to care so much about Catholic priests?"

"I care about the murder of two human beings."

"All you care about is yourself!" he snapped at her, immediately regretting it.

Nicole stood up. "If we're talking about being self-absorbed, dear Jack, you win the prize! And I'm sick of it."

"So am I." These destructive responses seemed out of his control.

Nicole stared at him for a moment. "Fine, then. There it is."

He did not return her look. She left him sitting in the courtroom.

CREED FOUND JUSTICE HARVEY in his office packing his briefcase for home.

"I know you've developed a certain kinship with them, Jack. It's only natural. And I don't believe they are evil men."

"Then commute the sentence, sir. Give them a term in prison, but don't kill them."

"My hands are tied. They've been convicted of first-degree murder. The mandatory sentence is execution."

"But surely there is a case for an appeal. If, Justice, you yourself put in a recommendation for mercy to Ottawa, it would have a huge effect. They would have to respond. You could save their lives."

Harvey stopped his preparations for a moment. "I'm not going to do that, Jack. I will be standing there when they hang, and I will observe the just and successful prosecution of the guilty."

IT WAS STILL WELL BEFORE NOON when the Calgary express pulled up to the platform in Edmonton with a long sigh, as if exhausted from the journey north. Among the passengers who disembarked were two soldiers in uniform. There were many men in uniform in the town, but these two, a captain and a corporal, were distinctive. The captain was short and wiry, with a full, well-cultivated moustache. The right sleeve of his jacket had been folded and pinned neatly over the place where his arm had been. He was attended by a brawny corporal carrying their kit bags, who stayed carefully behind him and to one side. They did not speak to each other. Each wore the distinctive white arm band of the military police.

AFTER THE VERDICT, Angituk sat with the hunters without speaking, for what encouragement could she offer? Uluksuk saw her distress and told her to go for a walk. She obeyed, and returned to the bank of the river.

She was somehow comforted by the contemplation of the muddy, swirling water. And there she reached a decision after everything that had happened. She needed someone to be with. After the pain and disappointment of the night before, and after the tragic verdict in the trial that morning, she knew she had been alone too long. The dream of her father and a family of her own had been destroyed, but she was left with deep yearnings. As she stared down into the dark current, she determined to set out and talk to Creed. He was a good man and she loved him, though he had been so distant lately. Now that the trial was over, maybe they could go north and rediscover what they had had before on the Great Bear and the Coppermine. It would not be with their friends Uluksuk and Sinnisiak, but they would burn sweetgrass for the hunters and remember them to the spirits up there, who perhaps could ease their pain.

Angituk suddenly realized, like a great bolt of wisdom, that the most important thing in the world was love. It was not to be taken for granted. It was not to be counted upon or even expected. It was hard to find—a special gift from the good spirits. And after love was family—not the family of a wealthy white man in Edmonton, but her mother's people in the North. And the family she and Creed could make.

CREED WAS WAITING in the hotel dining room. Nicole was late, but that she had agreed to come at all was a relief. He rubbed his temples to ease a headache. He needed his wits about him if he were going to save the lives of Sinnisiak and Uluksuk.

He had gone first to Superintendent Worsley to ask for his official support for clemency toward the two convicted, to stop the executions. Worsley was sympathetic but completely unwilling to take sides.

"We are police officers, Creed. It's not our job. You know, I hate to say this," Worsley told him, "but it might be for the best. What is the alternative? They're fine fellas, but ... they're wild. Like animals. How long would they last cooped up in a jail cell?"

Creed stared at him as he thought about this.

NICOLE WAS SILENT as he stood up and greeted her. She hesitated and then sat, and he pulled his chair over closer to her.

"Nicole. I was very rude to you. I apologize."

She was far from sold yet. He continued.

"This has been a long ordeal, but I had no right to take it out on you."

She looked at him for the first time. "You're right. I didn't appreciate it."

"They're my friends."

"And what am I?"

"I hope we can get past this. Do you think that's possible?"

He gave her a tentative smile and the corners of her lips responded ever so slightly. The angry fire in her hazel eyes cooled.

"You have been under a lot of pressure."

"You do understand me."

"Not easy sometimes." There was a legitimate smile beginning there now. "I'm hoping it'll get easier."

"I'll work on it."

He gave her a full smile then, and she shook her head in exasperated amusement. "You know, I'm sure when you go out alone into that wilderness without civilized people to talk to, your brain reverts to some primitive state. Some regressive phase of basic animal existence. I hardly know what to do with you when you come home."

"You're very patient."

"What choice do I have? I'm just pleased that this trial is over and we can now get on with life. There is something I wanted to talk to you about. You know the rumours are rampant that there are further advancements in store for you, and possibilities beyond the police force. Some say with a little polishing—maybe a little tutoring in elocution—you could pursue a future in politics. What do you think about that?"

"I ... I don't know. I've never considered public life."

"Just think about it. And not just municipal, or even provincial. I'm speaking about federal. You could run for Parliament, darling. Go to Ottawa! I'd go with you. And I could help you so much. You know old Hindmarsh in the North Edmonton riding is close to retirement. He may not finish out this term. You don't get opportunities like that very often. You will think about it, won't you?"

"Yes. Okay. I'll think about it. But I do have one request." Her eyes were impatient at the interruption of her vision for the future. "I would like you to go to your uncle and ask him to recommend that the death sentence be commuted."

"Oh, for God's sake. This trial again!"

"All the Attorney General needs is your uncle's recommendation and he can stay the death sentence."

"My uncle doesn't change his mind."

"He will for you. He adores you. You see how the public is reacting. They love the Eskimos. If they're hanged, there will be negative publicity. It will leave a bad taint over the whole case."

Nicole listened, and recognized his point.

"But if the sentence is commuted to a prison term," Creed continued, "the case will end happily. The press will say how the case represents both justice and compassion."

Nicole was thinking about it.

"And that is a good note on which to start my new career. My campaign. Don't you think?"

Nicole's smile suddenly beamed. "Good boy! Now that's the right kind of thinking. All right, then. I'll see him at tea this afternoon."

"Thank you, Nicole."

Nicole rose and moved to the chair beside him and took his hand. "Now, I have another idea to inaugurate your campaign. We announce our engagement! Now, after the trial. Remember we agreed?"

It had been the other worry at the back of Creed's mind.

"In fact, why don't you come to tea? He's always pleased to see you. We can talk clemency and politics and ... marriage. And wear your civilian clothes. You've always looked good in a uniform, but it'd be a nice change. An introduction to your future."

"So, you'll help me?"

"Yes, of course," she said with a sudden impatience that quickly passed. "This is all so exciting, darling. I knew we'd be good together." Nicole leaned forward, put her arms around him, and kissed him on the mouth with a passionate enthusiasm that surprised him.

THE TWO MILITARY POLICEMEN arrived at the courthouse. They heard the hammers ringing out in the still air as the new scaffold was erected. There were a few Mounties on duty, and the one-armed captain approached Constable Faraday.

"Constable, I'm Captain Crosswell." The little captain was British-born with a Yorkshire accent. "We are looking for John or ... rather Jack Creed. He's involved with the trial, correct?"

"The trial is over, sir. Finished yesterday."

"Oh. Good, then. Where is Sergeant ... or rather Corporal Creed? We'd hoped to have a chat."

"At the detachment, I would guess, sir. If you head east, then straight down Jasper to 101A Avenue. Or he could possibly be at the hotel. The Macdonald. It's on 100th Street, number 10065. Two blocks up and two to your right, sir."

"Very well, Corporal. Thank you."

"If I see him, what shall I say is the nature of the inquiry?"

"We just have a few questions for him. Carry on, Corporal, and thanks for the information."

"Do you want to know the verdict, sir?"

"What?"

"The verdict. In the trial, sir. They were found guilty. The two Eskimos. They're going to hang them."

"Oh. Good show. Well done. Always excellent when the case ends well."

ANGITUK WALKED to the hotel going over what she would say to Creed. She had seldom asked for anything in her life, but she was going to ask for this. There had to be a way to make this work. It was not just something she had imagined. He had told her he loved her, and when she remembered what he had said and how he had looked at her, she knew it was true. Now that the trial was over, there was nothing keeping them here. She wanted to leave this unhappy place. There was happiness and anticipation now in her plan, in finally telling the world who she was and what she wanted and going after it. And what she wanted was Creed.

Angituk entered the hotel foyer and popped her head into the dining room doorway. She cast a glance around the room and immediately recognized Creed at a table with his back to her. She started forward but stopped when she saw Nicole sitting beside him. She was smiling at Creed. And then suddenly she leaned over the corner of the table with her arms around him and kissed him on the mouth. They kissed as she and Creed had kissed, and Angituk froze there in the doorway. She watched as the embrace continued; saw the satisfied, possessive expression on Nicole's face over Creed's shoulder. She saw Creed touch her cheek. She turned and fled.

CREED WENT FIRST to the detachment to find Cowperthwaite and ask about civilian clothes. He had nothing suitable for high tea with the Justice. Cowperthwaite's two suits were too small for Creed, but Trooper Sedgewick, who was away on a patrol, had a fine-woven wide-lapelled suit. Cowperthwaite retrieved it in stores and it fit Creed perfectly. He showered and shaved at the detachment, tied the black bat-winged bow tie before the mirror, and put on Sedgewick's oxford shoes.

Creed had not seen Angituk all day and he decided to go by the hotel. He would buy her dinner later and talk of all that had happened. He hoped to be able to tell her of his success with the Justice and the appeal for clemency. He wanted to make her laugh and to ease the pain and worry that had so obviously plagued her during the trial. His pulse quickened at the thought of her and the desire was suddenly intense, to see her and tell her of his plans.

Feeling a little in costume in Sedgewick's suit and shoes, he entered the hotel, turned left in the foyer, and started down the hallway toward Angi's room. He saw them immediately: two military police, knocking at his door. Creed kept his head down, maintained his stride, and made a quick left turn down a convenient service hallway. Behind piles of trunks and baggage, he listened.

"Sergeant MacKay! JOHN MACKAY! Open up!"

Creed stood there, his head against the brocade wallpaper, staring down at the red carpet, his head dizzy, trying to think. They had found him. He had to get away. He heard them knock again on his door, and Creed escaped down the hall and through the kitchen into the empty service yard to decide what to do next. These men were the recurring nightmare that had haunted him for two years. These were the "dark spirits" Uluksuk had spoken of. It must have been the early photographs in the newspapers. Someone had identified him. They had found him and come to take him back.

It seemed impossible. Would the army use up its dwindling resources on searching for one deserter across an ocean and on the far side of a continent?

Yes. They would, to make an example of him. And he was far more than a deserter.

So should he run? He'd have to think about that. He had to do one last thing, though, before he did anything else.

WHEN CREED ARRIVED for tea on the spacious veranda at five minutes past four, Nicole was already with her uncle, their wide wicker chairs close together. They rose to greet him when he arrived. A gentle breeze off the river kept the bugs down as the maid brought the tray of tea and scones and oatmeal cookies. Justice Harvey was pleased to see him. His courtroom *gravitas* lifted to reveal the kind and friendly man underneath. They began by discussing the bright future ahead.

"You know, a life in politics can be a fine thing. The country is growing and it needs strong guidance," the Justice told him, his enthusiasm rising. "Men like yourself in positions of power are essential."

"Thank you, Justice Harvey. I'm very flattered."

"Old Hindmarsh in North Edmonton has a strong following,

but he'll soon step down. He has no sons or seconds-in-command to speak of. I think he'd like you. We'll have him over for dinner."

"I'd enjoy meeting him."

Now, for Creed, public life as an option had ceased to exist. The only two options in Creed's life were to run or to surrender, and the time for making that choice was narrowing quickly. Creed finally came right out with it.

"There is one thing that remains heavy on my mind, sir. I feel the need to ask once more if you could find it in your heart to recommend clemency for the Eskimos."

The Justice shifted in his chair and frowned as he considered Creed's request, but before he could answer, Nicole waded in as Creed had asked her to.

"You see, Uncle, our concern is about the negative public response to the hangings. You saw how popular the Eskimos are. Jack's image could suffer. I think the citizens would be much more positive about Jack as a public figure if he represented justice tempered with compassion. Don't you think?"

They made the argument from different points of view; clemency would be better for everyone.

"Consider your own legacy, sir. Do you want to be known as the justice who sentenced the Eskimos to death? I would think the priests themselves would advocate mercy."

After the initial resistance, Justice Harvey softened finally under Nicole's persuasive pout, and her hand on his sealed the bargain. Creed marvelled at the speed with which she'd convinced him. He unfolded a blank telegram form.

"I don't mean to rush you, Justice Harvey, but perhaps you could compose a telegram to the Attorney General. I can take it to the telegraph office. I think in this case there is no time to waste."

"I think it would be a wonderful gesture, Uncle. I would be so pleased."

With no more prompting from Nicole, to Creed's surprise and relief, the Justice complied. He even used Creed's argument that it was an example to the Eskimo people of both the just and the compassionate nature of the white man and it set a moral tone before the nations of the world. Creed thanked him with all his heart, and after a few more minutes of friendly chat, avoiding the subject of marriage, he left to get to the telegraph office before it closed.

Creed stopped at the garden gate and looked back at them, still at tea, talking intently. He was ashamed of his duplicity and his deception toward both of them. It was only a matter of hours before they knew all about him—who he was, what he had done. It crossed his mind then, as he looked back at them, all that once could have been. Before the Coppermine. He smiled bitterly to himself at the irony: he had gone north seeking anonymity and had found fame, which would soon become infamy.

He waved to them then turned and, with the telegram in his pocket, walked briskly back into town.

AS CREED ENTERED the telegraph office, Captain Crosswell and his corporal arrived at the Royal North West Mounted Police offices. Faraday had reported the presence of the military police and their interest in Jack Creed, and this had stimulated much speculation at the detachment. Where was Creed? The captain introduced himself to Worsley and asked to see him in private. Cowperthwaite stood near the door to listen.

"I'm afraid Inspector Creed is off duty."

"Inspector? He's done all right for himself."

"He's one of our most valued officers."

"Yes, well ... And it's Creed he calls himself? We saw it in the papers in London. That's how we picked up his trail. They published a photograph of him with the Indians."

"Eskimos."

"Yes. I was the one who identified him. His real name is Sergeant MacKay. Sergeant John MacKay."

"All right. And what do you want with him?"

"We have charges. Rather serious charges against him. We have papers for his extradition." The little captain took them from his breast pocket and quite deftly with his one hand opened them in front of the Superintendent for his perusal.

"And what are the charges?"

"Murder and desertion."

On the far side of the door Cowperthwaite was in shock.

"Very serious," Worsley agreed. "I take it this was the murder of an officer?"

"As a matter of fact, yes. He strangled his CO to death in the trenches in the middle of an action and then deserted."

"That can't be the Creed I know."

"I'm afraid it's true. He killed his CO."

"He must have made Creed quite angry."

"This is no matter for humour, Superintendent."

"Of course not. Where will you take him? Where will he be tried?"

"The court martial will be in Belgium, probably Ghent."

"And if he were convicted, what sort of sentence?"

"Not for me to say, but ..." The captain knew it was imprudent to speculate, but he could not resist the temptation. "This sort of thing, this serious, in times of war—they'll want to set an example. Similar cases in the spring resulted in the firing squad, immediately after sentencing. Fairly standard."

"I see."

"So I'll need your co-operation. In fact I must insist on it."
He unfolded another piece of paper with equal dexterity before
Worsley. "This is from your Commissioner in Ottawa, ordering
you to co-operate in every way."

Worsley looked at the paper. "Very well."

"So where is MacKay?"

"I'll send for him."

"I would recommend discretion in this case. It would be a
rare man not to attempt to run. Our orders call for lethal force
if necessary."

"I can't imagine Jack Creed running."

"Nevertheless ... we're counting on you."

"Cowperthwaite!"

Outside the door, Corporal Cowperthwaite waited a moment
then stepped into Worsley's office.

"Yes, sir!"

"Would you send a couple of the lads out to find Creed,
please."

"Yes, sir. What shall I tell him?"

"Just tell him to report to me immediately. Try Justice
Harvey's office or his home, then Wallbridge's office or the
hotel."

"Yes, sir."

"And Cowperthwaite, could you and ... anyone else out
there ... keep this quiet?"

Cowperthwaite was wondering if anyone else knew that
Creed was wearing Sedgewick's clothes, civilian clothes. He
didn't think so, and he wasn't telling.

"Yes, sir."

When Cowperthwaite had left, Crosswell turned to the
Superintendent. "I find it quite unnerving to see all of these fit
young men out here when there's a war on."

"I'm not sure what you mean."

"Why aren't they in Europe, at the front?"

"Well, there are a few other things to look after, Captain."

"Don't you understand what's going on in France? We are battling an evil menace. The future of the world hangs in the balance."

"I'm sure you're right."

"Look at you, for example. You must have some skill at leading men, and here you are having tea, marching around in your red jacket, while others are doing the heavy work in Europe."

Worsley stared at him, the blood rising to his face. He spoke calmly, evenly, over the fury he was feeling toward this man. "I had two brothers in France, Captain. One was killed at the Somme. The other is still fighting for the King, whatever that means in that stupid, murderous family squabble going on over there."

"What did you just say?"

"Someone has to keep law and order in this country so my brother and his colleagues will have something to return home to."

The captain was about to respond hotly but then thought twice. "I suppose."

ANGITUK SAT BEFORE THE MIRROR in her hotel room and stared at herself. For the first time since she was little, she was wearing a dress. On the trail she would often make skirts of leather or extra cloth while she washed and dried her trousers, but this was a real full-length cotton dress with a small floral print and lace at the neck like other women wore in this village. The lady in the shop had said the colour was good for her.

Angituk had taken some of her back pay and gone to the fashion stores on Jasper to become a real woman, like the white women, and the people she'd met there were very helpful. She had headed home with her arms full of parcels, studying the face and hair of each woman she passed so she'd know how to make herself look. First she had brushed her short hair and put it in small curlers like the other lady had shown her. She had powdered her face and rouged her cheeks and put the black stuff on her eyelashes and brows according to the instructions of the third, older lady, who had cautioned her toward subtlety with the makeup she had sold her.

So now she studied herself, unsure, so far, of the results. She reached for the heavy green bottle again and took a long pull of the sweet champagne. She was feeling better.

The curlers had been in for an hour and now she pulled them out impatiently. Her black hair still hung straight, but there was an appealing wave to it when she brushed it out. Yes, it was nice. A "smart" look. Now for the most important part: red for her lips. With a twist, she extended the stick of rouge from the little cylinder and pretended to kiss toward the mirror as she had been shown. She took another mouthful of the sparkly drink, wiped her mouth, and applied the lipstick. It looked pretty good, she thought, kissing at herself, admiring her bright red mouth.

She stood up, drained the bottle, touched up the rouge on her lips one more time, and set out to find a man to love.

Twenty-Four

At the telegraph office, Creed sent Justice Harvey's cable to the Attorney General and paid for it himself. There was some relief that that was done. Returning to the hotel, Creed ducked past the lobby to Angi's room. They would be watching his room but not Angituk's around the corner. And Angituk was who he wanted to see. He tapped quietly and whispered her name. Two sets of heavy footsteps were coming around the corner. He tapped louder, then pressed the handle. It held fast, but then suddenly gave way. He stepped inside, closed the door, and waited. The heavy footsteps passed by.

Creed turned to find Angi's usually tidy room in disarray. There were empty boxes and papers from a Jasper Avenue clothing store scattered on the bed and floor. Her clothing—her trousers and the flannel shirts she favoured, the suit she wore to court—was in piles on the rug where she'd shed it. He picked up her old discarded fedora and rotated the rim through his fingers. On the low dressing table, to his amazement, he found cosmetics containers, some spilled powder dusting the glass surface. His foot nudged something on the floor that rolled and clunked against the leg of the dresser. As he held up and inspected the empty champagne bottle, his alarm grew. He had to find her. Then his eye caught a piece of white paper on the floor crushed into a ball. He picked it up and spread it out on the dressing table and recognized Cowperthwaite's careful handwriting. It was a list of three addresses for Angus McAndrew.

THE MAID AT THE McANDREW HOUSE looked a little tentative until Creed identified himself as Inspector Creed of the Royal North West Mounted Police. He hoped to speak with Angus McAndrew. He was ushered into the parlour, where he remained standing despite the maid's invitation to sit. McAndrew entered in his shirt sleeves and vest holding a snifter of cognac.

"Inspector. How do you do? You're ... you're the one who captured those two Eskimos. I saw your picture in the papers. Wonderful work! You make us all proud. You know, I've spent a few seasons in the North myself, trapping and trading. In the delta. So I was following the trial rather closely."

"Yes. I know. Around Paulatuk."

"Yes! How did you know? They were good years. But it's a young man's game. These old bones couldn't take it now. Anyway, how can I help you? Name it."

"Have you had a visit from Angituk McAndrew?"

McAndrew was a little taken aback, then his eyes narrowed. "The little half-breed? Calling herself McAndrew, is she?"

"Then you have seen her."

"Yes, last night. Came in here bold as brass claiming all kinds of things. I almost called you boys to take her away. She's a fraud artist. She wanted money. Are you looking for her? What else has she done?"

"What did she say to you?"

"She was going on, claiming to be my long-lost daughter. Wanting money."

"Then what happened?"

"She's crazy. I wanted her out of the house. Away from my family. I took her out to the street."

"Do you have any idea where she'd be?"

"No. But you should keep an eye on her. She's dangerous."

"I plan to. Tell me something, Mr. McAndrew. Do you have a mermaid on your left forearm?"

McAndrew looked at him in surprise. "Yeah. I do. But anybody could know that. That's what I mean. She's smart. Using that information."

"Did you go with Eskimo women in the delta and over near Paulatuk?"

McAndrew glanced toward the door of the parlour, smiled, and dropped his voice to just above a whisper. "Sure," he said quietly. "We all did. You know how long and cold those nights can be. You must have too, I'll bet. We treated 'em well for the most part. Fed 'em. Gave 'em a little money. Sometimes they could be stubborn. Act up. A man has needs, as you know. But we never used a closed fist on them."

"Did you ever consider the possibility that Angituk could be your daughter?"

"Or the daughter of a dozen others. Those squaws knew what they were doing. It was just business."

Creed smiled at him, his eyes cold, furious. "I think Kunee was different."

"Look, whatever happened, some lying little half-breed is no daughter of mine."

Creed couldn't hold himself back any longer. His fist caught McAndrew under the chin, sending the cognac to the ceiling and McAndrew falling backwards over a fainting couch and crashing down on a tea trolley, scattering fine china. Creed considered going after him over the couch—his face could use a little more of Creed's fist—but McAndrew was smart enough not to get up. A moment later McAndrew's children were in the doorway, George and Portia and Cleo. Creed looked at the three sets of Angi's eyes and much of the anger drained out of him. He had to find her.

"If anything's happened to her, I'm coming back."

CREED SEARCHED SHOPS and restaurants along 98th Street, working his way down toward the bars nearer the river. The warm summer night had enticed people to stroll the Edmonton streets and there were hundreds of faces to study. What would she look like in the makeup and dress of a city woman? He feared for her now after the scene Angus McAndrew had described, and there was a growing urgency in his hunting.

Creed knew Dooley's Bar on 96th from foot patrols in the city. As he approached, he could hear fiddle music. He had helped break up a couple of fights there, the combatants usually too drunk to be of much danger to each other. He opened the door to the squawking fiddle, many drunken voices, and the familiar smell of sweat, tobacco, and beer.

The thin stratus of smoke floated just above their heads and glowed translucent from the ceiling lights. There was a commotion in a corner at the back, a sudden explosion of laughter. Creed moved through the smoke toward the sound. On the far side of the billiard table sat a circle of men taking turns tossing dice on the floor. If he had been in uniform, a lookout would have warned them and the dice and money would have disappeared long before. A heavy-set, older woman poured drinks at the table. Someone spanked her ass and she turned and slapped the man's face. Everyone in the circle laughed. A young, thin girl with a black eye stared at her drink and the man with his arm around her shoulders sang drunkenly and watched the dice throwers.

Creed was turning to leave when he noticed the figure of a slender young woman in a floral dress. Her face was turned away and she sat on a big bearded man's knee with her bare arms around the neck of another. The woman released him and sat back, taking a long drink from an open bottle of rum. She almost fell off the big man's lap. His heart stopped. It was Angi.

The man she had been kissing rolled a three and a two and groaned with the loss. The big man laughed.

"I win! I claim my prize." He stood up with an arm around Angituk's waist to keep her from falling down, then buried his full beard between her cheek and shoulder to kiss her neck. "Come on, cutie. Upstairs."

His big hand clamped onto Angituk's wrist, and he headed for the staircase leading to the rooms. She staggered after him. Her acquiescence shocked and infuriated Creed. He moved forward and grabbed her other hand and she turned to look at him, trying to focus through her inebriated haze.

"Creed ...?"

Feeling the resistance, the big man turned back too and snarled at Creed. "Let go, asshole. You can have her when I'm finished."

"I'm taking her out of here."

"Not till I'm done."

"You're done, you fat son of a bitch."

The big man released Angituk's wrist and stepped toward him. Two of the other gamblers came up on either side of him.

"You can't talk to Clarence like that. He won the squaw fair and square."

The bearded man ran his eyes up and down Angituk. "And we got more playing to do."

They came at Creed.

Creed had felt a satisfying surge of dark, unrestrained fury when he struck the furrier. A similar impulse had overtaken him long before that, in the trench near Ypres when he had killed his commanding officer. In that moment at Dooley's it came to him again, giving him speed and power. With his left hand he pulled Angituk back to safety and with his right he swung around at one of the gamblers and caught him in the side of the head. He went down.

The second gambler, his eyes wild, took a skinning knife from his boot, pointed it toward Creed's throat, and lunged. Creed's hand found a pool cue lying across the table behind him and swung it hard as the gambler came for him. It caught the man under the arm, cracking ribs and making him howl in pain. He dropped the knife and staggered away.

As big Clarence converged on him, Creed swung the cue again, but the backswing was limited. Clarence caught the cue in his meaty paw and easily pulled it away from Creed. He grabbed Creed by the throat, pulled him off his feet, and deposited him on the billiard table, where his immense belly pinned him. He pounded Creed twice in the face with his massive fist, bloodying his nose and tearing the skin from his cheek. His hands closed around Creed's throat.

Creed's vision of the ugly face in front of him was narrowing. He could feel the blood flowing down his neck and for a moment was idly concerned it would spoil the green felt on the table below. He was losing consciousness when he heard a little whack behind them. The whack came again, and again, developing into a steady rhythm. With each impact, a little of the anger left Clarence's eyes and the pressure of the massive hands around Creed's neck eased slightly. He looked up past Clarence to see the face of Angituk behind him with the cue ball in her hand, bringing it down hard in determined, repetitive, concentric arcs on the skin and bone of the big man's head. The sickening whacks continued until Clarence's eyes rolled up and his hands released. The big man slid off Creed and fell unconscious to the floor.

Angituk stood unsteadily with the bloody white cue ball still raised in her hand. The bar was deathly silent. Creed stood up and recovered quickly, picking up the pool cue again, looking warily around him among the circle of gawking faces for any other challengers. There was a large bartender with a hostile glare who came toward him, but he looked at the other damaged men and decided against it. There were no others.

Keeping the cue in one hand, Creed felt for the big man's pulse and found it. The skull was bruised but not cracked. He'd be all right. Creed put his jacket around Angi and lifted her up in his arms. She was light. He turned toward the door and made his way out into the street. As soon as the door closed behind him, the fiddle music began again as if Creed had never entered.

NICOLE OPENED HER UNCLE'S DOOR to the two military policemen. Their officious manner amused her, but she was gracious toward them and knew her uncle would welcome them with the special warmth he reserved for any English visitors. Although he was a nationalist, Canadian-born and proud, Nicole was certain that the captain's clipped English lilt would be a pleasure to Justice Harvey's ears.

She escorted them into the parlour, where her cousin Harold and his friend Richard Wilkerson were smoking with her uncle. She introduced them. The captain explained to the Justice that they were in Edmonton on army business. He suggested they talk alone, but Justice Harvey assured him everyone in the room was trustworthy.

"We've come to Edmonton to arrest a man by the name of John MacKay. We are to escort him back to London and then

Belgium for court martial. You know him by the name Jack Creed."

Nicole put a hand to her mouth. "Jack Creed? What has he done?"

"Murder, I'm afraid, and desertion."

"Good God. Not Jack," Harold said quietly.

"There must be some mistake," Nicole insisted.

"I'm afraid not, miss."

"Murder? Desertion?" Justice Harvey repeated. "I can't believe it of Jack." He was watching his future plans for the boy dissolve.

"I'm afraid the evidence against him is very strong, Justice Harvey. He strangled his commanding officer to death in front of an eyewitness."

"What had the officer done?" Nicole asked evenly, though she was deeply upset.

"Not at liberty to discuss it, miss. How well do you know Mr. MacKay?"

Nicole was suddenly cautious, hiding her distress. She could not help Jack if Crosswell suspected she was his lover. She answered with the casual air of one who has only a passing interest. "He's one of a number of friends I see from time to time. Chums with my brother and uncle. Seemed a decent fellow. I have to admit I'm shocked."

Harold, Justice Harvey, and Richard Wilkerson stared at her in surprise at her deception.

"Looks can be deceiving, miss. He's a very dangerous man. We've been to his hotel room and have men there, at the detachment of course, the courthouse, and now here. The Superintendent has extra officers out looking for him. Would any of you know another place we might find him?" After a moment's silence the captain continued. "And please do realize, we will find him sooner or later. I strongly recommend your assistance. Please understand, delay will only make it worse for him."

Justice Harvey dismissed his concerns. They would co-operate.

"No, of course, Captain. If what you say is true, you will have our complete co-operation. Mr. Creed—or MacKay—must face up to what he's done."

"But you have no idea where he could be? A friend's house, a tavern, a church perhaps?"

"Can't think of any place offhand," Harold told him earnestly. "Nicole?"

"No, nothing comes to mind other than the places you mention."

The captain's voice betrayed some impatience with their lack of information. "If you hear from him, could you contact me at the detachment?"

"Yes, of course, Captain. We will."

"Good day to you, then."

When the soldiers were gone, Nicole sat down, tears only then brimming. "I can't believe this is happening."

Justice Harvey sat beside her, gave her a handkerchief, and took her hand. "I'm so sorry, my dear. This is a terrible turn of events for you. But we must co-operate. I hope you'll agree."

Nicole wiped her eyes and nodded.

"I will use all my influence to ensure he has a fair trial. But Nicole, this looks like a very serious matter. I can't see how it could possibly end well for him. Or for you. You should prepare yourself."

"We have to give him a chance to tell his side of the story. You've seen trumped-up cases before, Uncle. I don't trust that captain. It could all be some kind of cruel fabrication."

"But you know," Richard Wilkerson offered lightly, "I always found something odd about Creed. Something just didn't add up for me."

Nicole stood. "Why don't you just shut up, Dick!" And she stormed from the room.

Richard raised his eyebrows in a gesture of innocent surprise. "Well, I did."

Twenty-Five

Creed carried Angi through the back streets and stuck to the shadows. A few of his colleagues on patrol passed them by and twice he turned away to feign an amorous embrace with her until they had gone by. In this way they made it back to the hotel without discovery or challenge. He knew the military police would be looking for him at the hotel, making it the most dangerous place. But if he could get to Angi's room, they'd be safe. The eye of the hurricane, he thought to himself. Keeping his head down, he entered through the crowded tavern and skirted the crowd at the bar.

The barroom was loud with the spirited conversation of men feeling their drink, and it distracted those who might have looked twice at a man carrying a young woman. Creed put her down, letting her stand unsteadily for a moment. His battered face was a natural disguise as the bruising came to full bloom. Mainprize, surrounded by other journalists, was holding court against the bar, and through the cacophony a repeated phrase finally caught in Creed's consciousness: "commuted to life." There were many here who knew him from the courtroom and he avoided their eyes, but he asked a young stranger: "Did they stop the executions?"

"Yes! A telegram from the Prime Minister. The mayor announced it."

Creed's heart felt suddenly lighter. At least there was that. He listened a moment to the conversation. Keedy and his Harvard students were there, scheduled to leave on the southbound train the next morning on their way home to Boston. Keedy spoke to several of the press, including Mainprize.

"No, the first verdict was quite a shock, revealing the faults of the prosecution and the subjective effect of the defence tactics, but it worked out well in the end. And now this pardon from execution I believe is the right decision. Don't think it'd ever happen in the States. Two good trials, though. An altogether satisfying study. Stone Age man meets modern law, and the law has been satisfied. It's given me quite the paper to write."

"Damn good case," Mainprize agreed. "Just wish there was a love story."

Keedy laughed. "Can't have everything."

Lifting Angituk up tight to his chest again, Creed hurried out of the bar and down the back hall to her room.

HER MEN'S CLOTHES were still on the floor as she had left them. Makeup dusted the dresser. He locked the door and laid her down on the unmade bed. She moaned, eyes closed, and murmured a few words of Copper. He gave her some sips of water from a carafe on the bedside table, and she took what she could and lay back again, eyes still closed. He looked at her and listened to her breathing for a moment, then he slowly, gently took off her stained dress. He smiled, despite his worries, at the red nail polish she had applied. He never thought there'd come the day he'd see scarlet nail polish on Angituk's fingernails, these fingers that gutted a fish or skinned a muskrat with such quick and practised skill. Then, smiling at how foreign they too seemed against her smooth brown skin, he unsnapped the garter belt and unclipped the stockings, rolling them down her long, slender legs. He wanted to bring back the Angi he knew.

She began to shiver in the cool of the night. He left her in the silk undershirt and the pretty lace undershorts she had bought and put the covers over her. He had her sip some more cool water and then brought a bowl of warm, soapy water to gently wash her face clean of the makeup. She was calm now, sleeping, her breathing shallow but regular, lips slightly parted, eyes lightly closed. He caressed her face again with the warm towel, then he placed the palm of his hand against her cheek, his thumb tracing the fine high bones. She licked her lips, her eyelashes stirred, and suddenly her eyes opened, slowly focused, and looked up at him. She frowned at his swollen cheek and battered nose.

"What happened?" she whispered.

"Had a disagreement with one of your boyfriends."

"Boyfriends? Oh." It was coming back to her, along with a pounding in her temples. "Oh, my head. Are you all right?"

"Yes. But Angi, I have some things to tell you. First, they've commuted the death sentence. They're not going to hang them."

"That's wonderful!" she said, her face beaming for a moment, and then her relief turned to concern. "But what will they do to them?"

"They'll put them in jail for twenty years."

"Twenty years!" she said, stricken. "They will prefer to die. Uluksuk will not last twenty days."

"Well, I know. But it's a start. I couldn't live with myself if they were hanged."

Angituk thought for a moment about the new fate of her friends. "What else were you going to tell me?"

Creed wondered where to start. "I'm in trouble, Angi. There

are men who have come from the army. They want to arrest me
and take me back to the wars for a trial."

"Like Uluksuk and Sinnisiak."

"Yes."

"You white men like trials."

"Yes."

"What do they say you did?"

"They say I killed someone."

"And did you?"

"Yes."

"Who was he, the man they said you killed?"

Creed stood on the threshold of the memory he had tried so
long to bury. He hadn't told the story to anyone. He dredged up
the memory of his crime, and with it the faces in the trenches,
the useless slaughter, and the soulless survival of living for
months in mud and misery.

"My name then was Sergeant John MacKay, and I was second-
in-command of "A" Company, Princess Patricia's Canadian Light
Infantry in the Second Battalion." Creed realized how little any
of this would mean to her, but he was telling it also for himself.
He spoke as if he were explaining not only to Angi but to Justice
Harvey, Nicole, Worsley, Cowperthwaite, and the others at the
detachment. As if he were making this first attempt to explain
himself, to confess to the world what he had done. Angi listened
quietly, intently.

"My third-in-command was Corporal Frank Banes, a farm
boy from Omemee that I'd known playing hockey. We had
joined up together. Banes was a good hockey player, and the
finest soldier I ever served with. He had played on the first
team with my brother, Charlie, and they were friends. They
could talk about hockey for hours, describe the blow by blow
of obscure games from years before. It had a way of putting the

war in perspective. He used hockey terms like 'taking the game to them,' 'playing your position,' and 'put the puck in the net.' Frank, my big brother, Charlie, and I had one leave together near Neuve-Chapelle. I sang all night long at the estaminet with my brother. We talked about everything." Creed smiled at the memory. "When Charlie had to leave to go back to his unit in the morning, he told me if anything happened he would come back and find me, and I told him the same thing. And we shared tears without shame because we knew what our chances were. Six days later he was killed by a sniper."

Angituk was shocked by this, but Creed said it without emotion. He was long past the emotion. He took a deep breath and continued.

"I had a unit of good, seasoned men, those that were left. A few months before, we had held the line in front of Ypres against a German offensive in what they later called the second battle of Ypres.

"When our battalion first marched through in the spring of '15 on our way to the front line, Ypres was a beautiful little town with gardens and fountains, an impressive cathedral, and the Cloth Hall. Civilians walked the streets. But then, after we stopped the Germans it became the favourite target of their long-range, fifteen-inch artillery. The citizens flooded the roads leading west. By the fall, Ypres had become a bombed-out ruin. We had saved the town only to watch it be destroyed behind us. This childishness didn't surprise me. We did the same. The whole massive show was a childish, vindictive squabble. Except people died in very large numbers in horrible ways.

"Our new trenches north of Ypres were good—deeper, fortified, and reinforced. We moved in and began to organize trench raids against the Germans.

"On this one warm night in October, the plan was

straightforward. British and Canadians would lay down a short thirty-minute barrage from our heavy trench mortars that had been brought into position. Then at 1:30 a.m. the shelling would stop and a large raid would be made through no man's land—crawling on our hands and knees—to the German trenches. They were only eighty yards away.

"My commanding officer, a very smart French-Canadian lieutenant from New Brunswick who had commanded us through Ypres and Kitcheners' Wood, had been shot in the head the day before by a sniper. We all respected him deeply, but we also agreed that there's a bullet out there for everyone. When it happens, it happens.

"The replacement for our lieutenant arrived that morning. He was a young British-born captain, an officer in the Canadian army but impatiently awaiting transfer to the British forces, and he made little pretence of his contempt for 'colonials,' as he called the Canadian troops. He was accompanied by a batman, an Irish corporal named McFee, who felt the same way. The captain, whose name was Blackborough, worried me. He had been transferred away from his original regiment for a reason. He issued orders that were redundant, and his voice rose suddenly in volume at the end of each command, as if expecting a challenge. He avoided looking at me directly, but the few times I saw his eyes they were filled with either contempt, accusation, or fear. He was always sweating and he had a sickly sweet smell that to me indicated illness. I guessed he was doped up on morphine, as a few of the officers on the line were. I didn't trust him.

"I knew my men well and my philosophy was to get as many of them as possible through each day alive, while still obeying orders. Apart from the back-and-forth attacks and the constant sniping, the Germans continued to throw a lot at us.

The mortars were straightforward. You heard a gentle 'thunk' from their lines and you had a few seconds to take cover. The whiz-bangs were nasty little shrapnel bombs that whined like mosquitoes as they came for you, and if they landed in a confined trench they could shred several men at once. Then occasionally, arbitrarily, they'd fire their fifteen-inchers, artillery that sounded like a locomotive coming and could take out an entire length of trench and everyone in it. From the fifteen-inch, there was no escape.

"Even in the midst of all this, there were ways to survive. But I had lost a lot of men. Far too many for what land we had gained and then often lost again. With each operation I found myself more hardened to the losses. My emotions were bulletproof and unreachable. I knew that this would be a challenge in the future, but after Ypres and Kitcheners' Wood it had become my means of survival. Like Blackborough with his opiates and Banes with his hockey, we had all found some means to live day to day."

Angi listened in studied silence, catching most of the story, trying to make sense of it, trying to place him in this bizarre world. He was deeply wounded, she knew, and she was staying quiet, trying to assess the best treatment, letting him continue so she could understand.

"Just before another barrage was scheduled to start, I walked the trench to see how the men were doing. Some jokes, some encouragement. I told Banes to give the order to fix bayonets. That night I estimated fifteen to twenty percent casualties. I was confident my men would go over the top at the appropriate time. The French had begun to shoot their men for refusing orders. The British too executed their deserters. Whether too stupid, too scared, or too eager, the Canadians hadn't recorded any executions yet for 'failure to obey.' So I could count on them to carry out orders, but still I felt I had to maintain their confidence in me, to keep the casualties as low as possible, if not for emotional reasons then for practical ones.

"I remember the mortars were positioned two hundred yards behind us and the shelling began. We'd press our bodies against the wall of the trench, feeling the impact eighty yards away through the earth. I remember thinking at least we had thirty minutes before we went over the top. Thirty minutes to remember the life lived, the girls kissed. But Captain Blackborough had other plans.

"Twenty minutes into the barrage, down the line, the new captain called out the order to prepare to attack. I turned toward him and checked my watch. Blackborough shouted his order to advance! No one moved. I ran down the line to where Blackborough stood in the widest section of the trench. I shouted at him over the pounding of the mortars.

"'We've got another ten minutes of this, sir! Then we go.'

"I remember the captain's eyes were wild and he had his revolver out and it worried me the way he waved it around. His adjutant McFee stood defensively beside him as if used to this dangerous behaviour.

"'That's what they expect! We go now! Surprise them!' he yelled at me.

"The accuracy of the British and Canadian mortars had improved in recent months, but the German trenches were only eighty yards away and often shells would land far short.

"I told him, 'Sir, it's a bad idea.'

"'Are you questioning an order, Sergeant MacKay?'

"'It's almost over, sir. Wait a few more minutes or we'll lose men to our own barrage.'

"'Are you a coward, Sergeant? All right, men! Advance!'

"Not a man moved. They looked at me. I remember Blackborough's angry, glistening face.

"'Do you hear me? I said attack! *Attack!*'

"His face was red. And again I waited and my men did not move.

"The mortars were firing so fast, a 'short' was inevitable. A shell fell forty yards from our forward trench and right behind it another at less than thirty. We would have lost half a dozen men to them alone if I had obeyed Blackborough's initial order. But still the fool screamed his order to advance.

"At that point there were two ways for it to go: Blackborough would back down until the end of the bombardment or the confrontation between us would escalate. Blackborough made his choice. He pointed his heavy revolver at me and yelled, 'Order your men to attack!'

"'No, sir.'

"The pistol trembled. 'You will do what I say!'

"I figured there were only a few more minutes until the shelling stopped. I closed my eyes for a moment, willing the big mortars to silence and all this would go away. But they didn't stop.

"I opened my eyes again and Blackborough had turned the revolver away from me and grabbed a young private by the name of McEwen, a good kid who got letters every week from a girl in Sudbury. He put his pistol to McEwen's head and looked at me. 'Order the raid!'

"'Yes, sir! Please be careful!' I shouted at him.

"Private McEwen was terrified. I remember he had closed his eyes, his lips moved in prayer. I turned to my men and commanded, 'All ready!' Each of my men knew what was being asked, but they would do it for me.

"'I'll order it, sir! Let McEwen go.'

"'No, Sergeant! First ... attack!'

"'Please, sir. Be careful with that—'

"'I said *attack!*'

"When Blackborough spoke the word, the Webley in his hand gave a kick, the shot unheard by most of us against the shellfire. McEwen's thin body fell down onto the muddy duckboards, blood flowing from a hole in his temple, dead before his knees touched the ground. I remember Blackborough staring down at the crumpled body as if the boy had offended him.

"The truth is, in that time since Charlie's death, I had been a little worried about myself. Sometimes my mind would go completely blank. Other times I found I had to resist impulses to poke my head up above the trench for a while, or take off all my clothes and stand facing the German snipers. Sometimes I had the impulse to pull pins from grenades and put them back in my pocket. I resisted these irrational behaviours for the most part, but I didn't resist the sudden and satisfying impulse to kill Blackborough. Before he knew it, I had knocked the revolver away and my hands were around his throat. I had him head down beside McEwen in the mud and I was squeezing the life out of this man with everything I had. I've never made a clearer choice. I killed Blackborough. It was the right thing to do."

CREED SHIVERED. His eyes were moist and his hands trembled. Angituk put her arms around him to keep him warm and calm because she knew he had to get the story out, like a bad spirit inside him. She nodded and hugged him for a silent moment. Then she told him, "Go on."

"I was surprised that I could kill a man like that. Also that Blackborough died so quickly. And also that no one stopped me. No one even tried.

"Well, that's not true. The Irish corporal, McFee, the adjutant, he tried. When I attacked his officer, he screamed and attempted to grab a rifle, but Banes disarmed him. I guess other soldiers helped because, when I was finished with Blackborough, McFee's hands were tied behind him and my soldiers held him there, on his knees.

"I remember McFee shouting at me, 'You killed him!' I remember we all stood there for a moment like a tableau, the big mortars still sending shells from behind us, the illumination from the hits so close along the German trenches that we were silhouetted. Then, as we stared down at the dead officer, Corporal Banes told me, 'Look, John, it's not a problem. We just drag the body with us when we go over the top. Just another body. No one'll know.'

"But I remember looking at McFee. He was terrified. Banes came closer, gestured to McFee, and told me, 'Same thing.' McFee knew what was up. He was whimpering loud enough to hear between the exploding shells. I shook my head at Banes.

"'No,' I told him.

"Banes moved closer to me and said, 'Look, John. Every soldier here is behind you. That bastard had it coming, and that's what we'd all say. But on the books, with this guy testifying, it's you killing an officer, and they won't take it kindly. They'll shoot you for it, John, sure as a pussy's a cat. So I figure in a couple minutes, when the bullets start, we just hold him up, right? Hold him up till he takes a couple. Problem solved. We get through the penalty.'

"But I told him I couldn't do it. I told him to let him go.

"Banes was very disappointed. 'Really? Don't you want to think about this?'

"I told him to let him go. The soldiers released McFee. Banes cut the rope around his wrists. I told McFee to get out of there. He was panicked, looking down at Blackborough's body, his eyes wild, then at me. He asked if I would shoot him and I told him again to run. The Irishman finally got it and ran like a maniac down the supply trench heading southwest. I knew he'd make a left at the St. Catherine's trench and head straight toward the high command. It was at that moment the mortars fell chillingly silent. Up and down the front lines came the orders as men lined up to attack.

"I shouted out for them to get ready. The bodies of Blackborough and McEwen still lay crumpled on the duckboards. I remember Banes was watching me. He asked if I was all right and I told him, 'No, Frank. I'm fucked. But maybe it won't matter.' Then I ordered the advance.

"When we scrambled over the top, there was no opposing gunfire. The shelling had had the desired effect. I had my revolver drawn. We started on our hands and knees, but then I quickly rose to my feet and led them at a full run. I remember wondering what fate would bring. The gods of the battlefield would be more benevolent than an army court martial for murder of an officer. We covered most of the eighty yards to the German line with my men behind me, without losing a single one. I wondered if the shelling could have been this effective. I knew the German trenches would be deep and give good cover, but for a moment I wanted to believe, as all soldiers want to believe, that either the enemy was dead or the objective had been abandoned.

"There was a rise up to the trenches with a slight hollow just before. The barbed wire had been cut and blown open by the mortar rounds and there were several clear passages. I scrambled through the wire and up just below the lip of the trench and opened the sack on my belt to get the Mills bombs. I turned and gestured for my men to move up—they were still some distance behind. As I found the grenades and pulled the pins with my teeth, I heard a whispered German voice close by, just beyond the mound of earth. Then the clink of a bolt released in the

magazine of a heavy machine gun. A flare ignited above us and
there were explosions inches above my head: the German belt-
fed Maxim was in place and firing. I had been too slow with the
Mills. Too slow.

"I had one bomb in each hand and lobbed them into the
trench on either side of the gun. I heard my men screaming. I
buried my face in the dirt and waited the three seconds while
the German gun fired over me. I could see it passing across
the field and returning to finish. How many would die in those
three seconds because I had been late?

"My two grenade detonations sounded flat by artillery
standards, but they were directly on target. The gun stopped
and the screams came then from the German side. I remember
standing up and climbing to the lip to look down. Two dozen
German soldiers had been massing behind the machine gun
crew for a counterattack. My grenades had killed most in the
packed trench, the Mills cutting through them, shredding limbs
and bodies with their arcs of razor-sharp shrapnel. I stood there
for a moment staring down at the carnage of shattered bodies
I had created. I checked up and down the German line, where
there was the sound of other battles under way. But here now, in
this place, it was quiet. Peaceful.

"I turned around and looked down on my own men behind
me. They lay across the rise in a uniform line. All fourteen
shot. What were the chances of me leading them point-blank
into a new machine gun nest? The first pass of the Maxim had
wounded or killed most of them. The second pass had finished
them off. The impressive efficiency of the Maxim had been no
less than that of the Mills bombs. I remember thinking that we
had, both sides, brought killing to an art form.

"I checked each man. Bailey ... Cassidy ... Caravaggio ...
Schmidt ... young Mallory, only a week with us ... the older

Preston, too old really for infantry. Now it didn't matter. When I found Banes, his lips were still moving. He had taken two heavy bullets in the stomach—they had passed through, opening up his back. I knelt down beside him, put my face close to his, and told him I was there. He said to me in a whisper, 'You know something, John, I don't want to kill people anymore. I've had enough of it.'

"And I said, 'Okay. That's fine, Frank.'

"He couldn't focus his eyes, but he gripped my arm and tried to speak. He said, 'John? Listen ...' He licked his bloody lips and concentrated on forming the words for me. He said, 'You ... gotta get away from here. Get as far away as you can. It's enough.' I told him okay, but he continued. 'No, John, I mean it,' he struggled to tell me. 'Game misconduct ... You're out of the game. Don't even look back. Far away as you can imagine ... far as you can dream. Promise it.'

"I promised him. Moments later he was gone. I remember standing and walking back up to the edge of the trench. There had been other successful Allied raids by Canadians and British farther up, at least where I could see. In front of me, fighting was still under way. A bullet whizzed by my ear. I looked down at the German dead, studied them a moment, then back at my own men. I felt alone. I wanted to join them. But Frank's words kept repeating themselves: 'Get away. Far as you can dream.'

"The truth was, there was no reason to stay. No more men to lead. No more enemy to fight. And then I was suddenly taken by one of my old impulses, and this time I did not resist. It just made all the sense. I took off my helmet first, then my webbing, belt, and jacket. I bent down to unlace my boots and unravel my puttees. I slid out of my suspenders, dropped my pants, and stepped out of them. When I was finished, I stood there naked, my fish-belly body glowing in the light from a lone phosphorous flare that still drifted above the carnage of the battlefield. I was a translucent target without any takers.

"Then I heard my brother's voice as clear as if he was standing beside me: 'Come on, Johnny. This way! Let's go see.' And I began to walk through no man's land toward the northwest with a sense of freedom ... of impunity. There were pockets of fighting, exchanges of gunfire. Further on, a dozen Allied soldiers passed in front of me on a raid. As I watched, German riflemen began to fire on them. They fell back and began to return fire within a few yards of me. I simply walked through the battle.

"A few soldiers stared at me as I passed. A few raised their rifles, but they couldn't tell what side I was on and I was obviously not armed. They all let me pass.

"Charlie then began to speak a mantra from our childhood: 'Second star to the right and straight on till morning. Second star to the right and straight on till morning.' I walked through firefights with bullets flying by. I sidestepped two soldiers in a knife fight. Mortars fell near me. A boy died an arm's length away, but I was not touched. I passed like a ghost among the living and the dying. I was blessed. A bullet clipped my shoulder finally. It spun me around, but I stayed on my feet. I looked at the blood on my hand, which had flowed down my arm—and I suddenly wanted to live.

"I walked for hours with more determination, within sight of the trenches, past towns and forests equally brutalized, past bodies of men and rotting beasts. Bits of shrapnel, glass, and empty shell casings cut my feet, but I stayed mostly in the mud or patches of grass. It was late October. The night was strangely warm and I was not cold. I met a full British battalion moving east and I felt invisible as they passed by me. Frank Banes's idea kept me moving west and Charlie's spoken instructions made perfect sense to me. 'Second star to the right and straight on till

morning. Second star to the right and straight on till morning.'
We should all have had such clear directions given us.

"At some point I found a horse standing to the side of a bomb
crater on a road, nosing around for clumps of churned-up grass.
There was an English saddle in place, reins trailing in the mud.
A short distance away her rider, a British captain, lay dead, face
down in the mud. Though my wound had opened no arteries, I
had lost a lot of blood and felt weak. I whistled to the mare and
her ears perked. I approached her and she seemed almost as if
waiting. The horse took two steps toward me. I mounted her
and rode west, still with Charlie's voice in my ear. 'Second star
to the right ...'

"By dawn, we were well to the northwest of the battlefields.
Coming over a rise, I made out in the distance the cranes and
factories of the port of Boulogne on the coast of the English
Channel."

NOW, ON THE WIDE, comfortable bed in the Hotel Macdonald
beside Angituk, Creed stopped talking for a while, looking off as
if from a clifftop into a distant memory on the horizon. Angituk
tried to smooth the furrows of his brow with her fingertips, and
when still he did not look at her she placed her hand gently on
the side of his face and turned it toward her. He smiled back
sadly.

"So? Then you became a mounted policeman and they finally
gave you some clothes?" She was pleased to see the smile without
the sadness for a moment.

"No. There was a barn near a sign that pointed to Cap Gris
Nez and I found some overalls. People were good to me. At the
docks in Boulogne I avoided the military police and found a ship,
almost empty, headed back to New York. They needed crew. I
spoke some French and no one asked questions. I stayed hidden

while a military policeman and a customs officer inspected the ship. America had not yet joined the war, but everyone knew they were sending supplies to the French and English. The first night the captain cauterized my wound. Did a good job." He showed her the small blue crater in his skin and muscle. She touched it and kissed it.

"Did your brother ever speak to you again?"

"No. He got me out of trouble. That's what he always did. I have not heard his voice since then. When I got back over here, I thought of going home to Peterborough, but there were just too many questions to answer. My brother was dead and my father and I were not on good terms. And that is the first place the military police would look for me. So from New York I made my way to Chicago, then north to Winnipeg. I took Frank's advice to heart and continued west. My money ran out in Regina, where I was informed by a Methodist recruiter that God had determined I should become an honourable member of the Royal North West Mounted Police. They needed good men. I liked the idea. It had been some time since God had said anything to me at all. In fact in Belgium I believed He was dead. So I became a new man and my name was Creed, and I had a mission: I would serve the force and bring order and law."

Creed looked at Angi's blue eyes studying him intently. He could see that she didn't understand everything, but she understood and felt his pain, and loved him as he was. He realized in that moment how deep and complete and overwhelming his love for her was. She was the one his life had brought him to, the essential friend and lover. In spite of his desire for solitude and independence, his selfish moods and carelessness, his insensitivity and his stupidity, he would die for her. Or die without her. She was the lost life force that he had been searching for. Through her he could believe in a god again. He placed his hands around her face.

"Angi." He spoke in an intense whisper. "I've been thinking what we should do. We'll get a couple hours' sleep then leave well before dawn. We'll pick up horses at Walpole's near the river and head south. Travel light. Cross country in case they're watching the roads. In four or five days, we'll keep the mountains in view and cross the border into Montana. Pick up the Missouri and follow it down west into northern California and head for San Francisco. I've always wanted to see San Francisco. And the Pacific Ocean. And they'll never find us there. What do you think? Will you come with me?"

She looked at him, caught up in the question, then her brows knitted. "What about Nicole? I saw you kiss her in the dining room."

Creed was surprised that she had seen them. "I needed her help to have the sentence commuted for Sinnisiak and Uluksuk."

"So you don't love her?"

"No, Angi, I don't love her. I love you."

In a sudden torrent of relief, she smiled at him and rubbed her face against his battered one, smearing some blood from his cheek onto her own.

"Yes, I will come with you." And then she kissed him tentatively, aligning her lips carefully with his as she was learning to do, nose to the right, eyes open to assess how their faces fit, then closed. He kissed her back, gentle but firm. Before he could withdraw, she took his lip in her sharp teeth and bit until he gasped and pulled free. Then she smiled. They kissed again, their passion ignited, mouths locked together, arms wrapped around each other until they had to stop to catch their breath.

"You really love me? Say it again."

"I swear it's true. I want to swim in the Pacific Ocean with you. Or any ocean. I want to be with you forever, Angi. I love you, I need you. I am yours," he told her, and she smiled again, eyes shining. She nuzzled him gently.

They knelt on the bed facing each other, their breath quickening together. She raised her slender arms and he slipped her undershirt from her broad, skinny shoulders and then slowly pressed the open palms of his hands against her breasts and cupped them gently. He was amused by the contrast between this elegant room, with its soft mattress and fresh linen, and the cold, wet love they had made in the Great Bear. Her undershorts disappeared and she helped him off with his. She pushed him back, climbed on top of him, and eased him inside her. Sitting on him with back arched, she made love to him as if at a gentle canter, her breaths quickening, pleasuring herself on his body until her eyes widened, muscles tensed, and a long breath escaped her in an animal moan. And then she laughed at her own pleasure and collapsed on him.

He rolled her over, exchanging places, and looking down into her eyes he held her beautiful face between his strong hands and kissed it and licked her lips and nose. He moved inside her for a long time, until they were both overwhelmed as if by the ocean tides surging up through the green ice caves. Then they collapsed side by side and floated on a dream into the deepest sleep of their lives.

Twenty-Six

Nicole Harvey conducted her search for Jack in a calm and authoritative manner. She did not show her desperation; she was too strong for that. And yet each time she said the charge out loud to herself, she could not believe it. Murder. She would help him escape. She had her own money and she had friends in Toronto she could count on. But first she had to find him. She started at the hotel, where she discovered several RNWMP officers waiting for him. She went to the detachment. They had sent out patrols. She took Cowperthwaite aside, but even he had no idea where Jack might be. She went to restaurants and two taverns Jack visited and called the houses of several mutual friends by telephone. But by then it was well after midnight and she didn't want to alarm anyone. If they sensed her anxiety, it could compromise her plans for Jack's escape.

Nicole was about to return to her uncle's house and wait for Jack to contact her when she had an idea. The half-breed boy. The translator. She sensed a bond between them. He might know where Jack was.

She made her way back to the hotel. It was very late and the bar was closed and the lobby quiet. She nodded to two policemen she didn't recognize at Jack's door and made her way down the hall and around the corner. It was the third door, she believed, where she had seen the boy enter once. She didn't want to disturb anyone else at this late hour or call attention to herself. She tapped as loudly as she dared, only then recalling the lad's name.

"Angituk?" she whispered at the door. "Angituk."

There was no response and again came her concern that she not wake any others in the hotel. She found her hand on the knob and turned it. It resisted at first but then, as she tried again, something gave way, the knob turned, and the door opened. She looked inside. She knew her presence in the boy's room would be a little awkward, but this was an emergency. She felt for a light switch but couldn't find one. As her eyes adjusted to the darkness, she moved slowly into the room, trying to sort out the tangled shadows on the bed in front of her.

"Angituk ...?"

The word caught in her throat in surprise when she saw the strong, bare, familiar shoulders of the man on the bed. Before she could call his name, her joy was overtaken by a dark foreboding. What was going on? She moved slowly, reluctantly toward him. He was on his side, naked, facing away from her, sleeping soundly. As Nicole moved closer, she saw that he held the boy in his arms. But her moment of shock and revulsion was cut short when she noticed the incongruous shapes of the boy's naked body. This was not a boy's body at all. There was no mistaking the feminine curve of the slender thigh. Angituk was a woman! Grief and rage consumed her at first, and she was on the very verge of screaming. Then Nicole abruptly regained control of herself.

She looked down at the two of them. Completely naked. What held her spellbound was the way they lay—his left arm protectively around her shoulders, her tattooed left hand gently on his chest as if in a caress, right hands with fingers entwined, their faces close, turned almost eagerly toward each other, breathing together the same air, all in their own world. When Nicole and Jack had made love that one time, there hadn't been this intimacy. She would have given anything she had, she thought bitterly, for a night like this with him. But he had chosen to have it with the half-breed.

She looked at them sleeping with the innocence of children. She hoped their dreams were sweet. She hoped it had all been worth it to them. Carefully she began to back away from the bed toward the door. Leaving them just so, she stepped over the threshold and closed the door silently behind her.

THE BIG MILITARY POLICE CORPORAL was the first one through the door. He was followed by four of Creed's fellow officers. The corporal drew his gun. They surrounded the bed. Creed sat bolt upright. Angituk awakened more slowly, looked at the man with the gun, and covered herself. Captain Crosswell was in the doorway. He stepped inside and approached the bed.

"Are you John MacKay?"

Creed took a deep breath. "I am."

"You are under arrest for murder and desertion. We are to escort you back to Belgium to face a court martial. There you will be assigned an officer for your defence. I suggest you say nothing about your defence until then. Get your clothes on."

Creed checked his watch: 1:45 a.m. He had planned to get up in two hours. How had they found him?

He sensed her presence before he saw her. Nicole Harvey stood in the doorway behind the officers, her face cold and aloof as she studied Creed. She had turned him in, he realized. There was pain and anger in her eyes, but no regret at what she was doing. He could not blame her.

The other policemen turned away as Creed and Angituk found their clothes, but the corporal and captain did not. Having spent so long and come this far, they weren't going to take their eyes off him. Creed discreetly held a sheet around Angituk while she slipped into her clothes. Nicole watched his gentle ministrations toward the girl: his steadying hand, his whispered words. He put on Sedgewick's suit and Oxford shoes. Two officers placed his hands behind his back and cuffed them. Corporal Dewey spoke for his colleagues.

"Terribly sorry about this, Creed."

The little captain turned to Dewey. "Shut up!"

Creed again caught Nicole's eyes. He was sorry to have hurt her like this. There was a moment of silence in the room and then Nicole suddenly, against her resolve, released a sob. She put a hand to her mouth, turned, and left the room.

BY 2:00 A.M., Creed was back at the detachment, locked in the cell beside Sinnisiak and Uluksuk by Captain Crosswell himself. Creed watched his nimble hand, marvelling at how agile the Englishman was with only one. Crosswell turned the key, slid it out, and gave Creed a thin smile.

"We'll take the noon train Tuesday. The long trip back to civilization."

"Is that what you call it?"

Crosswell ignored him and walked out into the main detachment office, closing the heavy door behind him.

The Eskimo hunters had awoken from a deep sleep. Sinnisiak was pleased to see him until it was explained why Creed's cell was locked. But Uluksuk barely acknowledged him. The old man was gaunt and very ill. Sinnisiak had learned more English from Cowperthwaite over the last few days and was able to explain his concerns about his friend.

"Uluksuk no eat. No talk. Say he better dead. And look." Sinnisiak lifted up Mainprize's pocket watch, which Koeha had given Uluksuk. It had been dropped, and the glass was cracked. "Watch broke. Uluksuk say sun no come."

Creed took the watch in his hand. It had stopped.

"Watch broke. Sun no come," Sinnisiak repeated.

It took a moment for Creed to understand. "There will be sun. The watch doesn't control the sun coming up. It's only a tool to measure. The sun will come up!" But neither of them believed him.

Creed, appraising the old shaman, hated to see Uluksuk suffering, but wasn't exactly in a position to help at the moment. The dire nature of his own predicament became crystal clear to him in the afterglow of his time with Angi. First, a long, lonely trip back to Belgium. Then a star chamber court martial at HQ within earshot of artillery. And last, a firing squad to make a strong example of him. There'd be no defence witnesses left. Only McFee for the prosecution. Maybe Frank Banes had been right; maybe Creed should have held McFee up to enemy fire. The charges would never have been laid. But Creed had had enough killing at that moment. McFee was just one too many. Or maybe there was more to it. Maybe deep down Creed felt he deserved all this.

Creed suddenly felt very weary. He and Angi had been so close to getting away. So close to the rest of their lives together. What hope had they now? He then heard her inquiring voice in his head. But it wasn't in his head. It was in the office beyond the door. She was here! He could hear Captain Crosswell's clipped replies.

"No. No visitors."

"I am the court translator."

In the detachment office, Angituk and the little captain stood nose to nose. She wore her trousers, boots, flannel shirt, and suspenders, though today she did not bother to hide or even subdue her gender anymore.

"That trial is over."

"I translate for the prisoners. I have information for them."

"They don't need your services right now. You have no official business here."

"I have as much official business as you."

"Superintendent! Would you deal with this ... individual."

Worsley was standing in his doorway, conflicted and rather irritated by the high-handed nature of this junior officer. What hurt could a visit do? But the Commissioner had ordered him to co-operate with the fellow.

"We'll restrict the visits for now, Mr., eh, Miss McAndrew."

"I'm staying here until you let me see him." Angituk sat down on a bench.

Beside Worsley, Cowperthwaite and the police officers who had arrested Creed had been listening to the exchange. The news of the charges against Creed had swept through the ranks like a hot chinook wind. *Creed.* It was difficult to believe. And though each man would have done his duty, if reluctantly, to apprehend him, the news of his capture had spread a deep malaise. The final revelation was Angituk's true identity. The boy, though he had kept to himself, was well known and liked. The shock was that no man had consciously suspected him. Slender, perhaps underdeveloped—the Natives seldom had much facial hair—and the thin, high cheekbones ... but a *woman?* Now, as with any brilliant idea, each man wondered how he hadn't come up with it. And then thoughts turned to Creed again. Wily old Creed. On patrol for months and months with a now admittedly comely young woman. It all gave the men a lot to think about.

Creed slept a few hours and awoke after the dawn he had

promised. "You see?" he told Uluksuk. "The sun has risen. The watch means nothing."

But the old man merely closed his eyes.

JUSTICE HARVEY AND NICOLE arrived after breakfast. Angituk still sat on the bench in the detachment office. She and Nicole held each other's eyes for a moment. Justice Harvey went to Worsley.

"I still can't believe this is true, George."

"It does seem to be a legal warrant for his arrest, your Lordship. The Commissioner is aware of it all."

Harvey studied the paper for a moment.

Angituk stood and spoke. "Justice Harvey? They won't let me see him. You could let me."

Harvey looked at Angituk. He had come to think highly of her, of her insightful services during the trial, but by the expression on the face of his niece he knew he had no choice.

"I'm sorry, Miss McAndrew. It is not for me to say. But I would like to see him myself."

"Of course, your Lordship," Worsley told him. Captain Crosswell seemed about to object but closed his mouth tight.

Cowperthwaite was opening the door for him when the Justice stopped and looked back at Nicole. "Are you coming in?"

"I'd rather not, Uncle. I'll be here if you need me."

THE JUSTICE ENTERED THE CELL area at the back of the office. He nodded to Sinnisiak and Uluksuk, though the old shaman's eyes were closed. Then he spoke a quiet inquiry without accusation.

"Jack. What do you have to say for yourself?"

"I killed a British infantry officer, your Lordship. It was in defence of my men. But I'm afraid the court martial won't see it that way."

"No." The old Justice shook his head gravely. The silence grew for a moment. "I'll give you and your lawyers all the advice I can."

"That's awfully generous of you, sir."

"Nicole is taking this very hard."

"I know, sir."

"Not just the charges, but the other thing ..."

"Yes. Of course. I'm sorry."

"So am I. You had made us all so proud, Jack. We thought you could very well have become ..." The Justice's eyes searched the distance as he pondered the possibilities now dead. The silence grew again. The old man moved to leave, then turned back. "Well, let us know if there's anything we can do, Jack."

"I will, sir."

"I'll see you before you go."

"I'll look forward to that."

Justice Harvey stepped out into the office. The other police officers had left except for Cowperthwaite. Harvey approached Worsley.

"Have you seen a copy of the discovery against him, George?"

"No, Horace. It wasn't provided."

Captain Crosswell interjected. "They're working on it in London. We do have a witness statement by the dead officer's adjutant, your Lordship. If you'd care to come into the Superintendent's office, you can read that, examine the extradition order, and I can outline the case for you as I know it."

"All right. You're leaving on the Tuesday train?"

"That's correct."

"I'm sure the Superintendent is giving you every co-operation."

"Very much so."

Worsley extended an open hand. "Let me have the cell key, captain. I'll lock it in the case in my office."

The captain patted the side pocket of his uniform and offered a thin smile. "If you don't mind, Superintendent, no offence, but I'll keep it myself. Just want to make sure he stays put."

Worsley bristled again at the impudence. He replied as evenly as he could, "As you wish."

The men all moved into Worsley's office.

NICOLE AND ANGITUK had listened to this exchange without a word. They were now left alone together in the outer office. Nicole studied the girl in silence. She could easily see how one might mistake her for a boy. Slender body. Wide shoulders. Minimal curves. Her black hair long enough to conceal high cheekbones in a face that was always averted. Angituk sat very still on the bench, rotating her fedora in her hands, staring at the floor. Nicole moved around the office. She stopped periodically and regarded the girl from different perspectives. What had Jack seen in her? Nicole studied her as she decided exactly how to begin.

"Angituk? That's your name—Angituk?"

"Yes."

"You know, I appreciate you have some feelings for Jack. Absolutely understandable. It's the one thing we have in common. But the truth is, you're just making this whole thing so much harder for him."

Angituk looked up at her in alarm. "What do you mean?"

"You are creating such a problem for him."

"No. I don't want to do that. I don't understand."

"Well, of course you know it was your fault he was arrested."

"No! What did I do? I didn't—"

"Jack's not stupid. He knew the military police were here. Do you think he'd still be in Edmonton if it wasn't for you? He'd be long gone. He stayed here for you."

"I ... I didn't want him to stay. I mean, I didn't know he was in danger."

"You weren't worried about him. All you cared about was yourself."

"That's not true. He told me he loved me."

"Of course. They always do. To get what they want."

Angituk was shaken by this. Her mother had told her the same thing. Angus McAndrew had told Kunee he loved her. But now she knew: people lied about love. "But I love him."

"All right. I'm glad you said that." Nicole moved closer, bringing a chair. She sat down, and they faced each other. "You say you love him?"

"Yes."

"Then help him. He's in trouble, Angituk. They could execute him. What good are you to him now? You can't do anything for him. He's facing a murder trial."

"I want to help him."

"Of course you do."

"How can I help him?"

"The truth is, you can do nothing for him. If you want to help Jack ..." Nicole paused. "... you have to get out of his life." She let this sink in. "I can help him face this thing. I know this world. I can find the finest lawyers, petition the government. I can use the press. My uncle has strong influence, as you know. I can get Jack through this. I can save him. I love him too. Do you understand?"

Angituk nodded.

"I will get him through this. But you ..." Nicole hesitated, and then her voice broke as she continued. "You must give him back to me."

Angituk stared at her. "Back to you?" she repeated. She was slowly realizing that even if all Creed's troubles went away, she could still never have him. The tears pooled in Angituk's eyes and her lips quivered as she tried to speak clearly. "He is all I have left."

Nicole had purged her voice of any emotion. She was all business now. "It is never easy to do the right thing."

Angituk's eyes overflowed and she hated herself for showing this emotion, this weakness, to the yellow-haired woman. She lifted her flannel sleeve to her face and aggressively wiped the tears from her eyes. She sat up straight and took a deep breath, and after a moment she could speak with dignity. "How do I do the right thing?"

Nicole took her hand in appreciation and held it in her lap. Angi let her.

"You won't see him again. That is important. You can write him a letter. I can help you with that. You have to tell him you don't love him anymore. We can do it now if you like. Then you will go back north, to your own people. He will understand that. That will give him what he needs so he can go on."

"But I can't see him?"

"No, Angituk. I can save him, but you have to go away."

Angituk thought about all this. The right thing to do. A wave of grief washed over her again, drawing her back with it into the darkness.

"If you really love him, Angituk, you will do this for him. Why don't we write the letter now? I'll help you."

Angituk nodded slowly as all hope inside her died.

Twenty-Seven

She filled two burlap sacks with the things she had bought: the dresses and blouses, lacy underwear, the makeup, lotions, and powders. She put them in the garbage barrels behind the hotel. She collected the $974 still owed her from her contract as translator with the Royal North West Mounted Police. Then she went to the court clerk, Ainsley, for another $127 for her work in the courts. She bought a fine three-year-old roan mare at Walpole's livery, which she named Kannokapfaluk, goddess of the animals. She had learned to ride years ago from some friendly Blackfoot south of Fort Norman and she was determined to bring a good horse up there when she returned. She bought a new Western saddle and generous saddlebags made in Calgary; a .38 Winchester rifle and three boxes of cartridges; two dozen small steel traps for muskrat, beaver, and fox; two real bowie skinning knives from Illinois; and a double-bladed axe forged in Montreal with a maple handle. She bought a couple of iron pots, two boxes of Bluebird wooden matches, three pounds of salt, three of flour, and three of tea. She could hear her mother laughing at the tea and flour. She was going white, she would say. But she wasn't. She was only taking a few things she liked from them. That's how her people thrived. By adaptation. By making practical selections. "We absorb some of their things, but they never absorb us," she told herself. "Never absorb us." As for the rest of the white world, she wished it would all slide into the muddy river.

She had her plan: to make her soul strong and independent, to learn to live alone, to not offend the spirits of people or animals, to make the necessary offerings, to use the magic words and songs and make the amulets as she had learned from Uluksuk. She would go again and live in Fort Norman, where her mother had died. There was a reason she had lived so long in Fort Norman. It was halfway between her mother's people and her father's people. For so long she had been stuck there without the courage to go either north or south. But now she could make her choice. Creed had given her that much, and she was grateful. She would stay in Norman for a while, run a trapline in the winter, fish in the spring, hunt in the fall, and maybe guide white men in the summer months. Then, after a year or two, when the pain of losing Creed had eased, she would go up the Coppermine again. She loved the country and the people. Her people. Slowly she would coax her mother's spirit north, back to their real home.

At Blowey & Henry department store she bought two fine new soft flannel shirts, green and red plaid, and corduroy and jean trousers, and new red suspenders. She bought long underwear, one pair of light natural cotton and one of thick red wool for winter, each with a buttoned flap at the back. She bought four pairs of wool socks, grey with white and red stripes at the top. She bought a good down-filled sleeping bag, though she knew she'd stitch together a warmer caribou one when she was far enough north to hunt again, and a small, thick-canvas one-person tent. She also chose three newly published books to take with her: *The Shadow Line* by Joseph Conrad, *The Rainbow* by D.H. Lawrence, and Henry James's last book before his recent death, *The Ivory Tower*. She filled the saddlebags. She had to tie the tent and sleeping bag behind the saddle with leather straps.

It was early afternoon when she mounted the packed roan. She would put the horse and her provisions on the Fort McMurray train at a livestock siding a few miles north of the city. She could not stop herself from looking up from under the brim of her hat toward the detachment where he was. Her head told her Nicole was right. No good could come now of seeing him again or hearing his voice or touching him. It would only make it worse and compromise her resolve. Her resolve to do the right thing. Her eyes brimmed again as she looked at the ornate detachment building, with towers and a stonework entrance like a castle she had seen in a book from a stupid white man's fairy tale. She wiped the back of her hand across her nose and turned the horse away from him. Under a hot afternoon sun she headed north with the determination of a wave in quest of a distant shore, out and away from Edmonton, along the ugly brown river.

CREED SAT IN THE CORNER of the cell for three days listening to the soft periodic chanting of Uluksuk's death song. The old man had given up eating and he spoke no more. He was slipping away into the dream world now and there was nothing Creed or Sinnisiak could do for him. No hope to offer. Creed himself had no appetite, and the songs that were a yearning for death lent a resonance to his own situation. Indeed, what was there to live for? The present was unbearable and the grim future offered little more. The girl was gone.

It was Cowperthwaite who delivered the sealed letter. Angituk had gone back to her people. This was not her world, she wrote to him. He was not her man. She wanted Creed to forget about her. And Creed knew that she was wise. In fact ruthlessly practical, and he had seen that feature in her before, the time she took the beating heart of the dovekie between her fingers and crushed it. So the message rang true. But still it surprised him. It pushed him deep into despondency. He would never see her again. He yearned to have his own death song and the comfort of the covenant old Uluksuk had made with eternity.

Nicole visited him twice a day. She held his hand through the bars. She was bright and optimistic, talking of the defence strategies she had developed with her uncle. There were no surviving witnesses to the crime but for McFee and Jack. There was not a lot of evidence still in existence. The captain's body had been recovered and a battlefield autopsy done at the insistence of McFee. Even so, it was his word against Jack's. If Jack confessed to killing the officer, there was still a defence to mount. To that end, she had been telegraphing doctors in Montreal and Boston who had expertise in the newly recognized mental condition called "shell shock." Doctors were confirming that it could manifest itself as irrationality. It was not just an excuse to be relieved of duty.

"I'm coming with you to Belgium, Jack. I'm going to see you through this. You have to keep your spirits up. You heard what I said: there is some good news in all of this."

She would then tell him she loved him and he would smile sadly at her, unable to bring himself to speak what was expected in return. He could not lie to her. The only thing he could think about was Angituk's slender body swimming to him under the surface of the Great Bear, her urgent breath, her delighted laughter, and that she had left him and he would never see her again.

"Are you listening to me? You have to shave. You have to maintain appearances, Jack. You have to speak with confidence. There will be journalists. They'll be watching you. We need them on our side. I'll help you, but you have to work hard and help me, too."

"All right."

"Jack? It's going to be okay. All right? We'll get through this together and then we have our whole lives ahead of us."

He would smile his sad smile and nod. "I don't deserve you."

On the third day, Nicole was discouraged. She had been giving him encouraging talks and discussing defence strategies and he just wasn't readying himself.

"Funny old Jack. Is it the memories of the war coming back that are making you so sad?"

"I think that must be it."

"Well, as I say, we'll use these new studies about what war does to people. How it can make you behave in irrational ways. We have a lot of reasons for guarded optimism. My uncle says Boddington, Rupert and Lang are some of the finest defence solicitors in London. And the military court has agreed to consider his request to allow them to represent you. That's a big hurdle."

Creed was listening to most of what she said. She had told him she was more or less recovered from the shock and anger over what she had seen in the bedroom. She could put that behind them.

"I understand men are simple creatures and have their needs. You were under stress. I mean, the girl was pretty enough, I suppose."

She had even told him she felt a little sorry for having turned him in to Crosswell. "In retrospect, I might have reconsidered."

"I understand, Nicole. I don't blame you."

"And you know, in the long run, it is probably for the best. I mean, to deal with the criminal charges head-on. You can't run forever. It's rather exciting, really, that I can help save you. And then we'll always have that. And we can put it behind us and be together."

Nicole took Creed's hand through the bars. "The train trip tomorrow will be a tonic for you. Hopefully, Captain Crosswell won't be a boor about things and will give you a little freedom. Maybe we could all go to one of those excellent restaurants in Montreal. Maybe the Château. And then passage across the Atlantic on one of those convoys. They say the German submarines are almost under control. I think we should look on it as an adventure. I'm rather excited to go to Europe again. I haven't been since I was a teenager, before the war."

As she spoke, Creed realized he was dreading the trip, not so much because it would take him back to Europe and that hateful conflict and the charges he would face and the potential penalties, but rather because it would take him so far from the girl. Even if she had gone back to her people, didn't love him anymore as her letter had stated, and would not have him, to be imprisoned on another continent so far away from her seemed more than he could bear.

Creed studied Nicole as she spoke to him, holding his hand. The practical Nicole. The beautiful Nicole. She was remarkable. It was true, if somehow they got through this thing, they could make a good life together. And she was the perfect agent for him with her uncle's knowledge of law, her persuasive manner, and this resilient intent to love him whether he deserved it or not. He'd be a fool not to accept her help. Without her he would be lost. But he had used her once to gain advantage and then clemency for Sinnisiak and Uluksuk; he could not bring himself to deceive her again. He would have to tell her the truth, and then she would have to make her decision.

"Nicole. You have been wonderful to me. I don't know what I'd do without you," he began. "You cheer me up and say you love me and you have your plans and strategies for the trial. But I have to tell you something."

He had her attention.

"You are beautiful and charming and any other man would say I'm a fool, but you should know this. I don't love you."

She stared at him in shock, her hazel eyes searching his. Then she looked down and sorted herself out. When her eyes returned to his, they were brimming. He hated himself.

"Well, you know ... sometimes there's a lot to be said for lies and pretence. Don't sell it short." She laughed and two tears traced their way down her cheeks. Then she sniffed them back and sat up straight and began to speak quickly and calmly. "You know, Jack, these things often work out over time. In a little while you could begin to love me. Often that's how it goes, Jack. Just more time. We've hardly had enough to really get to know each other, with you wandering all over the country. Love isn't like some magic spell or ... it's never the mythological 'at first sight' sort of thing. It develops, bit by bit, until one day you turn around and there it is." She was struggling now not to cry again. "I know I can make you love me, if you just let me. Please, Jack."

"I love someone else."

Nicole looked at him in shock. "You ...? Who else ...? Not the Eskimo girl! Over me? You love her?"

"I do."

"But she's gone, Jack."

"I know."

"She's left you."

"Yes."

"She's out of your life!"

"I know, but still I can't.... It means I'm not able to love you."

"You would sacrifice our entire life together because of this love for her?"

"You were right, Nicole. You said that love trumps everything. You were right."

Nicole thought about this for a moment. Her hazel eyes darkened, her tears were gone. Suddenly she was on her feet.

"You bastard. You stupid bastard, Jack Creed or John MacKay or whoever you are. I've had enough of your games. You can go straight to hell! And you probably will, or spend your life in a military prison. And that's fine with me. Go ahead. Throw yourself on the mercy of the army. You'll get no more from me."

She left the cells, slamming the heavy wood and iron door behind her, and Creed reflected into the evening on the future he had chosen.

JUSTICE HARVEY FELT COMPELLED by duty to have Captain Crosswell for dinner on his last night in Edmonton. He would take the noon train south to Calgary tomorrow with his corporal and the prisoner, John MacKay, then the Continental to Montreal. Nicole had told her uncle she would not now be travelling to Europe, and though he was surprised, he did not question her. Captain Crosswell was quite disappointed she would not be accompanying them, but he too controlled his urge to pry. Harold and Lieutenant Wilkerson joined them for dinner. They both had another eight days of leave in Edmonton. The staff served roasted elk, fiddleheads, and a very good rendition of Yorkshire pudding. The port helped the evening pass.

After dinner, as the clock tolled eleven, they all retired to the parlour. The men smoked cigars and Harold started up the gramophone with a Ziegfeld Follies piece sung by Fanny Brice. Nicole, normally the energy of the party, had been unusually quiet and thoughtful and the men felt compelled to draw her out. As they did so, she suddenly came alive.

"Captain Crosswell, you've spent some time in Paris and London?"

"Indeed I have, miss."

"We read in the news about popular dancing in the clubs. My goodness, what goes on! But I think it's healthy. This old world needs to give itself a shake. Stop being so serious about everything."

"Well, everything is rather serious these days, miss. If the Germans were to win, I can't imagine what would become of 'this old world.'"

"Yes. But we can't do much about it right here, tonight, can we? So what I want to hear about are the new dances. Do you dance at all, Captain Crosswell?"

"Funny you should say. I do, miss. The wife and I used to be quite the pair in London. And even with my disadvantage, I did cut a rug in Paris."

"Oh! You must show us! Show us a new dance. I've heard of one: the Trot."

"Yes, the Foxtrot. Very popular. But you know, it's not named after the creature. It's named after the man, Harry Fox, who invented it."

"Really?" Nicole was on her feet. "I can't wait a moment longer. Show us the Foxtrot."

Captain Crosswell hesitated, glancing at Justice Harvey. But when he sensed the Justice's approval, he rose dutifully to his feet.

"Right, then. I'll show you how it goes, but maybe first we warm up with something simple."

The captain put his good arm around her waist, and she placed her right hand on his waist and her left gently on his shoulder above his empty sleeve, which startled him for a moment until he realized it was the perfect configuration. And he smiled at her, this attractive, sensitive woman. Harold put a slower Dixieland jazz band number on the gramophone and they were suddenly dancing a two-step. The captain was smooth and confident. He did not seem to mind she stood more than half a head taller.

"We'll start with the easy version of the Trot. Some people approach it like a polka, but it's much more like an energetic waltz!"

He moved her around in circles, explaining when to do the little kicks. They danced smoothly all through one song and started it again. Halfway in, she stumbled and went down onto one knee, laughing. Alarmed at first, the captain knelt down to support her and help her up. As he did so, she grasped at his waist, leaning awkwardly against him. Her fingers slid unnoticed into the side pocket of his uniform jacket and emerged with the key to Jack's cell. A second later she was back on her feet, quite recovered. She danced once more with the captain and then they tried a little of the quickstep version, but she expressed her dizziness and sat down, thanking him.

With the only female partner available bowing out, the disappointed men left dancing behind and the focus turned to stories of the war. Justice Harvey reached for his best bottle of Macallan Scotch, which Nicole had positioned with glasses on the sideboard. She lit the small fire she had set as, she explained, the night was cooling and a fireside is always the best place to tell stories. Her uncle was fond of saying that the greatest lies are told before marriage, after the hunt, and during the campaign. When the Scotch was poured, the men drank to the success of the war effort, and to the Yanks who had finally joined the Allies, and almost immediately the conversation turned to artillery and tactics. Nicole claimed weariness, bade them all good night, kissed her uncle and cousin, and left them to their stories.

In her room, Nicole changed into her riding breeches, boots, and blouse and then went quietly out the back way to the stables. She could have taken the Ford, but it had a tendency to backfire. She harnessed up the grey gelding to the trap and, so she wouldn't be heard, led him slowly down the muffling grass beside the gravel driveway to the street. Nimbly, she jumped aboard the cart and gave the reins a snap and soon they were trotting down 106th Street into town.

AT THE DETACHMENT, Corporal Cowperthwaite was looking at the last inch of Hudson's Bay rum in the bottle. He had another bottle if need be, but it appeared by the heavy lids and slack jaw of the British corporal that the man had finally succumbed. It had taken a little persuading, that first sip. He was a by-the-book soldier and on guard duty after all, his chair positioned beside the door into the cells, and he outright refused at first. Cowperthwaite promised him his captain would certainly be enjoying the contents of the Justice's liquor cabinet, and the prisoner was locked away and asleep, so the NCO finally agreed to a ceremonial sip. Once committed, the big corporal took enthusiastically to the stuff.

As they drank, Cowperthwaite entertained him with talk of some recent research he had done. "You see, the Eskimo is a nomadic hunting society while ours is a stationary accumulative society. They are polar opposites, no pun intended. In our society it is the accumulation of material goods and land and currency which is the measure of a man's success. And this system then requires government and taxes and banks, the creation of class structures, competition, suppression of the poor and of women. But in Eskimo society, success comes from a productive hunt and to do that they require mobility, adaptability, skill, and planning, and an intuitive understanding of land and sea conditions, animal behaviour, and weather patterns. Touch more?"

He poured the corporal three more fingers. There was no protest. Cowperthwaite was warming to his dissertation.

"And it has always been the case that settled culture seeks to change nomadic hunting cultures, to make them stop and stay in one place and embrace their brand of civilization, but it is the very egalitarian nature of the nomadic society that defends against that. They have no real leaders as such. No organizations! Each Eskimo makes his own decisions. The best hunter leads by example. Others watch. No questions are asked. No one tells anyone else what to do. If anyone tried to give orders, it would be considered rude and improper. And you see, this individualism is an effective barricade against organized domination by one man, one class, or by an outside civilization like ... ourselves. You see my point?"

"Yes. Very inner-esting." The corporal drained his glass and Cowperthwaite didn't even ask to pour this time.

"You've never heard of Eskimo wars, have you? They'd be impossible to organize! And their very nature is to avoid personal conflict. They have enough to do to simply survive. So when conflict comes, they smile or ignore it or simply move away to a new camp, whereas we, on the other hand, must stay and defend our accumulated stuff! Result: war!"

Cowperthwaite had gone on along these lines for the better part of an hour, by which time the bottle was nearly drained. He himself was not feeling any pain, though he had subtly pushed the lion's share onto the corporal so he would be ready for the work at hand. He stood up straight and whispered to Nicole when she arrived, trying not to slur.

"I think he's good, Miss Harvey. Out for a while."

And as they both looked at the corporal, he began to

produce soft little snores, slow and consistent and growing in volume.

"Good work, Cowperthwaite."

"I gave it my best, miss."

When she went to go inside to the cells, Cowperthwaite was behind her and she suddenly turned back. "Can you give us a minute?" she asked him.

THERE WAS MOONLIGHT coming through the small window, illuminating the cells with an eerie incandescence. The two Eskimos were curled up asleep on the floor. Creed lay on his back along a narrow bench with one hand across his chest, the other trailing on the floor, his face turned toward her in childlike repose. Nicole lowered herself to her knees and studied him through the bars. She loved this man. Everything until then had been plans and arrangements, and now, in this moment of calm, this moment of reflection on what could and couldn't be, the grief came suddenly and she fought against the unstoppable tears and then for a moment she let them flow. Only a moment, only one breath-catching sob, quiet like a whisper, but enough of a release that she could then recover and function again. She was back in control just as Creed opened his eyes.

"Nicole?"

She put a finger to her lips. "The corporal's asleep," she whispered. "Crosswell is with my uncle. The men are out on patrols except for Cowperthwaite."

She held the key out to him in both hands like a sacrament. Creed took it through the bars.

"My trap is waiting outside. The train for Fort McMurray leaves in twenty-five minutes."

Creed held her hand through the bars, their faces close. "Why are you doing this?"

Nicole went to touch his face with her hand, then stopped herself. "Because I lied to you, Jack. I'm sorry. You ... you initiated this reckless new world of honesty. So here it is: I made her write the letter. I made her say she didn't love you. I made her go away. But the truth is, she does love you, Jack. As much as you love her. So if love trumps everything ... go and find her."

He looked into her eyes. "Nicole, I don't know what to—"

She put her fingers against his lips to stop him. He took her hand and squeezed it, then stood, inserted Crosswell's key, turned it, and the latch quietly released. Across town, the train whistle signalled the twenty-minute warning.

Cowperthwaite stepped inside anxiously. "You better hurry, Jack."

Creed looked into the second locked cell, where his friends were sleeping. "Cowper, I'm taking them with me."

His friend held up the chain of keys. "I thought as much."

Creed took the chain from him and opened the second cell. "Come on, you two. We're going home."

Sinnisiak was alert in an instant, but it took precious moments to get Uluksuk awake and standing. He was weak. Too weak to walk alone.

"You're going home," Creed repeated.

"You'll see your wives and children and grandchildren," Sinnisiak told him.

"Come home, Uluksuk."

The old man's dull eyes brightened and a new strength suddenly surged through his frail, starving body. "Home?" he said.

Creed helped him out of the cell and through the door, where Creed stopped and turned back toward Nicole.

"Are you coming?"

"No. No, I think I'll stay here, thanks."

Creed hesitated in the doorway, keeping Uluksuk on his feet. "Goodbye then, Nicole. Thank you. I'll never forget this."

"I know."

When they were gone, Nicole walked into Jack's cell. She reached down to place her hand on the bench, still warm where his body had lain. She noticed on the floor under the bench a silver circle and bent down to pick up the object. It was Mainprize's broken pocket watch, the hands still, a pretty thing, the face tragically cracked. She turned, reached out to grasp a bar on the cell door, and swung it shut, the lock clicking into place. Then, with the broken pocket watch tightly in her hand, she lay down on the warm bench where he had slept, to wait.

Twenty-Eight

They crowded into the little two-wheeled buggy: Creed, Sinnisiak, Uluksuk, and Cowperthwaite. Creed lifted the old man up and his body was as light as a child's.

Creed suddenly realized the risks his friend was taking. "You're going to get in trouble, Cowperthwaite. Aiding and abetting."

"I'll say it was all at gunpoint. Where's your gun?"

"They took it away."

"Oh, of course. Here, take mine."

"No, I'm serious. Accessory to an escape."

"I'll be fine. The corporal got me drunk."

They made their way with Nicole's grey gelding at a quick trot down the deserted streets toward the station. The train was in final boarding when they arrived. There were only a handful of people in the station. Creed and the hunters remained behind a closed concession stand while Cowperthwaite bought the tickets. The clerk was painfully slow about it. There was an RNWMP constable on duty near the gate and Cowperthwaite went over to report some drunken ruffians on the street outside the station. When the constable went to investigate, they all passed through the gate and out onto the platform.

At the steps of the final passenger car, they stopped while

Cowperthwaite gave Creed the tickets. A conductor called out to stragglers.

"ALL ABOARD! LAST CALL FOR FORT McMURRAY!"

Creed turned to Cowperthwaite. "Thank you for this, Lyle. I owe you my life."

"Just a letter from time to time, Jack. Let me know how you get on."

Creed shook his hand warmly.

"And take this." He handed Creed a brand new volume of Robert Service's poems. "He just gets more wonderful all the time!"

Creed laughed and stuck it in his knapsack. "Thanks, Lyle. I'll put it to good use."

Creed guided the hunters to the steps. Uluksuk could almost stand on his own now and with both hands on the railings, with Creed's help, he mounted the first step. They'd made it. Creed put an arm around him to help him up the final steps. In moments they would be on their way.

"Good evening, Creed," Superintendent Worsley called to him.

Three RNWMP officers—Dewey, Oberly, and Worsley—were suddenly standing on the platform behind Creed. Big Svenson appeared inside the train at the top of the steps, blocking their way. Creed turned to stare at Worsley then and stepped down onto the platform. It took him a moment to find his voice.

"Good evening, sir."

His heart plunged. It was over. He had involved Cowperthwaite and Nicole and he had failed. They would be punished. As for his own freedom, he had used it up long ago. He killed a man with his bare hands. Only moments ago, when Nicole revealed the way to him, did he allow himself to believe that it could be this easy. But freedom was never this easy. The worst thing about it was Uluksuk. The shaman would die now. He would die and there was nothing Creed could do about it.

"How did you know?" Creed asked Worsley, who seemed pleased at the question.

"Just a hunch. I couldn't be sure, but this train was one of your last options. If you hadn't arrived, no loss. But you didn't disappoint me, Creed."

Creed had never seen this cruel streak in Worsley before. Worsley turned to Cowperthwaite with an official tone.

"Corporal! What do you think you're doing here?"

"Ah, sir, I ... I was just about to apprehend these fugitives."

"Fugitives. Is that what you call them?"

"I'm happy to call them anything you like, Superintendent."

"I think you should call them 'men on assignment.'"

Creed and Cowperthwaite looked at Worsley with blank stares.

"Assignment, sir?" Creed asked. "I ... I don't understand."

Worsley spoke to Creed, his face devoid of emotion. "New orders, Inspector Creed. I think it's high time the Royal North West Mounted Police established a new post at the mouth of the Coppermine River. Would you volunteer for such a mission?"

Creed looked at him, astonished. "Yes, sir."

"Excellent. And these two will be your assistants: Special Constables Uluksuk and Sinnisiak. You can swear them in."

"Special constables, sir?" Creed stared at him.

Worsley leaned forward and spoke quietly. "Yes, Creed. Why don't you just take them home."

Creed was startled by the blast of the train's whistle. The conductor called out to Worsley: "One minute, Superintendent."

Worsley looked at Creed, waiting for a response. "Do you understand?"

"Yes, sir. I think I do. Thank you, sir."

Sinnisiak was helping Uluksuk on board. They went up the steps and entered the passenger car.

"I'll telegraph Fort Norman to have supplies ready for you. Find yourself a new name. Send me regular reports. Both the Anglican and Catholic churches have declared their intent to build missions there in the next couple of years, and Hudson's Bay wants a post. I need a good man to keep things under control."

"What will you do about Crosswell, sir?"

"Don't worry about Crosswell. I will receive word tomorrow you've been spotted crossing the Montana border." Worsley smiled for the first time. "Better get on board, Creed."

The whistle blew again and the train began to move.

Creed jumped onto the lowest step, pulling himself up. He looked at the amused faces of Svenson, Dewey, Oberly, and Cowperthwaite.

"Oh, and Creed—you're going to need to hire an interpreter. I would suggest, from what I've heard, you might find an experienced one in Fort Norman."

"Yes?"

"That's what I hear."

"I hope so, sir. Thank you, sir."

ON A SUNNY, warm afternoon late in September, the girl sat on a three-legged stool on the bank of the Great Bear River on the edge of the tumbledown, patchwork settlement of Fort Norman. The husky named Star lay at her feet. The flannel shirt and trousers were still a little big for her frame, but she liked the roominess. She hated any feelings of confinement. She was skinning muskrats, a slit up the front from tail to chin, side cuts up the legs and around the paws with her new knives, then working the skin off using her mother's *ulu* blade, which was still the best for parting fur from flesh without nicking the membrane. Her strong, slender fingers worked quickly. George Fish, a half-breed like her, who owned the tannery, was happy to have her back. He didn't care if she was Eskimo; she was the best skinner he had ever seen.

Angituk was still dressing and acting like a man since her return to Fort Norman, though it was more difficult to maintain the charade than it had been before her trip to the Coppermine. Her body had filled out in the last few months and her face had matured past the ambiguity of adolescence. Her short hair had grown, which worked more than anything against her male image—when it fell in her eyes, she would toss her head in an unmistakably feminine manner—and so it was impossible to assert she was now anything other than a beautiful young woman. But she didn't really care. Men, white or red, did not intimidate her anymore. She had a fine set of knives and it was known she could use them. Her clothing and manner were more habit and comfort now than masquerade. And George Fish and the good people of Fort Norman didn't care either. They were most of them running from something. They all had their secrets and eccentricities. They had offered her honest smiles and warm greetings when she had returned a few days before.

After her odyssey, Angituk had simply returned to life as she had known it. She didn't need the money from skinning, but she needed the simple purpose and a place to hole up for the few months. She put down her knife and wiped her hands on her jean trousers and felt her belly, still firm and showing no more than if she had just finished a big meal. It had happened on the Great Bear. The first time they made love. She massaged it in circles and sang a few words of the magic song to the baby inside. She could still be active for several months while the baby grew. She thought she would do some hunting in the fall.

A rich white man from the South had contacted her: he wanted to kill a bear. Someone had recommended her as a guide. But why would he want to kill a bear? They were brothers to humans, only to be killed if you were starving or if the bear was starving and about to kill you. To seek out and kill a bear was, as the priests at the mission school would put it, a sin. She could take the rich white man out and make sure he didn't find a bear, but probably she would just avoid him altogether and establish a trapline in the winter up near Great Bear Lake instead. The fishing would be good in the spring. Maybe she would even cross that great freshwater ocean and make her way through the Dismal Lakes as far as the Coppermine. If that far, why not all the way to the north coast? Would her mother's spirit follow her home?

Her mood lifted, thinking of that distant land of spirits where you put your ear to the stone earth and it asked you the question, *Il-viunna-hugi-vit?* Are you who you appear to be? That would be the best place to bring up the child, among her people. With Kingagolik helping her. But it was too far to go alone this year. She had to find a safe place to have the child and she had to have someone to help. There was Bessie Fish, George's kind wife, who helped mothers. She would ask her to be with her when the baby came.

Angituk rubbed her belly again. This child would become her world and she would never be lonely again. It was what he had given her, and she was thankful for the gift. But she had decided she would never take another man. She could never give her heart again like that, to a lover or to a father. She refused to experience that pain again. It was, at its simplest, a survival instinct. And so she would live free of men, with the child, as her mother had done for the most part. And that was fine. Now, in the North, away from Edmonton, she felt again the company of the spirits. She sensed that her mother was near. She and the child would be protected.

Angituk tossed another fresh pelt into the tub of water beside her. George had brought her two big beaver to do and she was pleased to have the variety. Thicker pelt, different cut pattern, and a nice rich, glossy texture. She hauled the first up on the stump, turned him over, and selected a wider-bladed knife, when she heard her name spoken. Often in the wind she heard her mother's voice speak her name, but it was not her mother who called her this time.

She turned and slowly rose to her feet, the broad-bladed knife in her hand, her wide-brimmed hat back on her head, hand to her eyes to block the glare of the low sun. Twenty yards away, near the tannery shack, he stood in civilian clothing, a tentative look in his eyes. Creed did not say her name again, he just looked at her, unsure of how she would react after what he'd put her through. The knife slipped from her fingers to the ground, and with everything she had, she ran to him.

IT WAS LATE FALL by the time they reached the Coppermine in two canoes on the broad, handsome river. A light snowfall defined the rocky banks. Creed had located two more sixteen-foot Peterboroughs at a mining camp on the Mackenzie downstream from Fort Norman. He and Angituk took the lead with Uluksuk and Sinnisiak behind. The baby was growing inside her but was still not big enough to diminish her paddle stroke or reduce her loads during portages. Whenever Creed's eyes found her, she was smiling, her face radiant as she sang little songs to the child.

Once they left Fort Norman behind them, the transformation

in Uluksuk had been dramatic. The old shaman began hungrily eating the meat they killed, made special charms, and chanted for their safety and success. He spoke to the spirits and happily reported the good tidings: they were welcomed back to this land.

All was well when they came to the smooth, quickening waters above Bloody Falls, and there was a short debate as to whether to portage or shoot the tubular rapids. The water was really too wild and cold to risk a dunking, so by mutual agreement they unloaded just upstream before the current became too powerful to resist. It was on the west side, the side where the priests had died, though no one discussed this choice. They each did two carries of equipment and supplies high on the cliff path above the turbulent waters on the loose, flat black rocks, slippery with frozen snow, and they put in below at a place where the frenzied waters spread out and calmed over a wide, rocky riverbed before their final nine-mile float to the sea.

There, on the pebble beach, they reloaded the canoes, including the delicate little leather sack with the bow and arrows Uluksuk had made for the child. Creed took a moment to survey the place all around him. This was where Samuel Hearne's Chipewyans had massacred an Eskimo camp of men, women, and children in 1771 as Hearne looked on. Franklin had reported still seeing many human bones here in 1821, but there were no bones now; all had been dissolved or washed away.

They had accomplished the portage almost completely without speaking, for even Creed felt the presence of the spirits in this place. They all hummed or chanted with each breath to keep any bad spirits out.

As his companions repacked the canoes on the rocky beach north of the falls, Creed hesitated. Then he turned suddenly, and with no explanation made his way down the hill and across the snow-tinged heather some distance away from the falls to find the wooden cross above the graves of the priests. Angituk followed him. Creed stood at the site for several minutes, considering the hopes and dreams that had brought the two men here, the character and passion of Father Rouvière, and the misfortune of their end. He wished them peace.

Angituk urged him in a whisper, trying unsuccessfully to keep the apprehension from her voice, "Let's go now." And they turned and, without looking back, made their way to the others.

They pushed off into the swift, smooth current, which bore them north, away from Bloody Falls, hardly having to dip a paddle, savouring these last hours of sensuous, effortless, burdenless travel toward the mouth of the Coppermine and home.

EPILOGUE

In 1919, the Royal North West Mounted Police established a permanent post near the mouth of the Coppermine River with the help of "Special Constables" Uluksuk and Sinnisiak, who lived out their lives in the Coppermine area.

With the complicity of a Hudson's Bay Company ship, which turned down the Catholic missionaries at the last minute, the Anglican Church was able to get construction materials to the mouth of the Coppermine ahead of the Roman Catholics, build a church in 1919, and baptize every Copper Inuit they could find. The Roman Catholics hired their own ship and built a church a year later to engage in a robust competition with the Anglicans, but the town of Coppermine, now known as Kugluktuk, remains predominately Anglican, the Christian religion folded well into the ancient, non-exclusive, and adaptable beliefs of the Copper Inuit who still live in tune with their own metaphors and love of the land.

ACKNOWLEDGEMENTS

In order of contributions, I would like to first thank Professor Gordon Moyles for his finely researched and written book about the case of the two Copper Inuit hunters, *British Law and Arctic Man*, which directly inspired this novel. My appreciation goes to Diane Lamoureaux and the Missionary Oblate Archives in Alberta for Father Rouvière's journal and letters. Credit also goes to the archives of Yellowknife and Edmonton. I wish to thank Deborah Bernstein and Slawko Klymkiw for commissioning the first development of Coppermine, which allowed me to travel, research, and craft the story. Thank you to the many who helped in those travels to Kugluktuk and the Coppermine: Becky and Luigi Torretti, Larry and Helen Whittaker, and Allen Niptanapiak and family, with whom my son Sean and I travelled to Bloody Falls and camped. My gratitude and respect to the elders of Kugluktuk who showed us the old ways and shared their stories. *"Quanaqqutit!"* Script editor John McAndrew was a strong early influence on the structure of the story. Kelly Dignan was instrumental and inspiring to me as an editor on the early draft of the novel. The project then came under the influence of the dynamic forces of my agent, Bruce Westwood (a man equally at home negotiating a book deal or an arctic river). My commissioning editor, Adrienne Kerr, at

Penguin, was both a passionate cheerleader and a major creative force in the work. For the finer points, I'd like to express my appreciation to my friend and fellow writer Ernest Hillen, and for the geography and methods and terminology of navigating rapids, Toban Leckie and Bruce Hodgins. To my daughter, Katelyn, thanks for your inspiration in creating all my young female characters. For the exquisite reference map, my thanks to Susan and Gordon Turner. Shirley Leckie gave me Edmonton in 1917. World War I historian Dan Murphy guided me through the Canadian trenches of 1915. I wish to thank Emily Angulalik of Cambridge Bay for her Inuinnaqtun translations and advice on the characters and story, and Monique LeRay for the sensitive translation of Father Rouvière's journal. Thanks also to George Wally for additional translations of letters and the journal. On becoming a writer, I am forever grateful to Stanley and Nancy Colbert for their guidance, and also to Timothy Findley, who supported my early funding applications and gave me great encouragement and inspiration.

There is a small library of arctic books that have influenced me in writing this novel. A few are *Inuit: Glimpses of an Arctic Past* by David Morrison and Georges-Hébert Germain; *The White Dawn* by James Huston; *People of the Deer* and others by Farley Mowat; *Prisoners of the North* by Pierre Berton; *Living Arctic* by Hugh Brody; *Coppermine: The Far North of George M. Douglas* by Enid Mallory; and *Afterlands* by Steven Heighton. My thanks to these and other northern writers. The Arctic is another world.

Coppermine

About the Book 448

An Interview with Keith Ross Leckie 449

Discussion Questions 454

A Penguin Readers Guide

ABOUT THE BOOK

Based on an actual murder investigation and incorporating historical documents and court transcripts, *Coppermine* by Keith Ross Leckie is a gripping story of adventure and survival in the tradition of Joseph Boyden's *Three Day Road* and *The Wars* by Timothy Findley.

The unforgiving icescape of the Arctic Circle is one of the most inhospitable places on earth, but for Corporal Jack Creed of the Royal North West Mounted Police, it is the perfect place to escape from the nightmarish trenches of the Great War and a from a dark secret buried in his past.

His assignment is a thankless task—to investigate the disappearance of two French Catholic missionaries who three years earlier had made the gruelling trip deep into the far North with the hope of converting the Inuit people of the Coppermine River to Christianity.

Creed hires young Angituk McAndrew to accompany him on the journey. Half-Inuit, half-white, Angituk serves as a guide and translator, and as the weeks pass, they share many incredible adventures and enjoy a growing bond of friendship and respect. But Angituk is not who he appears to be and soon reveals to Creed that he is actually a woman living out of necessity as a man.

Once they reach the Coppermine, Creed and Angituk find the bodies of the two priests, and the assignment becomes a murder investigation. The trail leads them to Uluksuk, a shaman, and Sinnisiak, a hunter, who both readily admit to killing the men in self-defence after one of the priests became violent and irrational. While the two Inuit express regret at what happened, they have little concept of the law or even of the country that white men call Canada. Creed is only the third white man they have ever seen.

Creed arrests Uluksuk and Sinnisiak, and they immediately set out for Edmonton, where the two men will stand trial for their crimes. Generally naive and unaware of what awaits them in the city, Uluksuk and Sinnisiak cheerfully go along on the lengthy trek. Along the way, all four must depend upon each other in order to survive the cruel dark months of deepest winter. As Creed learns more about the two men and their customs, he comes to understand the seriousness of their situation and pledges to help them receive a fair trial.

None of them is prepared for what awaits them in Edmonton. Creed struggles with returning to the demands of civilization and to Nicole, the woman he left behind but no longer loves, while Angituk sets out on a heartbreaking search for the father she has never known. Uluksuk and Sinnisiak are bewildered by the modern world of brick buildings and motorcars, and face a life-or-death trial in a legal system that barely recognizes let alone respects them. Then Creed must make the most important decision of his life when the secret he's been running from for years finally resurfaces. ■

AN INTERVIEW WITH KEITH ROSS LECKIE

Q. The *Coppermine* project began as a novel, then almost became a television miniseries, and finally came full circle when it was published as a novel by Penguin Group Canada. How would the television version of the story have been different from the novel?

If *Coppermine* were done as a movie, the structure would have been the same except we would have lost details, events, and characters, which the novel has room for. The biggest difference, however, has to do with the freedom to express a point of view. In a television show, we only know what a character is thinking and feeling by his behaviour, facial expression, and what he says. There is the exception of a voice-over, but this is rarely used. The novel, on the other hand, allowed me to get into the characters' heads and say, quite literally and intimately, what they were thinking and feeling.

At first I only used this point-of-view "monologue" with Jack, but in later drafts of the novel, I found I could be quite free with it and used the POV of several characters. For example, it was important for the reader to understand the POV of Sinnisiak and Uluksuk. You'll notice I only began to use the POV for those characters later in the novel. At the beginning we see them exclusively through Jack's eyes, and he views them as somewhat threatening and inscrutable. But during the trial, when it was time to get to know them better, I introduced their dialogue and their POVs. ■

Q. What sort of research went into writing the novel? Did you visit any of the locations in the story?

I'd been thinking about the Coppermine story for a long time. More than twenty years ago, I did some research into Arctic law and court trials for a CBC movie, and I came across a book called *British Law and*

Arctic Man by Professor Gordon Moyles, which described the murder trial of Sinnisiak and Uluksuk. I used this book extensively as a reference when writing my novel.

I found the story fascinating and determined it would be a great subject for a novel. I began to collect books on Inuit culture, particularly regarding the Copper Inuit, and books of the white explorers, geologists, priests, and police officers in the Coppermine area. Fifteen years later, I sold the story to CBC as a miniseries. This gave me enough funding to travel with my son to the archives in Edmonton and Yellowknife and, more important, to the Coppermine area. We met many Copper Inuit; interviewed elders about their customs, beliefs, and history; and paddled and boated up and down the Coppermine River. At Bloody Falls, where the priests were killed, we camped with the Niptanapiak family, who told us wonderful stories of hunting and survival. I got a good feel for the lay of the land and what it would have been like in 1913. I had a researcher send me photos of Edmonton in 1917 and newspaper articles about the city that summer of the trial. A World War I historian helped me with the sequences involving Jack's experiences in the trenches, and an Inuit teacher and linguist read the manuscript and made comments on the authenticity of Inuit behaviour and nuance. ∎

Q. Was it difficult returning to prose after such a long career writing for television? Did you find any advantages of one format over the other?

I was a little worried—it had been twenty years since my last novel. My structure and dialogue was good, but I wondered if I could write descriptive passages that would satisfy the reader. I was rusty at first but found it came back, helped in part by doing some intensive reading of contemporary classic novels. I'm proud of the book's prose. In scriptwriting the description should be direct and clear without wasting time on the creative, which no one beyond the cast and crew will ever read. I love the experience of seeing a script I've written realized as a film, but often one's vision is compromised by the budget or location, or reinterpreted by actors and the director. The thrill of a novel is that the writer has complete control of every word and experience presented to the reader. A film has its own satisfaction of collaboration with others, but with a novel, good or bad, the work all belongs to the writer. ∎

Q: You make reference in the Author's Note to taking some historical liberties in writing the novel. Describe the challenge of crafting an entertaining fictional story within the framework of actual historical events.

Most of my films have been based on or inspired by true stories, and I do take dramatic liberties with them, but there are lines I won't cross. I like to say I may manipulate facts, but I will tell the truth of the event. An editor once said, "Don't let the truth stand in the way of a good story." While I believe we have a responsibility to tell the truth, I also agree that we need to entertain and engage an audience. It is a balancing act. Someone else said that "human beings don't live their lives in a dramatically correct manner," and that is true. We have to condense events, make up composite characters, give characters sharp, clear objectives that in real life may have been muddy, and so on, so that the reader will be satisfied.

The fate of Uluksuk and Sinnisiak at the end of the book is the truth. Almost unbelievably so. They were found guilty in the second trial and sentenced to death, which was commuted to life in prison. But within a year, they were released from prison, made special constables, sent north again, and served the Mounties at a new detachment a few miles from where they had killed the priests! Here, truth was harder to believe than fiction. ■

Q: What can you tell us about the real Uluksuk and Sinnisiak? Did you try to present an accurate portrayal of these two men based on your research? Were the characters of Jack Creed and Angituk created especially for the novel, or do they, too, have historical inspirations?

Uluksuk and Sinnisiak are portrayed much as they were in real life. Uluksuk was the elder, a respected shaman, and Sinnisiak was the younger hunter. These hunting teams of unrelated older and younger men were quite common. There is evidence that in Edmonton Uluksuk became ill, depressed, and withdrawn. Sinnisiak was more outgoing but also more emotional. He broke down into tears quite often, and he also had a temper. A year before killing the priests, he and Jack Hornby had had a nasty but non-physical confrontation. In drama, characters tend to be either heroes or villains. I chose to portray Sinnisiak and Uluksuk as sympathetic, relatively innocent characters, which I believe they were, although their motives can be debated. Jack Creed is a composite character inspired by Inspector Denny La Nauze and Corporal Valentine Bruce, who lived through the type of experiences I give to Creed. The character of Angituk was inspired by a smart, young interpreter, Patsy Klingenberg (son of a Danish trader and Copper Inuit mother), a colourful character who travelled with La Nauze and later became a court interpreter. ■

Q: The first half of the novel is a fast-paced story of adventure and survival, while the second half combines a love story with a gripping courtroom drama. Did you find either section more challenging to write or more rewarding?

It's true the first and second halves are quite different, but I enjoyed writing them equally. The first half of the novel—freewheeling and adventurous—was fun to write. I had a lot of freedom in what is mostly a "road" story. I could put the characters through various dangers and challenges while sending them North and back. There was room for jokes, danger, reflection, storytelling, and romance. Once back in Edmonton, the second half was primarily a courtroom drama, although different subplots unfolded. I have written quite a few courtroom sequences in films and enjoy creating them. I wanted to write the trial accurately, and the court transcripts provided a structure. This meant I had less freedom in the second half. Also, I was juggling several subplots that all needed to advance successfully, so the second half required more precise writing in order to continue building tension toward the climax. ■

Q: You had access to Father Rouvière's journals as well as actual courtroom transcripts. Describe the process of incorporating those historical texts into the novel.

I basically went through the material, made note of important events that could be dramatized, and put them together in a linear assembly. Even though Rouvière's journal and the courtroom transcripts are exciting historical documents, much of the writing is rather boring. I had to expand on what was in Rouvière's journal in order to focus my story and make it relevant, all while maintaining the truth. Rouvière's last line was particularly riveting, however. When he was starving and the Inuit had turned against them, he wrote, "... and we don't know what to do." It's very evocative and provides a strong mood of desperation for recreating the scene. ∎

Q. What do you think contemporary Canada, as a multicultural society, can learn from this story? Do you think that our attitudes to the Inuit have improved much in the last hundred years?

I think Canadian society is much more enlightened and informed about Inuit people today than it was a hundred years ago, but of course it needs to improve. Today there are social problems among the Inuit in the North such as suicide, domestic violence, and drug and alcohol abuse that the rest of Canadian society doesn't understand. I like to think that as society finds out more about First Nations people—how they think and live, what their values are, how they treat their children and the elderly—a respect and empathy will develop for them and their needs, which will lead to improvements in their situation. I enjoyed getting to know about the Inuit belief system and their priorities in life. They have a different way of viewing the world. What we can learn from the Inuit in *Coppermine* is that there are other ways of finding a fulfilling life than by making money and accumulating property. ∎

Q. Canadians can be somewhat reluctant to explore or embrace our country's rich history. As a writer with a career of successful historical projects, what are your thoughts on making our past appealing to modern audiences?

In Canada we do have a remarkably rich history—amazing stories of individuals and events such as Coppermine that few people have heard of. I agree that Canadian media can be reluctant to embrace and promote these stories. I have had good luck with many past projects dealing with Canadian history, but for every one that has been produced or published, I have had a dozen that have been turned down.

I believe Canadians love to hear our stories. Part of the problem is living next to the United States. I think many publishers, producers, and networks believe that Canadian stories would limit their sales to the

U.S. market and may seem parochial and uncool to the lucrative youth audience they want. They believe the storytelling of Pierre Berton and Farley Mowat is out of style. There is also some truth to the observation that Canada is not a country of extreme violence, injustice, and intolerance, which makes for good drama. But I believe a great story is always in demand. Our task as creators is to make these stories relevant to this generation and the issues it faces. In *Coppermine* I deal with issues such as the futility of war, new approaches to the environment, religious fundamentalism, and even gender shifting. These are contemporary, universal topics that make *Coppermine* relevant to a modern audience. ■

DISCUSSION QUESTIONS

1. Discuss the themes and issues that *Coppermine* shares with other classic Canadian novels set in the same time period, such as Joseph Boyden's *Three Day Road* or *The Wars* by Timothy Findley.

2. Father Rouvière's final journal entry reads, "*Nous ne savons que faire,*" or, "We don't know what to do." Explore the relationship that white Canada has with the Inuit, in both positive and negative terms, as portrayed in the novel. How does the novel reflect the status of the Inuit in our society today?

3. "It was the freedom of insignificance within this enormous country that breathed life into [Jack's] ailing spirit and lifted the weight from his heart" (page 26). Jack finds solace in the North because of the sense of freedom that the open landscape gives him, but for some characters, like Father Rouvière or Eugene Begley, life in that unforgiving part of the world can lead to depression and violence. Discuss the role that dedication, determination, and faith play in surviving in such a bleak environment.

4. Angituk translates "*Il-viunna-hugi-vit?*" as the Earth asking, "Are you who you appear to be?" (page 69). Examine the reasons why Jack and Angituk initially adopt false identities and what it ultimately takes for them to answer that question truthfully.

5. Lieutenant Wilkerson coldly states, "Their world is now our world and they better damn well adapt to it just like the Indians have and like all the Aboriginals have in all the territories of the Empire. We made them" (page 326). Do you agree or

disagree with this statement? Do you feel that the government of Canada should have the right to impose and enforce its laws on the Inuit of the far North?

6. "[Jack] believed in humankind, despite the battering his faith in it had taken ... He looked to an improved future" (page 3). Even though he'd seen the worst of humanity in the trenches of World War I and experienced considerable violence here in Canada, why do you feel that Jack still maintains that faith in humanity?

7. As a reader, what are your feelings about Jack's admission that he had killed his superior and deserted the army? How does this affect your view of the character, not only as a Mountie investigating a double-murder case but also as the protagonist of the novel? Does this make him less of a hero?

8. Angituk is a thematically important character because she embodies the spirit and knowledge of both the Inuit and white worlds, yet she is not fully accepted by either community. She is also hiding her female identity within a man's persona. Explore what her mosaic identity contributes to the themes of the novel.

9. *Coppermine* is a fictional account of a true story and makes use of actual journal entries and court transcripts. Do you feel that this approach to storytelling is respectful to the historical figures depicted in the novel and to their legacies? What does it say about the malleable nature of history itself?

To access Penguin Group (Canada) Readers Guides online, visit the Penguin Group (Canada) website at **www.penguin.ca**.